AF486319

BREAKING
Cycles

Other Books by Nikki A Lamers

The Unforgettable Series

The Unforgettable Summer (#1)
Unforgettable Nights (#2)
Unforgettable Dreams (#3)
Unforgettable Memories (#4)
The Unforgettable One (#5)
Unforgettable Mistakes (#6)

The Home Duet

Dreams Lost and Found (#1)
Finding Home (#2)

BREAKING *Cycles*

MENDING SHATTERED HEARTS #1

NIKKI A LAMERS

atmosphere press

© 2023 Nikki A. Lamers

Published by Atmosphere Press

Cover design by Matthew Fielder

No part of this book may be reproduced without permission from the author except in brief quotations and in reviews. This is a work of fiction, and any resemblance to real places, persons, or events is entirely coincidental.

Atmospherepress.com

1

Grant

MOONLIGHT SHINES IN THROUGH THE CRACKED BLINDS, keeping me awake. I had been hoping to get a few hours of sleep, but tonight it appears an impossible feat. Turning my head to the side, I glance at the raven-haired beauty lying next to me, her tanned skin peeking out from underneath the sheet, barely covering her bare breasts. I take a moment, watching her chest rise and fall, making sure she's sleeping before quietly slipping out of bed, resigned.

Reaching for my backpack, I pull out clean boxer-briefs, slipping them on before stepping into my faded blue jeans. As I pull a white t-shirt over my head, my thoughts drift to the open road, my fingers already twitching with anticipation. I tug my shoes on, knowing it's time for me to go. Where? I'm not quite sure.

Taking one last glance at the beauty lying in bed, I sigh as I pull my black leather jacket on before grasping my black helmet from the table. Turning, I slip out the door, quietly closing it behind me, and make my way outside. Striding over to my motorcycle, I throw my left leg over, revving the engine. I pull out, heading northeast, out of Alabama, knowing in my head I'm already gone.

Soon, my body begins to relax as I cross the border into Georgia. Boundless roads appear in front of me as I cruise past endless seas of green. I don't exactly know where I'm going, but when someone tries to push too far into my life, I just can't stay, and she started digging. That was her mistake. Something inside me tensed, urging me to leave, to run, to escape. Honestly, I don't know how to do anything else anymore. She can't help me. No one can.

It's been a long time since I've been close to anyone. I almost don't remember what it's like. I huff a humorless laugh, knowing it's been years since I've allowed anyone in. I can't. Even my family doesn't know where to find me. My chest tightens as my thoughts drift to my parents and my little brother, Matt. I'm sure he's not so little anymore. It's been over ten years since I talked to any of them. I can't help but wonder what they're doing now and what they think happened to me. I grind my teeth at the thought. The truth is, I don't know what I'd do if they found me.

Leaving is inevitable. It's my reality. I no longer have a place I can call home. Admitting where I'm from is nearly impossible. I'll never look back at her or any of these places I've been or people who have crossed my path with any regret. She doesn't know me, and I don't know her, and I intend to keep it that way. I'm certain where to draw the line. I'm better off alone.

Wherever I stop next, I need to make sure I'm always in control of my situation when it comes to women. I'm always careful about the women I spend my time with. At twenty-nine, she's never someone older than me, and she's sure as hell not underage. She can never be the sweet girl next door, the one looking for something serious, nor someone who wants a husband and kids someday. She's never someone I work for, nor someone who asks a lot of questions I won't answer. I'm not a challenge or a game to be won by anyone. It doesn't matter who she is—I will disappear if she pushes me. She needs to know upfront it will never be more than a physical release for me. It can't be.

Of course, I have needs and my hand gets old fast. But I've

learned never to depend on anyone, and I won't allow anyone to depend on me. I can't be that man. Anyone who ever relied on me has only ended up disappointed. There's no way I can ever let that happen again.

As I cross the border into South Carolina, continuing northeast with palm trees interspersed among the trees lining the highway, my thoughts drift to the garage. Sighing, I exit to refill my tank at a 24-hour gas station. Pulling my phone out of my backpack, I tap my boss's number. "Hey, man. It's Grant. I'm sorry to do this to you at the last minute, but I had to leave town. Thank you for everything, and I'll talk to you soon." I disconnect, not wanting to explain. I'm going to miss working at that place.

I pull out of the gas station, my thoughts on what I might do for work now. I'm grateful to usually find work at a local garage with my experience, knowing it's a place where I don't have to do anything but my job. Besides, I love getting lost in my work, and working on bikes is my specialty. It's the one thing in life I still have that hasn't been tarnished, and without it, I honestly don't know if I would survive. Why some claim it's an empty existence, I'll never know, but I ignore them. When I'm working on or riding a bike, it's the one time I can truly relax and be myself. In those moments, I'm free of all the ties threatening to tear me down. I'm free to be me without judgment or consequence, whoever that might be; I don't even know anymore.

As I ride my motorcycle, watching the bright orange and yellows surface as the sun rises over the horizon, I'm calmed by the break in the mundane landscape as the deep blue of the ocean, the bright white of the waves cresting and the pale brown sand on the beach slide into view. Taking a deep breath as the wind whips against my face, I veer north for the first time in years. Summer is just beginning, after all. I could use some time near the beach. Maybe I'll find a coastal town to settle in for a while this time, but I need to be far enough away from the town I vacated in Alabama first.

About midmorning, I cross the border into North Carolina as dark clouds swiftly consume the sky. The wind picks up and rain begins to fall, pelting me and my ride. I should've checked the weather before I left last night, which reminds me, I'll have to pick up a new phone. I'm grateful for my jeans and simple black leather jacket, but it won't do me much good if this weather picks up.

It's not long before the roads become slick. The rain cascades harder and steadier and the wind gusts throw me off-balance, nearly knocking me over. I need to find a place to wait out the storm, and fast. My vision starts to diminish just as I see an exit up ahead, the sight nearly causing me to sigh in relief. Slowing, I lean into the turn just as a huge gust of wind hits me from the other side. I struggle to regain my balance and the wind whips again, pushing me past the point of no return. My breath catches in my throat and my heart stops, panic setting in. Desperately, I battle to streamline my bike, knowing I won't be able to compensate.

Time slows as I prepare for the inevitable. Hands clenching, I hold my breath, bracing for impact. The moment the first part of me collides with the ground, the air rushes from my lungs. A deafening bang followed by a high-pitched screeching rings in my ears. My right leg hits first, my bike crushing it, followed by my side and shoulder. Finally, my head bounces like a rag doll, my helmet cracking against the pavement on impact. As my bike begins skidding across the road, dragging my body along for the ride, my mind races, attempting to catch up to reality. My bike skitters away from me, as my body slows, finally coming to a stop, defenseless. My eyes widen, barely aware of my surroundings as I struggle to breathe. I feel myself losing consciousness.

A piercing scream fills the air just before a dark blonde angel drops to her knees at my side. "Oh, my God, are y'all okay? Of course, you're not okay, but can you hear me?" a sweet, soft voice asks, her slight southern accent laced with anxiety. Her shaky hands slip along my neck, probably searching for a pulse.

I grunt in response, "Ugh," not able to make any other sound as my breath finally comes back to me. I focus on breathing in and out, my lungs burning with the effort.

"Thank God, you're breathing." She states the obvious. "Hi, I need help. There was an accident. A motorcycle," she begins, sounding panicked. "He's breathing, but he doesn't look good."

Her statement causes pain to slam into me like a truck. My eyes squeeze shut and I can't stop the explicit scream coming out of my mouth, "Fuck!"

"Can you tell me what hurts?"

Rain continues pouring down on us like jagged icicles against my skin, causing me more agony. Instead of answering, I scream again, "Ah!"

She continues talking, but I can't make out what she's saying, too consumed with pain but not able to pinpoint any of it. Everything fucking hurts.

The soft, slick skin of one hand delicately skims my stubbled cheek as another covers my left hand, the touch pulling me out of my excruciating haze. Wait, when did my helmet come off? Licking my lips, the coppery taste of blood hits my tongue. "Helmet?" I grunt, barely able to force the single word through my lips.

"You're lucky, it didn't come off until the last bounce. I can't believe you're alive, let alone conscious right now," she mumbles under her breath, the words barely audible over the whistling wind, the gusts seeming to increase in intensity.

Neither can I, I admit to myself. Prying my eyes open, I will myself to look at the woman by my side, attempting to protect me. I stare into her deep blue eyes, the only thing that seems to be grounding me at the moment, trying to see through my pain. She has a heart-shaped face with a sweet button nose. Her cheeks appear rosy against her pale skin. "Beautiful," I murmur.

Her eyes widen and her cheeks turn a darker shade of pink.

"Can I do anything to help you while we wait for the ambulance?" she prompts, her plea desperate.

I try to shake my head, but moan in agony from the simple movement, my eyes reflexively closing. "C...can't..." I stammer.

"Just don't move." "I'll try to keep the rain off you as much as I can," she offers, leaning over me.

My eyes flutter open, squinting through the rain starting to come at us sideways and seeing a blurry, pale-yellow V-neck shirt completely soaked through and clinging to her body, her voluptuous cleavage on display. Attempting to lift my hand towards the perfect image in front of me, I groan in agony as if I'm being stabbed to death this very moment. Everything around me starts to feel like a dream except for my immense pain. There's no way she can be real. "Help me," I plead, asking her the one thing I haven't asked for from anyone in what feels like forever, but if she's not real, maybe she can give me a momentary reprieve before I die. Maybe that's why she's here, an angel to end my eternal pain.

The high-pitched wail of a siren sounds in the distance as if giving me permission to stop fighting. I honestly don't know if I care if the EMTs make it in time. It doesn't matter. I won't be missed. Will they tell my family? Will they care? My eyes slam closed. An image of my little brother, Matt, the way I remember him, flashes in my mind. He's crouching next to me and pretending to work on my bike as he smiles adoringly up at me; a look I don't deserve. He's better off without me. My angel's sweet voice attempts to comfort me, but I'm not able to take any more. Giving in to the pain, I finally let go, drifting into a dark, blissful abyss.

Ella

Leaning forward, I glance outside my living room window at the storm and grimace. It looks like the rain is starting to pick up. Reaching for the remote, I turn on the television and flip to the local weather station, hoping to get an update, when suddenly everything goes dark, making me groan in frustration. Losing my electricity is the last thing I need. At least it's daytime, so I'm able to see even with the storm clouds darkening the sky.

Setting the remote down, I reach for my phone. Just as I unlock the screen, my phone rings and my oldest brother's face lights up the screen. Sighing, I answer. "Declan, what a surprise," I grumble.

"Hey, little sis, I just saw the power went out all along the beach."

"How do y'all already know? It just went out!" I look around as if he's standing somewhere in the room.

"I know things," he teases, chuckling softly. "Actually, I was on the phone with the lifeguard station near you when it went out. I'm not sure how long it will be out with the storm, so you can come hang out at my place."

"I'm fine without electricity."

"Ella, if you don't want to come to my place, you know Mom and Dad don't mind if you go home," he emphasizes, knowing how I'll respond.

"I'm not going to Mom and Dad's."

"Look, you know Dad will come get you if you don't come here or even Charlotte's dorm room. I'm just warning you, though, Finn had a few friends from his team over last night, and I'm pretty sure they're all still at Mom and Dad's."

Groaning, I frown, knowing he's right. The last thing I want to do is hang out with a bunch of my younger brother's friends. I didn't understand high school boys when I was in high school, so at twenty-five it's not much different. "Alright, fine, I'll go to your house," I concede reluctantly.

"Great. Text me when you get there. You know where the key is. I should be home around four," he advises, pausing. "Drive safe."

"I will." I disconnect and set my phone down with a heavy sigh.

Standing, I begin going through my small beach house, making sure it's locked up tight. You would think since I'm responsible enough to have my own home, my family would trust me enough to make my own decisions about a little storm, but after everything we've been through, it's not the case.

The wind whistles, whipping past me as I step onto my large back deck, finding the picnic tables and chairs still tied down from the last storm. I wince, realizing the wind is already blowing harder than I thought. I'm sure it won't be long before the rain starts. I pick up my pace as I step over to my shed where I keep my bike, paddleboard, and things for my yard. Pausing, I give the lock a tug before rushing back inside my raised two-bedroom cottage.

I make my way through the house, unplugging small appliances and closing the shutters, grateful it's small and doesn't take me long to walk through. The house shakes from the wind, as if prompting me to hurry.

Stepping into my bedroom, I grab a pale blue duffle bag from the bottom of my closet and start tossing everything I think I'll need inside, knowing it might be a few days before I'm able to come home. My phone rings, my mom's face lighting up the screen. Grimacing, I ignore the call, already knowing she's just going to tell me she's sending Dad over to pick me up. My entire family nearly suffocates me with how protective they are of me. I get it, but I can't do it anymore. I'll call them in a little bit. In the meantime, hopefully, they won't call the whole town looking for me. You would think after I started making enough money waitressing and saving to get my own place, they would give me my independence, but sometimes I wonder if that will ever happen.

First pulling my bag over my shoulder, I grab my duffel with my other hand. My bare feet slap against the wood floors as I stride out to the living room, snatching my keys and phone off the table and slip them into my jeans pocket. I grimace at the sound of the rain pelting the house, alerting me to the growing threat outside. Snagging my purse sitting by the door, I hook it over my head, hoping I don't drop anything, but in the rain, I'm determined to do this in one trip.

Taking a deep breath, I inhale the scent of rain and saltwater as the choppy waves slam into the shore. I jump into my white Jeep Wrangler just as the rain picks up, coming down harder. "Great." At least I don't have far to go.

I love the peacefulness and simplicity here. It's perfect for me. But while we're in hurricane season, my family probably won't leave me alone, insisting I come stay with them. I'm sick of being treated like I'm incapable of doing anything for myself. I'm fine on my own! I just need to convince all of them.

Backing out of my driveway with a heavy sigh, I veer towards Ocean Highway to make my way across town. I slow and lean closer to the windshield, wondering if I'll even make it to Dec's before I have to pull over. "I can barely see," I mumble to myself, squinting.

Coming up to a stop sign, I notice a single headlight up ahead to my right. It takes me a moment to realize it's not a car with a headlight out, but a motorcycle out in this weather. That can't be fun, or safe for that matter.

The next moment seems to happen in slow motion as I watch helplessly in horror. The motorcycle turns towards me just as a gust of wind bursts through, rattling my car and pushing the man past the point to recover. My eyes widen as the motorcycle begins to slide, falling onto his right leg, his whole right side following along like a ragdoll and slamming against the pavement. His head, protected with a black helmet, joins in, bouncing like a ball. The motorcycle screeches and crunches against the concrete, sending shivers down my spine. Appearing to drag the man's body along with it, the motorcycle finally breaks free and skids to a stop. His body rolls another few feet as his helmet detaches, spinning to a stop, while the man's body slumps into the now cracked ground.

Throwing my car into park, I jump out into the pouring rain, a terrified scream leaving my lips. Running towards the fallen man, I drop down on my knees next to him, his jeans and black leather jacket shredded and covered in blood, dirt, and concrete. "Oh, my God, are y'all okay? Of course, you're not okay, but can you hear me?" I prod, trying to control my anxiety as I yell over the sounds of the storm. Shakily, I slip my hand along his neck, searching for a pulse.

A low growl falls from his lips in response. "Ugh." My eyes finally focus enough to observe the slight rise and fall of his chest.

"Thank God, you're breathing," I mutter as my body relaxes only slightly with relief. Pulling my phone out of my pocket, I dial 911. Hearing the dispatcher, I interrupt, loudly blurting out, "I need help. There was an accident. A motorcycle," I begin, breathing heavily. "He's breathing, but he doesn't look good," I assess. A chill runs through my body, already completely soaked to the bone, but I ignore it, attempting to focus on the man lying awkwardly.

"Fu..." he slurs in obvious pain.

"Can you tell me what hurts?" I inquire as instructed, feeling like I just asked an obvious question, but he only screams again in response. "We're just off Ocean Highway in Genesis Beach," I inform them as the wind continues whipping around us. "Please, hurry," I urge desperately, as my heart slams against my ribcage.

"We will. The ambulance is already on the way, but I need you to stay on the line, if you can, to keep us updated," the dispatcher requests.

I almost laugh at the ridiculousness of the request in this weather, but concede, "I'll leave you on speaker, but I'm helping him." I set my phone down near my knee, hoping to keep it as dry as possible. It better not stop working now. Gritting my teeth, I lean over him, attempting to shield him from some of the pouring rain, no matter how impossible the feat, as the wind blows it sideways, hitting me in the face. No matter which way I turn, I'm squinting, attempting to see right in front of me. Reaching towards him, I'm eager to do what I can to comfort him and pray he's going to be okay. I cover his seemingly uninjured hand with my right hand, letting my left fall just above the curve of his strong jaw, his light stubble scratching my palm.

His tongue juts out, licking blood and rain off his cracked lips. "Helmet?" he rasps.

"You're lucky, it didn't come off until the last bounce. I can't believe you're alive, let alone conscious right now," I mumble under my breath, unsure if he hears me through the raging storm.

He opens his eyes and looks into mine as if he needs me to survive, leaving me off-balance and causing my heart to irrationally skip a beat. Unable to tear myself away from his intense gaze, I stare back at him, desperate to help. I can't tell for sure in this light, but his eyes appear hazel with blues, greens, and golds.

"Beautiful," he murmurs, catching me off-guard.

My eyes widen as my cheeks heat, but there's no way he can really see me out here in this. He must be delirious with pain. "Can I do anything to help you until the ambulance gets here?" I prod, needing to do something useful.

He attempts to shake his head, but moans in pain from the simple movement, his eyes reflexively closing. "C...can't..." he stammers.

"Just don't move." My chest tightens. The last thing I need is for him to hurt himself more. "I'll try to keep the rain off of you as much as I can." I lean further over him.

His eyes are barely open to slits as he attempts to reach towards me, before groaning in utter agony, the sound hitting me harder than the wind and rain. "Help me," he stammers, begging and breaking my heart. I've never felt so completely helpless in my life, and that's saying a lot coming from me. Tears stream down my face as the sirens seem to be closing in. I only hope they get here in time.

2

Ella

THE MOMENT I STEP INSIDE DECLAN'S HOUSE, A CHILL RUNS through me and I breathe a sigh of relief. I drop my things on the floor and kick off my sandals, leaving them by the door and hoping they're not ruined. Reaching into my pocket, I pry my phone out from my wet jeans and the screen slowly lights up, bringing a smile to my face. I never knew I'd be so grateful to have a waterproof phone; hopefully it lasts.

With a tired sigh, I unlock my phone, notifications lighting it up like a disco ball. Quickly scrolling through, I notice several missed calls from my older brother and my parents, making me wince. "Great," I mumble under my breath. Not even bothering to listen to the voicemails, I tap Declan's name to return his call.

"Are you okay?" he asks franticly the moment the call connects.

"I'm fine!"

"Then, where the hell have you been?"

Knowing he will find out about the accident anyway in this small town, I admit, "I was on the way to your house like I promised when I saw a motorcycle crash coming off the ramp. So, I stopped to help him."

"In this weather?" he challenges irritably. "You should've called me! I would've left work to come help you, Gabriella!"

I flinch, annoyed by his use of my full name. "I couldn't just leave him there to die, Dec! And besides, I was on the phone with 911 the whole time," I emphasize, attempting to match his patronizing tone.

He groans in frustration, mumbling under his breath, "I swear you live to help other people." Pausing, he takes a deep breath, exhaling slowly. "I get it but are you sure you're okay?" he prods, his tone much softer.

"Yes, I'm fine! I wasn't the one in an accident! And besides, I'm safely inside your house, soaked and dripping rain all over your wood floors, so you can stop being a pain in my ass," I mutter in irritation. "It's not like y'all won't be able to make sure for yourself when you get home."

"Ella, I'm sorry you're annoyed with me, but you know we all worry about you, and it sounds like we had reason to be worried this time. You know we can't help it."

"Yeah, I know, Dec, but I'm not sick anymore. I've been in remission for a long time, and I know this time it's going to stick. I barely even have to check in with the doctor, so why do I constantly have to check in with all of you?"

"Ella."

"Fine. I'm fine and I can take care of myself! I'm just a little cold and a lot wet right now, but that's very little price to pay for doing the right thing and helping someone. So, I'm going to use your bathtub and take a hot bubble bath to try to relax and warm up."

"Okay, okay, I'm sorry," he concedes, resigned. "A bath sounds like a good idea. Do you need me to come home?"

"No, Dec. I don't need a babysitter or an over-protective big brother. There's no reason for y'all to come home early except to annoy the hell out of me."

Chuckling softly, he concurs, lightening the mood, "Yeah, but that's so much fun."

I scoff and roll my eyes even though he can't see me. "Yeah, yeah." Shaking my head, I request, "Would you do me a favor though?"

"Anything."

"Will you call Mom and Dad for me to let them know what happened and that I'm okay? I don't want to deal with them right now."

"Sure. No problem. Call me if you need anything."

"I will. I promise. I'll see you after work."

As I pick up my bag, I slip my phone in the side pocket. With my jeans sticking to my legs, I struggle to make it upstairs. I open the last door on the left and drop my bag inside, noticing everything is just as I left it. It's the perfect guest room, but we both know it's for me. I appreciate everything he does for me, and I understand why my family is so protective with me being in and out of the hospital for most of my life, but I'm twenty-five; when will they let me grow up?

A relaxing bath is exactly what I need to help me warm up and calm my anxiety. Seeing that motorcycle skidding across the pavement dragging his body is something I've never seen, and I hope I never do again.

I pour lavender bubble bath in with the stream of hot water before I slowly peel out of my wet clothes, revealing my cool and clammy skin underneath. Out of the corner of my eye, I catch a glimpse of my drowned reflection in the mirror. I'm a mess. I can't help but laugh as the stranger's words echo in my head, calling me beautiful. My smile soon falls, the accident replaying in my head, again making my stomach turn. Hopefully, he's going to be okay.

Slowly, I slip down into the bubbles and hot water as I shake my head, attempting to rid myself of my thoughts. Although I know it's not something I will ever forget.

My body soon warms and my muscles finally relax, as my mind drifts back to the man on the street. The moment I looked into his eyes and saw a look in them I don't know if I can explain, my entire body reacted. Suddenly, I had this overwhelming feeling of panic and desperation as well as the strongest urge to take care of him. The sound of his deep, raspy voice continues to echo in my ears as he muttered, "Help me." But what keeps gnawing at me the most is not what he said but the way he said it. There's an inexplicable feeling inside telling me he wanted me to help him with more than his accident.

It may have been too dark to tell if his eyes were truly hazel, but even through his narrowed gaze, they appeared to be saying so much. His haunted look practically screamed for me, as if he truly needed me, but that's crazy. I've never even met him before tonight. Maybe that was his fear talking; or mine.

Inhaling deeply, I lean back and close my eyes, again attempting to shake off thoughts of him skidding across the darkened road, and hoping the scent of the bubbles will help me relax. Maybe I'll check on him at the hospital after the storm passes. Just knowing he will be okay could do a lot for my sanity. Unfortunately, tonight, I'll have to settle for praying he will survive.

It's as if no time has passed when the water begins to cool and the sound of the front door closing prompts me to get out of the bathtub. "Ella?" Declan calls from the bottom of the stairs.

"I'll be out in a minute." I guess it's time to convince Declan I really am alright. Quickly, but carefully, I slip on my heather gray and white striped pajama pants and tank top before I make my way downstairs to find my brother, wondering how long I might be stuck here, and already missing my cozy little home.

3

Grant

IMAGES OF THE BLUE-EYED ANGEL KEEP FLASHING BEFORE my eyes. She's standing in front of me, rain pouring down on her as she hovers over me protectively, looking down at me with immense concern. I've never seen anyone so beautiful or anyone carrying so much of their emotions in their eyes. I can't stop myself from wondering if she was real or maybe she was just a dream, a way for me to deal with the shock and the agony until help came.

The steady beeping of machines echo all around me, urging me to do something. I attempt to move, but instantly, stabbing, burning pain slams into me as if I'm being beaten with iron plates. A groan escapes my lips as I agonizingly pry my eyelids apart, squinting into the almost blinding bright light until my eyes adjust, coming into focus.

Blinking a few times, I'm slightly disorientated as I attempt to take in my surroundings. My heart thunders as I cautiously look around, the stark white of a hospital room glaring back at me, making my heart plummet and my anxiety increase. I grimace as the reality of crashing my motorcycle hits me full force. I'm pissed for putting myself here. I'm usually so careful when it comes to the weather, but all I could think about was running. Exhaling slowly through my teeth, I hiss as I attempt to move again, but something is holding me down. I'm afraid to look over my body to see the damage I've done.

A slight squeak of a door opening reaches my ears, and I warily turn my head in that direction. A tall woman, presumably a nurse in her blue scrubs, appearing a few years older than me, waltzes into the room. She has a round face, short dark hair, and kind blue eyes she instantly directs towards me. "You're awake," she announces wide-eyed and smiling, evidently surprised. "How are you feeling, Grant?"

I gulp, realizing she called me by name. I guess they found my wallet. I open my mouth and force out a response over my dry, scratchy throat. "Like my bike threw me to the ground and ran over me repeatedly," I rasp, brutally honest.

She offers me a sympathetic smile as she presses a button near my bed, a voice instantly echoing through the speakers. "Yes?" a high-pitched voice crackles throughout the room.

"He's awake."

"Thank you. I'll advise the doctor," the voice replies.

Without another word to the speaker, the nurse looks back at me, informing me, "Your pain medicine goes in through your IV. I've been monitoring your pain the best I can without your help. But now that you're awake, on a scale of one to ten, with one being no pain and ten being excruciating, what's your pain level?"

"Nine," I grumble, knowing I felt worse in the moment.

She nods. Reaching for my left wrist, she asks, "Name and birthdate?" I watch as she reads my hospital band while I answer. Then she continues busying herself, taking my vitals and entering the information into a computer as I let my gaze drift to the ceiling above me.

I don't know what I'm going to do. I may not know what's wrong yet, but I know I'm fucked.

"Grant," the nurse calls, pulling me out of my spiraling thoughts. I drag my gaze from the ceiling to her caring eyes as she looks at me with a kind smile meant for a stranger. Then again, that's all I ever am anymore.

"Do you have someone you'd like us to call?"

"No," I respond vehemently, my blood pressure boiling. I can't help noticing the machine behind me briefly beeping faster before returning to a steady beat.

Pressing her lips tightly together, she nods in acknowledgment. "You can drink some water or suck on ice chips to help with your throat, but small sips to start. I'll get you some. Can I get you anything else?" she offers, arching her eyebrows.

I attempt to readjust, shifting on the bed and flinch from the stabbing pain hitting the right side of my body. "Eleven," I mutter my new pain number. "Something for the pain," I grumble.

Nodding in understanding, she informs me, "I believe you're at the limit for now. The doctor will be in to see you in a few minutes to discuss your injuries. She may update your orders now that you're awake and we'll readjust."

"How long was I out?"

"Three days," she confirms with a look of empathy, her words slamming into me.

"Fuck," I mumble under my breath.

"But you didn't miss anything besides a small hurricane," she advises, as if hearing my thoughts.

Just as the words leave her lips, a petite woman with soft brown skin, brown eyes, and long dark hair, wearing a white lab coat embroidered in black with what I assume is her name followed by the letters MD, strides into the room. "Mr. Young, it's good to see you with your eyes open." She grins.

"Wish I could say the same," I complain, terrified to hear whatever she's about to reveal. I don't even want to let my eyes stray to my right side, the same side most of my pain seems to be manifesting from, starting at my head, and traveling all the way to my toes.

"I can imagine. I'm Dr. Magi, and I've been taking care of you with my team. So instead of asking you how you're feeling, since that seems obvious, I'm going to start by asking you a few questions."

She pauses and I grunt in response.

"What's your name?"

"Grant Young," I rasp, my voice not sounding like my own.

"And do you know where you are?"

"I'm at the hospital, but I have no idea where or what hospital. I'll assume somewhere in North Carolina, since that's the last border I crossed."

"And why are you here?"

Huffing a humorless laugh, I grumble, "Because I fucked up and crashed my motorcycle during a storm."

"And it was quite the storm." She pauses, looking over the papers on her clipboard. "Okay, so I'm going to go right into your injuries. You're a very lucky man." She offers me a sympathetic smile.

I don't feel lucky at the moment and grunt irritably, "Ugh."

"I'll start with the easy things," she states, earning another scowl from me; nothing about this is easy. Holding out her right arm to use as a visual, she begins explaining, "Your radius is the bone that goes from your wrist to your elbow on the side of your thumb and the ulna is the one that goes from your wrist to your elbow on your pinkie side. Both of these bones were shattered, which basically means they were broken in several places. We needed to do surgery to remove some of the bone fragments and then repair the damage. Then, we had to insert three steel pins to make sure both bones would be able to heal properly."

"Great," I mutter sarcastically, my chest tightening with every word.

Ignoring my comment, she continues, "The bone from your elbow to your shoulder is your humerus. You were lucky there, as you only suffered a clean break. We were able to set it without surgery."

"Lucky," I scoff.

She disregards my outburst. "You broke two ribs on your right side, but they didn't do any internal damage. Your right leg also sustained serious injuries with your femur, tibia and fibula all shattering and needing surgery. We removed all the bone fragments and were able to use pins to assist in their realignment in hopes of proper healing. After the bones heal, you will need physical therapy, but with hard work, you should be able to return to full function on your right side," she enlightens me, finally taking a full breath.

"What's the hard part?" My body sinks further into the bed in anticipation.

"Excuse me?" Her eyebrows draw down in confusion.

"You said you would start with the easy part. If that's the easy part, what the fuck is the hard part?"

She gives me another sympathetic smile. "One of the spots you hit on your right side caused your kidney to rupture. You had some internal bleeding and the tear on your kidney was too much to be saved. We had to remove your kidney, but since your left kidney didn't sustain any injury and it's completely healthy, you should be able to thrive with just one." She pauses, assessing me, but all I can do is listen, resigned.

"You have seven stitches on your head just above your right ear, which is nothing considering the situation. We needed to shave your head around that area. You did have a concussion and some swelling on your brain from the impact. We left you sedated for the last three days in an induced coma until the swelling came down, but there appears to be no permanent damage. We'll know more in time, but your helmet seems to have done its job."

I scoff, attempting to process all the information she's throwing at me. "Sure," I mumble, wanting to escape but knowing I'm stuck.

Taking a step closer, she looks into my eyes, repeating, "You were very lucky. These injuries are nothing compared to what they could have been. This morning we removed your feeding tube, which is part of the reason your throat hurts, but we still need to remove your catheter."

Ignoring her comment, I question, "When will I be able to get out of here?"

She chuckles, shaking her head as her shoulders relax the slightest bit. "You're definitely here for a few more days." I breathe a sigh of relief. A few more days I can handle. "After that, as long as you have someone to help you at home, we will be able to discharge you, but you will still have to come in for follow-ups and physical therapy, but we can set that up at the therapist's office."

My heart stops beating. "I can take care of myself," I retort defiantly.

Her head falls back as she laughs at my response, at me. "I'm sure you can, Mr. Young, but you're not superhuman. If you don't have anyone to help, we can send you to one of our facilities until you can do the basics on your own or at least with a home care nurse." My stomach churns with increasing unease. I don't even know how long my insurance will last from my last job, and I don't want them to know where I am. Clearing my throat, I open my mouth, but nothing comes out. "You have time to figure it out. I'm not releasing you yet," she reiterates as if reading my mind.

I nod, the movement making me dizzy and causing my vision to blur. Attempting to lift my hand to rub my eyes, I gasp as I'm pulled back to the bed with gut-wrenching pain. "Ah," I croak, squeezing my eyes shut.

"I'll check your pain medicine, and Jennifer, could you please make sure the pain management team stops back to see Mr. Young today?"

Hearing those words, I seal my eyes and tune everything out. I'm overwhelmed with the amount of information Dr. Magi threw at me. What the fuck am I going to do? Maybe it would've been better if I didn't survive. It's not like I would be missed.

4

LIGHT SPLASHING RINGS IN MY EARS AS MY PADDLE SLICES the water, pulling through before moving to the other side of my paddleboard and repeating the movements. As I take a deep breath in, I carefully lower myself onto my pink and white board, decorated with a single, large pink hibiscus. Resting on my knees, I pause and look around with the sun at my back and the seas eerily calm after the storm.

Being out here always gives me a sense of serenity, a chance to remind me of all the beauty and good in the world, and I'm grateful for every moment. I know how lucky I am to be here. I'm thankful for every single chance I've been given, and I don't take those gifts lightly. I've fought hard for this chance, this life, my life, and I want to use it for good. I want to help others fight their fight like my family fought alongside me, but I struggle with what that looks like. That's probably why I'm still waitressing. At least I work with good people and make good tips. I do like it there, but the question constantly gnaws at me—what now?

Birds squawk as they fly overhead, veering towards the shore and pulling my attention. My eyes scan the sandy shore with the long seagrass as its backdrop. The beach appears to be filled with a lot more debris than normal; rocks, shells, seaweed, fish corpses, and some garbage all washed ashore, making me grimace. The mess only reminds me of the storm, of the accident, of him. I wonder how he's doing; I hope he's okay.

I think to satisfy my own sanity I'm going to have to go to the hospital no matter how much I don't want to. After an accident like that, he'll either be in ICU or on the third floor. I'll have to search if I want to find anything out; it's not like anyone can tell me anything. Besides I don't even know his name, but maybe there was a reason I was there. Maybe I can do something to help him.

With my mind made up, I carefully stand, balancing with one foot on each side of the board, and begin paddling back towards home. It will be my first time at the hospital since the last time I rang the bell; the thought leaves me uneasy. But I have to go, I need to know he's okay. The pained and haunted look in his eyes just before he lost consciousness keeps eating at me. I have the strongest urge to do something to make that look disappear, but I'm clueless as to how to make it happen. How could I? I don't even know who the man is or even if I imagined that look. But I will find out.

As soon as I make it home, I rush to get ready to leave, determined to go see him before I change my mind. I swipe the basket of baked goods I made last night off the counter on my way out the door and make the short drive to the hospital. It's not long before I'm taking the elevator to the third floor, hoping he's here because there's no way they will allow me into ICU. Taking a deep breath, I step off the elevator and pause. I gulp down the familiar lump in my throat, reminding myself why I'm here and forcing myself to move. As I make my way through the corridor, eager to find his room and escape the familiar looks of concern, I force a smile and murmur my greetings. Knowing so many of the staff, I hope to make it past most of them without being stopped.

"Ella! Ella, wait," a familiar deep voice calls out, worry lacing his voice. "What are you doing here?"

I grimace, halting my footsteps. Slowly spinning on my

heel, I face Nathan, offering him a polite smile. "Hi, Nate."

Stepping closer to me, he reaches for my chin and tilts my face up to meet his. I take a step back, attempting to put some distance between us, but hit the cold wall behind me instead. Not only do I have nowhere to go, but my hands are occupied with the baked treats for the nursing staff. "Are you alright? You look a little pale."

Frowning, I deadpan, "Gee, thanks."

Narrowing his eyes, he gives me a warning with only my name, "Gabriella."

"I'm fine!" I insist irritably. He leans in closer, looking deep into my eyes as if searching for the truth. "I'm just tired," I emphasize, hoping it will get him to back off.

"Then, what are you doing here?" Leaning over the tray in my hands, he attempts to get closer, so close I feel his warm breath on my cheek.

Straightening, I narrow my eyes. "Although it's none of your business, I'm here visiting someone."

I watch as his shoulders visibly relax and he finally takes a step back, giving me some much-needed space to breathe. "Who are you visiting? Is everything okay?" he probes like he has every right.

"Like I said, Nate, it's none of your business." I paste a fake smile on my face.

He heaves a sigh and looks away. "It's not that easy to just forget, and that wasn't my choice."

"Maybe not, but..." trailing off, I shake my head in annoyance. "I'm not having this conversation right now, Nathan."

"Ella, please," he begs, his hands falling to my waist. His pager goes off, interrupting him. He glances down, grinding his jaw in irritation.

"You have to go," I state the obvious.

"We're not finished," he claims. He leans back in and I turn my head to the side, grateful for the barrier between us as his lips fall to my cheek. He tenses just before he lets out a harsh breath. "We'll talk later, Gabriella," he grumbles in frustration. Without waiting for a response, he turns on his heel and picks up his pace down the hall without looking back.

Taking a deep breath and exhaling slowly, I attempt to push Nathan out of my thoughts and reclaim my positive attitude. I don't want to walk into his room with any negativity after his accident. Stopping at the nurse's station, I smile, seeing Julie's pale, freckled arm sticking out from underneath her scrubs as she types into a computer. I place the tray of goodies on top of the desk. "Hi, Julie," I call softly, trying to get the beautiful redhead's attention.

Looking up from her paperwork, she smiles, before her eyebrows swiftly draw down in concern. I love her, but I hate that look. "Ella."

"I'm fine," I interrupt before she has a chance to say anything. "I'm just here to see someone."

Tanya, a gorgeous woman three years older than me with smooth brown skin walks around the desk and sits down next to Julie, joining the conversation. "Oh, are you and Dr. Hull back together? I saw you two down the hallway." She wiggles her eyebrows suggestively. "You seemed to be pretty cozy," she teases, smirking.

Grimacing, I stress, "No, we are not back together. He saw me here and I guess he was worried about me for no reason because I'm fine." They both look at me with wide eyes and I shake my head lightly. "Sorry, I didn't get much sleep the last couple of nights. I've been staying with Declan for the last couple days." They both nod in understanding. "I got up early and went back to my place this morning."

"So, who are you here to see?" Julie questions.

"The guy from the motorcycle accident. I saw it happen. I was with him until the ambulance came. I would've come earlier, but the storm..." I begin, shrugging my shoulders, hoping their expressions might let me know he's here. "I just need to see for myself that he's okay," I explain, ignoring their looks of surprise. "How is he doing?"

They both look at me with eyes full of sympathy, letting me know he's here without saying a word. "Gabriella," Tanya begins, "you know we can't tell you anything."

Nodding, I heave a sigh. "I know." I glance down the hallway I assume he is located in before turning my gaze back to them with a grin. "These are for all of you," I mumble, tapping the edges of the tray.

"Thank you," they both reply in kind.

"You're welcome." I return their smiles.

Julie peels back the foil and peeks underneath, inhaling deeply. "Oh, my goodness these all smell so delicious and fresh. Mm," she mumbles appreciatively.

"I haven't been able to sleep since I saw the accident. I see him losing control every time I close my eyes," I mumble, shaking my head. "I just need..." I trail off, gesturing down the hall. Looking back at them, I paste a smile on my face and change the subject. "Anyway, I decided to keep myself busy and bake for all of you."

"You know we always appreciate it," Julie reiterates.

Nodding, I smile in acknowledgment. "I'm going to go," I mumble almost inaudibly. I feel their eyes on me as I turn away from the desk and continue down the hallway, slowing my pace and glancing into each room. As I approach room 314, I catch a glimpse of the man lying in bed and halt, believing it's him.

Gathering my courage, I round the corner and gently nudge the door further open. Cautiously, I step into the room, not wanting to wake him if he's sleeping. Licking my suddenly dry lips, I gasp, my heart stopping at the sight of the man lying battered and bruised in the hospital bed. He's wearing nothing but a hospital gown, and a white sheet barely covering him, his right leg sticking out and propped up, adorned with a white cast.

Taking a step towards him, I look over this man, gorgeous even in his broken state. His dark brown hair sticks up in every direction, except for the small strip where it's shaved and stitched. The side of his face is covered in black and blue. He has thicker facial hair than the light stubble he had the day of the accident. Tubes run from his arm and chest to machines sitting behind him. His strong arms stick out from underneath the hospital gown, his right enclosed in a thick white cast, but his left appears to be covered in nothing but black and colored ink to the middle of his forearm. I move closer, hoping to get a better look and maybe some insight into this sexy stranger.

Without opening his eyes, he mutters irritably in a low growl, "What now?"

My heart thunders in my chest and I gasp. "I'm sorry, I didn't mean to wake you. I just wanted to see how you were doing."

His eyes snap open, his beautiful green gaze meeting mine, overwhelming me. "It's you," he rasps in surprise. "You're real."

His words elicit a quick intake of air, causing my body to heat from head to toe. "Um, yeah." I nod. "You remember me," I add, a smile tugging at my lips.

"It's the only good thing I have to think about lying here in this fucking bed," he enlightens me, eliciting another shocked gasp from me. He chuckles softly, immediately wincing in pain, and momentarily squeezing his eyes shut.

Ignoring the heat in my body, I quickly step closer to his bedside, reaching for his uninjured hand and giving it a light squeeze. "Squeeze my hand if you need to," I offer, knowing what that feels like. "It can help ground you and get you through the pain." It always worked for me.

He does as I instructed, without squeezing too tight while I watch as he breathes in through his nose and out through his mouth, slowly getting the pain under control. His grip loosens and he grits through his teeth, "I'm no stranger to pain."

"I'm sorry, I was just trying to help."

I move to step away, but his grip tightens again on my

hand and his eyes open, meeting my gaze. "I'm sorry. Don't go," he requests. Briefly pausing, I offer him a slight nod. "It sounds like you know what you're talking about," he begins, assessing me. "Do you work here?"

Shaking my head, I reply honestly, surprising myself. "No, but I spent a lot of time here as a patient once upon a time." He opens his mouth, probably to ask more questions, but I don't know this man. I'm not ready to tell him my life story. Attempting to halt his inquiry, I ask, "What's your name?"

He gives me a crooked smile, making my heart skip a beat. "Grant, and you are?"

I glance down at our still joined hands, my face heating. "I'm glad I was there to help you. I'm Ella."

His eyebrows draw down in confusion. "Ella, like Cinderella?"

Even though I've been asked that question before, I can't stop a giggle from erupting and shake my head in amusement as those words leave this man's lips, surprised he's asking that at all. "No, like Gabriella, but I prefer Ella."

"Okay, Ella, but you're also my angel," he emphasizes, making my cheeks turn an even deeper shade of red. "Thank you," he mumbles, his intense gaze holding mine.

My heart jumps up to my throat and I swallow hard, attempting to gulp down my emotions. "So, what's the verdict?" I ask, needing to move on from this moment so I can breathe again.

Sighing heavily, he claims, "Just a few bumps and bruises."

Arching my eyebrows in challenge, I proclaim, "I call bull-shit."

His eyes widen and he chuckles, instantly regretting it. Freezing, he takes a few more deep calming breaths before he requests, "Okay, don't say anything to make me laugh."

"How do I know what will make you laugh?" I challenge. He looks at me out of the corner of his eyes making me giggle. "Okay, I'll do my best."

Barely nodding in appreciation, he mumbles, "Thanks."

"So, seriously, are you going to be okay?"

Heaving a controlled sigh, he concedes, "Yeah. I have a few broken bones, one less kidney and I got some much-needed sleep due to a minor concussion and a few stitches," he reveals nonchalantly.

"Okay, that's manageable," I murmur, feeling all the stress and anxiety drain from my body. Grant stares at me, his eyes appearing heavy. "I should let you get some more sleep then," I admit hesitantly. I have an urge to stay by his side, but I don't know this man, and I'm sure his family and probably girlfriend will be here soon. It's not my place.

"I'm okay," he claims. Arching my eyebrows in disbelief, he attempts to shrug and winces instead, sighing in defeat.

A tall and thin male nurse I've never met strides into the room, addressing him, "Hello, Mr. Young, I'm Joe. I'm part of your pain management team. Can I discuss your care in front of your sister, wife, girlfriend?" he questions, fishing.

Shaking my head, I answer for him, "Oh, no, I'm just a... friend."

The man grins and winks at me, making me blush. Grant immediately interjects, "You're more than that, Angel."

Goose bumps prickle my skin as my attention swings to Grant in surprise. "Um," I rasp, my heart pounding. Angel, as if it were my name. My phone rings, pulling my attention. Declan's face lights up the screen. Shaking my head, I hold up my phone, announcing, "I have to take this."

"Will you be back?" Grant inquires.

Licking my lips, I open my mouth to respond, not knowing what to say. Does he want me to come back? I glance at the nurse, his gaze flitting back and forth between us before making a quick decision and returning my focus to Grant with a nod. "I'll be back tomorrow."

I watch as what appears to be relief passes over his handsome, battered features, but I don't understand. A man as sexy and beautiful as that all beaten and bruised is probably more than I can handle, but I want to come back, to help him. Besides, I promised myself I wouldn't live with any more regrets. Life is too short. I don't have room for not taking chances, no matter what it might be. Even if I'm betting on a stranger like Grant who makes my blood boil before I know anything about him besides his looks and that he rides a motorcycle.

I'm in so much trouble, but after everything I've been through, I may not know what I'm doing with my life, but I plan on keeping my promises to myself. I at least deserve that.

Grant

GRATEFUL FOR THE MOMENTARY REPRIEVE, I STARE BLANKLY at the ceiling. I'm done with being poked and prodded. I know what my damn name is and I know I crashed my bike, but I'm still here. Stop asking me the same fucking questions. I just want to be left alone, even for a little while; at least by everyone but her.

I can't believe my blonde angel is real. The only thing about that night that feels like reality is the excruciating pain. I would've bet she was a hallucination, but I shouldn't be surprised. My imagination couldn't create someone like her. That woman is one-of-a-kind gorgeous. And yet, she stopped to help me. Little did she know I'm not worth the effort.

The moment her soft voice hit my ears, I knew it was her, I just didn't know if I was dreaming and I had to know. As our gazes collided, an electric shock traveled through my body, giving me life. Her bright blue eyes hooked me, offering comfort and hope, just like they did as I laid helplessly on the cold, hard ground. I would've given up in a heartbeat if it weren't for her. She saved my life, and although I'm not sure if I should've been given this chance, I've got it. Now, I have no idea how I'm supposed to thank her for that or if I want to.

When she held my hand, while I worked through the pain, her touch seared my skin even through my agony. She knew just what to do to help, and I craved to know why. After my pain eased enough to focus, I wanted to ask.

Instead, I stared, not able to take my eyes off her. Those blue eyes held me captive. I had the strongest urge to reach up, pull her into my arms and hold her close. Besides being partially incapable of doing so, I don't do things like that, ever, and I sure as hell can't start now. She's dangerous for me. I can feel it. Ella needs to be at the top of my list of things to stay away from. Getting too close to her could burn us both, and I don't think I would survive the inferno. But even if I did, I would hate myself for the ashes I left behind.

I sure as hell don't know why I told the pain management nurse she was more, challenging her, wanting a reaction. Holding back, I try not to laugh at myself knowing it would only hurt, but that's a fucking lie; I know exactly why I did it. The way he looked at her made my blood boil. Irrationally, I wasn't about to let him ogle her and flirt. I didn't like it. It may not be any of my damn business, but I felt the need to protect her whether she wanted me to or not. There's no way I was going to lay in bed and watch him ask out my angel and no way in hell I was going to turn her away from me before I knew anything about her—no matter how bad of an idea it is.

When I close my eyes, I see her standing over me, protecting me and pushing me to fight. It may be selfish, but I can't walk away from that, from her. Not yet anyway. I don't know what the fuck it is about her, but I want to see more of her. No, I need to see more of her, although she's probably the last person I should see. I'm not good for anyone, and the blaze she ignited inside me with just a glimpse is bound to be my destruction.

Then again, what harm can seeing her or talking to her really do? I'm in the hospital with my right side broken and completely useless in this state. Plus, it's either I'm under the influence of pain medication, or I'm in so much agony, I can't see straight. With me like this, it's not like I can do anything about it. But if I could, would she even want me to?

Sighing heavily, I attempt to shake off my thoughts, pushing away the what-ifs. Those things don't matter. They can't. That's not my life. I gave up the chance to hope a long time ago, and it's no longer mine to take back. I don't deserve it. I'll be gone soon enough, and everything will go back to how it should be; my normal. Ella will be here without me to darken her path and I'll be somewhere on my own, going through the motions before the time comes to move on again. I'll never be able to stop moving, leaving everything and everyone behind.

But for now, my body is broken like the rest of me, and I'm stuck here. I feel so fucking useless, powerless. Asking Ella to come back gave me a reason to look forward to tomorrow. Am I an asshole for wanting to take her offered kindness? Probably, but there's no way in hell I'm stopping it now, at least not yet. The day will come. It's inevitable, but in the meantime, I'm going to take what I can get to survive.

My eyelids fall, too heavy and weighed down for me to fight to keep them open.

"Mr. Young, sorry to wake you, but I need to do another test," a technician advises as he steps up to my bedside.

I do nothing but groan in acknowledgment, letting him do whatever he needs to while my eyes remain closed. I've endured worse.

6

Grant

"COME ON RICK, GIVE ME A BREAK! I'M IN THE FUCKING HOSpital! I need to keep my insurance," I plead, my desperation building.

"You were the one that quit by leaving me a fucking voicemail," he reminds me, making me cringe.

"I'm sorry, man. It couldn't be helped." I'm grateful he can't see my face. "I had an emergency and had to leave immediately."

"You left me high and dry, Grant! Were you even planning on coming back?" he questions accusingly.

I grind my teeth, knowing I can't lie to him. He was a great boss, and he's right. "Rick," I begin apologetically.

"Save it!" Heaving a defeated sigh, he proposes, "Look, I can keep you on until the end of the month, but at the start of July, you will be removed. That gives you time to come up with something."

"Thanks, Rick." I wish it could be longer, but I realize I'm a lucky bastard and it's better than nothing; it's more than I deserve.

"Good luck to you, Grant." I drop the phone next to me on the bed, growling in frustration.

Julie, my nurse, walks back into the room. "That bad?"

Sighing, I meet her gaze. "It's fine. Thanks for letting me borrow your phone."

"You'll have to get yourself a new one. What's left of yours is in a Ziploc in the drawer on your left." Glancing towards the drawer, I grimace. I guess it doesn't really matter. The moment I landed in a new place, I would've cleared it and started over anyway. "Your keys and wallet are in there too."

"Thanks." My gaze falls to my broken limbs, my mind still stuck on what I'm going to do. "How long until these casts come off again?" I'm already dreading losing my independence until these things are gone.

"About another seven weeks."

"Shit," I grumble under my breath as my insides twitch in misery.

"Getting antsy already?"

I move to shake my head and flinch, a shock of pain moving through my right shoulder. Hissing through my teeth, I attempt to control my breathing before conceding, "I'm just trying to figure out what to do about work."

"What do you do, Mr. Young?"

"I'm a mechanic. Motorcycles are my specialty," I reveal, narrowing my eyes. "I need both of my hands to work."

Her face turns soft, giving me a look of pity and making me cringe. I've had enough of that type of look to last me a lifetime. "Unfortunately, that will be a while, but maybe you can figure something else out in the meantime."

I huff a humorless laugh and mumble under my breath, "Yeah, right."

Ignoring my comment, she continues, "After the casts come off, you will need physical therapy. But everyone heals differently, and with hard work, you'll be back to yourself in no time." Smiling, she attempts to soften the blow. "According to Dr. Magi, you should be able to get out of here soon."

"Yeah, soon. But that's only if I have someone to help me at home, and I don't have anyone." I grimace, disgusted with myself. "I don't even have a fucking home!"

She visibly flinches, her face pinching tightly. I watch as

she struggles to get her emotions under control before speaking. It's always the same thing. Anyone who knows that about me suddenly looks at me completely different, and it fucking sucks. I deserve it, but it doesn't make it easier to take.

"That's okay. We do have a facility where we can move you after you're discharged, and the physical therapy would be done right in-house there," she advises, pasting an encouraging smile on her face. "Insurance normally partially covers it. You'd have to check with your insurance company to find out the details."

I gulp down the lump in my throat, hoping it will ease my anxiety as her words sink in. The more tense I am, the worse I feel, my head beginning to pound along with the rest of my body. But what the hell am I supposed to do with that information? I go to their facility until the end of the month, and then what? Then, they kick me out because I no longer have insurance? "Shit," I grumble on a harsh exhale. I can look into interim insurance, but I wonder if being in the middle of treatment will be an issue.

I'm so fucked.

"Is this a bad time?" a sweet, soft voice calls into the room as she knocks softly on the open door.

My stomach flips and I look up, meeting her hesitant gaze. Exhaling in relief, my lips instantly curl up. She has her hair pulled up in a high ponytail on top of her head, bringing attention to her high cheekbones and blue eyes, appearing a darker shade of blue today. She's dressed in faded cut off jean shorts and a pale blue t-shirt fitted to her curves, causing my mouth to water. Licking my dry lips, I clear my throat before I dare speak. "You came back." The sight of her helps ease my pain and anxiety.

A bright smile instantly lights up her face as her cheeks tint a beautiful shade of pink. "I told you I would," she taunts playfully.

"You did. I'm glad you're here. Come in," I urge, waving

her in with my good hand.

She steps into the room and smiles at my nurse, just finishing up with my regular vitals. "Hi, Julie."

Julie smirks. "Hi, Ella. You're back."

Instead of responding, Ella sucks in her lower lip. Her cheeks turn a deeper shade of red as she looks away from my nurse and towards the floor. She releases her lip slowly before lifting her gaze to me as I fight to hold back an audible groan. "Are you doing any better today?"

"I am now," I tease, thoroughly enjoying her blush.

"Okay, Mr. Young, I'll be back after Dr. Magi does her rounds," Julie advises.

"Thanks." I glance in her direction. We both remain silent as she walks out the door, giving Ella a pointed look as she exits, piquing my curiosity.

"A friend of yours?" I question, arching my eyebrow.

Blushing again, she nods. "Yeah, we grew up together."

"So, you're from around here?" I ask, wanting her to give me more.

"Yeah. Honestly, I've lived here all my life." She scrunches up her face adorably with displeasure.

"Hm, you don't seem too happy about it."

Shaking her head, she quickly disagrees. "No, I love it here. It's a beautiful area, and I love the beach. I don't know how people live without it. Plus, my whole family lives in the area, and I'm grateful to have everyone so close." She shrugs as if it's no big deal, pausing in thought. My chest tightens, remembering what it was like to be close to my family, but I quickly shove the memories away as she continues. "I guess I've just never really had the opportunity to go anywhere, but one day I will get my chance."

"Huh," I mumble under my breath. Ironic. My angel remained in her hometown most of her life, close to her family, but without an opportunity to see more of the world. Yet, she saved my life; the man who had to let his family go and lives his life roaming the world. Maybe I've seen more of this country than I ever planned in the last ten years, but I would give almost anything to have and deserve a place to call home again.

Unfortunately, that will never happen for me. Staying any-where too long would only give me time for my past to catch up with me. I don't ever want to relive my past, my nightmare; that wouldn't be good for me or anyone around me. Besides, I'm no angel.

Ella

THANKFULLY, HIS BRUISES DON'T APPEAR QUITE AS DARK today, plus I see a little bit of yellowing around the edges, indicating healing. I watch as his features morph from happiness when he sees me here, to sadness, making me wonder what he's thinking or even where he's been. Instead, I ask, "Why were you out riding a motorcycle in the middle of a storm, anyway?"

He momentarily presses his lips tightly together before bringing his focus back to me. "I didn't know there was a storm coming. I didn't watch the weather," he admits sheepishly, making my heart skip a beat. He doesn't seem like a man who's shy about anything. "I was looking for somewhere to pull over when..." he trails off, grimacing.

"I'm glad I was there," I admit over the lump in my throat.

"Thanks, but I'm sorry you had to see it. It couldn't have been easy," he concedes, wincing. "I'm normally so good with my bike." He smirks, attempting to lighten the mood. With a slightly stiff shake of his head, he sighs heavily, appearing defeated. Forcing a smile, he prompts, "So what do you do that you're able to come hang out at the hospital with someone like me?"

"I like hanging out with you," I insist, already knowing it's true. I want to get to know him.

Chuckling, he shakes his head in disbelief. "So? You didn't

answer my question."

"Oh, I'm waitressing for now." He arches his eyebrows in question, urging me to go on. "It's exactly what I want to be doing right now. Flexible schedule, great tips." I shrug. I'm not ready to explain the whole reason why I'm working in my hometown as a waitress to a man I don't know, but I'd sure like to, and I don't know why. Attempting to take the focus off me, I inquire, "What do you do when you're not crashing motorcycles?"

"Fixing them." I arch my eyebrows in surprise, eliciting a low chuckle from his lips. He sighs, resigned, and nods almost imperceptibly. "It's true. I'm a mechanic and motorcycles are kind of my specialty."

I scrunch my face in incredulity and confusion. Tilting my head to the side, I assess his features, wondering what he's thinking and trying to piece everything together. Without thought, I blurt out, "So, how are you going to work?"

He huffs a humorless laugh and releases a heavy sigh. "Now that's the question of the day."

"Sore subject?"

"Yeah, you could say that. I need both hands to do my job, and my right side is obviously incapacitated for about another seven weeks or so if everything goes okay." I wince, familiar with the helpless feeling I see in his eyes. "Then, I need therapy after that to get back my strength and range of motion. But I have no idea how the hell I'll make it that far."

"Why do you say that?" My heart goes into overdrive, filled with unsolicited concern.

"Honestly?" he questions, an almost guilty look on his face. I nod. "I guess you could say timing is everything. I just quit my job the morning of the accident," he confesses, looking down at his cast.

"That really sucks, but since you have to take the time to get better anyway, isn't that a good thing?"

"You'd think, but insurance," he emphasizes, my eyes going

wide with realization. "I talked to my old boss, and he offered to keep me on the company insurance until the end of the month, but I need to figure out what to do after that. Besides there's the fact that I don't have a phone to do any research to find some interim insurance. Mine was destroyed in the accident."

"I can do that for you."

He shakes his head in refusal. "You've already done enough. I'm not asking you to do anything else for me."

"You didn't ask. I offered." I'm grateful he's giving me a way to help.

"Ella, you don't have to do that."

"You're right. I don't." I narrow my eyes at him, letting him know I'm not taking no for an answer. "How much longer are you here for?"

Heaving a sigh, he relents. "I don't know."

Dr. Magi strides into the room with two interns following closely behind, announcing, "Hopefully, he will be out of here in the next two days. At least as long as all your tests keep turning out as I expect," she adds with an encouraging smile towards Grant.

He winces, making a face. Perplexed by his reaction, I can't help but question, "What? Do you want to stay here longer?"

"No, but..." he trails off with a slight shake of his head, not giving me an answer. Turning his focus to Dr. Magi, he greets her, "Good morning."

"I should let Dr. Magi do her job. I have to work in a little while anyway." I suck my lower lip between my teeth in hesitation. "Is it okay if I stop in tomorrow morning?"

"Sure." He gives me a crooked grin, causing my heart to skip a beat. "I'll see you tomorrow, Angel."

"Bye, Grant." I smile, my face heating as Dr. Magi looks between us, arching her eyebrows in curiosity.

I glance back into his room one more time, reluctant to leave, while his focus remains on Dr. Magi. Sighing, I spin on my heel, turning towards the elevators. My heart clenches tightly inside my chest, desperate to help him. At least I can investigate interim insurance for him.

Spotting Nate stepping out of the elevator, I sidestep, swiftly slipping into the bathroom, hoping he didn't see me. He's the last person I want to run into right now. Hovering by the door, I hold my breath, waiting a few minutes before peeking out into the hallway.

Glancing in both directions, I find the corridors quiet. Slowly, I release my breath as I step out, cautiously making my escape. Out of the corner of my eye, I catch a glimpse of Nate in one of the patient rooms with another doctor, relief washing over me knowing he's occupied.

Taking advantage of the short window, I call out, "Bye," as I wave to the nurses making my way towards the elevator. I push the down button, bouncing on my toes as I anxiously wait.

A hand falls gentle, but firm on my back, startling me. Spinning on my heel, I come face to face with the one person I don't want to see.

"Sorry, I didn't mean to scare you. I guess you didn't hear me call your name." Nate holds his hands up in surrender.

"Hi, Nathan."

Crossing my arms protectively over my chest, I wait impatiently as he slowly looks me up and down, assessing me. "You look much better than yesterday."

Narrowing my eyes, I mutter, "Gee, thanks."

Sighing in annoyance, he ignores my comment and questions, "How are you feeling?"

"Great!" I paste a fake smile on my face.

"Are you here to see your friend again, then?"

"Yup," I reply, popping the 'p.' I refuse to give him more than he's asking. The elevator dings and the doors slide open, causing me to release the breath I didn't know I was holding. Finally meeting Nathan's gaze, I offer him a genuine smile and quickly blurt out, "Thanks for asking. I have to go to work. Have a good day."

As I step into the elevator, he grasps my elbow, halting me. I glare down at his offending hand and he instantly removes it. "Sorry," he mumbles. I nod my head and swiftly retreat further into the elevator, the doors sliding closed before he has a chance to say anything else. I'm sure I'll get a text from him in the next few minutes, but it doesn't matter. He needs to leave me alone and just let me live my life.

The moment I step outside, I close my eyes, taking a deep breath and inhaling the saltwater air. As I exhale slowly, I feel my body release its tension almost instantly. I love that smell and the way I can taste the salt on my lips as the wind blows in my face. I'm lucky I live here and fortunate to be able to experience that every time I walk outside.

Smiling to myself, I make my way to my car in the front corner of the lot. I want to get home so I have a chance to check into the insurance information for Grant before I need to get ready for work. I'm glad I can do something for him, even if it's something small like this. He looked incredibly vulnerable when he told me what he does for a living, like the confession alone might break him. I already wish I could do so much more to help, and I vow to do just that as long as he'll let me.

8

Grant

I WINCE IN PAIN, ATTEMPTING TO DRAG MYSELF OFF THE FLOOR, *wondering how the hell I ended up here. No, that's not true. I know how it happened. I'm here because I thought with my dick instead of my head and now, I have no idea how to climb out of this deep, endless pit I've dug myself into.*

Stumbling up to my feet, I lean on the wall for support as I try to catch my breath. I groan in agony, hissing through my teeth. What the fuck am I going to do? I have a game this coming weekend. There's no way I can miss it. I have too much riding on it, especially now, but I need to be able to actually move fluidly to play football, let alone be able to play well. And the guys are depending on me. I don't want to disappoint them.

Trudging towards the back door, I attempt to remain as quiet as possible. I freeze at the sudden sound of her heels clicking on the tile floor as she approaches from the kitchen. Inhaling deeply, I hold my breath. I can't help but wish I were invisible but know I have no way of escaping before she reaches me. My body tenses, preparing to protect myself.

"Where in the hell do you think you're going, Mr. Young?" she challenges, her shrill voice echoing off the walls, sending chills down my spine.

Gulping down the lump in my throat, I begrudgingly turn towards her, attempting to keep my pain under control. I'm not going to let her win. "Home," I answer, my confidence lacking.

"Not looking like that you're not. If people see you like that, rumors will start spreading about you, and I'm not taking any chances when it comes to you."

I huff a humorless laugh and shake my head in disbelief, knowing she doesn't give a damn about me. She's only worried about protecting herself. "Let them," I mutter with disgust. "I'm pretty sure the rumors started a long time ago," I add defiantly, at the same time, wondering why the fuck I don't shut my mouth. I'm just making it worse.

She narrows her brown eyes at me and quickly closes the distance between us. "Do you really think right now is the time to push me, Grant? Even if you don't care about yourself anymore, you have your little brother to think about. Matt sure spends a lot of time here," she taunts, an evil grin tugging at her lips, reminding me of what I already know.

Then again, he's just a kid. What could she possibly do to him? I look back, attempting to read her intentions and my stomach plummets. I don't think I can take anymore, but there's no way in hell I can take a chance with Matt. I can't let her get near him. Instead of answering, I take another deep breath, announcing, "I'm going to clean up."

She grins, a devilish spark flashing in her eyes as she gives me a look meant to entice, but the only thing I feel anymore is repulsion. "That's my good boy," she croons, patting me gently on the cheek as I attempt to step around her.

With a low growl, I grit my teeth as she grabs my face in her hands and yanks it down, pressing her lips to mine. My stomach churns in protest as I remain still. Thankfully, she pulls away, taking a step back. Exhaling harshly, my shoulders begin sagging with relief as I again attempt my retreat towards the bathroom.

"We have a couple hours before Amy will be home. I'll be there in a few minutes to help you feel better," she offers, turning back towards the kitchen.

"I got it," I argue, my back instantly going ramrod straight.

Her head snaps in my direction, her brown hair flying around her before it settles. Glaring at me, she reiterates, "I will be there in a few minutes, Grant. Warm up the water for me." She licks her lips as she stares at me, devouring what she sees, making me clench my fists in frustration, a wave of disgust washing over me. An evil smile curls her lips. "I will also give you a chance to make it up to me for your wandering eyes. And Grant, you will make it up to me," she declares, leaving no room for argument.

Pinching my lips tightly together, I take a deep breath, gathering my strength before I nod in acknowledgment, feeling anything but strong. I move towards the bathroom on autopilot, her gaze burning into my back. I step into the bathroom and pull the door closed behind me, barely breathing as I feel my whole world slipping away from me.

My heart suddenly begins beating out of control as I gasp for breath. I squeeze my eyes shut, attempting to empty my mind, but it's no use. My hands start to shake and my palms become sweaty. Taking another deep breath, I exhale slowly, trying to relax my body, but nothing seems to help. A single tear falls without my consent, rolling down my cheeks as everything closes in on me crushing my lungs.

I don't know how the fuck I'm going to get out of this mess. That scholarship feels like my only fucking chance. I need it to escape without further repercussions! I need it to survive, but I have to not only impress the scouts, I also have to make it through the rest of the year afterwards to graduate. Fuck! I'm so screwed! I don't know if I can make it.

I gasp, panic consuming me as my eyes fly open, quickly searching my surroundings. The stark white walls and pale blue curtains let me know I'm not trapped in that bathroom. Exhaling in relief, I make an effort to move. I flinch, realizing my pain is real. Instantly, panic sets back in, fighting to take control.

Closing my eyes I focus on my breathing, pushing my nightmares out of the forefront of my mind until I calm.

It seems like my dreams are back, but there's no way in hell I can live like that again. I don't know if it's being trapped here in the hospital, feeling helpless over my body and my life, or the amount of pain I'm in that's giving me flashbacks, but they're coming full force since the moment I opened my eyes in this hospital bed, and that can't happen. I feel like I'm falling backwards into a deep, dark pit, getting pulled under by the devil herself. I'm being forced to relive my nightmares every time I close my eyes, and not the one that just happened a few days ago when I crashed my bike; that does nothing to rival my past.

I thought I dealt with this shit already. I thought those nightmares were gone for good. I can't go back to that place, that darkness. The pain I'm in now after crashing my bike is a walk in the park compared to that hellhole.

Taking another deep breath, I try to think of something good, shoving my memories back into their box. A small smile tugs at my lips as my blonde angel comes to mind, lightening my thoughts and helping my body relax, at least a little bit. The thought of her gives me a peace she will never realize. I only wish I could return the favor, but I can never be enough or do enough to repay her for what she's given me. Even when it's only a few moments of reprieve at a time, it's a gift I don't take lightly and treasure every second.

Closing my eyes, I focus on an image of Ella hovering over me. I lick my lips in anticipation as I drift back to sleep, letting my dreams turn wicked, as I imagine the things I would do to her if she would only let me.

9

Ella

I GLANCE DOWN AT MY SIMPLE, PALE YELLOW SUNDRESS, smoothing out the non-existent wrinkles. It's fitted to my body on the top and flares out at the bottom from the waist, with spaghetti straps tied in a bow over my shoulders. The heat practically demanded I wear something to keep myself cool; at least that's what I keep telling myself. I wiggle my freshly painted blush pink toenails, peeking out from my white sandals, my anxiety beginning to climb as I wait for the elevator to reach my destination, despite my time on the water this morning attempting to keep it at bay.

As the doors slide open, I hold my breath stepping into the hallway, grateful I don't see a familiar young doctor roaming the halls. I wave at the nurses behind the desk as they glance up from their work, returning the gesture. "Hi, Ella!"

I reach Grant's room, finding the door slightly ajar, voices coming from inside. Just shy of the doorway, I stop, not wanting to interrupt whoever is inside.

"I'm sure you will like the rehab facility, Mr. Young. It will be very convenient," Dr. Magi advises.

"Great," he grumbles, obviously annoyed.

Moments later, Dr. Magi strides right by me with another doctor at her side. She nods and smiles at me in greeting as she exits. "Hi," I murmur softly.

Squaring my shoulders, I step into the room, watching as Grant's focus remains on his good hand, clenching and loosening it repeatedly. My heart breaks for him, wishing I could do more to help. I can't imagine what it would feel like to have your independence ripped away in seconds. Then again, maybe I know exactly how that feels. Taking a step closer, I gently inquire, "Do you mind if I come in?"

His head snaps up and I see an instant change in his features as he meets my gaze. His eyes soften, appearing more green than golden, his brow smooths, his fist loosens, dropping to the bed, and his lips curve upwards in a crooked smile, making my heart skip a beat before he even says a word. "Please."

"How are you feeling today?" His smile immediately falters, making me flinch. Shaking my head, I start over before he even has a chance to respond. "I'm sorry, that's really the worst question in the world when you're in the hospital, isn't it?" I ponder, scrunching up my nose in displeasure. "It's the only thing anyone ever seems to want to know."

He relaxes, his easy smile returning. "That and if you've eaten or gone to the bathroom," he adds honestly.

Nodding in agreement, I offer him a small smile. "True. Sorry."

"Don't apologize."

"So, I'm sorry, but I overheard Dr. Magi say you would like the rehab facility. Is that where you're going when you're discharged?" The reality of what I just asked sets in, the question repeating in my head, causing my stomach to sink. Was he drinking that night? I didn't think he smelled like alcohol, but it was raining. Maybe it was something else. Was he on something? I may feel like I know him, but I need to remind myself I don't know anything about this man, no matter how much I feel pulled to him, pulled to help him.

His eyes narrow, assessing me as if he can read my thoughts. I swear I see disappointment flash through his eyes, and I fight not to flinch or shy away from his intense gaze. "For my occupational and physical therapy, yeah."

My face heats, embarrassment and guilt flooding me. I should know better than to jump to conclusions about someone. "Oh, um, yeah. That makes sense. But if it were something else, it wouldn't be a big deal. A lot of people need help with things like that," I blurt out, feeling worse with every word erupting from my mouth. "I don't judge," I emphasize, my nerves wreaking havoc on my insides.

Sighing, he lets it slide, muttering, "Yeah, sure, okay."

I suddenly feel uneasy and I don't like it. How am I messing this up? I just want to help him, not make him feel worse. He's obviously been through a lot with his accident alone, and I have a feeling there's so much more to it than that or he wouldn't be lying here alone. Taking a deep breath, I attempt to redirect. "Anyway, I thought they said you would be discharged?"

He grimaces. "That's only if I have someone for them to discharge me to. They think I will need help once I leave." He grins, shrugging dismissively on his good side.

Arching my eyebrows I challenge, "And you think you don't?" He just smirks in response, heating me to my core. "What about your family? Or a girlfriend?" I prompt, feeling my cheeks heat instantly. "Or someone?" I add awkwardly, but I want to know.

His smirk broadens as he answers, "No girlfriend."

My cheeks turn an even deeper shade of red, and I force myself to maintain eye contact. "Well, what about your family?"

He frowns, grumbling, "They're not around anymore." He looks away offering no further explanation. I watch as his Adam's apple bobs up and down while he attempts to gulp down his obvious pain, only increasing my curiosity.

"Oh." My heart clenches, commiserating and wishing I could do something more to help ease his pain, both inside and out. That already seems to be a pattern with me when it comes to this man. He obviously has a lot on his mind, and now he has to deal with getting himself better without any support. That's something I always had, even when I didn't want it. I can't imagine trying to go through something so difficult without anyone around for me at all. Although I'm curious as to what he means about his family, I know not to push his limits. I have no right.

"Well, I brought you some information on interim insurance," I inform him, giving him the reprieve he's searching for.

He forces a smile. "Thanks."

My chest tightens, hating that I made him uncomfortable, but proud of myself for asking. Handing the papers to him, I point to the one on top. "It looks like this one might be your best option, but you may have to pay up to fifty percent for some things. They make it difficult since you're already in the hospital and you had just quit your job." I grimace, commiserating.

"Fuckin' great," he gripes under his breath, but I don't blame him.

"Sorry," I mumble, although I know it's nothing I can control.

"You have nothing to apologize for. None of this is your problem. I appreciate all your help, but you didn't have to do this. I'll figure it out." He frowns, appearing resigned. Glancing away, he mumbles almost inaudibly, "I always do."

I flinch, an idea forming in my head, one I know my family won't like, but right now, I don't care. I blurt out the words before I have a chance to think it through, "Come stay with me."

His gaze returns to mine as his eyes widen in surprise, most likely mirroring my own. The corners of his mouth twitch up as he assesses me, attempting to read my thoughts. He huffs a laugh before he finally responds with a slight shake of his head. "That's not a good idea, Angel."

I press my lips tightly together, my body tightening with his response. "Why not?"

"You don't know me," he emphasizes, drawing out each word.

I arch my eyebrows in challenge. "So, are y'all a murderer or a serial killer?"

"No." He chuckles, the deep rumbling sound giving me goose bumps.

"A kidnapper or a rapist?"

"Fuck no!" he answers, his fists clenching at the thought. "And I don't do drugs or sell them. I'm not a pimp, or a thief. The only crime I ever committed was assault on an asshole who thought he could attack a woman outside my front door, but I didn't know the woman."

"That's good enough for me," I answer irrationally.

His eyes narrow, focusing on me as he slowly reiterates, "You don't know me. I'm not staying with you."

"I could help you." I step closer, seeing a flash of indecision on his face. He opens his mouth to respond and then snaps it closed, his jaw clenching. Turning his head, he looks out the window, seeming to consider my proposition. I perch myself on the side of his bed, careful not to jostle his broken limbs. "Let me help you, Grant." He doesn't even glance in my direction, so I boldly reach for his good hand, steeling myself for rejection. I gasp the moment our hands connect, heat shooting straight up my arm and electrifying my body as his head snaps in my direction, his gaze colliding with mine. "Please," I beg, my desperation to help him overwhelming.

A spark of light glitters in his eyes before he shudders, as if shutting himself down. He scoffs, shaking his head and dismissing my offer. "So, what kind of food do they have where you work?" he inquires, attempting to move on.

"Burgers, chicken sandwiches, wraps, seafood," I begin, giving him his out for now. "They have really good food," I claim, foolishly wishing I could bring him there.

"I'll have to try some when I get out of here. It will be good to eat some real food. I'm so fucking hungry!"

"I believe it. But you do know they have a lot more here than just the cafeteria food?" I arch my eyebrows in question.

His eyes widen in surprise, making me chuckle. I nod. "Yeah, they have a smoothie bar, a coffee bar and even a café with sandwiches and wraps."

"Seriously? Have you been holding out on me?" he teases, a sexy smirk lighting up his face.

"Holding out on him? Are you sleeping with this asshole, Gabriella?" Nate questions from the doorway, his disgruntled voice bouncing off the walls.

I gasp, instantly jumping up and spinning towards the door with my heart beating out of control. I move to pull my hand away from Grant, but his hold suddenly tightens and I stop fighting. "What are you doing here, Nathan?"

His eyes narrow on me, glaring down at our hands and then back at me. "I work here." He steps further into the room. "You didn't answer my question."

"Because it's none of your damn business!" I retort defiantly. I refuse to give him anything.

"Do I have another test or something?" Grant questions, irritably.

Nate glares at Grant, answering, "No," before returning his gaze to me. "What are you thinking?" he challenges, his disbelief clear.

I scoff, shocked by his reaction. He has no right. "Nathan," I begin, squaring my shoulders.

Grant interrupts, "I don't know who the hell you are, but I'd like you to leave."

"Excuse me?" Nathan probes, perplexed, prompting an eyeroll from me.

"I don't like how you're talking to my angel," Grant defends, causing my mouth to drop further open in shock.

"Your angel?" Nathan challenges with a quick intake of breath.

I exhale harshly, blurting out, "Yes! But that's none of your damn business. You're not my boyfriend anymore, Nathan, remember?"

He winces and takes a step back. Glancing down at the iPad in his hands, he grins mischievously. "Well, it says in here Mr. Young doesn't have any family, friends, or significant other to care for him upon discharge, so he's being admitted to our rehab facility tomorrow."

I open my mouth to respond and snap it shut, averting his burning stare. "Well, that's wrong," Grant advises, my eyes flying back to him. "I'm going home with Ella," he claims, causing my heart to pick up its pace. "We were just discussing what to have for dinner tomorrow night when we get home," he adds, his own prideful smirk in place.

"You're bringing this guy home with you? Do your brothers know? Do your parents know?" Nate pushes, stepping closer.

"Aren't you supposed to be doing your job, not harassing the patients?" I clench my free hand into a fist at my side.

"Gabriella, I just want what's best for you."

I snort, an ugly laugh escaping. "You don't know what's best for me."

I see his wince before I turn back to Grant. "I'm going home to get a few things done before you're discharged. I'll be back tomorrow morning." Feeling Nathan's eyes on me, I lean down, placing a chaste kiss on Grant's lips, taking us both by surprise. His eyes widen as a small gasp escapes my lips. My face heats and his lips begin twitching in amusement. Straightening, I repeat my words, trying to get my head straight, "I have to go. Get some rest, Grant."

Spinning on my heel, I quickly rush out of the room and towards the elevator before either of them has a chance to say anything else. "Well, that was unexpected," I mumble to myself, feeling off-balance. I may have gotten him to change his mind about coming home with me, but that may have been the worst decision I've ever made in my life. Why would I offer to bring a strange man home with me? It doesn't matter that he's gorgeous even in his current state or that he makes it hard to breathe just being close to him. Nate's right: I don't know him and my family is going to kill me if I survive. With a shake of my head, I remind myself, he's broken, and he needs help.

A soft sigh escapes as I let my fingers fall to my lips, gently running reverently over them, while I ride the elevator down to the main lobby. My lips tingle, the simple kiss I forced him to endure burning my skin. Well, I do say I refuse to live without regrets, and I know I would regret it if I didn't help him. He may not want to admit it, but he needs me. My heart skips a beat. Ignoring it, I push forward, suddenly in a hurry to get home.

10

Grant

"YOU'RE A VERY LUCKY MAN, MR. YOUNG," DR. MAGI EMPHA-sizes, repeating the statement for what feels like the hundredth time. I'm sick of it.

"Thanks." I smile stiffly, but I sure as hell don't feel lucky.

I glance down at my broken body, covered with a loose pair of black net shorts a male nurse was kind enough to gift me, along with a black and white graphic t-shirt. My entire body hurts, constantly throbbing when it's not numb, even my good side. Half my limbs are in casts and my motorcycle was totaled. I have no job and no chance of working on bikes anytime soon, let alone riding one. My insurance will soon be gone, and I'll be paying through the nose to get maybe half of it covered. Plus, I'm positive I'm making a huge mistake agreeing to go home with Ella. I'm anything but lucky.

"Good luck, Grant." I grunt in response, ready to get the hell out of here. "Please let me know if you have any further questions, or if something changes, or if you need anything before you come back in for your follow-up."

"I will," I mumble automatically, barely listening.

"Goodbye, Grant." Dr. Magi nods as she walks out the door.

I sit on top of the blankets, anxious to get out of this hospital bed and at the same time uneasy. While I wait to be discharged, I can't help but wonder if Ella will show up. I wouldn't blame her if she didn't, but if she does, should I go with her? My chest tightens at thoughts of my blonde angel.

What the hell did I even agree to? I'm supposed to be staying away from her. She must either really hate her ex or like trouble because that's all I ever bring to the table. I know why I did it. I didn't like how that asshole spoke to her and I fucking hated how he looked at her, but she's not mine. Luckily she's not his either, at least not anymore. But that's none of my fucking business. So, why do I even care?

Maybe I should tell them to change the paperwork right now before it's too late. Or am I actually going to do this out of jealousy over a woman who can never be mine? My door swings open and I look up, glaring at the doctor in question as he stalks back into my room. I instantly know, without a doubt, that's exactly what I'm going to do.

"Okay, Mr. Young," he grimaces, grumbling my name with disgust. "Dr. Magi already went over everything here." He glances at the tablet in his hands. "One of your nurses will be in to help move you to the wheelchair you've been provided from the medical supply company. You already went over the basics for your wheelchair and your crutch with physical therapy?" he verifies, checking off the remainder of his list.

"Yes," I confirm, not caring what's on his damn checklist. I just want this asshole gone before Ella shows up...if she shows up.

"And the nurse will have the notes for your"—he pauses, gulping down a lump in his throat. Clearing it, he continues as if the words he's saying are dirty—"She will have the notes for your caretaker."

I grin mischievously and mumble under my breath, just loud enough for him to hear, "Oh, don't you worry. Ella takes very good care of me."

I watch him grind his jaw, seething, giving me exactly what I wanted. He opens his mouth to respond just as a nurse strides into the room and quickly swallows his words, gripping the tablet in his hands so tight, his knuckles begin turning white.

"Right," he grits through his teeth.

Amused, I turn towards the nurse, one I've seen several times throughout my stay. "Good morning," I murmur cheerfully, knowing everything out of my mouth grates on Nate's nerves. Who am I to take that away from him?

"Good morning! So, are you excited to go home, Mr. Young?" She smiles.

My smug grin grows at the word home, while Nate visibly flinches. "Yes, I'm ready to go home."

"Good." She glances up at Nathan before focusing back on me, her lips twitching up in hilarity.

"I have another patient I have to go see," he grumbles, barely keeping his composure as he storms out of the room.

"Don't get too cocky," the nurse advises quietly, stepping closer to me. "It's still a long time before y'all heal."

Her words take the wind out of my sail. I shouldn't be getting cocky at all, even though I want to put this asshole in his place. I shouldn't be going home with Ella. She's too good for me. Maybe she won't show up. That would be a good thing, for her anyway. She doesn't need to deal with taking care of me for the next couple months. She doesn't owe me a damn thing. As it is, she already saved my life even though I didn't deserve it. I owe her more than I could ever repay and going home with her would only add to my debt. I don't want to owe anyone, especially not her.

"Do you have any other questions?"

"Yeah. When will the therapist come by for my first session?" I need to push this conversation along.

"Let's see," she mumbles as she glances at my papers one more time. "It looks like they will be by later today. That's good. We like to get them into the home to make sure they assist you and your caretaker to fit your needs and your injury right away. After a few weeks, they will reassess and see if we can move your therapy back to our facility." She repeats the same information they shared with me yesterday.

"Thank you," I grumble, my constant bitterness intensifying every time I think about how long I'll have to remain in these casts.

"Of course."

"Good morning, y'all," Ella calls brightly as she walks into the room. My resentment begins dripping away at the sight of her. She looks sexy as hell wearing a white sundress with a tiny blue flower print. Like the dress she wore yesterday, it's fitted tightly to her curves, with spaghetti straps and flaring at the bottom, hanging about three inches above her knees. Her legs appear long, smooth, and lightly tanned down to the same strappy white sandals she wore yesterday.

A low groan escapes my lips without my consent as I release my lower lip from between my teeth. "Damn," I mumble under my breath. My gaze slides back up to her face, her cheeks now a rosy pink as she smiles at me.

"Hi," she murmurs shyly, rocking on her heels.

Grinning, I reply, "Good morning, Angel. You look beautiful."

Her face turns an even deeper shade of red, heating me to my core, but she holds my gaze as she responds, "Thank you. It's been hot outside." I nod, wondering if that's the only reason she dressed up today. I'm so fucked.

She tears her gaze away from mine and turns towards the nurse with a bright smile. "Hi, Julie." She waves.

"How are you, Ella?"

"I'm doing well, thanks. Is he about ready to go?" she prompts, instantly taking the focus off herself.

Julie's eyes widen as her eyebrows arch in surprise. "Is he going with you?" She glances back and forth between us.

Ella smiles and nods with a mock confidence I'm already starting to adore. "Yes, he is."

"Oh!" She smirks. "I missed that change on the paperwork. I just thought Dr. Hull's jealousy was from you constantly visiting, but..." she trails off, blushing.

Ella rolls her eyes. "He can feel whatever he wants. His

opinion doesn't matter to me in the least."

"Hmm," she murmurs, watching Ella closely as if trying to read her. "Okay. Well, I guess I need to go over a few things with you then about Mr. Young's care," Julie advises, handing her some papers.

Ella takes the papers and begins looking them over as she nods. I tune them out and stare at my angel, taking in every expression. I can't believe I'm going to be living with this beautiful woman. There's no way I'm going to be able to hold myself back with seeing her every day. Maybe I won't try, but I already know she's not the temporary kind of girl. I can't go there with her. She deserves better than an asshole like me, but I'm what she's got. Now she's supposed to not only put up with me, but help take care of me for the next couple months? Damn. I want to figure out a way to do shit for myself as quickly as possible, but if I must deal with someone helping me, she will definitely make it a hell of a lot more fun.

She has no idea what she's gotten herself into, and honestly, neither do I.

<h1 style="text-align:center">11</h1>

Ella

I WATCH AS JULIE ASSISTS GRANT WITH GETTING INTO THE wheelchair, his jaw set in what I assume is both determination and agony. Waiting until he settles, she hands him a recyclable hospital bag with the few personal belongings he had with him. "These were still in the drawer. It's what they were able to salvage from your accident," she informs him, her face apologetic.

"Thanks." He grimaces and places the bag in his lap without bothering to look at what's inside.

My stomach begins churning, wondering what I've gotten myself into and how in the hell I'm going to help this giant of a man. I can't even imagine what he weighs with all that muscle! What the hell was I thinking? I was thinking that I need to help him, like I'm meant to be here for him. I'm sure anyone who heard me would think I lost my mind, and they might be right, but I can't help it. Taking a deep breath, I exhale slowly, attempting to pull myself together.

"Are you okay?" Julie asks, pulling me out of my thoughts.

I lift my head, meeting her concerned gaze, nodding. "I'm good. I just have a few things on my mind." She smiles, giving me a knowing look.

Turning away, I look at Grant staring at the ground, appearing deep in thought. "So, Grant, are you ready?"

He glances up at me with obvious indecision. "I don't think I'm the one you need to be asking that question."

"What?" I ask, slightly puzzled. Instead of answering, he arches his eyebrow in challenge and waits for my response. Realizing he's looking for confirmation that I'm truly okay with this, I take another deep breath, pasting a smile on my face. I nod firmly, letting him know I'm as ready as I'll ever be. "Let's go."

"Okay," Julie acknowledges. She pushes him down the hallway to the elevator as I walk along beside him, everything about this moment surreal.

Steps from the elevator, Nathan calls out, "Gabriella, wait!" I stiffen and my steps falter, but I continue the last few feet to the elevator before his hand tugs lightly on my elbow. "Please," he begs.

Reluctantly, I spin around to look at him, crossing my arms protectively over my chest. "What do you want, Nate? I don't have time for anything right now. We're leaving," I add, gesturing to Grant.

He grimaces and squares his shoulders. "Can I just talk to you privately for a minute?" he requests almost desperately.

"You can talk to me right here," I insist, unwilling to step away with him.

Heaving a sigh, he runs his hand through his hair and shakes his head, relenting. "I just want you to think about what you're doing. You're not being smart!"

"Gee, thanks," I mutter, deadpan. I don't care if he's right.

"Gabriella," he warns as if I was the one who just offended him. "Do you really even know this guy? How long have you been dating?"

"I know him," I claim vehemently, refusing to correct his assumption or give him any more information.

"Has he met your family? Declan?"

"That's none of your business, Nathan. What I do in my personal time is none of your concern!"

"I'll take that as a no," he mumbles, a cocky smirk twitching at his lips. "I'm just trying to protect you. You know I worry about you. Now you're staying with a strange guy, and it makes me think you don't have any idea what you're doing anymore."

I huff a laugh in irritation, shaking my head with disbelief. Why did I ever think I was in love with this guy? Attempting to control my anger, I emphasize, "Nate, it's not your job to worry about me anymore. I'm not your responsibility!"

"That doesn't mean I don't care about you, and it sure as hell doesn't mean I stopped loving you!"

I narrow my eyes at him, annoyed by his comment more than anything. It feels like he's only trying to get to me and Grant, not actually help. "Nathan," I seethe.

"I'm pretty sure she's asked you repeatedly to stay out of her business," Grant speaks up, taking me by surprise.

Both our heads turn to Grant, the knuckles of his good hand white as he grips the armrest of the wheelchair, glaring at Nathan. My body begins to relax as I smile at him, grateful.

"She can tell me herself," Nathan mutters.

I tilt my head to the side in disbelief. "I have...repeatedly!" Shaking my head, I lean over and push the down button on the elevator. Dismissively, I glance back at Nate. "You had your minute. Now I need to get Grant home. We're leaving."

The elevator doors slide open and Julie pushes Grant inside, while I follow right behind. As the doors close, I notice a look of determination in Nathan's eyes, already knowing that's not a good look for me. Sighing, I mumble an apology, "I'm sorry about that, about him."

"Don't apologize for him, Ella," Grant requests.

I glance at Julie, standing behind Grant with wide eyes and giving me a look I understand as, *See what I mean?* I can't do anything but shake my head and shrug dismissively.

We step off the elevator and make our way towards the front door. "I'll get my car," I mumble, hurrying ahead of them to the parking garage. I pull my car up in front of the hospital and hop out, jogging around to pull the door open. Forcing a smile, I inquire, "Okay, how do we do this?"

Grant chuckles softly as Julie gives me a few more instructions on assisting him. I'm grateful she's helping me now, but I have no idea what I'll do when I get him home. The seats are high with my beach tires increasing the height even further. I hope it's not too hard to get him out. "Thanks." He nods as I push the passenger door closed.

With a broad smile, I wrap my arms around Julie, hers immediately doing the same. "Thank you," I mumble, truly grateful.

"Of course. Anytime. You know I'll do anything for you, Ella. Call me if you need help with anything."

"Thanks," I repeat, releasing her. She sets the crutch right behind the seats before she easily lifts the wheelchair, folding it into the back before closing the back door.

I jog around the front and slip in behind the wheel, buckling my seatbelt. With wide eyes and my heart racing, I glance over at Grant, instantly taken aback by the man seated next to me. Forcing my gaze past him, I wave to Julie, mumbling under my breath, "Bye."

"Nice wheels," Grant comments as we pull onto the street.

"Thanks." I peek at him out of the corner of my eye. Butterflies suddenly take over my stomach at the realization that I'm taking this big man home with me to stay at my little house for who knows how long. What will it be like? What's he really like? Can I handle this? Can he? What have I gotten myself into?

"Are you sure you're okay with this? I can figure something else out," he offers, probably sensing my sudden panic.

Ironically, his suggestion helps me relax. With a glance at him, I answer confidently, "I'm okay with this. I want to help you."

I feel him staring at me, attempting to read me as I drive. "I know it's not enough, but thanks," he finally speaks.

My heart clenches and I smile, nodding in acknowledgment. As I run my hands anxiously along the smooth black leather of the steering wheel, I inform him, "My family will probably find out about you before the end of the day."

I see him nod his head through my peripheral vision. "I figured as much. The last thing I want to do is cause you any problems. If things change after you speak with them, I will understand."

"Thanks, but this is my decision."

"Who's Declan?" He arches his eyebrows in curiosity.

"My older brother. He'll probably be the first to show up at my door." I scrunch up my nose in annoyance.

"I wouldn't blame him," he concedes, shrugging his good shoulder.

Looking out the window, we get our first glimpse of the ocean, the waves crashing gently against the sand and bringing a smile to my face. The ocean aways does so much for me, bringing me peace, happiness, and contentment. The sight, smell, and sound of it gave me hope at a time when I struggled to find any. It's my happy place.

"You live near the beach?"

Grinning, I emphasize, "I live on the beach." Moments later, I pull into my driveway and park my car. "This is it," I announce, my pride obvious.

"Wow, you weren't kidding!" he declares with wide eyes, nodding towards the water behind my house.

I giggle in delight and hop out of the car, making my way around to the passenger side as he pushes the door open. "Okay, I have to admit, I'm a little nervous I'm not going to do this right and I'm going to hurt you."

"No worries, it can't be any worse than I already feel."

I frown and lean close to him, taking a deep breath to gather my strength, my first mistake. Under the scent of hospital soap, he smells fresh and salty, like he spends a lot of his time outdoors with a little bit of maybe car oil, but I wonder how that's possible; that's a long time for a scent to linger.

My stomach twists, realizing I'm staring at his hard chest, unmoving. "Um, ah, put your arm around me," I instruct. He does as I say and a tingling sensation slowly creeps up my spine, making it hard to remember what I'm supposed to be doing. I sling one arm around his back and let the other fall to his chest, feeling his muscles ripple underneath my touch. My breathing picks up and I feel him shift, sliding out of the car, but keeping his weight back against it. He lands on his good foot. "Um, okay, okay," I mumble trying to keep my thoughts straight.

"Ella," he rasps. The gravelly sound of my name on his lips causes goose bumps to erupt all over my body.

Slowly, I lift my gaze, his eyes dancing with liquid gold and green. Tilting his head down, he presses his lips to mine, taking me by surprise and igniting me. Keeping his lips firm, but fluid, he takes my breath away as I kiss him back. With my obvious consent, he tilts his head further to the side, deepening the kiss and pulling a moan from my lips.

Swiping his tongue over mine, I whimper, my legs going weak. I grasp onto him for support and feel a sudden shift. He pulls back, attempting to stop the momentum and yanking me back to reality. I gasp, "Ahh!" Letting go, I reach my hands back in hopes of breaking our fall. But even in his state, he's faster. Wrapping his good arm around me, he holds me close to his chest and spins, hitting the ground hard with me landing on top of him.

"Fuck," he grumbles in pain, as the air rushes out of his lungs.

My eyes widen in shock. "Oh, my gosh, I'm so sorry! I'm the worst!"

"It's not your fault," he groans, his eyes squeezed tightly shut. "That was all me."

My hands begin flying all over his body, desperately checking for further injuries, but not having a clue what I'm looking for. "Are you okay?"

"I'm fine, I'm fine."

"I am so sorry," I repeat, overwhelmed with guilt.

With controlled breaths, he thankfully opens his eyes, focusing on me. "Don't be sorry, Ella. Don't ever be sorry. If you are, I'll take that as you're sorry for kissing me, and I would hate that because I've wanted to kiss you since the moment I saw you in my dreams at the accident."

I inhale quickly, shocked by his admission, my face heating instantly. My heart skips a beat as I look into his eyes. I nod, not able to speak. Swiftly, I climb off him and gulp down the lump in my throat, trying to pull myself together.

Finally, I drag myself out of my stupor. "Let's get you inside," I prompt, afraid to comment on what he just claimed. If I do, I won't only forget he's hurt, I'll be making out with this man in my driveway.

12

Grant

I SIT AWKWARDLY ON THE COUCH WITH A PILLOW UNDER my broken arm and my broken leg propped up on the coffee table in front of me with another pillow underneath. My body is still vibrating from the feel of her underneath my fingertips. The moment she laid her hands on me, my skin seared from her delicate touch, and I knew instantly I was screwed. There was no way in hell I could hold back; I had to take control. I had to kiss her, take some of what I want, while trying not to scare her away. A light flick of my tongue is all it took for me to realize a small taste of sweet Ella will never be enough.

Although, I don't regret what happened, I'm almost glad I lost my balance and fell. It really fucking hurt, but I can handle pain. I always do, but I needed something to happen to drag me back to my reality. She's not someone to just take what I want without thought. She needs to know who I am and have the chance to make a conscious choice.

Heaving a sigh, I drop my head back against the back of the couch. I need to be honest with her before getting in too deep. I can already tell she's the type of woman who could make me lose control, and I can't let that happen. She's too good. I need to set some boundaries, especially now that I'm going to be sharing Ella's space, even if it is only temporary. I don't want there to be any misunderstandings between us, not with her. Fuck, I don't know if I can do this. This was such a bad idea.

She walks back into the room, giving me a hesitant smile as she hands me a glass of water and some medicine. "Here."

"Thanks," I mumble, my fingers lightly brushing hers as I wrap my fingers around the glass. Keeping my gaze on her, I swiftly gulp half the water down. Pausing, I toss the pain killer in my mouth, swallowing and hoping it works quickly. I lick my lips and set the glass down as I watch her lowering herself into the chair across from me. Every move she makes sets me on edge, but I'm not quite sure if it's this situation, being here knowing I'm staying, not having anywhere to go, not being in control or maybe it's just her.

"So, do you need anything else?" she questions, not looking at me for too long and constantly shifting in her seat. I shake my head in response, still contemplating what I need to say to her and wondering how she'll take it. "Please tell me if there's anything I can do to help. I'm kinda lost being on this side of things," she admits, piquing my curiosity.

"You mentioned something about that before. Any chance you'd be willing to share why? Have you been in my shoes?"

She grimaces, scrunching up her nose adorably and concedes, "Well, yeah, sort of. I got sick a lot when I was younger, and I ended up at the doctor quite a bit." She shrugs like it's no big deal, but her eyes tell a different story. "I guess you could say I'm used to having someone trying to take care of me, but I'm not quite sure what to do when it's the other way around. I always try to help, but I know everybody is different with what they want."

My body heats and I clear my throat, attempting to focus on what she means instead of where my head is taking me. "What do you mean when you say sick? What did you have?" Is it more than she's insinuating? Maybe even being here I'm taking advantage of her, and that's the last thing I want.

Shaking her head, she attempts to brush off my questions.

"It's really not a big deal. I just want to help you, and I know I never liked people smothering me when I was sick. Anyway," she mutters, changing the subject. I relent knowing it's none of my business. I don't want to push her for information about herself when I'm sure as hell not willing to reciprocate anything that might reveal more about me. "Are you sure you don't want to see the guest room?"

"Right now, the less I move the better. Plus, I don't think seeing you in any bedroom is a good idea at the moment," I tease, the corners of my lips curving up in a flirtatious grin. My words bring the instant flush to her cheeks I hoped for, causing my blood to pump harder and making me struggle not to reach for her. I need to have a conversation with her before I think about doing anything else.

"Um, about what happened outside," she begins, making me grimace. "I'm not apologizing," she swiftly spits out, surprising me. "I promised myself I would live without regret, and I'm not going back on that promise."

"Ella," I quickly interrupt. I'm not sure where she's headed with this, but I need to take control of this conversation. I need her to know what kind of man I am and let her decide what she wants. We both need to have a clear understanding right from the start. "Listen, I greatly appreciate what you're doing for me, and if I get in your way or if you change your mind at any time about having me here, I will understand."

"Okay…" she mumbles, drawing out the word, presumably trying to figure out what I'm getting at. I don't blame her. This conversation usually comes so easy, but I don't want to see the inevitable disappointment in her eyes. I just don't have a choice if I'm going to stay.

"I think it's obvious I'm extremely attracted to you. I want you, Ella," I state simply, enjoying the pink coloring her cheeks, "but I'm telling you now, I don't stay in one place for long, and that's not changing now. It can't. I don't know if it's a good idea for me to stay here with you at all; in fact, it's probably not, but I do know it's what I want." I pause, closely watching her reaction to every word I utter. "What I don't know is what do you want?"

My heart pounds as I watch her chest rise and fall with increasing speed, proving my words are getting to her; I just need to hear her say it, one way or another. "Ah, Grant," she begins, maintaining eye contact, although it's obvious to me she wants to turn away. Her determination and courage only makes me want her more.

I bite the inside of my cheek, watching her as she takes a deep breath before she continues. "I know I want to help you. Whether you believe it or not, I think you were thrown into my life for a reason, and I want to know what that reason is. I want you to stay here with me, and I want to take care of you and help you heal. I'll also admit I'm drawn to you, and I think you're hot," she claims, her voice hitching as her face deepens to a bright red, her gaze never wavering. At the same time her words make my heart race, like nothing I've felt before. This is such a bad idea.

"I'm not the kind of woman who jumps into a temporary..." She pauses, attempting to find the right word. "...relationship, but I have this strong feeling I will regret it if I hold myself back, and like I said before, I'm not big on regrets."

My eyes widen in surprise at her admission as my stomach twists. "We can't have that," I tease, the corners of my lips curving upwards as relief overwhelms me. I love her subtle confidence. It's sexy as hell, causing my entire body to heat. "Why don't you come sit next to me," I urge, patting the spot on the couch to my left with my good hand.

She rises, holding my gaze, my heartbeat instantly picking up its pace. "I don't move fast, and I don't want to do anything that might get you hurt or set you back in your recovery," she continues as she steps towards me.

"I can do slow," I concede, hoping it's true. If I'm going to be this close to her every day, I will take whatever she's willing to give me while I have her. I just need to be careful. Maintaining my control is key to my own sanity and to protecting her.

The loud ringing of the doorbell chimes, and she tears her eyes away from me. She sighs heavily and mumbles under her breath almost inaudibly, "What am I doing?"

I flinch, my heart dropping into the pit of my stomach as I watch her saunter towards the door. I shouldn't be here. I shouldn't be putting her in this position. I'm such an asshole.

I watch as she pulls the door open, revealing a man and a woman, both appearing to be in their twenties and dressed in pale blue scrubs. I guess they're here for me. "Hi," she grins, greeting them cheerfully.

"Ella! It's so good to see you!" The man grins from ear to ear, instantly wrapping Ella up in his arms, and picking her up, while she hangs on tightly.

"Laine! I can't believe you're here! I'm so happy to see you!" My stomach sours instantly as I frown at the vision in front of me. The man is fit with blonde hair, a little longer on top and gray eyes. "I didn't know you were back," she claims as he sets her back on her feet without letting her go.

I have the urge to go to her side, but I have no idea how the fuck I would even do that in my state. Then again, I have no right to be there. Instead, I narrow my eyes, clenching my jaw as I attempt to get my emotions under control as I watch his gaze glide down her sweet curves. She's not mine. I don't have the right to say a single fucking word. If I plan on staying while I heal, I better get used to this because with someone as beautiful as her, I guarantee that in any room, every man's eyes will be drawn to her, but she will never be mine to keep.

13

Ella

LAINE SETS ME DOWN, RELEASING ME, BUT KEEPING HIS hand gently on my arm as he speaks. "I got back a couple months ago, but I've been working a lot at my new job ever since." He shrugs his shoulders sheepishly. "I saw Declan. I asked him about you. He didn't tell you?" he questions, arching his eyebrows.

Blushing, I grin and shake my head. "Of course not. You know my brother. You should've called me."

He chuckles softly and glances past me at Grant seated on the couch. He arches his eyebrows. "Looks like I'm too late."

My face heats an even deeper shade of red, and I shake my head. Ignoring his comment, I step back to let them both inside. I take a deep breath and step towards Grant, introducing them. "Laine, this is Grant Young, your patient."

"Hi, Grant," Laine murmurs with a firm nod.

Glancing at Grant I explain, "Laine and my brother Declan were best friends growing up. I've known him most of my life."

He nods his head in acknowledgment. "Hey."

I look over at the woman standing with Laine for the first time, noticing how beautiful she is. She has long, silky black hair, pulled up in a ponytail hanging down to the middle of her back. She has olive skin, high cheekbones, coffee brown eyes and full lips. She's tall and even wearing scrubs, I can tell she's thin and curvy; every guy's dream. "I'm sorry, but I don't know your name."

She smiles brightly. "Hi, I'm Natalia. I'm Mr. Young's occupational therapist. Ella, was it?"

My stomach flips, a sudden and irrational spike of jealousy overtaking my insides as I imagine her hands all over Grant. I gulp down the lump in my throat and nod my head in confirmation. Forcing a smile, I reply, "It's nice to meet you."

She turns her attention to Grant, holding out her hand in greeting. He reaches up with his good hand, shaking it awkwardly and making her giggle, causing my stomach to churn. "It's nice to meet you both. You can call me Grant."

"So," Laine begins, dragging out the word, "how did you two meet?" he questions, glancing back and forth between us.

"I witnessed his accident," I reply, my stomach dropping and my face going pale at the memory of his body skidding across the road.

Laine reaches over and gives my hand a reassuring squeeze. I glance up at him, giving him an appreciative smile. "That must've been hard."

"Yeah, it fucking sucked," Grant retorts, pulling Laine's gaze away from me. "I'm lucky Ella was there. She saved my life. I wouldn't have survived without her." He glances in my direction and gives me his crooked smile, causing my heart to skip a beat. "She's made it even easier to push through this bullshit by spending time with me at the hospital almost every day since. You can't help but smile when she's around."

I gasp, taken aback by his admission.

"Hmm," Laine murmurs, nodding in acknowledgment as he slowly releases my hand. He stares at me, his eyes wide before he finally questions, "You spent a lot of time at the hospital?" He knows more than most that it's not my favorite place to be.

"I wanted to do something to help him." My face heats and I shrug my shoulders like it's no big deal, but Laine and I both know better. "Plus, I had to know if he was okay. I couldn't get the image out of my head."

He nods in understanding and offers me a comforting smile as he sits down on the couch next to Grant. With a deep breath, he clears his throat attempting to put his focus back on his work and begins taking things out of a black bag I didn't even realize he'd been holding. "Okay, I'm going to start by taking your blood pressure and your pulse while I ask you a few questions," he explains. "Full name and date of birth?"

"Don't you have that?" Grant inquires.

"Yes, but we have to confirm it every time," Laine answers.

"I thought that would end once I got out of the hospital."

I listen to the two of them for a few minutes, wondering if I should even be standing here, but nothing has been too personal yet. Eventually, wanting to escape, I take a deep breath and offer, "Can I get anyone something to drink?"

"No, thank you," they all reply in unison.

"Okay, well, um, I have a few things I need to do, so," I stammer, gesturing down the short hallway towards the bedrooms and bathroom. "Call if you need me."

"We will," Natalia answers for all of them, not even glancing in my direction.

I grimace and spin on my heel, striding down the hall, anxious for a few minutes alone to pull myself together. Stepping into my room, I close the door behind me. I sigh heavily and fall back against the door with a groan.

What am I going to do? That man is so much trouble. He just oozes testosterone! Even with all his injuries I feel like I'm on fire just knowing he's near me. Then the moment my eyes take him in, my whole body begins to vibrate with need. It feels like I'm tingling on every surface of my skin and being pulled towards him like a magnet. I shake my head at myself. So, the man is hot. It's not like I've never seen a good-looking man before. What the hell is wrong with me?

I flop down on my bed, staring at the ceiling. Then again,

there's a reason he's here. I can help him. He doesn't have any-one like I did when I was sick; like I still do. I'm in remission, now, and even if it's not exactly the same, I know what it's like to be in his position. He can't do it alone. Even if he can, he shouldn't have to. I believe I'm meant to help him.

Besides, I promised to live every single day for me and leave regret in my rearview mirror. Life is too short. You never know when something will unexpectedly crash into your life, good or bad, and take away what you always thought would be there. I refuse to be the one saying, *What if...* or *I should've done...* or *I wish I would've...* or any other combination of any statement holding even the slightest bit of regret.

I have lived through more physical pain than many endure in a lifetime. I've been given more looks of pity than anyone should ever have to endure. I have cried more tears than my friends, and I've also been the one to comfort those same friends, their time with me dwindling the longer I remained in the hospital. I don't hold grudges or judge when someone doesn't know what to say or do; most don't have a clue. But I know what it's like to be stuck, in pain, and relatively helpless. I know what it's like to not be able to do what you love or just something that helps you feel like yourself.

Thinking back, I remember watching my friends go out-side to play, be a part of a team, a club, or the school play. They went on dates and went to football games, parties, school dances and special events, all without me. Every minute of it was pure torture, but it was no one's fault. I shake my head, refusing to let the absence of memories drag me down; I'll just make new ones.

My phone rings, pulling me out of my thoughts. Seeing my mom's smile, I answer. "Hi, Mom."

"Hi, Gabriella. I'm glad I caught you. How are you feeling, sweetheart?"

"I'm fine, Mom."

"We haven't seen much of you lately. Dad and I were worried."

Grimacing, I repeat, "I'm fine, Mom. I've just been busy."

"Oh, working?"

"Yeah, and some other, um, stuff; normal stuff," I stammer, knowing Grant is a large part of that reason. But I'm not ready to tell them he's here; not yet anyway; not if I don't have to. They won't like him staying here. I don't blame them since they don't know him, but I don't want him to go. He doesn't have anyone. He needs someone. Why can't it be me? I don't want him to think he needs to leave when he just got here. He still has a long road ahead.

"Well, why don't you come over for dinner tonight? Finn will be home from practice around 6:30. We can eat then."

"I already got chicken out for tonight and I don't want it to go bad." My stomach twists into knots. I hate lying to them, so partial truths are my best bet. "Mom, I gotta go," I blurt out, knowing the longer I stay on the line, the greater the chance that I'll screw this up.

"Alright, Ella. We love you. Please let us know if you need anything."

"I will, and I love you too."

Sighing, I disconnect the call. I love my family, and I will continue to love and support them and be there for them, but I need my independence like I need air. They don't intend to hold me back, but they do. I know they're just trying to protect me, but after living like that for so long I started to feel more like Rapunzel trapped in a tower than my own person. I get that sometimes their fears get the best of them, but I'm the one who suffers. I don't have it in me anymore to placate them just to help them feel better. It's time for me to focus on my own happiness, my own future, whatever that might be.

"Stay strong, Ella. No regrets. No holding back. I can do this," I mumble to myself. It's time to create some memories with Grant, no matter the outcome.

I smile to myself, feeling a renewed sense of confidence at the same time, wondering how to handle this situation with the man in my living room; the same man consuming my thoughts and emotions. I just hope I'm able to do the right thing in caring for him. Although they showed me what to do at the hospital, I'm still unsure when he seems so much bigger than me. Plus, I struggle to maintain my composure every single time he's near me. Add touching to that and I'm done for.

I can't believe he kissed me. He kisses like no man I've ever kissed; every bit of it consumed all my senses. The look he gave me electrified every part of me inside and out. My lips tingled, my body burned, he tasted like mint and smelled like hospital soap, salt, and man, whatever that means, but it's true. He moaned into my mouth, or maybe I made that desperate sound, I'm not sure, but I know it's my fault he lost his balance. Even injured, he tried to protect me. I hurt him even more, and I'm supposed to be the one taking care of him. I'm such a mess.

My thoughts drift to him telling me he wanted me, but also admitting he would never stay. I could let my fear take over if I allow it. It's been a long time since I've been with anyone, Nathan my last. But when it comes to Grant, I can already see myself getting lost in this man, and I barely know him. It makes me wonder what I really want to do, knowing he will leave. I'm not sure, but no matter what I decide, I don't want any regrets.

My cell phone rings, startling me and interrupting my thoughts again. I sit up, glancing at the screen and frown at the sight of Declan's face, wondering if he already knows. Mom and Dad didn't, but Dec always seems to know everything first. I know I need to tell them, but I can't let them control this situation. They don't get a choice with Grant. They can check on me all they want, but I want him here and this is my house.

Instead of answering Dec's call, maybe it's a good time to run to the store and pick up a few things for Grant while he's busy with the therapists. I jump off my bed, happy to delay the inevitable conversation with my brother. With a quick glance in the mirror, I stride back to the living room.

"Hey, sorry to interrupt, but I'm going to run to the store and get you a few things while you're busy."

"Thank you, but I could go with you if you wait."

All three of us laugh and he shrugs. "Thanks, but I think it will be easier without you." And I could use the space. "Is there anything specific you need?"

"If you grab my credit card from my wallet to pay for everything, I could really use a new phone."

"No problem. I won't be long." I need to get out of here for a few minutes to think. I'm already finding him to be a weakness; I'm just not sure if it's good or bad.

14

Ella

I PULL THE FRONT DOOR OPEN, ALREADY KNOWING WHO'S on the other side. "Declan, I'm so surprised to see you," I murmur sarcastically. "What are y'all doing here?" I ask, monotone, letting him know he won't change my mind.

He narrows his eyes and his jaw ticks in irritation. "Where is he?" he balks, attempting to push past me.

"Who are you talking about?" I tease sweetly.

"Now is not the time to fuck with me, Gabriella," he grits through his teeth. I arch my eyebrows in challenge, the corners of my lips twitching up. He lets out a breath in exasperation. Then he steps into my space and picks me up, making me squeal in surprise.

"Declan," I scream, smacking his arms as he sets me down off to the side. He swiftly steps past me, barging in.

"Where's this asshole?" he demands, scanning the room.

I shut the front door and cross my arms over my chest, glaring at my brother. "He's in the bathroom and he's not an asshole."

"And you would know that because..." he challenges, dragging out the last word.

I heave a sigh and attempt to gather my patience. "What do you want, Dec?" I ask with pure exhaustion lacing my voice.

"I want you to explain to me why you would let some asshole come and stay with you! You need to take care of yourself, not some stranger."

"I beg to differ, Dec. You don't know what I need. As you can see, I'm fine and I will be just fine," I insist cheekily.

"You don't know that Ella," he mumbles under a barely concealed grimace.

"Yes, I do!" I snap, my blood beginning to boil. "I'm so sick of this same conversation over and over again. I'm fine, Declan! When will you guys understand?"

"We understand plenty. We were there too." I bite my lip, hiding my flinch. "This isn't some hurt animal you found on the side of the road. You don't even know him."

"I'll be fine. I used to help take care of you and Char and Finn when you guys were sick," I remind him.

He huffs a humorless laugh. "We all did that for each other! That's what we do, but he's not us. You know every single one of us would lay down our life for you." My heart clenches. "Can you say the same about him?"

"That's not fair."

"And he's not sick. He's injured from driving a motorcycle during a hurricane. It's his damn fault, Ella."

I wince, feeling like I'm losing this fight, but I refuse to back down. This is my life. "Go home, Declan."

He takes a step towards me. "I want to talk to that asshole."

I shake my head, defiantly. "You don't know him."

"You're right. I don't, and neither do you."

"Does it make you feel better to call him an asshole?" I challenge, tilting my head to the side, mocking him.

My brother glares at me and repeats, "I want to talk to that asshole." I huff in frustration and roll my eyes, annoyed we're not getting anywhere.

"So, talk!" Grant mutters, hobbling into the room, while leaning against the wall, surprising us both.

"What are you doing?" I rush towards him. "You're not supposed to be doing this! You're going to fall again!"

He chuckles softly as I carefully wrap my arm around his waist. "I was able to use the wall for support."

"I told you to call me when you were done and I would bring the wheelchair back for you."

"Yeah, but I'm fine," he grunts defensively, nearly falling into the closest chair.

"You seem fine," I mumble irritably.

Ignoring me, he focuses on my brother. "You wanted to talk to me?" Grant crosses his good arm over the broken one lying on his chest making his biceps bulge, obviously attempting to intimidate. "I assume I'm the asshole you want to see?"

"What are you going to do, Dec? He can't even stand up without help." I glare at him.

He doesn't even bother looking in my direction, making me roll my eyes again. He never takes me seriously. "Why are you here?" Declan asks.

Grant glances down at his broken leg and arm before quirking his eyebrows as if confused. "Isn't it obvious?"

Declan shakes his head in annoyance. "Don't fuck with me. This is my sister's house. That's my sister," he emphasizes pointing at me. "What are you doing here?" he repeats, pointing at the ground.

"Yeah," I concur, interrupting him, "it's my house!"

Ignoring me, Declan maintains his focus on Grant. "Look, man, I'm not fucking with you. I swear. The hospital wouldn't discharge me unless it was to someone's care, and I don't have anyone to help."

"I don't give a shit! The last thing she needs is to spend her time taking care of you!" he proclaims vehemently.

"Don't you think she can decide that for herself?" Grant argues, making my heart skip a beat. I admit, I like that he's sticking up for me, especially knowing it would be so much easier to placate my brother in his position, even temporarily.

"He's right, Dec, stop ignoring me! This is my house, my life, and my decision. And I've decided to help him. Y'all have no say!"

He finally turns his gaze to me, gesturing back to Grant in aggravation. "What do you know about this guy?"

I grimace and sigh heavily. "Look, just like you, I was taught to help people when they need it, and he obviously needs it, so that's what I'm going to do. It's not like he can do much harm with half of his body incapacitated."

"What about the other half?" he debates.

"I get where you're coming from," Grant begins.

"Do you?" Declan interrupts, spinning around and glaring at him. "Do you really? Do you have a sister? One that..."

"Declan!" I interject, attempting to stop him from saying too much.

Grant glances back and forth between the two of us in curiosity before he speaks. "No, I don't have a sister, but I had a younger brother and I would still do anything for him." Something dark flashing briefly in his eyes.

"Had?" I prompt gently, my chest tight.

Grant shakes his head, letting me know that's all I'm getting, for now. "My point is, I may not have a sister, but I know what it's like to want to protect your family," he explains, only causing my curiosity to grow.

"It's not the same," Declan argues, shaking his head.

I groan in exasperation. "Look, Dec, if y'all don't trust me, then sleep on my damn couch," I suggest, at the same time hoping he doesn't take me up on my offer. That's the last thing I want.

"It's not you I don't trust." Pausing, his eyes widen and he stiffens, immediately turning all his focus on me. "What do you mean I can sleep on the couch? Where the fuck is this asshole sleeping?"

"In the spare bedroom! I do have one of those."

His cheeks flush, but he doesn't apologize. Instead, he runs his hand through his hair, obviously irritated. "I'm just worried about you, Ella." His underlying meaning is clear only to me.

"I know, but I can take care of myself. I promise."

"I know it might not mean much, but I'm not going to do anything to hurt her. That's not me," Grant claims, his deep voice remaining calm. "And I really won't be doing anything for a while, I'm in these casts for about another seven weeks, and then I still have to go through physical therapy to get back to normal."

Declan eyes Grant, momentarily lost in thought. "Seven weeks, huh?"

Grant nods, his jaw twitching. "Yup."

Declan clenches and unclenches his fist, growling in defeat. "If anything happens to her, I'll break your other side," he threatens as I sigh in relief, grateful he's no longer arguing.

"As you should," Grant grumbles in agreement.

Groaning, Declan drops down onto the couch, glancing at Grant, and repeats his original question, "Why are you here?"

Heaving a sigh, Grant replies, "Honestly, I quit my job the day of the accident. I decided it was time for me to move on, and I was searching for a new place to live somewhere near the coast. I ended up here because the storm stopped me from going any further. It came on fast."

Nodding in agreement, Declan mumbles, "Yeah, it did. So, quit your job?" Grant pinches his lips tightly together and nods his head in confirmation. "What do you do?"

Grant flinches slightly. "I'm a mechanic and I specialize in motorcycles."

My brother winces, briefly commiserating with him as he glances at his casts. "Ouch. So, what now?"

"I don't know," Grant answers honestly, his head falling back on the chair looking defeated. My heart clenches, aching for him.

I see the moment in my brother's eyes he sees what I see and truly relents, at least for now. "Alright, Ella, fine. He can stay for now," he advises as if he were making the decision, but I let it slide. "But I'll stop in to check on you every single day."

Grinning, I taunt, "You just can't stay away from me, can you, big brother?"

He chuckles softly, shaking his head in amusement. Turning back to Grant, he gives him a look of warning. "If there's anything I see or hear that I don't like, even a little bit, I won't hesitate to hurt you or throw you out on your ass."

"Understood," Grant concurs with a firm nod.

Glancing at me with a similar but softer look in warning, he adds, "And if I question anything, I will tell Mom and Dad."

I gasp, my eyes widening in surprise. "Wait, they don't know?"

Shaking his head, he reveals, "No, they don't know anything yet. Plus, I asked Laine not to say anything."

"Laine told you?"

His eyebrows draw down in puzzlement. "Sort of. He didn't mean to. He asked what I thought of your new boyfriend staying with you. When I asked what he was talking about, he backtracked and told me to talk to you. Then when you wouldn't answer your phone, I decided it was better to show up to find out the truth. Who else would have told me?"

"Nate," I enlighten him, my nose scrunching up in annoyance as his name passes through my lips. "I ran into him at the hospital a few times while I was visiting Grant, and he all but threatened to call Mom and Dad."

He scoffs and shakes his head. "I should've known. Don't worry about Nathan. With all the patient privacy laws he'd have to get pretty creative to tell them anything. That's why I didn't get anything else from Laine, and that's probably why Nathan is giving you lip service. He wants you on your toes."

"I guess," I mumble in agreement. "Wait, so how did you know he was the one in the accident?"

He gives me a look as if I've lost my mind. "Because you're my sister and I know you."

Sighing, I sit down on the couch, opposite my brother. "So, what are you doing tonight?" I ask, hoping to pull focus away from me.

"I'm spending the night hanging out with my sister and

her new friend," he announces, grinning mischievously.

"Fantastic," I mutter under my breath just before a throw pillow comes flying at the side of my face. "Hey!" I yell, flinging it right back at Dec.

Grant

"YOUR BROTHER SEEMS LIKE A GOOD GUY, BUT I THOUGHT he would never leave," I mumble as I watch Ella walking back towards me.

"Yeah, he kind of does that sometimes. He can be a wee bit protective of me. Sorry about that."

"Don't apologize for something that's not on you. Besides, he's just watching out for you. I don't blame him."

I notice a slight grimace before she forces a bright smile. "Are you hungry?"

Shaking my head in response, I request, "Actually, would you mind helping me into the bedroom? I think I need to move."

She nods her head and I wait patiently, watching her as she moves the wheelchair next to my chair and locks the wheels in place. Scooting over to the edge of the chair I'm in, I attempt to slide into the wheelchair, maintaining as much of my weight on my good side and off her as possible. I wince, a sharp pain shooting through me in both directions on my right side. "Shit," I grumble under my breath as I try to lean on my left side.

"Are you alright? Do you want another pain pill?" Her eyebrows instantly draw down in concern.

"I'm fine, and I don't need any pain medication," I grunt. I need to start forgetting those pills even exist.

"It might help you sleep."

She may be right, but I don't give a damn. "I'm good," I grit through my teeth, momentarily keeping my eyes closed.

"I can see that," she mumbles sardonically.

After taking a few deep breaths and exhaling slowly, I'm able to pull myself together. I open my eyes and hold her gaze. "I can handle the pain. I will *not* depend on any kind of pills," I explain to the best of my ability, without giving her any indication as to my reasons. Let her assume the worst of me if she wants; that might not be a bad thing.

She narrows her eyes, staring at me, attempting to read me, but I remain neutral, refusing to give anything else away. She finally nods her head, acknowledging my comment, "I can do that if that's what you want."

"It is."

She steps behind the wheelchair and pushes it down the hallway. I hate that she has to push me, but if I try to push myself with one hand, I'll just end up going in a circle, and that's not going to help anyone. Besides, there's the fact that she's right; I barely made it out of the bathroom earlier without falling, but I wasn't about to let her fight my battles.

I need to do what I can to heal enough to get these casts off so I can take care of myself. I don't want to rely on anyone, but I don't have a fucking choice. I guess that means I'm going to have to depend on her sometimes whether I like it or not. I need to focus on controlling what I actually can or I'll never get through this.

She rolls me into a bedroom with pale blue walls and white trim. There's a large window on the outside wall and pale driftwood furniture. The quilt embroidered with large, pale blue seashells and matching pillows and coral reef lamp give it a homey but beachy feel. "You must like the beach."

"Don't you?"

"Sure," I mumble. Glancing towards the dresser, I spot a seashell picture frame and point. "Who's in the picture?"

Walking over, she picks it up and hands it to me, a small

smile on her face. As I look down at the picture in my lap, I instantly pick out the younger version of Ella with her infectious smile, standing between what I assume is a younger Declan, a girl who appears a couple years younger than her and an even younger boy. They're standing side by side, smiling wide and barefoot on the beach. All of them have varying degrees of blonde or light brown hair, the boy on the end the smallest, but their resemblance is obvious.

"That's me with my brothers and my sister."

"The ones you used to take care of?"

She blushes. "Declan's right. We all took care of each other. My mom would get so tired taking care of us when we got sick because she didn't want to sleep in case we needed something. So, she would accidentally fall asleep trying to stay awake. I remember one time when we were all sick and my mom fell asleep in my room, and I snuck out of bed to bring stuffed animals and soup to my brothers and sister. But then I fell asleep telling Char bedtime stories and my mom screamed when she woke up because she couldn't find me."

I chuckle softly, admiring the obvious love she has for her siblings. I know how that feels. My chest tightens, wondering what Matt is like now. "You met Declan," she begins, pointing to his image and moving down the line as I try to focus my attention back on her. "That's me, then my younger sister, Charlotte, and my little brother, Finn."

"How long ago was this?" I ask, my curiosity growing.

"I don't know, probably ten years ago," she estimates with a shrug. "Finn is actually bigger than me now. He's still in high school, but..." she trails off, momentarily lost in a memory. "Anyway," she mumbles, dismissing her thought as she takes the picture from my hands and places it back on the dresser.

She glances at the bag with my things sitting next to the dresser before looking at me. "We can go get you a few things more this week if you want."

"You've done more than enough. I don't want to inconvenience you more than I already have." There's definitely some more things I could use than what she bought me the other night, but I'm not asking her for more favors.

"You're not inconveniencing me," she insists, shaking her head dismissively. "Besides, I'm offering, and I really had no clue what to grab you for clothes. I haven't seen you in much besides a hospital gown since I met you."

She's right. "What about work?"

"I told them I needed to take a week off," she admits, her cheeks flushing a rosy pink as she looks away.

My eyes widen in surprise. She's doing so much more for me than I deserve, and I have no idea what to do with that or even how to feel about it. She probably wouldn't be doing it if she did know me. "Ella, you didn't have to do that," I mumble, shaking my head.

"I know, but I wanted to," she proclaims, her blush darkening to a deeper shade of red, "just for us to at least get into a routine or something...while you're here."

I muster a grateful smile, knowing I should appreciate what she's doing for me so much more than I do. She really is an angel. And I am thankful for her efforts, but...having to ask for help leaves me unsettled. I want to do things for myself; I need to. It's my life, and I want to be in control. I need to be to maintain my sanity. But because of my stupidity, I feel like I can't do anything; I've lost all power, and I have no clue what the fuck I'm supposed to do about that. "Thanks," I mumble, restless.

"You're welcome."

Suddenly completely overwhelmed, my chest tightens. Taking a deep breath, I exhale slowly as I move my hand to my chest, feeling the erratic beating of my heart underneath my palm. Clearing my throat, I prompt, "Would you push me next to the bed? I think I need to lay down for a little while." Honestly, I think I need some space from her and some time to myself to get my head straight before I lose it as everything crashes down on me, leaving me isolated and broken. Then again, that's not much different from what I've known since long before...I quickly shove the thought away and focus on her.

"Sure." She smiles, immediately moving behind me and doing as I asked. "Can I get you anything else?"

Desperate to lighten the mood and take a little bit more control of this situation, I give her a mischievous smirk. "Well, I'm good for now, but I'm sure I'll need some help taking a bath later."

I stare at her, watching as her eyes widen and her cheeks turn a deep shade of red, heat instantly bouncing between us. I grin, reveling in how my words appear to succeed in eliciting my intended reaction. I need some way to maintain some semblance of control, and this works for me; it's the one thing I know I've still got while the rest of me is useless.

She opens her mouth to respond, but barely a squeak comes out before she quickly snaps it closed, biting her bottom lip instead, causing my heart to pick up its pace. Without another word, she spins on her heel and stalks out of the room, closing the door behind her and making me chuckle.

With a heavy sigh, I awkwardly, but safely, maneuver my way onto the bed. Reaching for the pillows, I put one behind my head and one under each of my casts before finally relaxing into the mattress.

I close my eyes, my blonde angel unsurprisingly the first image I see behind my eyelids. I just can't seem to shake her out of my head no matter what I want. It's not going to get any better while I'm here and she's only a few steps away.

As I run my good hand over my face in pure exhaustion, I admit to myself, I'm thankful for the space she's giving me, even if it's only a door separating us. I think we both need it. But if I don't get my dirty thoughts under control soon, every day could become pure torture being in her space. Then it becomes not if I cross that line, but when. At least that's if she'll let me.

16

Ella

I CAN'T BELIEVE I DIDN'T EVEN THINK THIS THROUGH! HOW the hell am I supposed to help him with a bath? The thought feels more like a bad porno than reality. Not that I'm not attracted to the man, I absolutely am. Almost anyone who likes men would be. He's hot as hell with all that muscle, those tattoos and that damn sexy smile that leaves me feeling breathless every single time. Add in his dark hair with his ever-changing eyes as they devour you, and I'm completely done for before we even begin. I can only imagine what his firm skin looks like wet when I'm not standing in the middle of the road during a hurricane afraid for his life.

Shaking my head, I attempt to rid myself of the thought as I feel my body heating, beginning to vibrate with need. I'm tingling everywhere just underneath the surface of my skin as if I'm being energized from the inside, out, making me feel alive. Quickly, I try to tamp down my feelings, breathing slow and deep, attempting to pull myself together because that's definitely not the way I want him.

If we do decide to hook up, I need to know he really wants me, and if he does, it's not just because I'm the one who happens to be here. I'm no one's convenience. Having no regrets is not the same thing as saying I'll do anything to get what or who I want. That's not me. Although, he did say he wants me, but is it me he really wants, or would any woman suffice? He is a man after all, and I honestly don't know him very well...yet.

I grimace in irritation and remind myself, I should be worried about his health, not if he's interested in me and the possibility of seeing him even partially naked in the shower or bath. It's easier said than done. Besides, he can't even get in the bathtub. For now, I can bring him a bowl with some hot water, soap, and a washcloth. I guess he'll still need a little help, though, since he can only use one hand, but I'm sure more than anything he was trying to make me flustered. I can practically hear his low, sexy chuckle as he takes in my response to his over-the-top flirtatious comments. My body can't seem to help reacting to him no matter how hard I try to maintain my composure, and he seems to relish every second of it. I just don't know if he means what he says.

Trying to give him some space, I take my time cleaning up the living room and kitchen, listening to Taylor Swift as I go. Full of energy, I dance to the back door and to the front, making sure the house is locked up before I turn out the lights and make my way to my room to get ready for bed. I pause in front of my bedroom, turning and staring at the closed guest room door. Should I knock to see if he needs anything before I go to sleep?

My heart skips a beat, thinking about him sleeping just steps away from me. What is it about him that I can't seem to get out of my head? Is it the mystery? Is it how vulnerable he looked while lying on the ground asking me for help? Is it my own need to care for people? To help him, specifically? Is it the sadness in his eyes or the way his eyes turn bright when he sees me? Is it the way he sticks up for me or attempts to protect me? Is it his broad shoulders, his sexy laugh or maybe his tattoos peeking out from underneath his t-shirt drawing me in? Or maybe it's in his damn kiss that was halted way too soon because of my stupidity.

Thinking better of it, I tear my gaze away from the closed

door with a resigned sigh as I turn back towards my bedroom. Maybe he fell asleep, and the last thing I want to do is bother him. Sleeping in a hospital is not easy with nurses and doctors waking you up every couple hours to check your vitals, give you medicine and sometimes other necessary testing. He's probably exhausted. He'll call if he needs me. At least I hope he will.

Grabbing my soft, pale pink, cotton tank top with tiny white seashells embroidered into the stitching and matching short shorts, I make my way to the bathroom and take a quick shower, forcing myself to focus on the task at hand.

I'd be ready for bed if not for the unbridled energy still running through my veins knowing Grant is sleeping under my roof just on the other side of this wall. "Ugh," I groan, frustrated with my errant thoughts.

Pausing, I glance in the mirror, assessing myself. I feel the sudden need to check myself one more time before walking out. Looking down at myself, I instantly notice my taut nipples, making me grimace. I don't like to sleep wearing a bra or underwear. It's just not comfortable, and anyone who says it is, is lying. But I'm also used to being in this house alone, and that's obviously no longer the case. It's not like I'm sleeping at my brother's. There I make sure to wear them underneath just in case, no matter how annoying, but I don't want to do that in my own home.

Although, with how I'm feeling around Grant, this is either the best idea or the absolute worst. Of course, I want to know more about him, but I want so much more than that too, and I've never felt like that before, not even with Nate. With Nate it was just different. It's not even a comparison. Shaking my head, I easily push Nate out of my thoughts.

But with Grant, I can't shove him out of my head even if I try; not that I want to. I want to see every detail of his tattoos. Do any of them have a special meaning to him? Why did he choose to get each one? I want to run my hands across his firm body, tracing the lines of his muscles or his ink, admittedly, not just with my fingers, but also my tongue. My mouth waters, and I lick my lips in thoughtful anticipation.

I'm dying to know what it feels like to have his lips pressed against my skin, on every inch of my body. I want to kiss him and taste him again until my lips are swollen and I can no longer breathe. Imagining what it would feel like to really lose control, not just with anyone, but with him, has my heart beating out of control. I have no doubt that he's the kind of man who could make me do exactly that, for better or worse. Every single part of me continues to prickle with anticipation at the possibilities of what could happen between us. I want that so damn bad, but I need him to want that with me, too.

If that's how I really feel, why am I so concerned about Grant seeing me without my bra? Would it really be such a bad thing to push him over the edge if he catches a glimpse of me in my pajamas? I concede, it's not just me in my pj's, but without a bra it's hard to hide how he makes me feel. Maybe I don't care. I'm always the good girl, but I don't want to be anymore, not since I met this man. I'm ready to enjoy my life. Is that so wrong? Don't I deserve to be happy and have some fun after everything I've been through?

Taking a deep breath, I stand up straight, push my shoulders back, and smile to myself as I exhale slowly. Finally, I pull the door open with newfound confidence. I halt almost instantly, a sense of disappointment washing over me when I'm greeted with the closed guest room door and an empty hallway.

I shake my head at my reaction. Of course, the door is closed. Did I think he would have a miraculous recovery or something and come looking for me? The poor man is in severe pain and he can't do a damn thing with the whole right side of his body, yet here I am ready to pounce on him the moment he's in my house. What the hell is wrong with me? I'm horny and Grant is the reason why. That's what's wrong.

"Ugh," I groan under my breath, frustrated with myself. I

stalk back to my room, resigned to crawling between my sheets and praying for sleep. Then again, maybe I need to give myself an orgasm to relieve some of this built-up tension Grant seems to ignite inside me if I want a chance of sleeping through the night. I'm pretty sure thoughts of him would bring relief relatively fast and then I can relax. I already feel like I'm about to explode any second, and I haven't done a damn thing!

Leaning back against my pillow, I close my eyes, instantly drowning in thoughts of him. I tug my shorts down and my top up, letting my hands roam and trying to imagine they're Grant's, exploring my body. As one hand plays with my already hard nipple, my other hand begins stroking my tingling core, with his name a soft moan on my lips, "Grant."

17

Grant

"I CAN'T KEEP DOING THIS ANYMORE," I QUIETLY PROCLAIM. I *try avoiding her hard gaze as I pull my black t-shirt on over my head.*

She purses her lips, inching towards me in her red silk robe. "You can, Grant, and you will," she insists, the corners of her lips curving up in amusement.

Shaking my head, I reiterate, "No, I can't. I'm sorry, but this isn't working for me anymore. I won't be back."

"Why are you saying this?" she challenges as if I'm being irrational.

"You're married."

She arches her eyebrows in question. "That never bothered you before."

"You came on to me," I remind her, knowing that doesn't matter. I went along with it. I put myself in this situation. Sighing heavily, I shake my head, finishing tying my shoes before I force myself to turn, facing her. "Look, this isn't right and you know it. I need to focus on football and school," I begin, attempting to get her to see reason.

She laughs and climbs on my lap, straddling me. "Really?" she asks, wrapping her arms around my neck.

"Yes, really. Colleges are starting to look at me. Coach said I have a fantastic chance at a scholarship. If I could make that

work, I'd have some good schools to choose from. My grades are okay, but I need football to help me," I insist, attempting to untangle her arms from around my neck. "I need this!"

"You don't need to worry about all that." She shakes her head, dismissing me. "You already have a job working for me." She holds onto me tighter, her robe falling open, and my body instantly starts to react.

"I have so much I want to do with my life! I definitely want more than that!" I insist vehemently. "Stop!" I urge, telling both her and my body to halt as I grab one of her arms from around my neck and gently remove it.

She narrows her eyes, suddenly grasping my hair with her free hand and yanking my head back hard, making me gasp. Her teeth bite my neck and she sucks, leaving a mark. I swiftly pull her away and she claws at me, gouging my arm and neck, drawing blood. "What the fuck?" I attempt to pin her arms at her sides, to keep her from attacking me without hurting her.

"You asshole! Don't fucking touch me!" she yells, as if I'm the one instigating this. She squirms and then elbows me in the stomach.

Grunting, I release her instantly as the air rushes out of my lungs. I hold my hands up in surrender as I quickly stand and start for the door. "I'm not trying to hurt you. I just want you to stop," I reiterate, desperate. "I'm leaving!"

"Fine. Go ahead and leave! But keep this in mind as you walk out that door, I'm close with your coach, and he would do almost anything for me." She sneers.

Slowly, I turn back to her, wide-eyed, with my heart suddenly lodged inside my throat. My stomach twists into knots at the evil glint in her eyes. "What do you mean by that?" I ask, barely breathing, attempting to maintain my composure.

"To be seen by the college scouts, you have to actually play, don't you?" she questions with mock innocence. The blood drains from my face, her threat painfully obvious. "I have more power than you may think, Mr. Young. This," she pauses, gesturing back and forth between us, "is not over. I'm enjoying this *way too much to let it end. If you don't show up on Sunday to work, you'll see what happens, and I can guarantee you won't like it one bit."*

I grind my jaw, glaring at her before I spin on my heel and storm out the door. A guttural scream follows right after me with a high-pitched crash as shards of glass shatter on the door frame, my right side getting several of the pieces deflecting off the wood, making me gasp in shock. "Don't fucking test me!" she commands, seething.

My eyes widen as I sit up with a gasp, the nightmare startling me awake. I move too quickly and lean on my right side, forgetting my fucked-up situation. Instantly grunting in pain, I let out a curse, "Fuck!" My whole right side feels like it's getting pelted by boulders. I quickly overcompensate, rolling to my left and slip off the bed with a thud. I grind my jaw and scream in agony through my teeth, trying not to wake her as I remember where I am. Closing my eyes, I try to breathe through the pain. Carefully, I attempt to readjust my body, scooting back towards the wall so I'm able to lean against it and have enough room for my leg to stick out, while I catch my breath.

I hear knocking, but I can't open my mouth to speak. Instead, I maintain all my energy on pulling myself together. The bedroom door soon flies open and bangs against the wall. The sound of her footsteps slapping against the wood floor as she rushes to my side echo as if in the distance.

"Oh, my gosh! What the hell happened? Are you alright?" Her panicked questions come at me rapid-fire, but I still can't respond. I don't open my eyes, continuing to focus on my breathing to get my pain under control. "Grant! Grant! Please say something," she begs sounding more desperate with each breath.

"Just give me a minute," I insist through my teeth.

"Sorry."

Thankfully she waits patiently. I feel her kneel next to my uninjured leg anticipating my response. After a moment, without opening my eyes, I take another deep breath and finally speak. "Sorry for waking you."

She scoffs. "I told you to wake me if you need me. What were you trying to do?" she questions, attempting to piece together how I got here.

"I thought I'd be more comfortable on the floor," I answer sarcastically. She laughs, the sound sending chills down my spine and easing my pain. I take another deep breath and exhale slowly, before giving her a more honest answer. "Something woke me up, and I was disoriented."

"Ah, that makes so much more sense." She gives me a sad smile. "Bad dream?" she questions, taking me by surprise.

My eyes flash open instantly. "What? Why the hell would you say that?" I prod through narrowed eyes, her question leaving me exposed.

She gasps and her eyes widen as she mumbles, "I'm sorry."

Her apology makes me realize I'm coming off too abrasive. I don't need to take my shit out on her. She's only trying to help. Shaking my head, I insist, "Don't apologize." Resigned, I sigh. "Something like that."

"I used to get nightmares all the time when my pain was off the charts," she offers, giving me a small amount of insight. I open my mouth to ask her more, but she continues before I gather the strength. "Can I help you back into bed?"

I grimace, hating that I need the help she's offering. "Thanks, yeah. Just give me another minute."

"Sure." She lowers her butt to the floor, getting more comfortable and leaning back against the bed, staring at me from underneath those long eyelashes.

She looks so fucking sexy. I bite my lower lip and let it slip through my teeth as I allow my eyes to wander. My gaze glides over her creamy skin, finding her nipples hard underneath a thin tank top, suddenly making it difficult to breathe. "You're not wearing a bra," I observe, wanting to see her squirm, desperate to gain some control of this situation.

As I'd hoped, her cheeks turn pink, and she bites her lower

lip anxiously, only succeeding in turning me on more. "I don't like wearing one to sleep," she surprisingly admits, turning a deeper shade of red.

My chest tightens and my cock begins to harden, making me groan. "Show me." I attempt to push her limits.

"What?" Her eyes widen further.

Staring at her, I take her in, momentarily letting down my guard. I lick my lips, wanting a taste of what my angel is dangling in front of me. "Show me," I repeat breathlessly, wondering what she'll do.

She shakes her head as if ridding it of its dirty thoughts. Ignoring my request, she takes a deep breath and prompts, "Come on, let's get you back in bed."

I sigh heavily, hating the roadblock she places in front of me, but conceding to her wishes, knowing it's probably the right thing. "Fine."

She crouches down next to me and pulls my good arm over her shoulders. "Lean on me and the wall and we'll slide up." I do as she says, balancing on my good leg. "Good," she encourages, my body heating from her close proximity. "Now, lean on me, and if you can take two jumps over towards the bed, we'll spin you back around and you can fall back."

"Okay." The corners of my lips curve up in amusement, knowing exactly what I'm about to do. I take the two jumps towards the bed as instructed. Leaning on her, I spin, lowering slightly before falling back on the bed and purposely taking her with me.

A soft gasp of surprise escapes her lips. Halting momentarily while she stares into my eyes, her hands begin mindlessly running over the ridges of my bare chest. I feel her taut nipples against my skin through her thin tank, but I'm sure she feels my hardening length against her stomach as well. I slide my hand still wrapped around her and weave my fingers into her hair, gently tugging her towards me. With a low growl, I crash our lips together, my tongue diving in to explore, licking, tasting, devouring her sweet mouth.

She kisses me back with fervor, her hands continuing to roam over my skin, over my muscles, over my ink, setting me on fire with her soft touch. I pull back, kissing and licking along her jaw, down her neck, behind her ear. "Tell me you want this, Angel," I demand.

She whimpers, goose bumps prickling her skin with each kiss. I slide my hand down, gliding it along the curve of her breast. "Grant," she moans, her breaths coming out faster.

I slide my hand lower, skimming over her thin cotton shorts and finding no sign of her underwear. My heart momentarily lodges itself in my throat. "Are you wearing any panties?" She shakes her head, eliciting a groan from me. Without further preamble, I emphasize, "I need you to tell me you want this."

Breathlessly, she gives me what I desire. "I want this. I want you, Grant,"

With her permission, I don't wait another moment. Sliding my hand up and slipping it underneath her tank top, I tug it over her head, taking the cotton with it. She hovers over me as I run my good hand over her breasts and pert nipples, my insides a tight bundle of anticipation. I pinch one lightly, rolling it between my fingers, before jutting my tongue out for a taste.

"Ah," she moans, her body arching towards me. My hand slides to her other breast and begins playing as I cover the first one with my mouth, swirling my tongue around her nipple and sucking gently, her sweet and salty taste driving me crazy.

Her body curves into me, her knee coming up and colliding with my hard cock. My head instantly falls back to the bed as my hand moves to cover myself. "Fuck!" I mutter, cringing from pain as I feel myself go pale.

"Oh, my gosh! I'm so sorry!"

She tries to get off me quickly and accidentally hits the cast on my right leg, eliciting another groan from my lips. "Ah!"

"Oh, my, God, I'm so sorry! I can't believe I just did that! I'm so sorry." She continues apologizing as she cautiously moves away from me.

Focusing on my breathing, I again try to get my pain under control and regain my composure. I barely feel the bed move as she climbs off, moving away from me. Of course, this isn't going to be easy anymore. Why would it? And here I thought it was the one thing I still had left. I should've known better. Why the hell would I be that lucky?

Or maybe that's another indication that trying anything with Ella is a bad idea. I already know she's way too good for me. This only helps confirm it.

18

Ella

MY STOMACH TWISTS INTO KNOTS, COMPLETELY MORTIFIED. What the hell is wrong with me? I'm supposed to be helping take care of the man and I hurt him instead because I can't keep my hormones in check! "I'm so sorry." My cheeks turn bright red with embarrassment. Reaching for my tank top, I swiftly pull it back over my head, covering myself. I watch as color slowly begins returning to his cheeks and his muscles release their tension. "I'm sorry, Grant. What can I do to help?"

Shaking his head, he doesn't look at me as he forces out his reply, "It's fine, Ella. Don't worry about it. I'm fine."

I grimace and shake my head, my guilt practically overwhelming. "It's not fine. I'm so sorry I hurt you."

He takes another deep breath, exhaling slowly, before finally opening his eyes and bringing his gaze to me. "It's fine. I'm already better, but maybe we can take it easy for a little while until we both get the hang of these fucking things," he grumbles irritably, glaring at his casts.

"I think you're right." My heart clenches, protesting, but all I can do is ignore it. "Are you sure you don't want some pain medicine?"

"No! I'm fine."

I flinch at his reaction, puzzled by his stubbornness. He's obviously in pain. "Okay," I mutter, dragging out the word. "Maybe you should try to go back to sleep. The sun is just barely beginning to rise." I nod towards the window covered by the closed blinds.

"Great idea, but it's not going to happen. I'm wide awake at this point." He sighs heavily.

I wince. If I had put a bra on...I shake my head, knowing I should've just helped him get back in bed so he could go back to sleep. "This is my fault. I'm sorry."

"Please, stop apologizing. It's not your fault. I wanted this. I mean, I want it just as badly as you...probably more if we're being honest."

I glance down, the corners of my lips twitching upwards as my cheeks heat. Shrugging, I bite my lower lip and release it before admitting, "I don't know about that."

He gives me a crooked smile and chuckles softly, making my heart skip a beat. My stomach suddenly growls, causing my face to heat again. "You hungry?"

As I look into his eyes, I'm overwhelmed at their uniqueness, appearing to be a smooth combination of green and gold. Clearing my throat, I look away and proclaim, "Obviously. Would you like some breakfast?"

"Sure." He nods. "Could you maybe help me into the bathroom before you go make something, though?"

"Of course!"

I assist him with getting out of bed and help him into the bathroom using extreme caution and care. I grab a washcloth and hand towel, leaving them next to his things. "Here."

"Thanks. Would you mind grabbing the bag I brought from the hospital and the whatever you grabbed at the store?"

"No, problem." I run and grab everything, leaving it next to the towel.

"Thank you."

"You're welcome." I tear my gaze away from the ridged muscles of his chest and arms, attempting to keep my focus on what he's doing instead of on him. I watch as he pulls everything out, and sets them on the sink, one by one. "Do you have everything you need?"

"Actually, would you mind grabbing my cell off the nightstand for me? That way, I'll just call you when I'm done, so you don't need to wait close by to hear me."

"Sure." I rush back to his room and grab it. As he takes it from my hand, his fingers lightly brush mine, pulling a gasp from my lips. I gulp down the sudden lump in my throat, quickly needing space. "Anything else?"

Taking another look around the bathroom, he shakes his head. "I think I can manage." I nod and spin on my heel. "Ella?" he calls, halting my footsteps.

Briefly hesitating, I slowly turn, facing him and arching my eyebrow in question. "Yes, Grant?"

Straightening, he stares at me, his gaze holding an intensity I'm not sure I understand. "Thank you. I'm not always good at showing my appreciation, but I don't want to even imagine where I'd be if you weren't there to jump in and help me."

My heart clenches tightly as I smile, goose bumps prickling my skin. "You're welcome. I'm honestly happy I'm able to help you. Just, please, let me know what you need. I don't want to leave you hanging."

He smirks, his eyes suddenly sparkling with mirth, making me shake my head in amusement. "Anytime!"

Spinning on my heel, I pull the door shut behind me as I quickly make my way to my room. Grabbing a white bra out of my top drawer, I slip it on underneath my tank top, the feel of Grant's hands and mouth on them prevalent in my mind. Stop it, Ella.

Sighing, I walk out of my room, retreating into the kitchen. I breathe a sigh of relief, ready to have some space between us, if only for a little while. It's especially needed when the man sits half naked and looks at me like he's ready to devour me. My stomach twists with anticipation at the thought. Things were just getting good when I had to go and ruin it all with my clumsiness and stupidity. But he did give me a small taste of what it could be like between us, only succeeding in making me want him more. Great.

I shake my head, again attempting to push him temporarily out of my mind while I figure out what to make us for breakfast. The distraction will probably be good for me. I can't keep lusting after the man; it's time I take care of him.

I start the coffee first, craving my first cup with this unexpected early morning. Opening the refrigerator, I begin scanning its contents, realizing I never asked him what he likes to eat. Well, I guess I'll just stick with some basics today and hope it works. I begin pulling out some food and quickly getting to work.

The coffee maker gurgles, signaling a full pot. Immediately, I stop what I'm doing and stride over, grabbing a raspberry pink coffee mug adorned with white hearts on the way and pour myself a steaming cup of coffee, adding sweet cream. Wrapping my hands around the mug, a small smile tugs at my lips as I take a deep breath, inhaling the scent as I take my first sip, enjoying the bittersweet taste on my tongue.

My phone pings, pulling my attention. I lower the cup carefully as I glance at the screen. Smiling at the sight of Grant's name, I immediately open his message. My eyes widen and I inhale quickly in surprise. "Ah!" I lick my suddenly dry lips as I look at his photo message.

"Clean and ready," he declares in white block lettering across the bottom of a photo of his hard abs and chest. The picture angles slightly down towards the sexy V dipping down into his shorts, making my mouth water.

I take a deep breath, exhaling slowly as I shake my head, attempting to clear it of my sudden lust-induced fog. "Damn. This man is trouble," I mumble under my breath, a grin tugging at my lips.

19

Grant

"THANKS FOR BREAKFAST," I MURMUR, STARING ACROSS THE table at her. Damn, she's beautiful in the morning.

I watch as she takes another bite of eggs and sets her fork down. She nods in acknowledgment as she finishes chewing, hiding her mouth behind the palm of her hand. "You're welcome." She cradles her coffee cup in her hands, taking a sip before leaning back against the chair. I can't take my eyes off her, watching her every move. She tucks a loose strand of her blonde hair behind her ear and lifts her gaze to mine, eyeing me quizzically.

"What?" I ask hesitantly. My stomach turns, wondering if I'll like where this is going.

With a shake of her head, she contradicts herself, mumbling, "Nothing, I'm just curious."

"Curiosity can be dangerous," I grumble, my body tensing protectively. Talking about myself isn't always a good thing when you don't want to get in too deep with someone. Besides, there's no way in hell she would stick around long enough to even take care of me if she knew the truth about me. She tilts her head to the side, giving me an unimpressed look, making me chuckle. I shrug, nonapologetic as I smirk in response.

She rolls her eyes dramatically. "Not everything has to be too personal, you know."

"Are you sure about that?" I taunt playfully, attempting to push the conversation in a different direction.

She leans towards me, asking, "So, since you won't be working on or riding a motorcycle anytime soon, what else do you like to do for fun?"

A devilish grin lights up my face as I crassly respond, "Fucking is a hell of a lot of fun." I watch her closely, anticipating her reaction. Her breath hitches, her body stiffens, her skin flushes and her mouth parts as she licks her lips in surprise, giving me the heated and innocent response I was hoping for, my own body igniting with her reaction.

Pushing aside my comment, she takes a deep breath, attempting to maintain her composure, before turning the conversation in her intended direction. "Do you like books, or cards, or puzzles, or games or movies or shows?"

Relenting, I answer vaguely with a shrug of my shoulders. "Sure, I like some of those things sometimes. Don't most people? Why?"

"Well, we need to do something to entertain ourselves. You obviously aren't much at answering questions, although I'll still continue asking," she enlightens me, pausing to watch my reaction, but I give nothing away. "I got really good at finding things to keep myself occupied when I was sick. There were times I started to feel like I was ready to bounce off the walls if I didn't do something. For me, I could only spend so much time on my phone, or tablet, or even watching TV before I needed to find something else to do. I love reading, but I would play cards or games with my brothers and sister and my mom and dad. Sometimes Char would bring in things like Mad Libs or crossword puzzles for us to do together," she elaborates, a thoughtful smile on her face.

"How long were you sick?" I hope approaching her sickness from a different angle will be enough for her to give me something about her past. She continues to refer to her illness without really giving me any information, and it's gnawing at me.

She bites her lower lip anxiously as she gazes at me from underneath her long eyelashes, making me want to jump over the table and suck her lip out from between her teeth, but I steel myself to my chair and wait for her to respond. Sighing heavily, she finally answers, "I was in and out of the hospital from the age of ten to twenty. Then, after that, I still had to go in for regular check-ups for a while before I ended up sick again, but I've been doing really well for over a year now. I only have to go in twice a year at this point."

I nod slowly, attempting to process all the information she revealed. It obviously had to be something serious to be in and out of the hospital for that long. Leaning forward on my good arm, I gently probe, "Can I ask what's wrong?"

She grimaces and defensively retorts, "Nothing is wrong. I'm in remission."

"I'm sorry. I didn't mean it like that." I hold up my good hand in surrender. "I really don't mean to pry."

She presses her lips into a thin line as she leans forward, mirroring me. Her elbows move to her knees, pushing up her cleavage and putting it on display. I bite the inside of my cheek, holding back a groan. "How about this, for every question I answer, you have to answer something for me?" she proposes, arching her eyebrows in challenge.

"What if I refuse to answer a question? Will you punish me?" I tease, attempting to keep the conversation light.

She rolls her eyes again, giving me an apathetic look and making me laugh. "I'm not going to force you to answer anything you don't want to, but maybe I'll reward you for answering questions honestly."

My eyes widen in surprise as I watch her cheeks turn pink almost instantly. "Are you going to share what the rewards are?"

"Umm," she mumbles, rubbing her lips together in thought.

I grin, hesitating for barely a moment before conceding with a smirk, "Alright. I'll agree, but you have the same terms."

Her eyes widen as she bites her lip, obviously unsure if she wants to maintain the same terms for herself. She doesn't know me and she's obviously not sure what I'm capable of. Smart woman. "Okay, fine."

"Sweet." My grin grows as she takes a deep breath and straightens her spine, attempting to regain her composure. I like this deal. "So, when do I get my rewards?"

"We'll figure that out after." I nod. "So, you already asked me something, now it's my turn to ask you a question." She grins wide in satisfaction.

"Go ahead."

"How old are you?"

A burst of laughter erupts from my chest. "You can ask me anything at all and you ask me how old I am?"

She shrugs. "Well, yeah because I'm done trying to guess."

I nod. "Twenty-nine. What about you?"

"Twenty-five, but I'm not done." I arch my eyebrows in surprise and she shrugs, claiming, "I get another question. I answered a couple for you already."

"Fine. Go ahead."

She bites her lower lip again, eliciting a soft groan from my lips. Her eyes widen, flashing to mine, but she swiftly schools her expression. Clearing her throat, she questions, "Why did you and your last girlfriend break up?"

I sit back, shocked she jumped from age to exes. "So much for not making it too personal," I joke, my nerves churning in my gut.

"That was before we made a deal. I figure with the possibility of being rewarded it's worth trying for a few real answers."

Chuckling softly, I concede with a nod of my head. "Of course," I mumble under my breath, slightly amused. I purse my lips, not sure how I want to answer. "Well," I begin dragging out the word, "I haven't had a real girlfriend since high school, so..."

"Since high school?" she echoes, her disbelief evident.

Nodding, I concur, "Yup," popping the 'p.' "I think we broke up because I had a lot of shit going on at the time, and it was too much dealing with a girlfriend, too."

"What do you mean?"

I grin and shake my head in refusal. "That's too many questions."

She pouts, sticking out her lower lip. "Fine."

I lean towards her, a wolfish grin on my lips. "You're adorable when you don't get your way."

"I must be adorable a lot then," she jokes, deadpan.

"I find that hard to believe."

"It's true, especially when it comes to my family. Since I was sick for so long, they always think they know what's best for me," she proclaims bitterly, giving me insight. "It's like they think I'm still a child, but I have two younger siblings," she spits, clearly irritated.

"I definitely don't think you are," I murmur wickedly, making a point of raking my eyes up and down her body.

She smirks, already getting used to my innuendos. I just can't seem to help myself with her, eager to see every reaction. "Thanks. My turn."

"No, it's not," I argue, shaking my head. "You gave up that information voluntarily. I commented, but I never asked a question."

"Ugh, okay. You're right."

"Damn straight I am." I grin and she rolls her eyes, the corners of her mouth twitching up in amusement. "What did you have when you were sick?" I ask, rephrasing my earlier question, hoping to get the answer I'm looking for this time.

Her smile falters, and she sighs heavily, mumbling under her breath, "Why did I want to play this game again?"

"You don't want to answer?" I chuckle softly.

She drops her hands into her lap and meets my gaze. "That's not it. Whenever I tell someone, they look at me differently."

I arch my eyebrows in question. Surprising me, she holds my stare. "They start to look at me with pity or as someone who needs help and can't take care of herself. They make me feel like I'm my sickness, that who I am is no longer important, like I'm not the same person because of it."

My heart clenches, understanding her pain. It may not be identical, but I've gotten similar judgmental looks. It's obviously not for the same reason and half the motivations behind those looks towards me were self-inflicted, but for me, all of it stemmed from the same problem. *She* was a sickness that brought all the rest of my pain, bad decisions, and judgment. "I would never do that," I declare confidently with a firm shake of my head.

She stares into my eyes trying to read me, suddenly seeming to come to a decision. She relaxes her shoulders as her hands slide to cup her arms, seeming more protective than defensive. "So, I'll give you the extremely short version. When I was ten, I was diagnosed with non-Hodgkin lymphoma. It grew quickly, and I was on and off chemotherapy treatments and had to spend a lot of time in the hospital. Then, I finally went into a full remission only to find I had a tumor on my spinal cord a couple years later. They were able to remove it, but I had to go through more treatments, and now I'm back in remission."

I nod in understanding, at the same time wishing I could do something to help her, not put more burden on her by having to take care of me. "You asked that I not look at you differently, and I said I wouldn't, but honestly, that's really hard to do," I confess. She stiffens, instantly trying to rebuild her wall. "But not how you think," I continue, watching her carefully.

Her eyebrows draw down in confusion. "What?"

"I already knew you were incredible. After all, you saved my life." I smirk. "I think about you going through something like that for years and it just shows your strength and courage." I shrug, trying to put her at ease.

She blushes, smiling. "Thanks."

I nod my head firmly. "I'm just being honest."

Taking a deep breath, she drops her hands into her lap and shakes her head. Then, she quickly changes the subject, attempting to move the focus off her. "What happened to your family?"

My body instantly tenses. Hearing that question brings me crashing back to reality. I shouldn't be doing this with her. "Um..."

A knock sounds at the door, giving me a much-needed reprieve. She glances at her phone and back up to me. "Wow, I didn't realize we were talking that long. That must be for your therapy." I breathe a sigh of relief as she stands and strides to the door, not ready to tackle those demons. I don't know if I ever will be.

20

Grant

I SIT ON THE COUCH, KEEPING MY EYES CLOSED AS I LISTEN to the clattering of dishes, the opening and closing of doors and the sizzling of something that smells absolutely delicious. Inhaling deeply, my stomach grumbles, impatiently waiting to be fed, at the same time grateful I'm not in the kitchen trying to do it myself.

Then again, I worked hard today with an occupational therapist just trying to do simple things, things I've taken for granted my whole life. Attempting to cook wouldn't only be comical, it would be completely out of the question. Although, it's strange having someone do so much for me.

Not being able to do the little things is what's pushing me towards the edge. It shouldn't be that hard to open a fucking tube of toothpaste just to brush my teeth, or to make myself a basic peanut butter and jelly sandwich or even to pull my dick out of my pants to take a piss, but every single bit of it is utterly exhausting and so fucking painful. I hate it. It's like my body is betraying me, sending white hot stabbing pain throughout any limb I try to move, my broken limbs twitching, begging to do their job, but completely useless.

Unfortunately, I have these damn casts, these barriers on my right side making me constantly feel off-balance, let alone, uncoordinated. I feel so helpless and out of control, the exact opposite of my life since I left home. I'm completely out of my element and I have no idea how to handle it, only causing me to grow exceedingly uneasy.

The one bright side of everything is Ella. She's not only my angel, she's also incredibly sexy, gorgeous, kind, caring and surprisingly funny as hell. It's probably a good thing I'm not constricted by jeans all day. Every time I see her, smell her, or even sense she's close by, I feel myself begin to harden in anticipation. Her full curves and luscious lips call to me like a siren as she easily pulls me in without even trying. Maybe that's part of my attraction to her. She's not like women I'm used to being with or even around. It's a good thing.

But after our epic fail the other night, I don't know what I want to do about it or if I should do anything at all; at least not until I'm functioning in relatively normal working order. I definitely don't want either of us to get hurt. Plus, I'm not one to push for complications or put myself in a situation where I don't feel like I have any control, and right now, putting it mildly, I feel dependent, weak, and completely at her mercy. After everything I've been through, that's the last place I ever wanted to be again, and I'm not sure what the fuck I'm supposed to do.

The soft sound of her footsteps approaching reaches my ears and I take a deep breath, inhaling her light, clean scent, dusted with the same savory-sweet smell wafting from the kitchen. Gulping hard, I force myself to blink my eyes open, quickly readjusting to the light. "Hey," I mumble, smiling up at my blonde angel.

"Hi." She grins back at me, causing my chest to squeeze without my consent. "Are you awake? Dinner is ready."

"I'm awake. I've been listening to you work."

She blushes a beautiful shade of pink as she glances towards the ground, a small smile on her lips. Squaring her shoulders, she returns her gaze to me, informing me, "Since it's such a nice night, I decided to set the table up outside on the back deck." I watch as she nervously bites her lower lip, staring at me, assessing me, and waiting for my response.

My eyes widen in surprise. I didn't think I heard her opening and closing the back door at all. Plus, the idea alone seems more personal, possibly even romantic. "I haven't been out there yet," I state the obvious, not sure what to say. I don't know if this is a good idea.

"Well, now's a great time. Don't you think?" she prods, hopeful, as she flutters her long eyelashes at me. Shit, I can't say no.

I nod my head and grin up at her, not able to stop it. Carefully, I slide myself to the edge of the cushion, checking to make sure the wheelchair is locked in place. I definitely learned my lesson when it comes to locking the wheels, and I'm sure as hell not up for any more injuries. Ella stands behind me, looping her arm underneath my broken one, giving me just enough support that I'm able to slide into the wheelchair without falling on another part of my broken body. I exhale in relief the moment my ass hits the seat. "Thanks."

"You're welcome."

She rolls me through the kitchen and out the sliding glass door off the back of the house onto a wide-planked teak patio overlooking the sea grass, the sand, and the ocean. "Wow," I murmur under my breath as I take in the spectacular view. Just off the steps of the patio to the right, I spot a narrow sand pathway through tall sea grass swaying on both sides. Then, beyond the path, the golden sand stretches endlessly down the water line with the dark blue waves of the ocean softly cresting, edged in white foam as they crash into the shore before the water is pulled back out to sea.

"It's really beautiful, isn't it?" she prompts reverently.

I nod my head with a quick glance in her direction before I continue staring in awe. It's not that I've never seen the ocean before, but it's the first time I've gotten close enough to let myself admire and appreciate the water since the moment I left home. It feels different somehow than it was back then. But I guess a lot can change in over ten years. I wonder what Matt is like now. Does he have a motorcycle or play football? Did he go to college? I push the imagined image of my brother out of my head and respond. "It is," I rasp, suddenly overwhelmed with emotion.

She sits down next to me, gazing out at the water. Focusing on my surroundings and the woman next to me, I relish what feels to me like a perfect moment. My body remains aware of her by my side as we look out at the blue and purple sky meeting the waterline, the bright orange, yellow and white of the sun angling towards the horizon. Priceless. I don't have moments like this anymore.

After a few minutes of comfortable silence, she quietly admits, "I love the water, whether I'm in it, out on it, or just coming out here to think and listen to the waves. It feels so peaceful, and sometimes I just need that calm, you know?" She glances at me out of the corner of her eyes.

I laugh humorlessly, understanding her more than I want to. I've been chasing that calm, peaceful feeling for over ten years, almost desperate for it, but haven't gotten a glimpse in forever. Yet, in this moment, while physically broken and defeated, I feel more at peace sitting next to Ella than I have since long before the day I left home. The knowledge causes my insides to quiver restlessly. Taking a deep breath, I exhale slowly, attempting to get my emotions under control. Dragging my eyes away from the ocean, I focus on the beautiful woman sitting next to me. "I get it. Do you surf or boat or something? You said whether you're in it or on it."

"Not exactly. I spend a lot of time on my paddleboard more than anything."

"Is that where you disappear to when I'm in therapy?"

She nods, a thoughtful smile on her face. "Yeah."

I wondered where she went, but I was so focused on what I was doing and either sore, pissed off, or both afterwards that

I didn't dwell on it. I've been isolating myself, thinking it was better for both of us. Well, better for her anyway.

Out of the corner of my eye, I notice the wide, white bowls edged with royal blue, filled with colorful food, drawing me in. I turn my head towards the table, and Ella immediately steps behind me, helping to spin me in towards the picnic table, placing me at the end, overlooking the ocean. "Thanks."

"You don't need to thank me for everything I do."

I give her a crooked smile and shrug in response. Glancing around the table, I ask, "What is all this?" Admittedly, I'm impressed with the spread she has laid out before us even without taking a single bite.

She shrugs like it's no big deal, her cheeks turning a light shade of pink. "I just made teriyaki pork and veggie stir fry over white rice."

"Well, it looks and smells absolutely incredible. Thank you," I emphasize. "I could get used to this." The corners of my lips curve upwards as my stomach growls loudly in anticipation.

She giggles softly, her cheeks turning a beautiful shade of pink. Glancing at me, she encourages, "Please, eat."

Nodding, I do as she says. I take a bite, my eyes closing as the sweet and spicy flavors burst in my mouth. "Mm," I mumble, chewing slowly, as I savor the bite before I swallow my food. Glancing up at her, I grin, attempting to show her my sincerity. "Ella, this is absolutely delicious." I lick my lips and stuff another bite of food in my mouth.

"Thank you. I'm glad you like it."

"I more than like it," I mumble around my food.

She blushes and begins pushing her food around on her plate as she gives me a little more of herself, causing me to sit up and listen. "I'm usually only cooking for myself. But I spent a lot of time reading when I was sick and I really enjoyed looking through different kinds of cookbooks, thinking about what I would make one day. So, when I moved in here, I finally started trying some of the recipes, but unless one of my brothers or my sister comes over for dinner, I'm the only one who enjoys it, and I end up with way too many leftovers."

I chuckle softly, enjoying finding out more about her. "Well, I get by when it comes to cooking, but this is fantastic. You can cook for me anytime." I grin playfully, taking another bite. "And if you have any leftovers, I'll probably devour those too along with a few other things I want to sink my teeth into."

She gasps, blushing deeply, and quickly takes a bite of her food, attempting to pull herself together. Damn. I love seeing the look of pride, excitement, and satisfaction on her face. I can think of a few other ways I'd like to put a similar look on her face without even speaking.

What the hell? This girl really does have me all tied up. I need to find a way to get my head straight when it comes to her because I can't go anywhere until I'm strong enough to drive, and that's not happening anytime soon. In the meantime, I can't let her break down my walls, but it feels like they're already crumbling. I can't let that happen.

21

Ella

I PULL THE FRONT DOOR OPEN, FINDING DECLAN ON THE other side. Narrowing my eyes, I plant my hand on my hip, grumbling, "You really don't trust me."

"You know I do," he retorts.

I roll my eyes as I take a step back, letting him in. "We just finished dinner. There's some more in the kitchen. I haven't even cleaned up yet."

He walks in, closing the door behind him. Looking around, he narrows his eyes. "Where is he?"

"Out on the back deck."

He nods and turns to me. "Good. Listen, I just got a call from Mom and Dad," he begins, running his hand through his hair.

My heartbeat increases along with my sudden anxiety. "Yeah, and?" I prompt, ready to beg him to continue.

"Well, they went by the restaurant for dinner tonight. They asked for you and James told them you called in for the week," he enlightens me, watching me carefully for my reaction.

"Ugh!" I grunt in frustration, already knowing what's coming as my hands fall to my sides.

"They called me thinking you haven't been feeling well and were maybe trying to hide it from them. I told them I've been hanging out with you and you're fine, but..." He grimaces and shakes his head. "You just need to call them. I guarantee they will be stopping by even with a phone call, so I think it's time you tell them you have a temporary guest," he states, emphasizing temporary.

I groan in irritation, wishing I had more time. I'm still not sure how to approach this conversation with my parents. Then again, I probably never will. It won't matter that he was in an accident or that he's hurt. He's a strange man staying with me in my home. I get it, but he doesn't feel like a stranger to me. Besides, I can make my own decisions, and I'm going to see this through. Now, I just need to come up with something to say that will appease them. Sighing heavily, I reluctantly agree, "Fine, I'll call them."

His shoulders fall, relaxing as a broad grin lights up his face. "Good." Turning towards the kitchen, he inhales deeply and calls over his shoulder, "Let me know what you tell them so I don't fuck it up."

Chasing after him, I probe accusingly, "What do you mean? Why do you think I won't be completely honest about how I know him?"

He reaches for a bowl from the cabinet and begins serving himself. "Honestly?" I nod as if that answer is obvious. "I think you'll be better off not telling them everything this time," he claims, taking me by surprise.

"Seriously?" I arch my eyebrows in challenge. Our parents raised us to be honest, but Declan always emphasizes the importance of honesty and trust. After everything he went through with his ex-girlfriend, I don't really blame him.

He glances at me and shrugs his shoulders. "If you tell them everything, they're going to want you to kick him out, and I know you won't do that, no matter how much we don't trust him. This way we can all help keep an eye on you and get to know him." I narrow my eyes at him as he sets his now full bowl down on the counter and holds his hands up in surrender. "You know we're going to worry about you. We always will, Ella. That doesn't mean we don't trust your judgment."

Frowning, I nod in understanding, still slightly taken aback by his comment even with his explanation. But I'm also grateful he can see this from my point of view. As I glance out the back door, I take in Grant sitting with his back to us, staring out at the water, my mind beginning to race. "Yeah, I get it. It's just I've been through something similar as him in a way, but this is also completely different. I honestly can't imagine what it's like to be in his position."

"What do you mean by that?"

"Besides the obvious?" He nods, waiting for me to continue. "Well, he was in the process of moving when this happened. He can't work. He's insinuated that his family isn't around anymore, whatever that means for him. Plus, I don't think I've heard him talking with anyone besides his old boss, insurance companies and people from the hospital or doctors' offices following up on his care." I sigh heavily, wishing I could do more to help him.

"So, you're saying he doesn't have a lot of friends?" I glare at him, making him chuckle. "You can't save everyone, Ella; no matter how much you want to." His hand falls to my shoulder in support.

I flinch at his choice of words and then straighten my shoulders, quickly attempting to brush them off. Shaking my head, I retort, "I don't want to save him, Dec. I just want to be there for him while he tries to get his life back, whatever that looks like for him. Everyone should have someone. It's like I just know I'm supposed to help him," I emphasize with conviction.

"I get it, I do. Like I said, maybe they don't need to know everything this time." He shrugs his shoulders.

My phone rings, interrupting our conversation. I pull it out and glance at the screen, grimacing at the sight of my mother's light brown hair and green eyes looking back at me. "It's Mom," I grumble.

He chuckles softly and picks up his bowl of food. "I think

I'll go outside and keep Grant company while I eat this. You should answer that before they end up on your doorstep in the next few minutes," he advises, arching his eyebrows.

I groan, knowing he's right, and slide my finger across the bottom of the screen to answer the call as I watch him walk outside, his amusement clear. With a deep breath, I paste a smile on my face, hoping it reflects in my voice. "Hi, Mom."

"Gabriella! Hi!" The relief in her voice is obvious, making me wince. I hate that I made her worry. She deserves some reprieve. "I'm so glad I finally caught you. How are you feeling, sweetheart?" she cautiously probes, her voice soft.

"I'm feeling good, Mom. I promise," I state, immediately attempting to give her some reassurance.

"Are you sure? You can tell us if something is wrong. It's better for all of us if we know right away. I can come over to help you."

I wince, sick of repeatedly having the same conversation. "Mom, I'm fine." I close my eyes briefly, trying to keep my temper under control. "And Dec is here now, anyway."

She sighs in relief. "Declan said as much, but then why did you take off work this week? Dad and I stopped at the restaurant to see you and have lunch, but Noah said you took the whole week off. Why do you need so much time off if you're doing so well?"

I sigh heavily, still struggling to come up with a reasonable scenario to portray. "Well, I'm helping someone out," I begin, cutting myself off.

"Helping someone out?" she echoes. "Who? What are you doing?"

"It's, um, it's a friend of Julie's," I stupidly blurt out. "You know, from the hospital?"

"Oh, yes, she's such a sweetheart. What are you helping her with that you need time off work?"

Taking a deep breath, I gather my courage, correcting her assumption. "Well, he was in an accident and..."

"Wait, he?" she interrupts.

"Yeah, Mom. He was in a motorcycle accident the night of the hurricane, and he was hurt pretty bad."

"Oh, that's terrible," she commiserates. "But who is he?"

Shaking my head, I ignore her question, knowing I need to tell this my way. "Well, he was discharged from the hospital the other day, but he doesn't have anyone that can help him out since Julie works all the time, so I offered to let him stay here since I have the extra room, and I thought I could help him out because I know what it's like to be stuck focusing on trying to get better and not being able to do anything else," I ramble, the lie rolling off my tongue.

"Slow down, Gabriella," she urges, probably trying to process what I just threw at her. "Are you saying you have a man staying with you at the beach house?"

"She what?" my dad's voice booms in the background.

My heart drops into the pit of my stomach. I take a deep breath, exhaling slowly as I try to pull myself together. I've got this. "Yes, Mom. Grant is staying here with me while he heals from his accident," I confirm, surprising myself with my confidence. "He needs my help, and I plan on being there for him."

"Gabriella," Mom gasps.

"Mom, Declan is here. In fact, he's constantly here," I emphasize trying not to show my annoyance. "You have nothing to worry about. Besides, his right arm and his right leg are both broken, so he's not very mobile. But that's also one of the reasons he needs my help."

"But...he's not a lost puppy or a bird with a broken wing."

"I know!" Why do they all say the same thing?

"Do you? Taking care of someone like that is a lot of work," she emphasizes, making me flinch. She quickly changes direction, realizing her slip. "That's not what I mean, Ella." She heaves a sigh before a gasp falls from her lips. "You're not helping him with private things?"

"What the hell, Kathryn?" Dad yells.

My face heats in embarrassment even though they can't see me. "No, Mom," I answer, refusing to elaborate. I huff and shake my head. "I'm fine. I will be fine. He's a good man who's in a shitty situation and he needs help."

"Gabriella!" she gasps at my language in warning.

Ignoring her, I push forward, needing them to know how important this is to me. I'm an adult and I can make my own decisions. They don't have to agree with me, but they have to accept them. "He's staying here, and I will help him."

My mom sighs heavily, relenting, knowing I'm not giving in. "Well, if he's friends with Julie," she mumbles hesitantly, making me wince. Of course, that's the reason she finally gives in. I need to call Julie the moment I hang up the phone to fill her in. Hopefully she's okay with it. "Just be safe, Gabriella, and please call us if you need anything!"

"I will," I concur, "and Mom?"

"Yes?"

"Please, give him time to feel a little better before you and Dad show up and give him an inquisition."

"I wouldn't even think about it," she claims, both of us knowing she'd happily barge in if I didn't speak up.

"I love you, Mom, and tell Dad I love him too."

"I will. We love you, honey."

"I gotta go, but I'll talk to y'all tomorrow," I murmur, done with the conversation.

"Okay. Tomorrow. Goodbye, sweetie."

"Bye."

I disconnect the call and drop my head in my hands, mumbling to myself, "What did I just do?" Sighing heavily, I pull up Julie's number and connect the call.

"Ella, Hi!" she answers almost instantly.

"Hi, Julie. I'm sorry for bothering you at work."

"Oh, I'm not working and you're not bothering me."

"Thank you."

"So, what's up? Everything okay?"

"Um, yeah, I just, ah, kinda need a favor," I stammer.

She laughs. "It sounds like it's something big." I remain silent, biting my lower lip in thought. How do I even ask something like this. "Just tell me, Ella!"

"Ugh, fine. It's about Grant. So, I didn't want my parents to freak out, and Dec suggested I not tell them everything, so I kinda told them that I'm helping Grant because you're so busy at work and..."

"Wait," she interrupts, laughing. "Why would it matter if I'm working?"

"Because he's a good friend of yours," I squeak out as more of a question.

She laughs harder, the corners of my lips twitching up in amusement at her reaction, but I hold my breath, still waiting for her response. "Yeah, we're so close," she finally comments, deadpan.

"I would owe you for this, Julie, please?"

"Yeah, I can do that. That's what friends are for."

"Really?" I squeal.

"Of course!"

"Thank you, Julie!"

"Listen, Ella, I know we lost touch while I was in college, but it had nothing to do with you, and I really do regret that. I just had a lot going on and with school..." she trails off and my heart squeezes. "I realize I've probably felt more like a nurse to you the last few years more than anything, but we are still friends, Ella, and I'm happy to cover for you."

"Thank you," I rasp, emotion suddenly overwhelming me.

"So, how is that beautiful, broken man?" she asks, teasing, lightening the mood.

"Tempting," I retort, and she laughs again.

Declan peeks his head inside the door, arching his eyebrows. "Everything okay? Are you coming outside?"

"Yeah, I'm coming. I'm just talking to Julie."

His shoulders relax and he calls, "Hey, Julie."

"Speaking of beautiful men…" Julie mumbles.

"Ew." I grimace, feeling more normal than I have in a long time. "She says hi." Her laughter rings in my ears, enveloping me in a sense of peace. I've missed this.

I SIGH AS I FINISH PUTTING A BREAKFAST TRAY TOGETHER for Grant. Grabbing a knife, fork, and spoon, I set them down next to the plate with a veggie omelet and cinnamon toast before I go in search of napkins.

My thoughts drift to Julie as I look. I owe her for this one. In fact, I should stop at the hospital to drop more treats off for her to let her know how grateful I am for covering for me. Or maybe we could get together on one of her days off. She's right, she has felt like more of a nurse since she returned from school and I miss our friendship. It felt good laughing with her again. I am glad I got ahold of her when I did, especially since she ran into my mom at the coffee shop the next morning. Of course, Grant was the first thing she asked about.

The moment I pull my junk drawer open, I spot the napkins. I shake my head, knowing my brother left them there. Thankfully, Declan has given me a little more breathing room now that he's had the chance to spend some time with Grant, but I'll admit I'm thankful for his help, too. Maybe he'll stop over while I'm working tomorrow. I grimace, knowing I'm running out of time to come up with a plan for when I'm not around.

I pour a glass of orange juice and a cup of coffee, setting them on the tray. Taking a deep breath, I pick it up, strolling cautiously as my thoughts drift towards Grant over the last few days. I'm disappointed he hasn't tried to collect on his rewards for answering my questions. Admittedly, neither have I, and we never agreed on what they would be, but he's definitely taken a step back. He's still as flirtatious as ever, but he hasn't even tried to kiss me since I nailed him in the groin and then almost immediately hit his cast. It seems my clumsiness might've taken away his lust for me. Unfortunately, it did absolutely nothing to get rid of mine. I still want him. I'm extremely attracted to him, and I don't know what I'm supposed to do about it.

I've been enjoying spending time with him playing games, watching TV or movies, or just sitting on the back deck and watching the water while we talk. He seems to like it out there as much as me. But I imagine he's starting to go a little stir-crazy. I'll escape to the water, spending time on my paddleboard when he's in therapy, but he doesn't have the chance to get away. He needs help with so much, and I can see it getting to him. If I were in his shoes, I know I would be antsy, especially if I started feeling better like he seems to be, even with his casts. Sometimes he gets that look, as if he's ready to crawl out of his own skin. I just hope he doesn't want to get away from me.

Carefully balancing the tray, I knock softly on the guest bedroom door and smile at his rumbling response, "Come in." I walk in and gasp as I take in the sight of his bare, ridged chest. His good arm stretches above his head, his bicep and tricep firm, while his cuts and bruises have almost completely disappeared from his body, leaving a few dips and lines of pale and darkened, puckered skin. He drops his arm, running his hand through his hair, messy from sleep before he lets it fall into his lap.

"Good morning," I mumble, not able to stop ogling him.

He looks at me with a panty-melting smile, making me forget why I'm here. "Good morning. Is that for me?" He arches his eyebrows in question.

I glance down at the tray in my hands and instantly feel my face turn three shades of red. Nodding, I mumble, "Um, yeah, I made breakfast and thought it might be easier to bring it into you today before you get dressed."

"Thank you." He smirks as he watches me force myself to approach him.

"You're welcome." Carefully, I lower the tray next to him on the bed. "Can I get you anything else?"

"You do enough for me, but I'd love for you to keep me company while I eat." He tilts his head to the side, assessing me. "Did you eat?"

I nod. "Yes. I didn't want to wake you."

"You're too good to me, Angel."

I shrug. "I know what it's like to not be able to do things for yourself that you're used to doing. Plus, I had a family who was always around to assist with whatever I needed, even when I didn't want them to be." He presses his lips together and a crooked grin tugs at my lips. "I told you I don't mind helping you, and I meant it."

He nods and takes a bite of the omelet. "Mm," he groans in appreciation. "Damn, this is delicious."

"Thanks," I mumble, rocking awkwardly back and forth from heel to toe.

"Please, sit with me," he urges again, nodding towards the other side of the bed.

I nod and move closer, my heart starting to speed up as I sit on the end of the bed, facing him. "I have to go back to work tomorrow," I blurt out.

He gives me a crooked smile. "I appreciate you taking the time you did. You didn't know me. You didn't have to do that."

"I wanted to."

The corners of his lips twitch up in amusement. "So, you've said."

He takes another bite of his omelet and I watch, my mouth watering as his tongue juts out, licking his lips. Suddenly realizing I'm staring, I tear my gaze away, my face flushing. "I was going to ask my brother if he could stop in to check on you while I'm gone. He was probably going to anyway."

He chuckles. "True. I am getting pretty good at balancing though," he claims, shrugging. "I want to let you know, with my new interim insurance, I will have to go into the office for OT and then PT when I get to that point. Hopefully that will be sooner rather than later."

"When do you need to go?"

"Don't worry about it. I'll text you when I won't be here, but I'll probably just grab an Uber or something," he mumbles dismissively.

I scrunch my nose. "We have Uber, but there's not really that many around here. Y'all are welcome to try, but it's kinda hit or miss..." I trail off before adding, "Y'all probably be better off with a cab if I can't drive you or convince Dec to do it."

"No problem. I don't want you to worry about me. I can handle it." I lick my lips, biting the bottom one and running it through my teeth as I desperately attempt to keep my eyes on his golden gaze. He groans, giving me goose bumps. "You have to stop looking at me like that."

My eyes widen, taken by surprise, with my face suddenly on fire. "Wh...what? What do you mean?" I stammer.

Setting his fork down, he leans towards me, staring into my eyes. "Like you're ready to have me for breakfast."

My heart pounds so hard, I barely hear anything besides its thundering beat and the flow of blood in my ears. "Um, I... ah..." I gulp down the lump in my throat, focusing on breathing in and out.

"My fingers and mouth are itching to feel you, to taste you," he mumbles, the deep sound of his voice vibrating through my body and heating me to my core. "I just need a little more time to get at least one of these damn things off," he declares, glaring at the right side of his body.

Speechless, I stare at him, processing his statement. He's

pulling back because of his casts. The doorbell rings, taking me by surprise, pulling me out of my stupor and causing my eyebrows to draw down in puzzlement. "Um, ah, why don't you eat while I go see who's at the door?"

He smirks. "Sure. Can you toss me a shirt on your way out?"

"Absolutely." I stand and grab a black t-shirt off the dresser, setting it down on the bed near him. The doorbell rings again and I spin on my heel, making my way towards the door. "Coming!" I yell, irritably. I feel his eyes on me as I quickly stride out of the room before I decide to ignore his request and jump him now.

I pull the door open, my eyes widening in surprise at the sight of my younger sister. "Charlotte! What are you doing here?"

She plants her hands on her hips and asks sassily, her southern accent strong, "Is that any way to greet your favorite sister?"

I smile and pull her into a hug she willingly returns. "Hi, Char, it's so good to see you." As I release her, I take a step back and let her in, shutting the door behind her. "What are you doing here? Shouldn't you be in class?"

She spins, facing me. "No, I'm right where I'm supposed to be." I arch my eyebrows in challenge, prompting her to roll her eyes dramatically. "I'm done for the day. I'm only taking one class over the summer."

Her light brown hair hangs down her back with a few loose curls, her green eyes looking innocently back at me, indicating I'm in for her kind of trouble. She's dressed in dark blue jeans, an off the shoulder ivory top embroidered with small, ivory flowers and short, black leather, ankle boots. "You look nice."

"Thanks," she murmurs, grinning appreciatively as she takes a mini curtsy. "I thought I should look good when I come over to meet this man y'all kidnapped and are holding captive," she teases, wiggling her eyebrows.

I groan, dropping my head in irritation. "I'm not holding anyone captive," I argue.

"So just kidnapped then?"

"Ha-ha. I'm helping someone who needs it."

She smirks and nods her head, placating me. "Mm-hm. Whatever y'all have to tell yourself to sleep at night. So, where is he?"

Shaking my head, I burst out laughing. "Well, I guess I can't hide him forever. Come on, do you want a cup of coffee first to give him time to eat and get dressed?" Her lips curve up in a mischievous smile, making me laugh. "He's too old for you, Char."

"I didn't say anything."

"You didn't need to." She shrugs without apology, grinning wide. Laughing, I shake my head in amusement. "Anyway, it takes him a while to do things with his injuries, and he likes to try to do things for himself."

"Oh." She frowns, appearing irrationally disappointed. I burst out laughing at her reaction, my sister quickly joining in.

We walk to the kitchen as we catch our breath. "So, let's have coffee then, while you tell me what you really think about this guy."

23

Grant

"DAMN," I MUMBLE TO MYSELF, MY GOOD HAND REFLEXIVELY falling to my cock as I watch her practically run away from me. I need to get these fucking casts off. I haven't jacked off with my own hand this much since I was thirteen, and that's not an easy task with my left hand. She seems so sweet and innocent one minute and the next she looks at me like that, igniting every part of me and my dick responds, turning as hard as stone. She's my angel and my wet dream all rolled into one. It really can't get much better than that. However, I can't have her; at least not yet.

Her laughter echoes down the hallway. Another female's voice joins hers, igniting my curiosity. Groaning, I readjust and reach for the shirt she left for me, swiftly pulling it over my head. I'm getting pretty good at maneuvering a few things, helping me feel a little more like myself, but I'm more than ready to take back control of my body and my life.

I take another bite of the omelet, enjoying the savory flavors and the light texture. Soon, there's a knock at my door, followed by Ella's muffled voice from the other side, "Grant?"

"Yeah?" I mumble between mouthfuls.

"My sister stopped in to see me and she thought she'd introduce herself to you if that's okay. Are you decent?"

"Come in."

The door slowly swings open, Ella peeking in, glancing at me before she pushes the door all the way open, causing my mouth to tug up in amusement. I'm not a modest man.

A girl a few years younger than Ella steps into the room behind her grinning ear to ear. She strides confidently up to me as she pushes her light brown hair behind her shoulder. "Hi, Grant. I'm Charlotte, Ella's younger, smarter, and more beautiful sister."

Ella rolls her eyes with a small smile on her face. She obviously adores her sister. "Nice to meet you," I mumble, chuckling.

"It's so nice to meet you," she croons. Stepping closer, she juts her hand towards me to shake, blushing almost instantly, realizing her mistake.

I reach my left hand out, twisting it, taking her small one in mine, and shaking it awkwardly. "Sorry, my right hand isn't exactly in working order," I apologize, nonapologetic, the corners of my lips curving up in a smirk.

She giggles, shrugging her shoulders sheepishly, the action reminding me of Ella. "Yeah, I'm sorry about that," she mumbles biting her lip. "You look good for someone who totaled their motorcycle over a week ago."

"Char!" Ella admonishes, blushing a deep shade of red.

"Thanks." I chuckle humorlessly.

"It's a good thing Gabriella was there," she murmurs.

My chest tightens momentarily, remembering wanting to let the darkness consume me in that moment, until I saw her, the moon giving her hair a reflective glow like a halo. It felt like she was there for me, giving me a reason to fight or to bring me peace; I honestly wasn't sure which at the time. I'm still not, although I'm still alive. Gulping down the sudden lump in my throat, I take a deep breath and nod in agreement. "She's my angel."

Charlotte nods, glancing back and forth between us, her smile growing, appearing almost gleeful. "She is an angel. It's like it was fate or something," she taunts, a mischievous glint in her eyes as she glances at her sister.

"Don't you have to go study for a test or something?" Ella grumbles, crossing her arms over her chest as she glares at her sister.

I chuckle softly as I watch the two of them banter. I used to react the same way to my brother. Matt would follow me around doing everything he could to be involved in anything and everything I was doing anytime I was around. He'd flirt with the girls I brought around, he played football and he even used to try helping me work on my motorcycle. I remember getting so frustrated with him sometimes, which only made him more determined. A sad smile crosses my face as my good hand drops to my chest. I rub the ache, hoping to diminish the feeling, desperately missing my brother, with the same questions consuming my mind, wondering what he's up to now.

Movement appears out of the corner of my eye, just as Ella's hand falls gently to my shoulder, pulling me out of my dark thoughts. "Are you okay, Grant?"

I glance up, her eyebrows drawn down in concern. Nodding, I gulp down the lump in my throat and take a deep breath, attempting to calm the brewing storm inside me. "Yeah, yeah. I'm fine." I force a crooked smile.

My heart clenches seeing her worry for me as her brows furrow further, obviously not believing me, but I can't go there. "Grant..."

Clearing my throat, I interrupt, swiftly stopping her. "I was just thinking about my motorcycle," I claim, telling a partial truth. I can't bear to talk about my family, especially Matt. It hurts too fucking much. I need to remember why I left and remind myself why he's better off without me. Hopefully, things are going well for him with me gone. He deserves to have everything he's ever wanted. The only thing I ever really did for him put him at risk. I will not be the man who puts my little brother in danger.

"Ah, I understand," Ella murmurs, yanking me further back

to the present. "Have you started looking for a new one?"

I shake my head. "Not yet. I'm waiting to see what I get from insurance. Plus, I want to be able to do some of the details and custom work myself, and I obviously can't do that yet." I glare down at my casts, hating how much restriction they're putting on me. "I'll start looking for something I'll be able to mold into my own soon enough." I need to or I'll lose my damn mind.

She grins back at me, her look easing some of the ache in my chest. "I think that's a great idea. You're welcome to use my computer if that helps."

"Thanks."

"You're still going to ride a motorcycle after such a bad accident?" Charlotte challenges with wide eyes.

I shrug my shoulders and answer honestly. "Absolutely. It's in my blood. It's a part of me." It's almost overpowering how much I feel the loss.

"Huh," Charlotte mumbles, pursing her lips in thought. "Your eyes lit up when you said that."

"I made a mistake. One I don't plan on ever making again. I'm not about to let a little storm, a bad decision and some broken bones hold me back."

The girls laugh, Ella shaking her head. "It was a hurricane, not a little storm." I shrug like it doesn't matter, making her laugh again. I crave that sound.

"I wish I had a passion for something like that," Charlotte murmurs dreamily, garnering our attention. "I'm in college, and I still haven't found something that I really feel is a part of me."

"You will, Char," Ella mumbles, her hand falling to her sister's back in support. "You're so talented. You just gotta keep looking."

Charlotte smiles appreciatively at her sister and gently pats her hand laying on her arm. "We've got all the time in the world to figure it out."

"Yeah, we do," Ella agrees softly, a smile tugging at her lips.

Watching the two of them together is becoming over-whelming. It's both beautiful and heartbreaking, causing my muscles to go taut. Fuck. I would give almost anything to get away from here right now.

"So where are y'all from, Grant?" Charlotte asks, pulling me out of my head, but not with a question I want to answer.

"All over." I shrug, forcing a smirk.

She laughs. "An answer without answering."

Ignoring her comment, I glance at my angel, peering at me from underneath her long lashes, assessing me. Her curious and concerned look tells me I need this conversation to end. "Ella, I'm sorry, but I think I need to go back to sleep for a little while before they get here for my OT. My body is really sore and I'm getting a headache." I need some time to myself, or at least away from her. I can't force myself to talk to her sister right now or answer any more questions. I'm not even ready to tell Ella. Charlotte seems nice, but I'm not Ella's boyfriend. Hell, we're not even friends. I don't need to do this. My head begins spinning everything happening into chaos, and being social is the last thing I want to do.

"Would you like me to get you some aspirin or something?" she offers, knowing I won't take anything else.

"Thanks, that would be great." Glancing at Charlotte, I nod my head in acknowledgment. "Nice meeting you."

"It was good meeting you, too, Grant, and I promise, I will be seeing y'all soon," she emphasizes happily.

I grunt in response as I carefully lay back and close my eyes, draping my good hand over my forehead before they even step away.

"Are you done eating?" Ella prompts softly as I feel her hand lay tenderly on my bicep, heating my skin, but I try to ignore it.

"Yeah, I'm all done. Thanks, Ella. Breakfast was delicious as always," I mumble without lifting my gaze.

Ella's hand slips away from my arm, leaving me cold. Right after, I feel her step away from me, taking the breakfast tray with her. "I'll be right back with your aspirin and some water," she proclaims, her voice soft as she walks out.

These are the moments I wish I could leave, to escape. I'm desperate for control, yet I feel utterly helpless; my life nothing but chaos, but I'm still here, surviving. The more time I spend with Ella, getting to know her, I feel myself falling down the rabbit hole, and I don't know if I'll be able to dig my way out, or if I want to. That's dangerous; she's dangerous.

I shouldn't be here. Ella doesn't need to see me this way. She deals with enough of my bullshit already when she shouldn't have to deal with any at all. At least she will be working more often now and she won't feel obligated to spend so much time trying to entertain me and take care of my sorry ass. She deserves so much better.

24

Ella

I PULL INTO THE GRAVEL PARKING LOT, DRIVING MY CAR INTO the back corner next to the other employees' vehicles at the restaurant. As I open my door and step out, a gust of wind slaps me in the face, just as a wave crashes into the shore, the booming sound echoing in my ears and bringing a smile to my face. Pausing for a moment, I take a deep breath, inhaling the scent of the salt water and fresh air, exhaling slowly. Most of the time, I love that smell, and today is one of those days. It gives me a sense of calm knowing I'm still standing strong, putting myself out there and moving forward, relishing the happy moments.

Tearing my gaze away from the ocean, I glance up at the large, square, cedar shake building adorned with a wide wrap-around porch on all four sides and a massive outdoor patio on the side opposite the parking lot with a bar we open for events and most weekends. The aqua blue shutters of the picture windows are folded back for customers to take in and enjoy the beautiful view. The restaurant is slightly raised on massive stilts to assist with keeping it safe from erosion and storms, especially hurricanes. Long ramps leading up to the building sit on the parking lot side, as well as the back with a set of stairs located on both sides of the front, or the side facing the water, giving us easy access to the beach.

I make my way towards the back door and pull it open, step-ping inside between the dining area and the kitchen, instantly struck with the scent of seafood and burgers. Pausing, I look towards the square bar made of a reclaimed wood, similar to the floors, located in the middle of the restaurant. Spotting James, one of the managers, I lift my hand and wave, smiling. James towers over the bar as he wipes it down, his black hair recently cut close to his head. His warm brown eyes meet mine, and he smiles, the kind of smile that makes me feel spe-cial. How does he do that? He gives me a head nod in greeting and continues working.

James grew up here, and although he's always been friendly with Declan, he's a year younger than him and they never really hung out. Honestly, I don't know if I could've worked here if one of my brother's friends had been my boss. It would be another thing for Declan to hold over me. I think he would control everything I do if he could. Sometimes he's worse than Mom and Dad, but that's probably because he hears more than they do. Or maybe it's the fact he gave up so much for me, although he still claims it's what he wanted. Doesn't mean it was easy for anyone.

Glancing around, I quickly assess what still needs to be done. I grin, grateful the place looks clean; it means less work for us to set up for dinner. It must've been a quiet lunch crowd today for it to look this good. I weave my way through the high-top tables surrounding the bar, as well as the shorter and wider ones interspersed between. Tall booths with the same treated wood as the bar line the walls by the windows. I walk towards the back right corner, finding the area with the two pool tables and dartboards appearing spotless.

As I walk past the kitchen, one of the chefs sticks his arm through the narrow window where they place orders for the runners. "Ella, good to have you back."

"Thanks, Mario. It's good to see you." Glancing at James, as I pass, I ask, "Were you guys closed for lunch today? This place looks nearly spotless."

He laughs. "Just a small crowd and some extra help today."

"Nice." I spin on my heel, striding into the locker room to put away my keys and purse before I check in. The moment I open the door, I scrunch my nose up in disgust, assaulted with the overwhelming scent of sweat and body odor. "What the hell is that smell? What idiot didn't bring their clothes home?"

I'm greeted with a woman wearing the same aqua blue fitted t-shirt as me with the white writing and logo of the restaurant, Mackie's, paired with light, frayed jean shorts, much shorter than the ones I'm wearing. "Ella, you're back," Ginny croons. She grins broadly as she wraps her arms around me. Ginny grew up here like me and graduated a year behind me in school. She went to college and came back after she graduated to help her mom and younger brother. During the day she works with them at the general store in town and she picks up shifts here at night, calling it her social life. Her long, dark brown, curly hair, flawless olive skin and tawny brown eyes all add to her beauty. She's five-feet eight-inches and thin with subtle curves as well as the kind of confidence I try to emulate, and a fiery spirit to match.

Smiling, I return her kind gesture, squeezing her tight. "I'm back," I concur, lacking enthusiasm. I don't know if I want to be back, but I'm here. It's not a bad job. In fact, we usually make good tips and I like being around the people. With the customers at work, I'm usually treated like everyone else, and I like feeling normal, but I want to know what to do next. I need more. But while everyone else seems to be starting their lives, I'm still trying to figure out the basics of my future.

It probably doesn't help that I've really enjoyed being able to be home to help Grant and spend time getting to know him. He's so much more than he seems to want to let people know. So many times, I don't think he means to tell me something, but the more I'm with him, the more I learn. Plus, now I feel like I can't stop worrying about him, and I left barely twenty minutes ago.

"I think it's in the locker in the corner," she informs me, pointing and sticking her tongue out. "I'm not touching whatever the hell it is. The way it makes this place smell, it could be growing something poisonous. That's something I don't ever want to see, let alone have to clean up," she complains, shaking her head.

"Ew," I mumble, scrunching up my nose in revulsion. "I'll tell Devon about it, if y'all haven't already," I mumble, thinking about the sometimes janitor and sometimes porter.

"Good idea. I didn't say anything to him yet. How are you feeling?" She looks at me, her eyes suddenly full of concern.

I wince, releasing her and gently wiggling away from her hold. "I wasn't sick." I shake my head. Every single time I miss anything, everyone assumes I'm sick again. I hate the look of pity that crosses everyone's face when I'm asked a version of that same question. "I took the week off because I was taking care of..." I pause, not sure how to explain Grant or if I even want to, "someone who needs my help with something," I finish vaguely.

She smirks and arches her eyebrows in question. "Someone? What kind of someone? A man? Is he hot?" she blurts out her questions, rapid fire.

I chuckle softly. She loves to gossip about men. An image of Grant without a shirt instantly comes to mind, making my mouth water. I lick my lips, fighting a groan. Instead, I shrug and quietly admit, "I definitely think so."

Her high-pitched squeal pierces my ears as she bounces up and down on her toes in excitement. She looks at me with her eyes wide as they light up with pure glee. "What did he need help with?" she taunts playfully. "Spill!"

I open my mouth, not quite sure what I'm going to say, yet feeling like I could talk about him all day. "Well..."

The locker room door swings open and Hannah sticks her head inside, glancing at both of us with a wide grin. Hannah is petite at five-feet, two-inches. She's barely twenty-one with dark brown wavy hair, green eyes, and a chest the men love, but she hates. She claims they make her unbalanced and causes guys to talk to her chest instead of her, assuming her intelligence is in the weight of her boobs. I don't blame her; I've seen it happen and even I've been tempted to kick many men in the balls in her defense. It's just not right.

"Hey, y'all."

"Hi, Hannah," we reply in unison.

"Welcome back, Ella!" she proclaims cheerfully.

"Thanks."

Glancing back and forth between the two of us, her face turns apologetic. "I'm sorry to interrupt what looks like a fun conversation, but James wants everyone up front for a quick staff meeting before shift."

"Okay, thanks, Hannah. We're coming," I respond for both of us. "I need to get away from that smell anyway before I really do get sick," I tease, only half joking. If I can't make light of it, people would really start walking on eggshells around me, and that's the last thing I want.

As I spin around, Ginny gently grabs my arm, halting me. I arch my eyebrows in question as her eyes narrow on me. "Y'all are not getting out of this. I want to hear everything about this guy you spent your week off with," she states as if in warning.

Chuckling softly, I concede, nodding. "Okay, okay. We will talk later."

"Promise?" She arches her eyebrows in challenge.

"I promise. But we gotta get out there before James gets pissed. Besides, now we can tell Devon about that," I add, nodding towards the offensive odor in the corner.

"Well, then, let's go," she prompts as she releases my arm. We both step out of the locker room and take a deep breath, needing to get the stench out of our nostrils.

23

Grant

I GRIN, FEELING ON TOP OF THE WORLD, MY ADRENALINE still running through me. Offering a wave, I finish up with the reporters, giving them an apology, "Sorry, but I have to hit the showers before talking to Coach." Spinning around, I jog towards the locker room, my black cleats clicking on the tile floors. As I approach, the locker room door slams open, the smell of sweat hitting me in the face. A few of my teammates, already showered and dressed, file out, playfully shoving one another as they continue congratulating each other, talking animatedly about our winning play.

"Young, man, fantastic game tonight! Your arm was on fire!" Dudley calls out, smiling wide. Dudley is a big guy, tall and broad. He's incredibly strong and surprisingly fast and agile, making him one of our best defensive linemen.

"Thanks, Dudley! You too, man! It's a good thing Valens knows how to catch," I joke, feeling my adrenaline increase again.

Valens, my six-foot two wide receiver laughs humorlessly. "Yeah, it's a good thing," he mumbles sarcastically. "It's also a good thing we have a quarterback who thinks he knows what he's doing." I smirk and shrug my shoulders like it's no big deal.

"Are you coming to the party at Denvy's later? Everybody

will be there," my teammate Langley prompts, halting to wait for my response.

Nodding firmly, I reply, "That's the plan when I'm done here."

He grins. "Later, then."

"Later!" I nod, stepping further into the locker room as the last of the guys straggle out, passing by me and knocking my shoulder pads in celebration.

Ignoring them, I make my way to my locker, ready to peel out of my uniform in the suddenly quiet room. I'm always the last player in here, and since it will be a little while before Coach gets away from the media and parents, I know I have a little time to myself. I set my helmet on the wooden bench next to me and turn towards my locker. Quickly spinning the lock, I yank the door open with a click before I tug my red and white jersey off over my head, immediately followed by my pads. I toss them on the ground next to me at the same time someone smacks my ass over my white, tight, padded pants, taking me by surprise.

"I thought all you assholes left," I mumble, spinning around.

A petite woman stands in front of me, causing my eyes to widen in surprise. "Mrs. Stone? What are you doing in here?"

She lets her head fall back as she laughs. "You know exactly what I'm doing here, Grant. I came to congratulate you for playing such a great game."

Gulping, I shake my head. "Thanks, but you have to leave."

"Why is that Grant? All your friends left," she reiterates, making me grimace. "You've got me all to yourself."

"No. You can't be in here." I glance around the locker room anxiously, even though I know she's right; we're all alone.

"Don't worry so much. I'll be gone before your coach comes back if you're good," she emphasizes, "and all of your team-mates are already long gone," she declares as if in victory.

"This is the men's locker room!"

Laughing, she murmurs, "Oh, I'm very aware." She steps towards me, reaching for my cock and hitting nothing but my cup.

I have a quick intake of air, tensing in reaction anyway and instantly pushing her away. "You can't do that," I mutter uncomfortably, my anxiety skyrocketing and making my stomach churn.

She smirks, pressing her body into mine. "That's where you're wrong, sweetheart. I can do whatever I want when it comes to you, especially if your sweet, innocent, little brother still wants to hang out with Amy. They seem to be quite close, and I would hate it if he got himself into any trouble."

I clench my jaw, narrowing my eyes at her. "I've told you to leave Matt out of this! He's just a kid." I grit through my teeth, my blood boiling.

"And I've told you, you're already in too deep to pull out," she murmurs, licking her lips, her innuendos clear as she attempts to seduce me.

"I have somewhere to be," I grumble. My brain goes into overdrive as I continue to untangle her arms from around my neck.

Irritation flashes in her eyes as a sudden look of determination covers her face. "You need to learn to listen to me, Mr. Young. You don't control what happens between us. I do! It's time you understand that!"

"No!" I shake my head vehemently in denial.

Ignoring me, she pushes up on her toes, pressing into me. Her tongue juts out, licking my neck, my breaths coming out in pants. "You had your chance and you took it. Now you're mine," she stresses. With one hand, she reaches up and slides her fingers into my hair at the back of my head. Suddenly, she grasps a handful of my hair, jerking my head back hard and slamming it into the locker behind me, taking me completely by surprise.

Grunting in pain, I lift a hand to my head, muttering, "What the fuck?" Feeling off-balance, I reach up with my other hand and try to gently pry her off me.

Suddenly, the sound of the locker room door opening as

someone walks in hits my ears. My eyes instantly widen in panic, pleading with her to leave. "Please," I rasp, desperately.

She grins, a devilish gleam in her eyes as she leans towards me, whispering in my ear, "You could just give me what we both want..."

"I don't want you."

She stiffens briefly before her voice lowers in warning, "Or with one yank on my shirt, I could ruin you." I glance down at her hand, playfully twisting pearly white buttons between her fingers. "Who do you think they'll believe?" she challenges, arching her eyebrows in question.

My heart races with anxiety, causing me to freeze, unsure what to do. She suddenly bites down hard on my neck, just above my collarbone. Gasping, I reflexively shove her off, harder than I mean to, causing her to fall back, hitting her back on the bench on her way down.

"Young?" Coach calls. "Is that you?"

All the blood drains from my face as I inhale a swift intake of breath. Before I respond, I think about what she just said and how this would look to anyone else. What would Coach say? I could be kicked off the team and lose my chance at a scholarship for college. Plus, if she really pushes it, I could go to jail. It would ruin my family and put my little brother at risk from her wrath. She doesn't take kindly to losing, me included. I'm fucked.

Gulping down the lump in my throat I force out my response, "Yeah, Coach, it's me. I just tripped on the bench. I'm just about to jump in the showers now," I inform him, attempting to keep my voice from shaking.

"Alright, come see me in my office when you're done," he calls back. "I need to see you before you leave."

"You got it!"

We both wait, listening to his retreating footsteps before moving. I reach down and hold out my hand, helping her up. "I'm sorry," I apologize, my nerves taking control of my insides.

"I didn't mean for you to fall."

"Hm, you owe me for that," she grumbles, her eyes narrowed with doubt and accusations. As soon as she's back on her feet, I release her, but she instantly steps closer, crowding me. "I expect you at my house on Sunday morning. You have some making up to do."

Shaking my head, I open my mouth to refuse when she narrows her eyes, giving me a look of warning. Snapping my mouth closed, I grit my teeth and nod my head in defeat, my whole world closing in on me. Taking a deep breath, I give her the verbal response I know she wants, grunting, "Got it."

She grins in triumph, making my heart sink. "Good boy," she murmurs smugly. As she leans towards me, I attempt to lean back, but I have nowhere to go, my body hitting the lockers. She pushes up on her tiptoes, giving me a chaste kiss I don't return before she taps my cheek lightly and sneaks out through the back door.

Clenching my fists, I turn, slamming my hand against the locker next to mine. The whole row of red metal rattles loudly as I growl in frustration. Instantly, a fist-sized dent glares back at me. I'm already feeling the bruising on my knuckles, but I don't give a fuck. I'd give almost anything to just get my life back.

My eyes fly open and I gasp for breath. Frantically, I look around the darkened room lit only by the moonlight. Anger courses through my veins before I finally realize where I am. Knowing I'm safe, my eyes close in relief. I focus on breathing in and out, attempting to calm myself down, and hoping to release all my built-up tension.

After a few minutes, I rub my good hand over my face and heave a sigh, grateful I didn't yell and wake up Ella. I don't want to explain my nightmares to anyone, especially not her. She wouldn't understand; no one would. I don't ever want to see that look of disappointment and disgust on her face directed at me. I'll be gone before I let that happen.

It's been years since I had that nightmare. I guess my thoughts about Matt brought back memories of her trying to control me by using my family, my little brother, football, basically anything that really mattered to me. I hate myself for being stupid enough to get involved with her in the first place. If only I had never...wincing, I shake my head, my self-loathing strong, cutting off the thought before it finishes. I can't go there. I'm already in a sinkhole after my accident. If I think about her, I'll never be able to claw my way out.

Unfortunately, I'm not very mobile, yet, and I'm stuck here. But at least Ella had to go back to work. Without her here all the time, I'll need to figure out how to do this on my own. That will only help me get back to myself much faster. I need my independence back.

Besides, there's no way I can allow her to keep taking care of me. She does too much for me, and everything about it feels too personal, too intimate. I can't rely on anyone but myself. It's not fair to them, and I just can't do that to my angel. Especially since, when it comes to her, I seem to always want more, and I won't be sticking around; I can't.

26

Ella

OVER THE NEXT FEW WEEKS, WE FALL INTO A ROUTINE, starting the day with me making breakfast before eating together. The days I don't have to work, we find ways to pass the time, and I enjoy every single minute, whether we're playing a game, doing a puzzle, watching a movie, joking around or just talking. So many of the things we've found to do, he's admitted to me he hasn't done in years, but the far off look he gets in his eyes when he mentions it makes my heart clench. That look nearly brings me to my knees. It makes me want to reach for him, hold him, comfort him and be there for him in any way he will allow me to be. I just wish I knew what's causing him all that pain. Is it his family?

Luckily, he's surpassed one hurdle, no longer needing the home care nurse to come to the house for checks. At least that's one less thing for him to do. And with both his occupational and physical therapy temporarily halted while he waits for his casts to come off, he doesn't have much left to do but eat, sleep, take care of his personal hygiene and hang out with me.

Admittedly, time with him has become the best part of my day, even better than my time on the water, I think, as I set my paddleboard down in the corner of my shed. I wonder if he'll ever try going with me when he's better, but I swiftly push the thought away, trying not to get ahead of myself.

I make my way inside, knowing the house is empty with Grant at his doctor's appointment, and it's likely too early for Declan to pop in. He still stops by regularly at all hours of the day, depending on his work schedule, but he seems to be getting more and more comfortable having Grant around. I'd even say they're becoming friends, but I don't think he would ever admit it. I'm just confident my eyes don't deceive me. I smile, remembering when I walked inside the house the other day, just getting home from work, and I heard the two of them laughing about something; the deep sound warming my heart.

Charlotte is so busy lately, it's rare I get to see her at all. I need to call her later to see how she's doing.

Grabbing my phone, I glance at the screen, seeing a missed call from my mom. I'm honestly surprised, but also grateful neither of my parents have stopped in to meet Grant or just to check on me, but I haven't missed their daily call either, or I'm sure that would change immediately. It probably helps that Declan keeps them updated too.

When my family is quiet, I start to wonder if they have a rotating schedule to check on me. I chuckle and shake my head. I wouldn't put it past any of them. They've been relentless when it comes to being overprotective of me. Realistically, I'm positive Declan is the only reason my mom didn't move in with me the moment she found out about Grant. Eventually, I'll have to pay him back for all his help.

I glance at the time again and make my way to my room to shower and change, Grant at the forefront of my mind. Most of the time when we're together, we fall into easy conversation. I must admit he attempts to keep our interactions light, never getting too deep, but I'm almost desperate to know more about him, not just what's on the surface or what he's currently willing to share.

Occasionally, a haunted look passes through his eyes just before he shuts down on me, claiming he's tired or sore. I don't doubt he is, but I also don't believe that's his reason for pulling away from me. My heart clenches painfully every time I see that look on his ridged face. I feel helpless, wanting to pull him into my arms to comfort and protect him, but he won't allow it.

It's obvious he's been through so much, I just don't know what. His actions only make me more determined to figure out a way to help him, and not just with his physical injuries. I will break down his walls.

Although I've been attempting to ignore it as much as I can, Grant still ignites an inferno inside me, drawing me to him like a moth to a flame, afraid of getting burned, but I believe it's worth the risk—*he's* worth it. Besides, like I've said many times since I was first diagnosed, I promise to live my life without regret. Not taking a chance on him would be one of my biggest regrets. I'm absolutely sure of it.

Now clean and dressed, I glance at my phone one more time, checking to see how long Grant's been gone. Heaving a sigh, I step back outside, and begin pacing my back deck, not able to sit still. I look out at the ocean, even the soft roar of the waves not able to calm my mind. I walk back and forth, impatiently waiting for him to return like a child wanting to see Santa. "He went to the doctor, Ella." I know I'm being ridiculous, but I can't believe he refused to allow me to go with him, insisting he didn't need my help; even taking a cab instead of letting me drive him. The man is stubborn as hell, but I'm determined to find a way to change that, at least I want to change how stubborn he can be when it comes to me.

Briefly, I think about doing something productive from my long list of things to do, but not surprisingly, my brain remains focused on him. I can't get him out of my head, for better or worse. Then again, I don't want to. I'd rather be spending my day off with him instead of doing errands or cleaning my house. I don't care what we do.

My eyes swing back and forth from the ocean to the front of my house, hoping he'll suddenly appear. Groaning, I shake my head, unsure why I feel so uneasy, except for the fact I've gotten used to him being here whenever I'm home. Although, I wish it were just the quiet house leaving me on edge.

My phone rings and I answer without looking at the screen. "Hello?"

"Ella? It's Laine."

"Hi!" I squeak in surprise. "Is everything okay?"

"Yeah, of course. Everything is great. Listen, I know you're seeing Grant, and I don't want to step on anyone's toes, but I have this opportunity I thought you might want to get involved in with me."

Not wanting to think about the first half of his statement, I ignore it for now. "What are you talking about? What opportunity?"

"Well, we have a program called Break For Fun Saturdays or BFF'S."

"Cute."

He huffs a laugh. "Yeah. Well, it's a group of kids we work with on Saturdays down at the park. They're all in various tough situations, and we spend the day hanging out with them, playing games, talking, having fun. Every single kid has a lot going on in their life like being sick, or a parent in the system, or going through rehab for something. Of course, some have a really hard-working parent, but maybe they have been home-less or wonder where they will get their next meal. Whatever it is, it's a lot for anyone, let alone a kid. Saturday sessions are one of the few times they have all week where they can really be a kid."

"Oh, wow, I can understand that."

"I know, and you're always so good with helping animals and people, especially kids. I've been wanting to call and ask you, but..."

"I would love that," I interrupt.

"Yeah?"

"Absolutely. What do I need to do?"

"Well, are you free Saturday?"

"I can make sure I am."

"Great. How about I pick you up and I can bring you with me on Saturday? I'll introduce you to everyone and get you all settled."

"Perfect. What time?"

"I'll pick you up at 8:30. Wear something comfortable and definitely sneakers."

"Got it. Thank you for thinking of me, Laine. I'm really looking forward to this." I grin, truly excited.

"You're the first one I thought of when we got the program going."

"Thank you. I'll see you Saturday."

"See you Saturday, Ella."

I disconnect the call just as the low rumble of a car motor sounds in the distance, causing me to hold my breath in anticipation. The crunching of gravel underneath tires hits my ears just before I see the cab round the corner and pull into my driveway.

Excited to tell him about BFF'S, I walk around the side of my house, forcing myself to take it slow. As I approach the drive with a smile, my fingers twitch at my sides, wanting to assist him, or maybe I just want to see him. He leans forward, seeming to pay the driver, before pushing the door open. Keeping my eyes towards the back of the car, I stare as he emerges on the other side. Shielding my eyes from the suddenly bright sun, I watch as he shuts the door, the car blocking my view. He moves back as the car backs out of the driveway, leaving him exposed.

"Grant!" I audibly gasp, startling at the sight of him.

He's standing in black net shorts and a white graphic t-shirt, leaning on crutches with the sexiest grin I think I've ever seen, taking my breath away. "No more cast," he happily announces, holding his arm up for inspection.

I run the last few steps, throwing my arms around his

waist, careful not to knock him off balance. After all, he's still sporting a cast on his leg. "That's fantastic!" I exclaim, my excitement palpable. Releasing him, I step back, smiling up at him. "We need to get you out of the house to celebrate!" Telling him about Saturday can wait. Tonight should be about him.

"I'd really like that. I'd love to have some good food down by the water. I love your view here, but it would be fun to have a different perspective after so long."

"I understand. I like my house, but when you can't really go anywhere, even my house can be depressing." I hated any kind of confinement when I was sick.

"Not when you're here." My cheeks heat instantly, making him chuckle. "Well, as long as you're with me, I know I'll have great company."

Rolling my eyes, I admonish, "Grant." He smirks. "Is there somewhere you want to go? I could suggest a few places." A wave of guilt washes over me, knowing I asked my parents to give him time and now I'm taking him out. But I don't exactly want to bring him to my parents' house the first time we finally get to go out together. I'm an adult; meeting the parents is not something you do on a first date. Is this a date? My stomach twists and I run my lower lip through my teeth, my nerves suddenly trying to get the best of me.

"What about the restaurant you work at? I know some people don't really like going where they work on their day off though."

"I don't care where we go, and that never bothers me. It's good food and a great view. Plus, this is your celebration, you pick," I reiterate, knowing my family will be asking me about it if we go anywhere within a ten-mile radius of town, and that's the best seaside restaurant in the area. Besides, I don't think my first date nerves could handle driving too far. It doesn't matter to me where we eat. I'm just happy he wants me to be the one to celebrate with him.

"Then, let's go there. I would love to see where you spend so much of your time when you're not with me."

My heart flutters and my cheeks heat further, turning a deeper shade of pink. "Mackie's it is," I agree, smiling up at him.

"I just need to clean up again first, if that's okay with you?"

"Of course!"

"After they took the cast off, I washed my arm while I was there, but it still stinks from being in the cast for so long. Sorry."

"You have no reason to apologize." I look down, taking a closer look at his arm, noticing his pale skin pucker slightly. Glancing back and forth between his right and left arm, I realize the obvious difference in his muscle definition from lack of use. I imagine that will take some time to rebuild.

"It looks so damn strange," he mumbles, inspecting his own arm.

"I'm sure it looks how it's supposed to."

He shrugs, glaring at his arm. "I guess."

"Does that mean you'll get more serious about replacing your motorcycle now?" I'm more curious than anything.

I watch as the corners of his lips curve upwards. "Maybe. I just gotta finalize everything with insurance."

"Well, at least you'll be able to work on whatever y'all find now that you have two functioning hands." He's mentioned having his two strong hands again to do a lot more than just work on his motorcycle, I think, my face heating at the thought. But the truth is, I would love to see him do his thing.

As he watches me, his grin grows, hopefully not reading my dirty thoughts. His eyes sparkle with something I don't think I've seen in him before, the beauty making my heart skip a beat. Looking at his fingers, he flexes and stretches them slowly a few times, staring, fascinated with the simple action. "It may be a little while before my hand works like I really want it to, but I'm sure as hell going to try."

27

Grant

MY EYES SLOWLY DRIFT DOWN ELLA'S GORGEOUS BODY. She changed out of shorts and a t-shirt, I assume thinking we would be hanging out at home again tonight, into a sexy, little dark green sundress with white daisies on it and thin spaghetti straps looped over her shoulders. Even her simple white sandals look hot as hell. I'm struggling to take my eyes off her and focus on the uneven ground as we make our way across the parking lot with my crutches and my right arm, not yet much help.

I glance out at the spectacular view, the sun still high above the horizon before looking back at her. "This place really has a sweet spot."

"Yeah, it does," she murmurs, glancing out at the ocean before smiling up at me.

We finally make it up the ramp and she reaches for the door and tugs, attempting to hold it open for me. But I take her place, leaning back on my crutches, wanting to do something for her, even if it's just standing in front of the door. She steps by me mumbling, "Thank you."

I nod and shuffle to her side, the door closing behind us. Pausing, I look around Mackie's, taking in the casual atmosphere. This is my kind of place, but finding it relatively busy tonight almost makes me second-guess our dinner plans as male eyes instantly roam over her luscious curves. I clench my fists in irritation, intensifying the stiff feeling in my right hand.

"Grant, are you okay?" She assesses me, biting her lip in concern.

Nodding, I reach up, tucking a lock of her blonde hair behind her ear, enjoying the darkening of her cheeks as my fingers skim her neck and shoulder, lingering. "I'm fine. It's just crowded. I wondered for a moment if this was the best decision."

She smiles, making it difficult to breathe. "We can sit outside on the porch. It will be quieter and a little less crazy out there; hopefully not as many prying eyes."

"Sounds good." A sense of relief washes over me.

"Ella! What are you doing here?" a girl wearing a Mackie's t-shirt questions as she steps up to us. Her eyes veer towards me, leaning on my crutches. She smirks, giving me a small wave. "Hi, I'm Ginny. I'm a friend of Ella's. You must be Grant."

I grin, nodding in affirmation. "That's me."

"Is there a table for us out on the deck?" Ella interrupts.

Ginny giggles and nods. "Yeah, but it will be easier to get there from outside with his crutches. Come on." We follow her back outside and around the deck to a table in the corner, giving us plenty of extra room for my broken leg.

"Thank you," Ella states, breathing a sigh of relief. Ginny leans towards Ella, whispering something in her ear. I can't hear, but I'm able to enjoy my angel's cheeks turning three shades of red as she looks anywhere but at me, piquing my curiosity. "Bye, Ginny," she mumbles, gently nudging her friend away.

Ginny bursts out laughing as she glances back at me. "It was wonderful finally meeting you, handsome."

I chuckle softly. "You too."

Ella huffs and drops down into a chair before I have a chance to pull it out for her. "I would've gotten your chair; I'm a little slow these days."

Her eyes widen in surprise. I lean my crutches against one

chair and carefully lower myself into the seat across from Ella with my right leg sticking out. "So, what do you think?" she inquires, glancing around apprehensively.

I tear my gaze away from her and let my eyes sweep over our surroundings. "It's definitely a beautiful location and casual; just my speed." I return my eyes to her, a smile tugging at my lips. "I trust you with the food, and as I've said before, I have beautiful company." She blushes. "You do look absolutely gorgeous, Ella."

"Thank you," she mumbles, appearing slightly uncomfortable with my praise. "What are you in the mood for?"

I lick my lips and run my teeth over my lower lip with a low groan as I take her in. As I stare at her, I smirk, arching my eyebrow in challenge. "You. I'm feeling a little playful now that I have both my hands," I proclaim, wiggling my fingers. I let my eyes drag up and down her body, relishing the sudden deep red color of her skin.

"Hi, Ella! What are you doing here on your night off?" another waitress questions, stepping up to our table.

Ella gestures across the table to me, announcing, "We're celebrating. Grant got one of his casts off today."

"Nice." She nods in my direction. "Congratulations."

Chuckling softly, I mumble, "Thanks."

"Grant, this is Hannah, and Hannah, Grant," Ella introduces us.

I flash her a smile as she responds, "It's nice to meet you, Grant." With a quick look back at Ella, she informs us, "Looks like you're stuck with me tonight. You guys know what you want?"

A devilish grin lights up my face as Ella blushes instantly again, making it impossible to hide my amusement. "I know what I want," I reiterate, licking my lips as I stare at her. "Do you want to order for us?"

I watch as she takes a deep breath, pulling herself together. Attempting to ignore me, she orders, while I watch her every move. I can't take my eyes off her. The moment Hannah walks away, Ella narrows her eyes on me, not able to keep a straight face no matter how hard she tries. "You have to stop looking at me like that."

Grinning wickedly, I murmur, "Not going to happen, Angel." I don't even bother to pretend. "I like looking at you."

"Gabriella," a deep voice calls softly. Ella's whole body stiffens as we both look up, finding her ex stepping up to her side. My eyes narrow and my fists clench as he leans towards her, kissing her on the cheek without an invitation. She immediately begins to squirm, obviously uncomfortable with his actions. "What are you doing here?"

"She's eating with me," I answer.

He frowns as he looks at me, unimpressed. "I see you got one of your casts off," he mumbles dismissively.

She reaches for his arm, pulling his attention back to her. Standing over her like that, he has a perfect view down her dress to her cleavage, and I don't fucking like it. "What do you want, Nate?"

"I saw you walk out here and I had to come say hi."

"Great. Well, you saw me. Now you can go. I'm on a date," she emphasizes, dismissing him with a flick of her wrist.

My heart stutters as I quickly inhale in surprise. Her words both satisfy and startle me for completely different reasons. I guess this is a date, but I don't date, not the way she deserves. Then I glance at Nate, leaning towards her, getting in her space, and I feel my blood boil, ready to claim her as mine no matter the consequences. Taking a deep breath, I exhale slowly, attempting to remain calm before I say a word. "I believe my *date* asked you to leave."

He turns his head, clenching his jaw and straightening his shoulders as he looks at me through narrowed eyes. "I'm talking to Gabriella."

"Well, I'm the one who told you to leave," Ella repeats, her frustration growing.

He sighs heavily, gently resting his hand on her shoulder. "I'll go, but how are you doing?" She glares up at him and he continues, "Are you getting enough sleep? You look tired."

"Gee, thanks," she mumbles, monotone. "I'm fine." He looks at her, his doubt clear as she shakes her head. "Goodbye, Nathan!" she declares, overly cheerful with a fake smile plastered on her face.

Nodding reluctantly, he brushes his lips along the top of her head. I swear he's trying to piss me off. "Please call me. We need to talk."

She huffs a humorless laugh. "Not likely," she grumbles under her breath, making the corners of my lips curve up.

"Have a nice night," he mutters, glaring at me again before he stalks inside, going directly towards the bar.

Sighing heavily, she apologizes, "I'm so sorry about him."

I huff a humorless laugh and shake my head. "You don't need to apologize for him. What he does and says is not on you, unless you provoke him for some reason, and even then, I'd bet he's to blame."

"Thanks."

"Maybe this was a bad idea. Do you want to go?"

"No!" she insists with a firm shake of her head.

"Okay, let me know if you change your mind." She nods, sinking into her chair. "What happened with you two anyway?" I question, remembering too late why I don't like to ask these kinds of questions. It's easier not to answer for myself when I don't ask.

She grimaces and glances up at me, uneasy as she begins to fidget with her fingers. "Are you sure you want to know?"

I nod firmly, suddenly anxious, but also desperate to know the answer. "I want to know."

"I think our biggest problem was he treated me like a patient instead of his girlfriend," she confesses, surprising me. "It's hard to explain, but when we would fight, I used to say that he cared more about my sickness than he did about me and what I wanted. He was a resident when we started dating, and his career was important to him. I didn't blame him for that, but he became more of an overcautious doctor who was constantly on call, instead of my boyfriend. I felt like a case instead of just me. Does that make sense?" She glances up at me from underneath her long eyelashes.

I nod my head as my heart clenches seeing the pain he obviously caused her. "It does."

Sighing, she shakes her head, dismissing the topic. "We didn't come out tonight to talk about my ex, though. I'm not about to let him ruin my night."

My heart drops into my stomach, taking her statement for so much more than her pure intentions. My fingers twitch with my hands itching to touch her. I'm instantly over this change of scenery. I want to go home and wrap her in my arms. I lick my lips, sucking my bottom lip into my mouth and letting it slowly slide through my teeth, wishing I were kissing her lips, her neck, her breasts, her pussy. I groan involuntarily. At this rate, I'm not going to make it through dinner.

"Are you okay?" she prods innocently, causing my cock to twitch in response.

"Fantastic," I growl, my voice low. Her eyes widen and set ablaze as she holds my heated stare. "I think we should make it a quick night."

28

Ella

ATTEMPTING TO BE DISCREET, I GLANCE AT GRANT OUT OF the corner of my eye as I slip the key into the lock of my front door and twist. He no longer seems to be holding back, making the air feel electric. It's like he's a different man tonight. I assume it's the cast, but he even looks different, more confident, more content. It kind of makes sense. I can't imagine finding something you love to do and know you're really good at it, but then it's suddenly ripped away from you. Now, he'll be able to get that piece of himself back with the use of both his hands again. It's a good look on him.

He does look damn good in his long-sleeve black t-shirt with three buttons open at his neck and white net shorts. Seeing him in long-sleeves makes me wonder what he'd look like in blue jeans. The last pair I saw on him were almost completely shredded, hanging off his body and covered in blood, dirt, and concrete. I guess I'll have to wait to see him like that until his cast comes off his leg. I wonder how much longer he'll have to wait.

"Need some help with the door?" He arches his eyebrows in question as the corners of his lips twitch upwards. The deep timbre of his voice goes through me, making me squirm as my body heats in embarrassment.

Tonight, there's not just a spark or even a fire between us, but an electrical storm that can't be tamed without the other. Shaking myself out of my stupor, I gulp and focus back on the door, attempting to brush off the rush of hormones slapping me in the face. "No, I've got it, sorry. I was just thinking about something."

He leans towards me and my body heats instantly at his proximity. Licking his lips, he whispers in my ear; his warm breath on my cheek giving me goose bumps as I attempt to maintain control of my breathing. "If the look on your face is any indication, I know what you were thinking about, and unless you want me to press you up against your front door and kiss you right here, right now, I think you should let us in."

My eyes widen as I gasp in surprise, feeling my face flush. He leans back, the corners of his lips twitching up in amusement as he chuckles softly. Taking a deep breath, I force myself to move. I wiggle the key, forcing the door open and tossing the key and my purse inside the door. "It's open," I announce in triumph. Smiling, I step inside, holding the door open for him.

A grin lights up his face as he follows, and I close the door behind him. The moment I spin around, I find him standing in front of me, making my breath catch. He sets the crutch in his right hand down, leaning it against the wall by the door before he maneuvers closer to me, backing me against the door. I tilt my head up, watching his expression as his right hand glides up my neck and along my jaw, weaving his fingers into my hair. His tongue juts out, licking his lips in hunger as he meets my gaze. "I've wanted to do this again for so fucking long," he emphasizes on a groan.

His head tilts down until I feel his heated breath against my lips. My breathing picks up its pace and my heart begins to thrash against my ribcage as he hovers over me, the seconds dragging. My hands slide up his chest, desperately grasping the front of his shirt. "Grant," I whimper, begging him to kiss me.

Granting my wish, he presses his lips to mine. A small

whimper escapes my lips as I melt into him. He moves slowly as if savoring our kiss. His tongue juts out, licking and tasting my lips, asking for entrance I willingly give. I open my mouth, pushing closer as our tongues collide, twisting and exploring with a soft moan. I feel the moment everything shifts, intensifying and deepening our kiss, causing my whole body to vibrate with need. My nipples harden, drawn towards him, begging for his touch, while my core heats and my juices begin pooling, soaking my panties with only his mouth on mine. I want more of him. No, I need more.

He pulls back, leaning on his left crutch still in his hand, eliciting a whimper from my lips. Pausing, he leans his forehead on mine as we both pant, catching our breath. He leans back just enough to hold my gaze. "You know this is only temporary. I can't stay here forever," he reminds me, seemingly from out of nowhere.

My heart skips a few beats in response, hating the truth. I attempt to gulp down the sudden lump in my throat as I nod my head in acknowledgment, not meeting his eyes. Licking my lips, I exhale slowly, my calm returning as I regain my confidence. "It's hard to forget when you keep telling me, but I want you, Grant."

A slow grin eases onto his face as he stares down at me with a glimmer in his eyes. "And I want you, Ella," he rasps, his deep, gravelly voice rumbling through me and heating me to my core. "But I'll be honest, we won't be doing everything tonight." I scrunch my nose up in annoyance, bringing a sexy grin to his lips as he shakes his head in amusement. "You know I want to, but I can't; not with my leg still in a cast, but I sure as hell need more if that's what you want."

"I'm good with more," I concede breathily.

He chuckles softly, pressing his lips to mine as I hum in satisfaction. Barely pulling back, he mumbles, "You are so fucking adorable, Angel."

I feel my cheeks heat, loving his compliment and enjoying

his nickname for me even more. "Grant," I whisper.

"What do you want, Angel?" He brushes his lips lightly back and forth over mine making them tingle.

That's a loaded question. I suck my lower lip into my mouth to keep the words in that want to spew from my mouth without thought. That's not something he should be asking me if he really does plan on leaving. My stomach again twists in protest, wondering if I could change his mind, but I can't make this decision based on 'what if.' I need to be confident in what I want without regrets, knowing what he's willing to give. Instead of answering him, I clear my throat, proposing, "Will you come with me to my room?"

He pulls back, attempting to get a better look into my eyes, assessing me. "Are you sure that's what you want?"

Nodding, my hands fall to his waist as I hold his gaze and confidently confirm, "Yes, please, Grant."

"Alright, then," he murmurs, grinning at me. "How can I say no when you ask so nicely?" I barely huff a laugh as I watch his deliberate movements. Tipping his head down, he presses his lips to mine as I easily relax into his kiss, but all too quickly he leans back and slowly untangles his hand from my hair as he reluctantly pulls away and my hands drop to my sides.

Tearing his gaze from me, he reaches for his other crutch, leaning against the wall, tucking it back under his arm right arm. "I have to admit, it's much easier to get around with two crutches, although it still sucks."

Grimacing, I mumble, "I imagine." I slip my sandals off, abandoning them by the front door before strolling towards my room. Looking back at him, I give him a crooked smile and playfully prod, "Are you coming?"

"No, you always come first," he responds, a mischievous sparkle in his eyes. His comment causes my insides to tingle as flames instantly engulf me. His low chuckle at my reaction sends shivers down my spine as he follows me towards my bedroom, my heart pounding in anticipation with whatever he has in store for us.

29

Grant

BALANCING ON MY LEFT FOOT, I LEAN MY CRUTCHES AGAINST the wall and spin around, sitting on the side of her bed. Lifting my gaze, I look at her, seeing a touch of anxiety or maybe anticipation in her movements. I bite my lip and release it slowly, feeling her energy with every breath. "Come here," I urge, gesturing for her with barely a flick of my head.

She takes a deep breath and holds it as she cautiously approaches, standing between my legs and successfully avoiding my cast. I watch her carefully, wanting to see every single reaction to my touch, no matter how big or how small. Slowly, I let my hands slide up her sides, over the curve of her breast, along her collarbone, up the sleek curve of her neck and into her silky soft hair, leaving a trail of goose bumps in its wake. Gently, I tilt her face towards mine. Cupping her face in my hands, I search her eyes for any ounce of hesitation, and thankfully find nothing but need and want.

Without another thought, I tug her to me as I swiftly close the distance between us and cover her mouth with mine. My lips burn as she kisses me back with fervor, her hands tightly gripping my sides. She opens her mouth in invitation and I quickly sweep my tongue inside, kissing her deeply, devouring her delectable taste, her touch, her sounds and craving so much more. She tastes a little salty like her dinner and a little sweet like her. I can't get enough! She whimpers softly, eliciting a groan from me and causing me to pull back.

I look into her eyes, seeking consent and watch as her blue orbs deepen to a darker shade of blue, like the ocean underneath a night sky. My hands slide back from her face and slip around to her back, over her shoulders and down towards the back of her dress, brushing over her soft, velvety skin just above her zipper. "May I?" I growl, my voice a low rumble as my body burns hotter with every single touch; hers or mine.

She gives my hips a gentle squeeze as if prompting me to do something. As she licks her lips, she nods her head, dreamily murmuring her assent, "Mm-hm."

My fingers fumble with the zipper, making me grimace, annoyed my fingers aren't as nimble as before my accident. But the moment I glance at her, I see nothing but lust, anticipation, and patience, giving me my own sense of reprieve as well as perseverance to continue trying what's normally a simple feat. I'm finally able to grasp the tiny zipper and carefully tug it down, my shoulders relaxing right along with it.

Trailing up her spine and over her shoulders, my fingers slide the straps of her dress to the side. Leaning towards her, I inhale deeply as I brush my lips along her collarbone. I slide the straps down her arms, until her dress falls, pooling at her feet. She steps away from her discarded dress as I lean back and look at her, standing in a strapless, pale yellow, lacy bra and matching bikini underwear, taking my breath away. Her creamy skin appears flawless against the delicate yellow lace. I let my eyes drag over her curves, feeling a fire churning in my gut. "You are so damn sexy."

Her skin tinges pink from head to toe, only making me more gluttonous, wanting all of her. I need to control myself; I can't get carried away. Stealing myself, I reach out, pulling her towards me and pressing my lips against the hollow of her neck. My tongue sticks out, licking and kissing down towards her breasts, loving the taste of her skin. Slowly, I slide my hand up, cupping her breast, suddenly desperate to get rid of the thin barrier between. I slip my hands behind her back, searching for the clasp, but find none. Pulling back, I glance down between her breasts, seeing only a tiny white bow. As I bite my lip, I arch my eyebrow in question.

She giggles at my confusion before attempting to make a deal. "I'm already feeling a little bit naked next to you."

I grin, dragging my tongue between her breasts as an appreciative moan leaves my lips. "I'm okay with that."

She grins wide, not able to hide her amusement or desire. "Well, I'd like to balance things out a little bit. How about you take your shirt off and I'll show you how to take this off."

"You're blackmailing me," I mumble, attempting to get a reaction out of her. "I can work with that this one time," I emphasize, chuckling, only half joking as she blushes that beautiful shade of red. I reach down with my left hand, having gotten used to doing things that way recently, and grasp the hem of my shirt, pulling it over my head and tossing it to the side.

I stare at her, and her eyes widen. She inhales a quick intake of air as her eyes blatantly ogle my chest. "I kept my half of our bargain. Now it's your turn." The corners of my lips curve upwards, knowing I got the better end of this deal.

"There's a small clip under the little bow in front," she murmurs, her voice barely above a whisper.

"Sweet." My teeth rake over my lower lip as my fingers move to her sides. Her breath hitches as I run my fingers right underneath her breasts, stopping right in the middle of her chest. Carefully, I lift the bow, finding the clip and immediately flick it open. Slipping my hands between her breasts, I move them in opposite directions, pushing the material away as my hands slide over her breasts, pausing to circle each nipple and let my thumbs brush over the tips. "So, beautiful," I mumble in awe. A groan of satisfaction falls from my lips and I immediately take her breast into my mouth. She releases a soft whimper as my tongue swirls around her nipple, sucking lightly, while I take her other nipple between my thumb and forefinger, rolling it gently and burning my calloused skin.

She arches into me, pushing closer. "Grant," she rasps, the soft, breathy sound igniting me further. I release her breast with a tender nibble, giving the other side the same treatment. "I can't stand."

Her statement brings attention to her weakened state in my arms. I'm thrilled to be the one doing this to her, but I can't hold her up in my state. Twisting, I flip her onto the bed, wincing at the awkward angle of my broken leg. Quickly, I readjust, trying to get more comfortable. I lean up, kissing her lips, my tongue diving inside as I continue playing with one of her breasts. I feel like I can't get close enough, listening to her soft sounds, her desperate pleas, her body curving into mine like she's begging for more. "I need to touch your pussy. I need to see how wet you are for me, and then I'm going to make you cum with my name on your lips," I inform her, watching her closely for her reaction.

Her face turns a deeper shade of red, seeming more in anticipation than embarrassment. She whimpers again, barely whispering my name, "Grant."

My breathing picks up its pace. I'm fraught with need, grateful for my loose shorts as my cock hardens further, beginning to feel like a steel rod and eager for relief. "Do you want that, Ella?" I probe, needing to hear her say the words.

"Yes, Grant."

Relief, joy, and lust flood me as I kiss her again, harder. Her hands dive into my hair and she holds me close, lightly tugging. I moan into her mouth as my hand moves down her belly, pausing as I run my fingers along her panty line. Her hips arch towards me, urging me. My hand slips underneath and over her smooth mound. Suddenly breathless, I break our kiss. I curse, surprised and thrilled by my discovery. "Fuck!" Dropping my head against her forehead, I state the obvious, "You're completely bare."

"Do you like it?" she asks, sounding timid.

"I fucking love it!" I need her to know the truth.

She grins, breathing heavy. "Good."

I continue down, slipping my fingers over her wet folds. "You're fucking soaked," I mumble breathily, my whole body humming with every touch.

"For you," she claims, further fueling me. "I've wanted this for a long time with you." She seals her words with a kiss.

Her comment hits me in the chest, overwhelming me. It's a little too much. I tell myself she's just talking about our attraction to each other, but I'm not stupid; I know better. Gritting my teeth, I attempt to ignore her words, focusing on her expressions of bliss as I slip one finger inside, curling it in search of her g-spot. Her head falls back, as she arches towards me with a groan, bringing a satisfied smile to my face. Pulling out, I add another finger, slipping both inside. Her smooth walls clench my fingers, giving me insight as to how good it will feel to be inside her. "You're so tight, Ella," I mumble, wondering how long it's been for her.

"Grant," she gasps.

I chuckle softly, her desperate plea going straight to my cock. My thumb slides over her clit, moving in gentle circles as I move my fingers in and out of her wet folds. Her mouth drops open and her eyes fall closed as her hips arch towards me, matching my rhythm. "Grant, I'm...I'm gonna..."

"Yes, Angel. I want to see you cum. I want to feel your walls squeeze my fingers. Cum for me, Angel." I stare at her, taking in every sound, every expression, every movement.

"Grant," she groans loudly on a harsh exhale. She thrusts her hips towards me, just as I feel her fall over the edge. Her body begins to convulse around me, squeezing my fingers. She moans, a beautiful look passing over her face, clenching something inside my chest as well as my dick as she reaches her climax and slowly begins to come down from her high.

Exhaling slowly, she finally blinks her beautiful eyes open, meeting my gaze. "Wow," I mumble in awe. "You're absolutely stunning."

As she blushes again, she reaches for me. She runs her hand over my hard length inside my shorts, her eyes widening. "You're so big."

I groan, pulling my hand out of her panties and nudging her back. "Easy. I'm gonna go quick, Ella. You got me so worked up and it's obviously been a long fucking time."

She arches her eyebrows in question. "What do you mean, obviously?"

"It's been six weeks since my accident." I shrug my shoulders.

"So, it's been longer than six weeks. That's not long," she comments, looking down. I arch my eyebrows in challenge, wanting to argue. "I don't know..." she pauses, suddenly looking anywhere but at me. "Oh," she grumbles, a look that I can only describe as disappointment flashing across her face before it's quickly gone.

I attempt to ignore the way her reaction hits me in the chest as if I were punched. "You don't have to do anything you don't want to," I reiterate, needing a response from her. Seeing the question and vacillation in her eyes, I exhale slowly, making the decision for both of us. "You know, I'm a little sore. I think we're done for the night."

As she lifts her head, her gaze instantly meets mine. "But you don't look too comfortable," she mumbles, reaching for me again.

Grasping her wrist, I stop her, knowing it's the right thing to do. "Thanks, but don't worry about me."

She blushes a deep shade of red as her eyes cast downward, letting me know her thoughts are heading in the wrong direction. I give her wrist a tug, pulling her towards me and cover her lips with mine. I slip my tongue inside, tangling with hers before I slow the kiss and break away. "That was perfect for now. I just need to get some rest."

Her look turns puzzled, obviously unsure if she should take me at my word. Smart woman. I press my lips to hers again trying to distract her. As I pull back, I request, "Would you mind helping me back to my room?"

She stares at me for another moment before she shakes her head as if clearing the fog and nods in agreement. Reaching for my shirt, I grasp it and tug it over her head, grinning as her head pops through; I want her covered so I can walk across the hall without losing my balance with my focus on her sweet body, but I'm not going to tell her that. I need to get across the hall to finish what we started, without seeing the uncertainty in her eyes. She's right to not be sure about me. I'm not worth the trouble.

She returns my smile, looking adorable and making my heart momentarily fracture, wishing we could be more than this, whatever this is, but knowing she deserves so much more than I can ever give. I already feel like I'm taking too much, but I just can't seem to stop myself when it comes to her. Plus, I can't tell her no. That could put us both in a corner, unable to get out without destroying everything in our path.

30

Grant

I SKIM THROUGH THE MOTORCYCLE LISTINGS USING ELLA'S computer, searching for anything that piques my interest. I want to find something I like, but also something that I'll be able to work with, giving it my own touch. I don't mind doing the work, in fact I love it, but I also don't want to have to rebuild the whole bike, not this time. It's not that I can't do it, but after my accident I'd like to save time and money so I at least have something to ride. Plus, why would I bother starting with a base if I'm building it from scratch? I can play with a new design after I get a job and make some more money, so I'll have some to live on and put into a bike.

A motorcycle comes across the screen with a woman on the back. The image only makes me think about how good Ella would look on the back of a bike with her arms wrapped around me. My mind strays from the motorcycles on the screen and focuses on the girl in my thoughts, like it seems to do almost constantly.

I keep thinking about last night. My stomach twists and my chest aches thinking of Ella in that moment. She's beautiful and sexy; the sounds she makes set me ablaze. Damn, I wanted her more than I wanted air to breathe, but with my broken leg still in a cast and her slight hesitation, I had to push back. I needed to maintain control. But would I have done things differently if my cast weren't an obstacle? I'm honestly not sure. Of course, I would never push her to do anything she didn't want to do, but she sure as hell seemed disappointed when I stopped us from going further.

Then again, being with her at all breaks every rule I've ever had regarding women. She's the kind of woman I don't only stay away from, but I make sure to avoid for a reason. I've been upfront with her from the beginning; she knows I won't stay. She claims she still wants this, whatever it is. She says she wants me. Maybe that's true, but she deserves more than I've given to women in the past. She merits more than me.

I treat her differently because she deserves to be cherished and taken care of in every way. She's special. Even if I can't stay, I should handle her like the angel she is, so that's what I tried to give her last night, but it felt like too much. Every touch, every kiss, every taste, every moan, every quiver slowly began to overwhelm me in a way I don't know if I can even comprehend, but I do know I didn't want it to end.

Admittedly, I want more, but do I have a right to take it? She says I do, but I'm already dreading the day I'll have to leave her behind. It will arrive, and I will force myself to keep moving forward like I've always done. I may not like it, but I will survive. I don't know if I can say the same about Ella if we keep this up. Will she feel betrayed when I go?

"You're looking at motorcycles," Ella states the obvious, stepping up behind me and pulling me out of my thoughts. My body stiffens as I take in the light scent of her floral perfume, letting it waft over me with a deep breath. "Have you had any luck finding anything you like?" She places her hands on the back of my chair, looking over my shoulder.

"A few things." I shrug like it's no big deal. "I might go down and talk to the guys at the garage, see if they have any information on anything local. I'm sure they would know the best deals around if there are any."

"Good idea. Have you had any luck figuring everything out with insurance?"

I huff a humorless laugh, shaking my head at that living nightmare. "Nope." Running my hand through my hair in frustration, I drop it into my lap. "Insurance crap seems to be the bane of my existence lately."

She gives me a look filled with empathy. "I understand."

Briefly, my chest clenches, comprehending her meaning. As I spin around, her hands drop to her sides. Leaning back, I look up at her, wanting her to forget about her past and my present as much as we can with my broken leg. "Are you working today?"

"No," she replies with a shake of her head. "But I do have plans." She bites her lower lip, letting it slide through her teeth, the motion leaving me uneasy.

The doorbell rings, interrupting. "I'll get that and then I'll come back and tell you." She spins on her heel, walking away.

Reaching for my crutches, I stand, hobbling after her, my curiosity overwhelming. Laine stands in the doorway dressed in black shorts and a white graphic t-shirt. My eyebrows draw down in confusion. I've never seen him out of his scrubs. "Did we have a session or something today that I missed?"

He chuckles, shaking his head. "No, man. I'm off today. I'm just here to pick up Ella." He nods in her direction.

My heart plummets to the pit of my stomach and my entire body goes taut. "Oh." She's going on a fucking date?

"Grant, I was just about to tell you about today," she begins, stepping towards me, her eyes soft, apologetic.

I grip the crutches so tightly, my knuckles turn white. Fuck that. I don't want to hear her excuses. With a slight shake of my head, I interrupt, "No worries. You don't have to tell me anything, Gabriella. You can do what you want."

She flinches at the use of her full name and I hate it, but I can't stop myself. I'm pissed. No matter how much I wish I weren't. I know I've been telling her I'm leaving, that we're only temporary and that's all we can ever be, but after last night... I didn't think she would go out with another guy the next day. What the fuck?

Stepping closer, she lowers her voice, "But Grant..."

"Go, have fun. Don't worry about me. I'm just fine on my own. I have some shit to do, anyway." I hear the angry, dismissive tone in my voice, but it doesn't matter. I want her to feel bad. Does she not give a shit? Why the hell would she push so hard to claw her way into my life just to leave my insides broken and bruised.

Why the fuck did I let her in?

This is one of those times I wish I didn't have these fucking crutches. My fingers twitch, desperate to run. I need to get out of here, but I have to settle for getting out of this room, away from them; away from her even though it's the last thing I want. She's not mine. I have no right to step between them.

"Grant," she calls one more time. But I slip inside the room, without looking back. I can't talk to her about going on a date, especially not with him in the same damn room, even if he can't hear what we're saying.

Barely a moment later I hear the front door close and I throw my crutches on the floor, grunting in frustration. Maybe she isn't who I thought she was. Maybe I didn't need to be so worried about her and stop us from going too far. Maybe next time I'll just listen to what she says. If there is a next time. She obviously doesn't think anything of last night. So why the hell do I? Maybe she is just like the other women I usually spend my time with. My stomach twists, refusing to believe my disturbing thoughts. She's not like that, but what else am I supposed to think?

I hate this acidic feeling in my gut, telling me I fucked up and I shouldn't have let her go as I mentally rebuild my walls. I didn't even realize how much she had broken me down until this overwhelming feeling of betrayal punches me in the chest. Does she just feel sorry for me? Have I been some kind of charity case to make herself feel better, or maybe to piss off her parents or her ex? She used me. I swore I would never let anyone do that to me again.

How could she?

As I look around the room, I suddenly feel trapped, the walls closing in on me with no way to escape. It's like I'm back at day one of my accident, but my thoughts and my heart are what are tearing me apart. How could I let this happen? I know better.

The silence deafening, I tap my music on my phone.

Desperate for a way to rid myself of my frustration, I reach underneath the bed, yanking out the dumbbells Laine let me borrow from therapy to strengthen my arm and balance myself out. Fucking Laine. He's probably better for her than I'll ever be, but I don't care. The moment he said he was there for her, I just wanted to claim her as mine. Instead, I didn't only let her go, I pushed her right into his waiting arms.

My arms start moving on autopilot, attempting to not only strengthen them, but also rid myself of my anger, frustration, jealousy and hurt; feelings I'll never express out loud. I can barely admit them to myself. I need to get them under control—tame them without looking back.

31

THEO JUMPS UP, GIVING ME A HIGH-FIVE AS THE LAST OF THE other tween boys and girls leave for the day. "Great game, Miss Ella."

"Thanks, Theo. I couldn't have done it without y'all showing me the ropes."

He stands taller, grinning from ear to ear. "It's no big deal. Wanna come with me to get my little brother?" He gestures to a group of four- and five-year-old boys and girls sitting in a circle in the shade of a massive oak tree; the perfect place to take a break from the sun.

"Sure!"

We cross the grass field and I glance around the park at the different groups of kids. Most of the teenage boys are still playing basketball on the polymeric rubber crumb court in various shades of blue, a few teen girls joining in, one of them sinking a shot from the three-point line while the other teens still here remain on the sidelines, watching. The eight- and nine-year-olds left continue playing freeze tag, while the six- and seven-year-olds hang off the jungle gym.

As we approach the group, we hear Theo's little brother, Donnie, talking. "Tomorrow is visiting day, and I can't wait to tell my daddy about my goal!"

"I'm sure he'll be so proud. We're proud of you," Laine proclaims.

"He's in jail," Theo admits, smiling sadly. "Sundays are family visiting day." My heart breaks for these kids; I feel so helpless.

Donnie grins and tosses the ball to a little girl sitting across from him with short, blonde curls and big blue eyes. "My mommy says I have to go back to the doctors this week. I don't want to, but she promised they would give me a Nintendo Switch to play with again. I just hope I feel good enough to play." She frowns and my chest tightens further. I know how she feels. "Daddy!" she screeches as she jumps up, dropping the ball. Giggling, she runs to him.

Laine laughs. "Annie was the last one. It looks like circle time is over."

A few adults standing on the sidelines step up to the group for pick-up, while Donnie waves to his brother. "Hi, Theo!"

"Hey." Theo grins. "Hi Mr. Laine."

"Taking good care of Miss Ella?" he asks.

Theo nods and I grin, answering, "He sure is."

He blushes, waving to an older woman behind his brother. "Our grandma is here. We'll see you next time!"

"Bye!" Donnie waves.

"Thank you," their grandmother murmurs, smiling at Laine and me.

"They're great kids," Laine declares.

"Yes, they are," she agrees, as she turns to catch up with them. "I'm not as fast as you boys. Slow down."

I laugh. "They have been running all day. How are they still going?"

Laine chuckles and stretches his arms above his head. "They are full of energy. Looks like those two were the last ones besides the teenagers; they might be a while. Oh, wait, one is coming back." He laughs, pointing behind me.

"What?" I ask, turning towards the parking lot.

I spot Annie sprinting towards us, her blonde curls bouncing, bringing a smile to my face. She crashes into my legs full force, wrapping her little arms around them and squeezing me tight, warming my heart. "I'm going to miss y'all," she murmurs in her sweet voice.

I reach down, my hand patting the back of her head. "I'll miss you too, Annie. I'm so happy I got to meet y'all today."

"Me too. Are ya going to come back?"

"Yeah, are ya going to come back?" Laine echoes, fighting his amusement.

"Please?" she begs, dragging out the word.

"If y'all will let me."

"Yay!" she shrieks and lets me go, sprinting back towards her dad, watching from a safe distance.

As I help Laine and two of the other volunteers, Sidney, and Derrick, pack up the rest of the balls, he looks at me, his grin lighting up his face. "So, what did you think?"

"I think this is pretty incredible. These kids are amazing, and their stories...I know I only heard a couple, but they really hit home, you know?"

He nods, somber. "I do." He stuffs another ball in the bag. "You were really great with them, you know. I knew you would be."

"Thanks. They make it easy. I honestly wish we could do more for them. I kinda know what it's like to be in their position. It's not the same, but..."

"Annie's story is similar to yours."

My eyes go wide. "I heard her say she had to go back to the doctors. What is she fighting?"

He grimaces. "She had a brain tumor. She had surgery and then chemo and radiation. Her hair has just been growing back." I gulp, my chest tight, emotions overwhelming me. "They think they got it in her last treatments, but she is just barely in remission."

"She's so strong, so young."

"So were you," he claims, giving me a pointed look. "And you're still one of the strongest women I know, Ella."

My cheeks heat, appreciating the compliment. "Thank you, Laine."

He nods, tying off the bag of balls and slinging it over his shoulder. "It's true. Ready?"

"Troy and Mandy will be okay with all of them?"

"Yeah, they don't mind. Taryn is Mandy's sister."

"Oh, I didn't know." He shrugs like it's no big deal, and I turn to Sydney and Derrick. "It was nice meeting you guys. Thanks for letting me help out today."

"You too, and y'all are welcome anytime," Sydney states.

"Definitely!" Derrick agrees.

We wave and walk back to his car. I settle into the seat with a smile on my face as we pull out of the parking lot. "You look really happy, Ella."

"I am. Thank you for thinking of me for this."

He nods. "I knew this would be a perfect fit for you. Do you want to go grab dinner or a drink or something?"

"Umm..."

"No pressure, Ella. I know you're seeing Grant. I just really enjoyed spending time with you today."

I bite my lower lip, running it through my teeth. Am I seeing him? He was acting so strange before I left. He wouldn't even let me tell him where I was going.

"Everything okay with you guys?"

"Huh?"

"Does he treat you good?"

"Yeah, he does, but..." I pause, not sure what I want to say. "I guess I just don't know what was up with him earlier."

Laine chuckles, his shoulders relaxing. "You're kidding, right?"

My eyebrows draw down in confusion. "No. What are you talking about?"

"Seriously, Ella? Wasn't Nathan ever the jealous type?"

My eyes widen in surprise. "You think Grant is jealous?"

He nods. "I know he is."

Wow. Maybe I am getting to him.

"Why didn't you tell him where you were going today anyway?"

I shake my head. "It wasn't on purpose. I was going to tell him the day you asked, but then he came home with his cast off and we went out to dinner to celebrate. I wanted it to be about him, not me. Then I just got preoccupied with everything else, and before I knew it, you were at the door picking me up." I shrug.

"I get it. So, that means we're not going for dinner?" he asks again, giving me a crooked smile as he glances at me out of the corner of his eye.

I laugh. "I'm going to say no but thank you."

He nods. "Okay, but if you ever need anything, Ella, I'm here."

"Thanks, Laine, and thanks for today."

"Thank you and let me know when you can come back." I nod. He leans across the center console, giving me a hug I easily return.

"Bye, Laine." I climb out of the car and stride to the door, wondering what Grant was up to all day while I was gone. Was he really jealous?

I push the door open, finding him sprawled on the couch, a few empty beer bottles sitting on the coffee table. "Hi," I greet him, hesitantly.

"You're back."

"I am. How was your day?"

"How was your date?" he asks without even looking in my direction. I don't respond right away and he adds, "Must've been good. You've been gone all fucking day."

I shake my head. "It wasn't a date."

He huffs a humorless laugh. "What does that even mean?"

"It means it wasn't a date!"

He pushes up on his elbow, his eyes narrowed. "You looked pretty cozy in the car when he pulled in to drop you off."

"You were watching me?"

He shakes his head, rubbing his chest. "I couldn't. Isn't that the fucking kicker? I can't stand even the thought of you with anyone else."

"Grant, you've got it all wrong."

He sits up, glaring at me. "Do I? Then you're not using me?"

"Using you? No! What are you talking about? Why would someone do that? I've been taking care of you!"

He flinches. "Yeah, you have, and yet you go on a date with Mr. Wonderful tonight."

"It wasn't a date!"

"So, you've said."

"He said you were jealous, but this is ridiculous."

"He said I was jealous? What the fuck for? I could have you anytime I want you." I slap him hard across the face, stinging my palm and leaving a red mark on his cheek. He stares at me open-mouthed, momentarily stunned.

"Do you know what I was doing today, Grant? I was playing with kids who were sick, or in foster care or only have one parent who's always working to try to survive. Every single kid I was playing with today has a tragic story. But they let go and had fun today. Even as kids, they are doing what they can to not let their tragedy decide who they are or how they live. It's not easy, but they're trying.

"I know you have your own tragic past and I have mine. I'm not asking you what it is, but no matter the circumstances, I don't ever deserve to be treated like you're treating me right now. You're being an asshole." I shake my head in disappointment. "Maybe I was wrong about you."

He flinches. "Ella," he begins, his voice apologetic.

I stand up and walk towards the front door. "I'm not doing this with you. I don't even want to be around you right now."

Fuming, I walk outside and get in my car before I text Julie.

Are you available for dinner?

Yes! Mexican sound good?

32

TOSSING THE PAPER TOWEL IN THE GARBAGE CAN, I GLANCE down at the breakfast tray, wondering if this is really a good idea. But I feel like an asshole. I need to do something to show her I care, I'm sorry and I won't ever do something like that again. My guilt is eating me alive, like nothing I've ever felt. Besides the fact it was none of my business, I had no right, and she's the last person on earth that would deserve anyone being an asshole to her. She really is an angel. I just wonder if she'll have it in her to forgive me. I don't deserve it, but I sure as hell want it.

Now I just have to figure out how I'm going to carry this to her room with one good leg.

"Grant?" Ella questions, as she steps in through the back door in light blue board shorts and a white and blue long-sleeved rash guard, her blonde hair pulled up in a ponytail.

"You were out paddleboarding already?"

"I woke up early. What are you doing?"

"Trying to figure out how to bring you breakfast." She grimaces, unimpressed. I heave a sigh, determined to just get it all out there. "Ella, I'm sorry. I know that's not even close to enough, but I'm so fucking sorry. You're right. I was jealous. I thought you were going on a date with Laine, and I did everything I could to push you away because it hurt. I haven't

190

felt that in a long fucking time, and when I thought it didn't matter to you, I didn't know what else to do. It's no excuse, and I know I don't deserve it, but all I can do is beg for forgiveness. I just want to prove to you I mean it."

Warily, she opens her mouth to answer, but I interrupt. "Please let me do something for you, to show you I care and make it up to you. I'll do anything, Ella."

"Anything?"

"Yes."

"Is that for me?" she asks, eyeing the scrambled eggs and bacon.

I grin. "Actually yes."

She sits down at the kitchen table and begins eating. "Mm, this is just what I needed."

A smile tugs at my lips. "Does that mean you forgive me?"

"Because you made me breakfast?" she asks, incredulous.

I feel my face uncharacteristically heat and shrug. "What can I do?"

She sighs. "All I need from you, Grant, is to be honest and treat me with respect. If you want to know something, ask instead of accusing me. Talk to me."

I nod. "I can do that. I'm so sorry I was such an asshole. With my past...I have a hard time trusting." She looks at me waiting for more. I don't know how much I can say, though, before she turns and runs the other way. I don't want her to go, at least not yet. "Give me time, Ella. I'm trying."

"I know." She smiles. "But you talk to me like that again, and I'm not putting up with it."

I nod, my heart skipping a beat. Giving her a crooked smile, I ask, "Does that mean you forgive me?"

She laughs. "You're getting there."

"I can work with that." I lean towards her, kissing her on the corner of the mouth, grateful she doesn't pull away. "So, what are you doing today? Do you have time to spend with me?"

She sits back and begins fidgeting, looking around the

room instead of anywhere in my vicinity. "Yeah, I have some errands to do and well, um, my ah mom called, and she wants me to go over there for dinner tonight, but she also asked if I would, um, bring you. So, I um, was actually wondering if you would, um, go with me? You don't have to come," she awkwardly rambles. "It's not a big deal. It's just going to be my parents, Declan, and Charlotte, who you already know, and my little brother, Finn. It's just you've been staying here for a while now, and if it weren't for Declan, my mom would probably be sleeping on the couch here every night," she explains, her cheeks turning a beautiful shade of pink.

I chuckle softly and reach out, tucking a lock of her blonde hair behind her ear, instantly halting her movements. I nudge her chin in my direction until she meets my gaze. "You want me to go to dinner at your parents' house?" I'm surprised she wants me to go.

Gulping hard, she meets my gaze and nods. "Yeah, I do."

My anxiety starts to take over my insides, making my stomach turn. Honestly, I haven't met anyone's parents since high school. I don't want them to get the wrong idea about us, but I already know there's no way in hell I can say no to this woman, not when she looks at me like that. I don't want to disappoint her ever again, not when I can easily do something about it.

Without further hesitation, I agree. "Okay."

Her eyes widen as her body jolts in surprise. A hopeful grin lights up her face. "Okay?"

Returning her smile, I nod. "Okay, I'll go with you."

She squeals in pure happiness and throws her arms around me, making me grateful I'm already seated. I chuckle softly as she eases down onto my lap, sitting on my good leg. Holding my face in her hands, she presses her lips to mine, taking me by surprise. My hands come up, holding her hips still as I kiss her back. She eagerly pushes her tongue inside, as if searching for its mate. I groan and slow the kiss, attempting to regain my control quickly slipping away. As I hold myself back from pushing for more, I kiss and lick her lips in slow, easy strokes, savoring her sweet taste. She whimpers into my mouth, sending shivers down my spine.

I pull back, looking into her eyes, seeing both happiness and desire. Taking a deep breath, I exhale slowly to pull myself together. "If you want me to go to your parents', I want to finish cleaning up my mess while you do your errands, and then I need to shower, and it will still take me a while with my cast."

She reluctantly releases me with a heavy sigh, her shoulders dropping. "Fine," she grumbles. "Do you need some help?"

A playful smirk dances on my lips. "Well, I don't really need help, but I would never turn you down if you want to shower with me."

Her face instantly turns beet red as she attempts to backtrack. "Um, I ah, that's not...I mean that's not what I meant. I just meant that I...I thought you might need help with cleaning up, I mean, your mess and your, um, cast. I mean with wrapping your cast, to um, keep it dry," she stammers adorably, eliciting a deep chuckle from my lips.

"I know what you mean," I concede, letting her off the hook as another deep chuckle escapes my lips. "You're so fucking adorable when you get flustered."

She purses her lips and scrunches up her nose in a way that tugs at my gut. "Besides, I figure after last night I lost all my rewards and built up quite a debt."

"True." She takes a deep breath and looks back at me, her eyes showing her appreciation. "Thank you, Grant. This really means a lot to me."

I gulp down the lump in my throat, trying to shove down my emotions. "Thank you for giving me another chance." She smiles and I lick my lips, giving her a chaste kiss.

"You're welcome." She grins happily, looking down at me. "Are you sure you don't need help with anything?"

I smirk. "As I said, that would kind of defeat the purpose.

Don't you think?" She blushes again, bringing a smile to my face as I hobble out of the kitchen on my crutches.

She forgives me, almost, anyway. I can't fuck up again. She deserves to be treated like the angel she is. I can't believe I was such an ass. She's not like other women. I just hope today will go okay. I can't believe I'm meeting her parents. My nerves are already brewing a storm. Shit, I have no idea what I just got myself into.

33

Ella

I GLANCE OVER AT GRANT AS HE EXPERTLY MANEUVERS himself out of my car with his crutches. He looks hot in a navy-blue t-shirt loosely fitted over his hard chest and light gray cotton shorts. He may have a limited wardrobe with his cast, besides the fact that he obviously travels light and lost what little he had during his accident, but he makes anything look good. Clearing my throat, I prod, "Ready?"

He nods, offering me a stiff smile. "As long as you are." He gestures for me to lead the way.

I nod and glance up at my parents' white colonial home, the property just shy of an acre. "I used to spend a lot of time out here," I murmur, gesturing towards two white wicker chairs accented with cherry red cushions on the front porch.

"I can imagine. It's a great spot." Out of the corner of my eye, I notice he seems lost in thought as he looks around.

It is a great spot, especially when you're restricted in how far you can go. The memories make my stomach turn and urge me forward in the same breath. I'm not in that position any-more. It's my turn to live, no holding back. I glance at Grant again, smiling to myself, knowing that's what I'm trying to do.

Before he has a chance to catch me staring, I turn and stroll up the paved walkway, my thoughts going to our fight. I can't stop thinking about how his demeanor changed so quickly. How do I really know he won't do it again? Can I trust that? Trust him? That's what I'm asking him to do with me, so how can I not?

I gulp back the onslaught of emotions trying to break free. Honestly, I don't understand. I feel like if I knew his story, I would have a better idea of where he's coming from, but he hasn't let anything slip. Makes me wonder, how bad it is. I quickly push the question away. That's not what I want to be thinking about when I walk into my parents' house.

"Hello! Mom, Dad, I'm home," I call out as we walk in the front door.

My mom's feet tap against the wood floors as she rushes into the room, her dyed blonde hair pulled back into a bun. She claimed she had to start dying it with all the gray hair she got from worrying about all of us kids, but I'm sure she meant from worrying so much about me. She's dressed casually in tan capri pants and a sleeveless navy blouse with matching navy sandals. Holding out her arms for me, she grins like she hasn't seen me in years instead of just last week. "Gabriella, I'm so glad you're here! How are you feeling?"

I wince, sick of hearing the same question every time I walk in the door. Heaving a sigh, I grumble, "I'm fine, Mom." I step into her arms, returning her hug, instant comfort washing over me.

"Good."

Leaning back, I wiggle out of her embrace and glance at Grant, instantly feeling lighter as he smiles at me. "Mom, this is Grant Young. Grant, this is my mom," I introduce them, my voice filled with pride at having him by my side, even if he's not mine.

He leans on his left crutch and holds out his hand, giving my mom his panty-melting smile, making me bite my lower lip to hold back my groan. I don't even think he realizes he does it. It just seems to come so naturally. "Hi, Mrs. Howard, it's so nice to meet you. Thank you for inviting me today."

"Of course! I'm so glad you could come. It's wonderful to finally meet you, Grant. I've been wanting to stop by Gabriella's, but I didn't want to impose, especially with Declan stopping by every day." She pauses and he smiles, nodding in acknowledgment. "I heard your accident was rough, and you needed your rest to help you recover. If anyone understands what that's like, it's our family," she declares, a sad smile on her lips.

I cringe, hating how everything always seems to return to my illness no matter what the conversation is or who the focus is on. Grant's recovery has nothing to do with my health! "Where is everyone else?" I inquire, attempting to change the subject.

Tipping her head, she gestures towards the back yard. "They're all out back waiting for you."

"Thanks."

"I'm so glad you're feeling better, and I heard Ella was able to show you around town some." I blush, knowing I wasn't the one who told her anything about our date at Mackie's. Of course, she would already know.

"Just a little bit," Grant concedes.

"We should go say, hi," I announce as I take a step in that direction, needing to get away from the conversation. My eyes flit behind me, making sure Grant follows.

The moment we step outside, my gaze meets Grant's and I apologize under my breath, "I'm sorry about that."

He takes a hobbled step towards me as his eyebrows draw down in confusion.

"It's about time you showed up!" Charlotte proclaims, interrupting.

Spinning around, I face my family, all dressed in shorts and t-shirts. I grin. "Hi, Char."

She gives me a quick hug. Then steps back, her golden ponytail slapping me in the face as she twists away and hugs Grant, taking him by surprise. "Hi, Grant! I'm so glad you came with Ella!"

"Hi," he replies awkwardly.

Declan steps over to us, grinning wide. "It's great to see you with just one cast. I bet you can't wait to get rid of the other one."

Grant huffs a laugh and mumbles his agreement, "You got that right."

My dad sets down the spatula in his hand as he steps away from the grill and over to us. He wraps his arms around me, squeezing me tight before he lets go with one hand and pulls me into his side with the other, holding me captive. "You must be Grant," he states as he straightens his shoulders and narrows his eyes accusingly.

Grant nods. "Yes, Sir."

"You may be a friend of Julie's, but I don't like that you're staying with my daughter."

My heart stops as I see a flicker of confusion pass over Grant's features before it's gone. I open my mouth to say something, but I don't know what in front of my dad. Thankfully, my dad continues. "But she's old enough to make her own decisions, and I trust her." The look he gives Grant makes me uncomfortable, but Grant doesn't even flinch as he stares back at him, waiting patiently for what he might throw his way. "I heard about your accident," he states, letting him know that's the only other reason he has a partial pass. "Are you treating my daughter with respect?"

"Yes, Sir, Mr. Howard." His cheeks flush, and I can only imagine he's thinking about our fight.

"Dad, please leave him alone," I request, my stomach churning with anxiety. Maybe this wasn't a good idea. "Grant has been nothing but kind and respectful."

He grumbles under his breath, but I can't hear what he says. Then he holds out the hand not holding onto me. Grant mirrors him and they shake. "She's special," he emphasizes, intentionally trying to intimidate him further.

"Dad!" I complain.

Grant nods his head, not breaking my dad's intense gaze.

"Yes, Sir, she is," he concurs. I gasp softly, feeling myself blush and butterflies take flight on my insides at the compliment, even if my dad had to drag it out of him.

My dad nods, satisfied for now, and releases me. Placing a kiss on the top of my head, he lovingly mumbles, "Hi, Gabriella," before turning back towards the grill.

"Sorry," I murmur on a sigh. Grant smirks and shrugs like it's no big deal, but to me it is. It's not getting past me that he's willingly standing here taking everything from my family like the boyfriend I wish he were, making my heart stutter, but I'm too afraid to read too much into it.

My little brother, now just over six feet, saunters over, spinning a football in his right hand. "Hey," he mumbles uninterested. "I'm Finn."

"Hey," Grant replies, glancing at the football before focusing back on Finn. "Do you play?"

A cocky smirk covers Finn's face before he responds, making me roll my eyes. "Yeah, I play. I'm the quarterback on Varsity this year," he announces confidently.

"Sweet. That's what I used to play," he enlightens all of us.

My eyes widen in shock as Finn's eyes instantly flip a switch, lighting up with curiosity. "You used to play football?"

At the same time, Finn questions, "You played quarterback?"

He chuckles and nods his head in confirmation. "I haven't played since high school, but yeah, I was the Varsity quarterback."

"Were you any good?" Finn probes, continuing to toss the ball in one hand and catch it.

"Finn!" I admonish, narrowing my eyes.

He chuckles softly and smirks, shrugging his shoulders like it's no big deal. "What? It's a valid question."

Chuckling, Grant nods as he glances at me, insisting, "Don't worry about it, Ella. It's fine. He's fine."

I force a smile in appreciation, feeling my heart stupidly clench again inside my chest at the gesture. "You don't have to placate him."

He grins and shakes his head. "Don't worry, I'm not placating anyone. I promise. I like talking football, and I haven't been able to in a while, not like this." He glances at my brother. "You're right, it's a valid question. I made Varsity as a freshman, and I was the starting quarterback by my sophomore year. I had college scouts from all over starting to look at me by the end of that year to recruit me."

Both mine and my brother's eyes widen in shock. He was that good and yet he didn't bring it up in conversation before now? Why? He just said he hasn't played since high school. Why didn't he play in college? Maybe he had an injury like this that held him back, I ponder, my curiosity overwhelming.

"Wow! That's really fucking cool!"

"Finn," my mom admonishes.

He tosses her an apologetic smile before he looks back at Grant. "Do you want to throw the ball around with me after dinner? Maybe give me a few pointers?" Finn requests, suddenly bouncing on his toes in anticipation.

"I don't know how well that will work with a broken leg, but I could at least try to give you a few tips?"

"That's awesome! Thanks!" Finn exclaims, his eyes lighting up with his smile.

"No problem." Grant nods his head in response as Finn strides quickly over to Dad still standing at the grill, his excitement palpable.

Looking away from my brother, I gaze at Grant. "That's really nice of you. You know you don't have to do that."

"I know, but I want to," he insists, shrugging his shoulders, a relaxed smile on his face. "It will be fun."

My heart jumps and lodges itself in my throat. I gulp hard and paste a smile on my face. My heart falling faster for the man in front of me. It doesn't seem to matter that he plans on leaving. I already know when it happens, it will completely blindside me, no matter how prepared I am. But I refuse to give up even a moment of something I want more than any-thing. "No regrets," I mumble under my breath.

"What?" he questions, not hearing me, but he wasn't meant to.

"Just, thank you," I murmur, grinning up at him.

34

WE WALK IN THE FRONT DOOR AT THE BEACH HOUSE AND I hobble over to the couch, setting my crutches down as I drop onto the cushions. I glance up at Ella, still standing near the door staring at me with the corners of her mouth curved up in a thoughtful smile. "What?" I want to know what she's thinking.

She sighs happily as she strolls towards me. "Thank you for coming with me tonight," she repeats for what feels like the tenth time.

"You need to stop thanking me. I had fun and the food was great. Besides, I like your family," I admit, my chest tightening at the thought. I shrug my shoulders as if it's not a big deal, when we both know tonight was a huge deal for me. It's been years since I went to a family dinner; that reality causes another lump to form and my chest to ache.

She sits down next to me, her leg brushing against mine. The way she's looking at me has my heart racing on top of making it difficult to breathe. She places her palm on my cheek and rises to her knees, maintaining eye contact. I watch in anticipation as she leans towards me, our breathing rapidly becoming ragged. Her warm breath mingles with mine, giving me a light taste of the peppermint she ate on the way home. Her tongue juts out, licking her lips before brushing them against mine, a soft whimper escaping between her parted lips.

I lean towards her, pushing her back on the couch and taking over, prowling over her the best I can until I'm able to readjust my broken leg. I kiss her hard, almost desperate for the physical touch as my tongue dives into her mouth, meeting hers, licking and playing in a slow sensual rhythm. She pushes back with her tongue, giving as good as she gets.

I let my hand slide down her side and slip underneath the hem of her t-shirt, my rough fingers skimming across the velvety soft skin of her belly. My hand slides up, covering her breast, kneading tenderly as I continue kissing her soundly, not able to get enough of her mouth. She arches her back, curling into me as I brush my thumb over her hardened nipple, a frantic groan falling from her lips.

Her hips buck up into my groin, begging for more, and I desperately want to give it to her. I pull back, looking down at her luscious curves, both of us gasping for breath. While one hand remains on her breast, I lift my other hand, running my thumb over her full, kiss-swollen lips. "You're so fucking sexy."

She blushes, pushing up towards me. She kisses me again. I pull back, fueled by the fire in her eyes. Pushing her shirt up, she holds onto me, lifting off the couch so I can pull it up further, dropping back to the couch as I pull it over her head. Easily unhooking her bra in the front, I brush the fabric aside, exposing her breasts long enough to cover the first with my mouth, licking and sucking the taut peak before giving the other side the same attention.

I allow my fingers to explore her breasts as I glance up at her, urging, "Move up for me." Her eyebrows draw down in confusion, not understanding my command. I slide my hand down to her navy shorts, unbuttoning it and then tugging down the zipper before I repeat my demand. "Move up for me. I want to taste you." Her skin tinges a gorgeous red from her head to her toes, further igniting my lust for her. I chuckle softly, savoring the moment.

She doesn't comment, but she does as I instructed, letting me tug her shorts and panties down as I go. I drop them to the floor and shift my body, getting a little more comfortable between her legs. My fingers graze over her folds, and a whimper escapes through her lips. I glide my fingers back and forth between her folds, watching her reaction to my touch as her juices begin to flow. I look into her eyes, now a darker blue, as her lower lip runs through her teeth. "Grant."

"You're already wet," I mumble in appreciation.

Sticking my tongue out, I lick her from the back of her core to front and back again, causing her to moan louder than I've ever heard her and only making me crave more. I push my tongue inside her, hungry for her salty-sweet taste as my mouth covers her pussy. "Grant," she gasps as she grasps the side of the couch.

Pulling my tongue out, I rasp, "I've got you." Immediately sliding my tongue back to her clit, I suck gently before slipping it back down and inside her folds. Slowly, licking back up to her nub as my fingers take over thrusting and curling inside her. As I watch her body react, I lick and swirl my tongue over her clit, again and again, watching, feeling, tasting, and relishing every response to my welcomed assault on her body.

Her fingers weave into my hair and tug as she moans my name, "Grant." Increasing my speed and pressure, my heart thrashes against my ribcage as her moans get louder and her hips thrust up, desperately attempting to get closer. Suddenly, I feel her walls closing in on my fingers, prompting me to press my tongue to her clit and suck hard as I curl my fingers inside her, trying to hit every sensitive spot on her body. "Grant, Grant!" she screams, the sound of my name on her lips jolting me. Her head falls back as her walls clench over and over, squeezing my hand with her sweet juices flowing onto my tongue. I continue my movements until she collapses like a jellyfish beneath me.

I place a soft kiss to her core and lick my fingers clean

with a satisfied moan as she glances at me slightly dazed from underneath her long eyelashes. "Fuck, that was hot!" I love that I can make her lose control like that. "Are you okay?" I smirk.

She giggles in response. Taking a deep breath, I slowly make my way up her body, kissing a trail back to her lips. She pries her eyes open and looks at me with something I can't quite place. "I'm good. I just need a minute to catch my breath," she claims, closing her eyes again.

"Just good?" I ask, arching my eyebrows in challenge.

She giggles again, the sound going straight to my heart, but I shove the feeling away, attempting to ignore it. Forcing her eyes open, she stares at me with her cheeks flushed, looking incredibly gorgeous. "How come you're overdressed again?" she teases as she glances up and down my body.

Grinning, I reiterate, "I told you before, you always come first."

"Well, I already did, hard," she emphasizes, taking me by surprise. "So, can you please get rid of some of these clothes?" She tugs at my shirt.

I grin and lean up, pulling my shirt over my head with one hand and tossing it on the floor. "Since you asked so nicely."

Her fingers begin skimming over the thorny vines on my tattoo. It twists around from my back, over my shoulder and bicep, before stopping on my upper pec with a bleeding heart. I tense, hoping she doesn't ask questions I don't want to answer. If she looks closely, she'll see a football, scattered stars, and my little brother's initials. That's not something I want to explain to anyone, not even her. Ella's lips brush over the bloodied thorns near my heart. I push back, feeling vulnerable and unsure. She instantly sits up, following me, staying close. She presses her breasts into my side, instantly bringing my focus back to my need for her.

She lets her hands slide down over my shorts, pressing firmly against my hard cock making me groan in response.

"Angel," I mumble in warning. She bites her bottom lip and watches me as she slips her hand into my shorts, her hand stroking my dick before I reach out, grabbing her wrist to stop her. She lifts her head, holding my gaze, puzzled. "You don't have to do this." I barely get the words out. I may like to be in control, but I don't ever want her to feel pressured to do anything she doesn't want to do.

She nods and insists, "I want to." As I stare at her, I see the truth in her eyes. I nod and let go of her wrist, allowing her to pull my shorts and boxers down, joining our other clothes on the floor. Leaning back, I readjust again, resting my broken leg on the couch and the other placed firmly on the floor with her between my legs. She looks up at me with wide eyes, making my cock jump in anticipation. She slides her hands up my thighs, careful to avoid my cast, before cupping my nearly full balls with one hand as she caresses my already thick cock with the other; hard and ready for anything she has in store. Tingles consume my insides as my breathing turns erratic. Her tiny, delicate hand barely wraps around me as she rubs the sensitive skin.

"Fuck," I mumble, already struggling to maintain my control as I watch and feel every touch, every stroke she makes. She sticks her tongue out, licking my tip and eliciting a groan from my lips, overwhelmed with what she's doing to me. Her mouth covers my head, her tongue swirling around before she takes me in until I feel the back of her throat, her hand still wrapped around my base, moving in firm strokes along with her mouth. "Angel," I mumble, trying to contain myself as I stare at her with her lips wrapped around my cock and try to commit the salacious image to my memory.

"I've got you this time," she murmurs as she pushes me back. Then, she takes me in and sucks before slowly pulling back, taking me all the way in and out. This is so much more than I imagined.

My head falls back on a groan as I feel myself getting closer.

My breathing picks up, her lips and tongue overwhelming me. I'm not going to last. I bring one hand to the back of her neck as my hips arch towards her reflexively, fucking that sweet mouth. "I'm going to cum," I rasp in warning, nudging her back. She holds me tighter, sucking harder as her tongue slides and swirls over my cock. "Fuck," I grunt, as I feel myself hit the back of her throat. My body goes taut, igniting as she sends me over the edge and makes me explode in a flash of heat and desire like I've never felt before.

Surprising me further, she holds me deep and sucks me dry. I exhale harshly and my body relaxes. She glances up at me from underneath her long eyelashes with a look that's somewhat shy and somewhat mischievous, causing laughter to erupt from my chest. "Damn."

"That was funny?" she asks with snark and challenge as she wipes the corners of her mouth, driving me further insane.

Chuckling, I shake my head and exhale in utter satisfaction. "No, Angel. That was fucking perfect. Come here," I urge, tugging her towards me. I press my lips to hers, kissing her soundly as she climbs on the couch next to me, attempting to get closer. I pull back, my head falling back with a satisfied sigh as my fingers trail mindlessly up and down her back.

Her hands begin exploring my chest again, inching towards my tattoos, causing me to tense. She peers at me from underneath her eyelashes, attempting to read me, while I hold my breath, hoping she doesn't get a glimpse of my demons. I'm not ready to let her go.

She licks her lips and takes a deep breath, before she finally approaches the subject, albeit with caution. "I really love your tattoos," she mumbles in reverence. Her fingers graze over the roughened skin of one of my scars underneath the ink, and I fight to hold back my flinch.

My hands stop moving, freezing on the middle of her back. "Mm," I grunt, a nonresponse, my jaw clenching, hoping it will deter her.

Bravely, she gulps down the lump in her throat and pushes forward. "Do they mean something?" she asks innocently.

My heart sinks as I huff a humorless laugh and drop my hand to the couch, suddenly feeling nauseous. That's a loaded question if I've ever heard one. She may have the courage to ask the question, but the answer remains deeply embedded in the darkest pit of my soul. That's not something I'm willing to share with her; with anyone. Lightly tapping her shoulder, I prompt, "Can you hand me my boxers, please?"

She pushes back, her eyes full of concern, making me wince. I hate that look. I don't need her pity. I turn away from her and push her up. Quickly, I reach for my boxers, fumbling as I attempt to pull them over my cast. "I hate this fucking thing!"

"Grant?" she prods, the strain in her voice obvious.

"I'm sorry, Ella, but I can't do this," I grit through my teeth, suddenly feeling like I'm drowning in a pit of tar. Shaking my head, I glance at her, hating the instant tears flooding her eyes. I put those there. It's my fault she's hurting. As her tears overflow onto her cheeks, my chest aches as if I'm being stabbed. I hate myself more in this moment than ever before. "I'm sorry," I reiterate the simple words, knowing they're not enough as I force them from my lips, but I have nothing else I can say. It's too much.

I reach for my crutches and push up, standing on my good leg. Glancing over my shoulder, I give Ella one more look of apology, hoping she sees the sincerity in my eyes, but maybe it's better if she doesn't. As quickly as I'm able to move, I make my way to the guest room, leaving the rest of my clothes behind, along with my sweet angel in tears.

Gritting my teeth, I hobble inside the room and slam the door behind me, disgusted with myself. As I collapse onto the bed, I throw my crutches to the ground in frustration and rub my chest for relief I know will never come. I'm such an asshole. I don't deserve even a small piece of her; I never did and I never will.

33

Ella

AS I TAKE A DEEP, RAGGED BREATH, I WIPE THE TEARS AWAY, pulling his shirt on over my head. I bring it to my nose and inhale deeply, ironically his scent calming me. But it's not him I'm upset with. It's the pain I see in his eyes and his visible reminders I've been too blind to see and know nothing about. I should've seen it sooner.

I've been so focused on the hard ridges of his muscles, I didn't take a closer look at his tattoos. I can't believe I didn't notice his scars underneath until now. I guess that's probably part of the reason for his ink in the first place. Maybe that's why he doesn't want to talk about it or share that with me. The thought stabs at my chest.

I wonder what his scars are from. They don't really look like something that happened from playing football, but then again, I wouldn't really know. Maybe they're from some kind of accident. The way he reacted tells me they might be from something unexpected or maybe it's just hard for him to relive it. Tiny pinpricks take over my insides and spread like wildfire at the thought of him living through anything so traumatic that he can't even talk about it. The idea alone makes me so desperate to help him, my body begins bouncing with anxiety.

Running a hand through my hair, I heave a sigh in temporary defeat, hating that he pushed me away, but I have no idea what to do about it. How do I get him to open up to me when his eyes look so haunted, and he seems like he's suddenly ready to run away? I grimace and scoop the rest of the clothes up off the floor. Spinning on my heel, I trudge towards the mudroom off the kitchen and set our clothes on top of the washing machine, not bothering to toss them inside.

Today was such a perfect day besides my mom being hurt I brought him to Mackie's before meeting them. I loved watching him with my family. He laughed a lot and completely charmed my mom and Charlotte. I loved seeing a smile on his face; it made my heartbeat faster. He joked around with Dec, and Finn was probably enamored with him more than anyone. I'd even say he seemed to idolize him, but he would never admit it. I've never seen my brother listen so closely to anyone; it felt surreal.

I'm thrilled everyone seems to really like Grant, even though my dad threatened him regarding my honor and safety when we went to leave. Thankfully, Grant took it in stride, but with my dad, that kind of thing is to be expected. He's so protective; my age isn't a factor when it comes to me. I think he'll still be doing it when I'm fifty. Sometimes it's stifling, especially when they all do it, although they have gotten better. I can only imagine what would happen if my dad really knew what was going on between Grant and me. A heavy sigh escapes my lips, filled with regret, remembering that nothing is happening between us anymore, no matter how much I want it to.

Suddenly, my body drags, weighed down with emotional exhaustion. Might as well get ready for bed. I step into the kitchen and grab a bottle of water before making sure the doors are locked.

Pausing, I glance at the couch, my body heating instantly as I picture what we did to each other on those cushions tonight. I'm overwhelmed, barely able to contemplate the way he made me feel and the things he did to my body. I don't only want that again; I want so much more than he seems to be willing to give.

Then again, he's been honest with me from the start. I truly don't know if it's a good idea to keep pushing this with him no matter what I want. Just when I think he's opening up, he insists he's going to be leaving, and pushes me away. I need to accept it, and either way, I need to figure out a way to fix this. I'm not letting him shut down on me, especially while he's still in my house. I want every minute I can get with him while he's still here, even if I break my own heart in the process; that fact is inevitable. But I can't let it go; I can't let him go.

My phone rings, pulling me out of my head. I dig it out of my pocket and glance at the screen, answering, "Hi, Mom."

"Hi, Gabriella. Just making sure you made it home okay."

Sighing, I mumble, "Yeah, I'm home. Sorry I forgot to call you guys. I was talking to Grant and then I just started cleaning up before I went to bed."

"So, he went to bed already?"

"What do you want, Mom?"

"I wanted to say I'm glad you brought him over for dinner tonight. He's a nice young man, and I'm glad we finally got to meet him."

"Okay," I mumble, dragging out the word, knowing there's more.

"I just...it's just...I see the way you look at him, Ella, and I don't want you to get hurt," she finally blurts out.

I drop my head as my heart plummets into my gut, flooded with embarrassment and disappointment. Even my mom can see how much I'm into this guy, but she didn't say a word about him being interested in me. "Mom," I begin, not quite sure what I'm going to say.

She interrupts before I have a chance to continue, "I know you said he was a friend of Julie's, but..." she hesitates, but I refuse to correct my lie. "It's just that you told me he would be leaving when he was better. Is that still the case?"

Sighing heavily, I sadly concede, "Yeah."

"Then, no matter how he looks at you and how much he

makes you smile, remember that his time here is temporary."

"The way he looks at me?" I probe, needing her to explain and ignoring everything else she said.

My mom chuckles, bringing a smile to my face. "Of course, that's what you hear." She laughs again, the sound magical. After being without laughter in our family for so long, it's now one of my favorite things in the world. "Yes, Gabriella. I'll admit that boy looks at you like you alone brought the sunshine to the day and color to the flowers. He's absolutely smitten with you." I inhale quickly as my body heats with my mom's words, wondering if they hold any truth. "Which is another big reason you need to be extra careful."

"I am careful, Mom."

"No, Ella, you're not. When it comes to your heart, you jump in with both feet. You did that with Nathan, and you're still dealing with the aftermath."

"I'm over Nate. I've been over him for a long time."

"That's not what I mean," she mutters with a heavy sigh.

"I know, Mom, but he's not Nate."

"You're right. He's not, and even though he's staying with you, God help us, he's not staying. You may be old enough to make your own decisions on who stays with you, but I'm still your mom, and I'm still going to worry. You've been through so much, sweetheart. I just want you to be safe and happy. You deserve to be happy."

"I'm not the only one who deserves happiness."

I can hear the frustration in her voice as she replies, "Of course not, but you've been through more than many people go through in their entire lives. I think it's time you've had some peace. If love finds you, reach out, take it, and hold on tight, but don't ever settle for less than you deserve, like a man who's not willing to stay."

I wince and take a deep breath before I speak. "If I fall in love, it will be with someone who will do anything for me, just as I would willingly do anything for him. In the meantime, I promise to take care of myself."

Sighing, she concedes, "Well, I guess that's all I can really ask for. I know I won't be able to talk you into or out of anything you want to do when you have your mind set, Gabriella, but just keep in mind what you really want, and be careful."

"I will, Mom. I promise."

"Okay, well, I better go before Dad starts to wonder what I'm doing out here. I love you, sweetheart."

"I love you too, Mom, and thanks again for dinner."

"You know you're welcome anytime. We've missed having you around since Grant has been here."

"I know. I've missed you too. Bye, Mom," I mumble and disconnect before she has a chance to say anything else. Of course, she would see the interest in my eyes, but my mom is not about to change my mind about Grant. I will get through to him. He was put into my life for a reason.

Pausing in front of my room, I glance at his closed bedroom door, my stomach turning, wondering what's going through his mind. What is he trying so hard to get away from? To forget? I need to figure out a way for him to open up to me, and hopefully talking won't be his reason to run. Sighing again, my shoulders sag as I whisper my declaration in his direction. "This isn't over, Grant, not by a long shot."

36

Grant

"THANKS, PETE. I GREATLY APPRECIATE YOUR HELP," I DECLARE to the garage owner appearing just a few years older than me. I lean on my crutches and look up at his tall, lean build as I hold out my hand. He shakes it before returning his hand to rest at his jaw, mindlessly brushing his dark brown, neatly trimmed beard.

I'm grateful I came in before my physical therapy a couple days ago to talk to him about buying a motorcycle, hoping he might know someone who had something local and affordable. He claimed he knew a few guys who might have something I'd be interested in.

While I was working on strengthening my arm and hand in physical therapy this morning, he left me a message on my cell phone saying he had a few things for me, and to stop back in at the garage as soon as I had the chance. I'm fucking glad I did. He explained that one of the guys who works at the garage goes to an invite only auction once a month. He buys Harleys and other motorcycles that come out of the factory with something wrong, making it so they can no longer sell it as new. He gets them at a fantastic price and then he does what I like to do and fixes them up before selling them.

At the last auction, he found a Harley CVO Road Glide Ultra, and he was thinking about keeping it, but he agreed to sell it to me 'as is' if we could come to an agreement. Thanks to Pete, I'm meeting him for lunch up the road at a food truck parked near the water.

"No problem. I'm glad I could help you out. I'm sure Aidan will be able to help you with what you need. And Grant, if you decide to stick around and need a job, I'd love to see what you can do."

"Thanks." I nod in appreciation. I can already tell I would love to work with Pete, although I don't believe I'll ever take him up on his offer. Staying so close to Ella would only make things more difficult.

I maneuver my crutches into the back of the cab before I climb in, pulling the door shut behind me. Leaning forward, I tell the driver where I'm going. Then I sit back and relax, staring out the window, anticipating my conversation with Aidan.

I really hope this works out because I can't fucking wait to have my own ride again. It will be good just to be able to drive, have some of my independence restored. I'm ready to take back control of something I love, but apparently also something I took for granted. I've never felt more helpless than I have since my accident, and with everything I've been through, that's saying something. I honestly don't know what I would've done without Ella's help.

I wince the moment thoughts of Ella push into my mind. I've been doing everything I can to avoid her the last couple days, making me feel like shit, but I don't know what else to do. The more time I spend with her, the more I want her, but even without her standing in front of me, I can't get her out of my head, so I continue evading her.

This morning I left early for physical therapy, grabbing breakfast while I was out. I spent quite a while at the garage with Pete talking about cars, motorcycles, and different builds I've worked on after getting his call. Like a pussy, I returned when I knew she'd already left for work. I hate myself for it, but I can't help it, every time I see her, I want to pull her into my arms, cherish her and beg her for forgiveness, but to what end? We both know I'm no good for her. I would never be able to give her all of me. She deserves so much more; she deserves everything.

Yesterday, she attempted to talk to me, but like a fucking coward, I claimed I wasn't feeling well and retreated, hibernating in my room. So, when I took off early today, I couldn't stop hoping I wouldn't see her—at the same time, wishing I'd be blessed with a small glimpse of my angel. My chest tightens, reminding me I'm trying to do what's right, no matter how much I want to do so many things wrong when it comes to her.

We pull up by the red and white food truck and I climb out, pulling out my crutches before paying the driver. The scent of seafood, spices, and saltwater slap me in the face the moment I take a deep breath, exhaling as I spin around. My crutches hit the pavement, dusted with sand, broken rocks and shells from the beach. After merely two steps, one of my crutches starts to slip, instantly halting my movements as I pull myself together. "Shit," I grumble, forcing myself to slow down, so I don't fall on my ass.

"Grant Young?" a deep voice calls out.

Looking up, I spot a guy who I assume yelled my name approaching with his focus clearly on me. He's dressed in dark blue jeans, a fitted black t-shirt, and sneakers, standing about five-feet, ten-inches tall, with a stocky build. He has short, red hair, a little longer on top, a goatee, blue eyes, and a square jaw. "Are you Aidan?"

He nods in confirmation halting his footsteps right in front of me. "That would be me."

Leaning on my crutches, I hold out my hand to him. "Thanks for agreeing to meet up with me."

"No problem." He grasps my hand firmly as he nods towards my broken leg, arching his eyebrows in question.

"I totaled my motorcycle during the hurricane," I grumble in explanation as I release his hand, my own falling back to my crutch.

His eyes widen further in surprise. "And you think you're ready for another motorcycle?"

Shrugging my shoulders, I concede, "I know I can't ride until I get this fucking thing off, but hopefully that happens this week." I pause, glaring down at my cast. "I honestly can't imagine not riding. It's not just a part of me, it's in my blood. In the meantime, while I'm forced to wait, I would love to be able to work on my new ride."

He presses his lips tightly together and points in my direction. "See, that right there is the only reason I'm considering selling you this ride. It's a sweet motorcycle and needs to be taken care of properly. Pete mentioned you're a mechanic." He crosses his arms, his fingers sliding up to stroke his whiskers in thought.

Nodding, I emphasize, "I am a mechanic, and I'm a damn good one, too. But my specialty is motorcycles, and I'm even better at those," I brag, knowing he needs to hear it if I want him to consider selling me this bike. "I've rebuilt quite a few different rides or added special features, and I even have a few designs of my own."

He nods, seemingly impressed. "Okay," he mumbles, pausing as he processes my words. "I'd love to see some of the things you've done."

"I don't have anything on me, but I do have a drive with some of my work back where I'm staying." I hope it still works after the accident. I didn't bother to check.

He nods. "So, how long have you been riding?"

I shrug, the corners of my lips tugging upwards. "Since I was old enough to get my motorcycle license, and honestly, even before that."

He chuckles, nodding in understanding. "Kinda sounds like someone else I know," he mumbles under his breath.

"Do you know anyone who does motorcycle art around here?" I ask, changing the subject. "That's the one thing I've always depended on others for, and I'm obviously not from the area and would need referrals."

"The artwork is my favorite part," he claims, a slow smile spreading across his face as he drops his hand to his side.

I grin, suddenly feeling like we have a lot to talk about. "Sweet, I'd love to see some of your work."

"Absolutely! I have some of my work on my phone, and I have a website with most of the stuff I've done."

"That's perfect. Then, why don't we grab something to eat, and we can talk in a little more detail and I can take a look at some of your work?" I suggest, nodding my head towards the food truck behind him.

"Sounds good to me, as long as you're the one buying." He smirks. I barely have a chance to shrug before he turns around and joins the end of the line.

Chuckling, I hobble after him, eager to hear more about the motorcycle he acquired and his talents.

37

Ella

I'M EXHAUSTED. IT'S BEEN A ROUGH NIGHT AND AN EVEN tougher couple days with Grant doing a great job of avoiding me, and I hate it. I can't believe my curiosity pushed him so far away. It makes me wonder how deep his scars cut. Everything was going so well until I pushed for more, but I can't help it. I want to help him. Whatever did that to him obviously caused him pain, or at least the memories of what happened seemed to yank him back under. I need to figure out a way to drag him back to the surface, whether it's me he allows to be there for him or not. No one deserves to live like that.

With a heavy sigh, I shove Grant out of the forefront of my mind and take a quick glance at my phone, frowning when I don't see any missed calls or messages. I don't know what I was expecting, but I need to try harder not to think about him.

"Are you alright, Ella?" James questions, his eyebrows furrowed in concern.

Shaking my head, I stammer, "Yes, I'm fine. Sorry. I was just, um, checking on my friend. You know the one who was hurt. Um...sorry."

"Okay, I'll let it slide, but let's keep your phone in your pocket unless it's an emergency or you're on break. Alright?"

"Yeah, sorry."

He nods and gestures to a table behind me. "Now that everything is good, why don't you greet table three?"

"Of course, sorry," I repeat.

The corners of his lips quirk up as he spins on his heel and heads back to the bar. Quickly, I slip my phone back into my pocket and stride over to my next table. While I lift my gaze, I paste a smile on my face, wincing at the sight of Nate sitting with one of the doctors I remember from his residency along with a woman I don't recognize.

He smiles broadly and leans back in his chair the moment he sees me. His eyes swiftly drag up and down my body, making me stiffen before he meets my gaze. "Hi, Gabriella. You look really good. How are you doing?"

"I'm fine, Nate. Are you guys ready to order?" I prompt, glancing around the table.

"Can we order our drinks first?" the woman requests.

"Of course. What would you like to drink?"

"Umm..." she mumbles, dragging out the word as she scans the drink menu.

"Do you get off soon?" Nate questions, trying to pull my attention.

"I can come back later," I begin, ignoring him. With no response, I spin on my heel to retreat towards the kitchen.

Nate stands, blocking my exit route as he rests his hand on my elbow, stopping me. "Ella, please wait. I just want to talk."

"I'm working!" My body heats in irritation.

"I know, but you won't return my calls, and we still have some things we need to talk about."

Shaking my head, I mutter, "No. I don't think we do. Take the hint, Nathan."

James steps over to us, towering over me as he glares at Nathan in warning. "Do we have a problem here, Ella?"

"No, no problem, James. It's fine," I mumble quietly, my voice shaky. I only hope we're not drawing any attention.

"Then, I'm going to ask you kindly to remove your hand and step back from Ella," he growls at Nathan.

Nate's eyes widen as he holds his hands up in surrender. He cautiously takes a step back, appearing defeated. "I'm just trying to talk to her. She's my ex."

I wince. He didn't need to announce that; I'm pretty sure everyone already knows. Does he think that gives him power over me or something? I glance at James still glaring at Nate without saying a word and smirk, appreciating his intimidation tactics at the moment. "Thanks, James."

"I'm here if you need me," he states, taking a step back.

I straighten my shoulders and glance at Nate. "Call me when you're ready to order." Then I spin on my heel and stalk towards the bar, wanting to scream. Instead, I drop my empty tray down on the bar with a heavy sigh.

James walks around me and slips back behind the bar. "I can have Hannah take over their table if you want."

Shaking my head, I respond, "No, thank you. It's not worth it. He's not worth it, but thanks for the rescue, James."

He smiles and nods in acknowledgment. "Why don't you take off early? We're not busy tonight. Go home to that man of yours."

I scrunch my nose up in annoyance, as I feel my face heat in embarrassment. "I don't have a man."

James quirks a brow, giving me a skeptical look as he wipes down the bar. Instantly, I attempt to argue, "What? I don't!"

"Sure," he mumbles, chuckling softly. Then he tosses the rag in the sink under the bar before moving to the other end to take a drink order.

I huff in annoyance again. "Doesn't anyone listen to me?" I mumble under my breath. I glance at Nate's table and groan, his gaze continuing to drift in my direction. He grins when he catches me glaring at him, putting me over the edge. He's the last thing I want to deal with right now. I'm ready for the night to be over. Turning my back to the room, I wait until James returns to this side of the bar before I tell him, "You know what? I think I'll take you up on your offer. I'm leaving."

"Good decision." He smirks. "Have a good night, Ella. Tell Hannah she has your tables and give her what she needs."

"Got it. Thank you!" Spotting Hannah, I reach out, halting her. "Hey, I'm headed out. You have my tables, but they're all new except for table nine, but I just gave them their food five minutes ago. Unfortunately, table three is Nate and company." I scrunch my nose up in displeasure.

"Okay, thanks for the warning, but I've got your back. Have a good night, girlie!" She grins and waves goodbye.

"Thank you!" Turning around, I quickly make my way to the locker room to grab my purse and rush out the front door before anything else can happen. It's been one of those days where so many little things have gone wrong. I dropped a drink tray, broke a few glasses, mixed up an order, spilled a drink on myself, had beer spilled on me more than once, and had some asshole slap my ass. James definitely had his hands full tonight. By the time Nathan had shown up, I think every single one of us had already hit our limit of douchebags.

I sigh with relief the moment I get into my car, ready to get away from work and Nate. I can't believe he came here with colleagues and expected me to talk to him while I'm working. Why won't he just move on? Tossing my bag next to me, I start the car and pull out of the lot, my stomach churning as I turn towards home.

Several possible scenarios begin to run through my mind. I wonder if Grant will still be up and if he'll even talk to me if he is. I wonder what he's doing or if he's hanging out with someone else. He wouldn't bring someone to my house, but is he dating other people now? I know he's not mine—he has every right to—but he says he doesn't date. My heart sinks like a lead weight in my stomach, hating the idea of him out with someone else for nothing other than sex. I hate the idea of him out with another woman, period, but thinking of him naked with another woman makes me queasy. Where would he go? To her place? I shake my head, attempting to stop my destructive thoughts. Those won't help anyone, especially me.

I pull into my driveway and park. Grabbing my purse, I look up, feeling an overwhelming sense of relief at the sight of a light on inside the house. That should mean he's home. Slowly approaching my house, I think about what I should say when I see him. I'm barely up the front steps when another car pulls in, parking behind mine, confusing me. I turn around, waiting until the headlights flip off, and I'm able to make out Nathan's black SUV, my blood pressure instantly skyrocketing. I grimace and cross my arms over my chest in irritation as I wait for him to get out of the car.

"What are you doing, Nathan?"

He straightens, looking determined, causing me to stiffen. "So, you're not working anymore. Can we talk, now?"

"Fine," I grumble, exasperated, hoping we can end this here and now. "What do you want?"

He steps towards me and looks into my eyes, his own gaze softening. "I miss you, Ella," he murmurs with surprising gentleness. I startle from hearing my nickname on his lips. It's been a long time since he called me anything but Gabriella.

Shaking my head in denial, I retort, "No, you don't. You just miss controlling me."

He visibly flinches as if I just slapped him, quickly pulling himself together. "I never controlled you. I did what I had to do to protect you, to take care of you."

I heave a tired sigh. "Nathan, this is the same conversation we always have. It doesn't do either of us any good to keep doing this."

He takes another step towards me, getting in my space. I back up as he continues to advance until my back hits the wall next to my front door. He stops in front of me, caging me in. "Can you move please?" My heart begins racing, and my breathing picks up along with my anxiety.

Ignoring my request, he reiterates, "Everything I have ever done for you has been because I love you."

Shaking my head in denial, I refute his statement, straining to hold my voice steady, "You don't love me. I'm more like a case study to you."

He winces and shakes his head, pressing me into the wall. "Don't you remember what it was like to be together, Ella? To kiss me?" he pushes, his lips hovering over mine.

Tears spring to my eyes in frustration. I don't believe he would intentionally hurt me, but he never listens to me either. I raise my voice just slightly, hoping to get him to pay attention, repeating, "I asked you to please move!"

The front door suddenly swings open, slamming against the house and startling both of us, causing Nate to take a step back. Grant leans against the doorframe in a white t-shirt and black shorts, his cast sticking out, but no crutches in site. Taking in the scene in front of him, he glares at Nathan before turning his focus on me. He grins wide, giving me his mega-watt, panty-melting smile causing my breath to catch. "Hey, Angel. I thought I heard you out here. I'm so glad you're home."

He holds his hand out for me and I take it, stepping towards him with a grateful smile. "Hi, Grant."

Turning towards Nathan, his eyes narrow and his fists clench at his sides as he demands with quiet rage, "It's time for you to leave."

"You're still here," Nathan grumbles, matching Grant's glare.

Grant responds with his sexy smirk as he waits, gripping my hand and watching as Nathan retreats down my front steps and back into his SUV. The moment he drives away, I feel my body sag with relief.

Grant tugs me inside, his eyes roaming over my body from head to toe. "Are you okay? Did he do anything?" he inquires, sounding frantic. "I'm sorry I didn't hear you sooner," he apologizes as if Nate's behavior is his fault.

"I'm fine. I promise. You were there before he really tried

anything. I'm just more frustrated than anything."

He nods in understanding and exhales a heavy sigh of relief. "That's good," he murmurs, his whole body seeming to relax in respite, confusing me even more.

"Thank you, Grant." The look he gives me squeezes my heart. Ugh, this man. Please, just let go.

38

Grant

I CLIMB INTO THE CAB, LEAVING MY DOCTOR'S APPOINTMENT for the first time in what feels like fucking forever on my own two feet! I may be stiff as hell, slightly uneven, and nowhere near as strong, but I'm thrilled to finally get that fucking cast off. Now I feel like I'm ready to take back control of my life, although even walking feels a bit surreal and awkward.

The doctor did tell me not to overdo it. Plus, when I tried to leave my crutches behind, he stopped me and told me to use them when my leg needed a break, but I don't plan on using them no matter what they suggest or how much it hurts. I'll just find a different way to do things if it gets to be too much, but it won't. I can handle it. I've been through so much worse than this. I'll burn the damn things if I have to.

He says I still need to go to physical therapy for at least the next month to work on strengthening my muscles and getting back my range of motion, let alone my balance. My legs look like the legs of two different men standing side by side, one with defined muscles and the other thin and weakened. It's truly comical to look at, but if the progress I've made on my arm since they removed the cast is anything to go by, I'll look more like myself sooner rather than later. I'll definitely work my ass off to achieve it. I want to feel and look like myself again, and I'm not about to let a little bit of pain or discomfort get in my way.

I glance down at my pale, slightly puckered skin. A new jagged scar adorns both my lower hip and the side of my calf, adding to my unwanted collection, but at least these are self-inflicted in a sense. After all, I was the one who was stupid enough not to check the weather and crash my motorcycle during a hurricane.

Thoughts of my accident bring forth thoughts of Ella. Then again, she's never too far from my mind. I remember the way her fingers explored my scars, both old and new, with her tender touch. She knows what the new ones are from, but how could I ever tell someone as wonderful as her about the nightmares behind each one from my past? She shouldn't hear a single word about how I got those old wounds. She's too good.

A grimace tugs at my lips as my mind briefly drifts back to the old scars scattered across my chest, my back, my arms and even my legs. A dark cloud surrounds me as I remember how I got each one, feeling as if a weight is pinning me down. I flinch, feeling the pain of every intentional infliction as one of her ways of trying to keep me in line and devoted to her. Hell, she fucking succeeded for a long time. It's not like anyone believed me when I tried to confess, so what was I supposed to do? I was trapped. I had no way out, and I had been the one to put myself in that position in the first place. Little did I know, one stupid fucking decision would ruin my whole damn life.

With a heavy sigh, I close my eyes, attempting to shove my dark thoughts from my mind. Taking a deep breath, I exhale slowly, opening my eyes and scrunching my nose up in disgust. My leg, like my arm when the cast first came off, smells like shit, although I washed it the best I could at the doctor's office. I need to try to take a shower to hopefully get rid of this stench. Maybe I can even put some actual pants on. I'm sure it will feel strange to even be able to wear jeans again, but I'm so damn ready to have some normalcy back in my life, even something as simple as wearing blue jeans.

Shades of brown and green from the grass and trees fly by in a blur as I look out the window. Noticing the familiar landscape, I realize we're getting close to her house. I gulp, suddenly anxious to see Ella and take in her reaction to my leg being out of its cast. Then again, I'm nervous to see her response to seeing me at all, especially after last night.

I was ready to explode when I saw her ex-boyfriend pull up right after she got out of her car. At first, I assumed she invited him over, and that knowledge felt like a punch to my chest, making it difficult to breathe. I was livid at the same time, completely defeated, even though I know I had no right to be, especially after I spent the last few days avoiding her. I can't act without thinking like before with Laine.

Cautiously, I snuck over to the door, standing just barely out of sight and listening in on their conversation like a creeper, but I'm sure fucking glad I did! I can't believe that asshole didn't want to listen to a word she said, making me see nothing but red. She claimed he wouldn't have done anything, but I don't have as much faith in him as she does—meaning none. I don't have any doubt he would've tried something if I hadn't yanked the door open when I did.

I'm grateful just being there was enough to deter him. I didn't feel very intimidating with a fucking cast on my leg, but I would've hit him without a second thought if he touched her without her permission no matter what my current state. My blood boils again just thinking about the douchebag being near her, and he was way too fucking close.

After he left, I needed to see for myself that she was okay. The fire in her eyes along with her verbal outrage let me know she was just annoyed and pissed off, and she had every right to be. When she said thank you, I finally began to settle as relief flooded through us both.

Unfortunately, things quickly changed as the air thickened around us, everything becoming slightly awkward. After all, I'm the one who had been staying clear the last few days because she was getting too close and asking too many questions about my past I didn't want to answer. I'm not sorry I kept my mouth shut; I'm just sorry I hurt her in the process.

Regrettably, our whole situation is my fault. No surprise I put us in this position, but I'm also the one that let it get too far between us in the first place; I couldn't seem to help myself. I shouldn't have gone there with her, and I fucking knew it. There's a reason I have my rules when it comes to women, and my angel easily obliterated every single one of them without even trying. Now I need to figure out a way to repair the damage I've done without making it worse.

The cab driver pulls Into the driveway and stops, throwing the car in park. I glance up at the house, hesitant to get out. Ella crosses in front of the window, making my chest tight with barely a glimpse of her. "I need to fix this. What the fuck am I going to do?" I grumble to myself.

"The hell if I know, but we're here. Are you getting out?" the driver asks, staring at me through the rearview mirror.

"Sorry." My cell pings, indicating an incoming text. "Just a minute," I mumble as I pull out my phone. Unlocking my screen, I see a message from Aidan.

> I'm available now if you want to come take a
> look at the motorcycle I acquired at the auction.

I grin, feeling as if some things are finally starting to look up. Quickly, I text him back.

> I'm on my way. Be there in fifteen.

Leaning towards the cab driver, I redirect him to my new location. I relax against the black leather seat as he backs out of the driveway, heading towards what I hope will be my new ride, giving me back even a little piece of me and my freedom.

Figuring out how to fix things with Ella will just have to wait. Unfortunately, I don't think more time can help me out of this hole, but I'm going to take it anyway.

39

Ella

THE MUFFLED SOUND OF A CAR PULLING INTO THE DRIVEway causes me to jump up from the kitchen table, anxious to talk to Grant. Although I hate what happened with Nate, Grant seemed awfully protective of me last night, and I loved that feeling! But is he protective of me because he's being nice and just watching out for me, or is there more between us? I can't help but feel it's his past holding him back.

As I walk by the window, I see a cab out of the corner of my eye but keep moving, not wanting to look like I'm waiting for him. Honestly, I don't understand how he could be immune to the inferno I feel every time he's near me. I know he's attracted to me with everything that's happened between us, but he also told me from the start he doesn't do relationships. Does that mean I'm just like all the other girls he's been with? Has he been using me this whole time for my generosity and for sex?

I shake my head, refusing to believe it. That doesn't make sense. We haven't even had sex. Admittedly, we've gotten close, but we've just been fooling around. Besides, if that were true, wouldn't he be in my bed a lot more often, and wouldn't we be doing so much more? He's the one who stopped us every single time from going further. He's been the one with control. I've been a willing and eager participant. I grimace, annoyed with myself.

Still not seeing the front door open, I step closer to the window, curious as to what's taking him so long. I peer through the blinds, just in time to watch the cab backing out of my driveway, but I don't see Grant anywhere in sight. My eyebrows draw down in confusion. "What the hell?" I grumble aloud, a slight pang in my chest. Did he see my car here and decide to leave so he didn't have to see me? Why would he do that? Is he still avoiding me?

Groaning in frustration and annoyance, I stalk back to the kitchen table and pick up my phone, tapping out a quick message to him.

> Good morning! I hope your doctor's appointment
> went well this morning. I'm not working today,
> so I'll see you when you get back.

I want him to know he's not getting away from me so easily. He's going to have to talk to me sooner or later, and I have all the time in the world to wait today. I sound like a damn groupie or something. What the hell is wrong with me? Maybe I shouldn't have sent him a message, but it's too late now.

I sigh heavily, feeling like my time on the water this morning did nothing for my state of mind. I set my phone down on the kitchen counter opposite the sink, attempting to keep it away from me so I'm not constantly tempted to look at it or send another stupid message that makes me feel like a stalker. "No regrets, Ella. You did nothing wrong." I spin around towards the sink and start cleaning up my dishes from breakfast, knowing I need to find something to do to keep my hands busy and my mind occupied. Too bad it's not a program day; I would love to see Annie, Theo and all the other kids.

The doorbell rings, catching me by surprise. I reach for the faucet, turning the water off and drying my hands on the blue and white dishtowel next to the sink. "Coming," I call out, striding towards the front door. As I pull it open, my eyes widen and I gasp in surprise. "Nathan. What are you doing here?"

He stands on my front porch with his hands stuffed into his dark blue jeans, rocking back and forth on the heels of his brown loafers. He looks up at me from underneath his wavy brown hair, a dark lock hanging in his blue eyes, appearing brighter against his light blue button-down shirt. He has his shirt pulled out of his jeans, with the top two buttons open, appearing more vulnerable than I've seen him in a long time, and I'm not sure how to take it.

"I came to apologize," he proclaims, appearing sheepish and throwing me off-balance. "May I come in and talk to you for just a few minutes?" I open my mouth to respond, not quite sure what my answer should be. "Please, Gabriella?" he begs.

He's been asking me to talk constantly lately. Maybe if I give him the uninterrupted time he's been asking for, he'll finally leave me alone and move on. Besides, right now, he looks more like the man I fell in love with than the Nate I've seen as of late. Reluctantly, I heave a sigh and take a step back, allowing him to come inside.

Taking a deep breath for strength, I close the door behind him and follow him over to the couch. He pulls his hands out of his pockets as he sits down on one end and I sit down on the other. "Okay, Nathan. You're here. What do you think we could possibly still have to talk about?"

He winces at my tone and runs his hand through his hair, pushing it out of his eyes. "First, I need to apologize for what an asshole I've been since this guy"—he grimaces at the thought of Grant—"has been around. I especially need to apologize for last night. I know it's no excuse, but I had a few drinks before we even came to the restaurant. They told me it wasn't a good idea, but I refused to listen. I wanted to see you."

I cross my arms over my chest defensively and urge him to continue. "Go on."

He sighs, conceding defeat, looking into my eyes before he

speaks. "To put it simply, I was jealous," he admits, surprising me.

"Jealous?" I echo.

"You're not the kind of woman a man gets over easily, Ella. I know I fucked up with you. I was so focused on my career and making sure your disease never came back that I stopped thinking about how you were really feeling. Instead, I looked at the technical side of things." He pauses, shrugging his shoulders. "Maybe that made it easier for me to handle. As I'm sure you already know since you put up with me for so long, I'm not good with the emotional side of things, but I've been trying because I know that's what you need. Then I realized you started seeing someone and I'm already too late to make things right between us." He pauses, gulping down the lump in his throat as he shakes his head. "I don't know, I guess I kind of lost it. I wanted to be the one to be there for you. I wanted us to be together again." He laughs humorlessly.

"Nate," I murmur softly, my heart full of empathy. I drop my hands into my lap, no longer feeling the need to be so defensive.

He shakes his head, glancing in my direction. He gives me a look full of regret. I know that feeling, and it's one I refuse to have anymore. "I still love you, Ella," he declares, his eyes shining.

My heart clenches for our lost love. I don't believe we were meant to be together even when we were at our best. I may not want to be with him anymore, but things between us were good once. I just want us both to move on. I smile sadly. "I still love you too, Nate, but not like either of us deserves."

He looks away momentarily before bringing his gaze back to me and staring into my eyes. "Do you love him?" he inquires, his pain written all over his face.

I wince, his question giving me pause. Do I love Grant? "I don't know," I answer honestly. I look at Nathan and a wave of guilt washes over me, suddenly hating myself for lying to him. I shrug my shoulders, and before I can think about it too much I admit, "He's not my boyfriend. I don't even know if he'll stay."

Nate gasps while his eyes widen in shock at my confession. He opens his mouth to respond, but quickly snaps it shut before he tries again. "Were you ever together?"

I bite my lip, hesitant, thinking about our time together and how much I really do care for him. I want to see him. I miss him when he's not around. My heart aches knowing he might leave. I want to know every little thing about him, the good and the bad, and help him heal if he'll let me. We definitely have the sexual chemistry—I feel myself blush—but how does he feel about me? I'm not sure if I know his true feelings or if I ever will. I do know that every minute I've spent with him has been real for me. "Yeah," I confirm, not leaving any room for doubt.

He offers me a sad smile and reaches for my hand, giving it a light squeeze. "Well, I've learned a lot from you, so let me say this, say everything you want to say. Don't leave anything out because you never know if you'll have another chance. Take the risk for anything and everything you want. If he's what makes you happy, fight for him. Spill your guts until there's nothing left to say. No regrets, right?" He gives me a half smile, warming my heart.

"Right," I mumble, surprised by his words and support, knowing this doesn't benefit him. "Thank you, Nathan," I tell him, still holding his hand.

"And if he's stupid enough to walk away from you, I'm still right here waiting, and I wouldn't fuck up again if you ever gave me another chance."

I tilt my head to the side and shake my head, forlorn. "Nathan," I mumble, shocked and overwhelmed with his confession.

He chuckles softly. "No worries, Ella. I'll be fine...eventually." Sighing, he requests, "Can I have a hug?"

"Sure."

He immediately drops my hand and scoots closer, wrapping me in his arms as my hands slide around his back, returning the gesture. Being here with him, I feel safe and cared for, even comfortable. We could be good together again. I do love Nathan, but I'm confident it's not the kind of forever love I want to fight for. Is Grant that kind of love for me? My stomach twists, wondering if my growing love for Grant is unrequited like mine is for Nathan. I feel him kiss the top of my head, and I disentangle myself from his arms and gently push back.

He loosens his arms and looks down at me. "I love you." Leaning in, he kisses me on the cheek.

Placing my hands on his chest, I gently push him further away. "I think you should go."

He nods, standing, and I follow him to the door. He pauses, turning around and looking me in the eyes, holding my gaze. "I really am sorry, Ella."

"I know, Nathan. Thank you."

"I'm sorry I didn't say it sooner, and I'll try not to be such an asshole to your *friend*." He smirks.

I huff a laugh, giving him a small wave and a tight smile as he opens the front door. He steps outside and smiles dejectedly, stuffing his hands back in his pockets before he turns to leave. Without watching him walk away, I shut the door with a heavy sigh, stunned and a little overwhelmed by what just happened. I definitely wasn't expecting that, especially with his behavior over the last few months, but I'm grateful it did.

My phone pings from the kitchen, and I shake myself out of my stupor and quickly stride into the kitchen to grab it. I glance at the screen as I pick it up and smile, my heart skipping a beat at the sight of Grant's name. Tapping the message, I read,

I'm on my way home and I have a surprise for
you.

I gasp at his words, my hand falling to my tightening chest as my stomach flip-flops. It happens every time I hear him refer to my house as home. I only wish it were true, and this wasn't just a temporary home for him.

The corners of my lips curl up in a smile, as he did say he has a surprise for me too. That sounds more like the Grant I've been spending time with and less like the one who's been avoiding me the last few days. Then again, the Grant who has been avoiding me wouldn't have texted me at all.

I wonder what his surprise is, I ponder, biting my lip. My excitement begins to grow as I text him back,

I'll be here.

40

Ella

I PACE BACK AND FORTH, IMPATIENTLY WAITING FOR GRANT to return. My heart pounds, anxious to know what surprise he has for me. Although, I know I still need to talk to him, it's no longer my priority after his text. Plus, now I probably should tell him about Nate coming by and what happened with him. I know I don't need to tell him because he's not my boyfriend; he's made that painfully obvious. But I don't want to keep anything from him, especially something like this. But any kind of serious conversation can wait.

"What is going on, Grant?" I mumble to myself.

The front door opens and I release the breath I didn't know I was holding as I spin around, hopeful. Grant steps further into the room with his panty-melting smile in place and in full-effect. "Hi, Angel!"

I look him up and down and my eyes widen as I gasp in shock. A smile lights up my face as my hand falls to my chest. "Oh, my gosh! No cast! Grant, you got your cast off!" I screech, stating the obvious, my excitement palpable. Swiftly, I close the distance between us and throw my arms around him without thought.

He chuckles softly as he staggers backwards, catching himself and me as his arms instantly wrap around my back and he pulls me close. I smile to myself, taking a deep breath in, inhaling his musky scent, and enjoying the moment of being in his arms again. It may have only been a few days, but I missed this; I missed him. "No more cast," he repeats joyfully.

"I'm so happy for you," I mumble into his chest, giving him a tight squeeze before I reluctantly let go. I step back, looking into his golden eyes sparkling with a touch of green. "I didn't know you were getting your cast off today."

"I didn't either, but I'd hoped."

"That's a pretty great surprise."

He nods in agreement. "Yeah, it is." Smirking, he adds, "But that's only part of it."

My eyes widen and I arch my eyebrows, my curiosity instantly overwhelming. "What do you mean only part of it? There's more?"

His grin widens as he nods in confirmation. "Oh, yeah, there's more," he growls, sending shivers down my spine. Reaching for my hand, he entwines his fingers with mine, sending a shock to my system and heat throughout my body as he gently tugs me towards the front door. "Come with me outside and let me show you."

My eyebrows draw down in confusion, but I willingly follow him out the door, smiling at his exuberance. "What do you want to show me?" I question, just before I see it propped on its kickstand in the driveway at the end of the walkway. I gasp at the sight of the sleek black and silver motorcycle. Grinning, I turn back to the man who looks like a kid in a candy store, feeling my heart race inside my chest at how much I feel for this man. I love seeing that look of pure joy on his face. I'd search for ways to see it every single day of our lives if he'd just let me. The thought causes my heart to skip a beat.

Giving myself a mental shake, I force myself to redirect and declare the obvious, "You got a new motorcycle!"

He grins proudly. "I did. Some of the insurance came through, and I've got to drive something to get around, right?"

I smirk, wondering why he thinks he needs to explain himself. "Guess you don't need me anymore," I joke, the words making my stomach twist in a way I don't like. Swiftly, I shove the thought away. "I admit, I don't know anything about motorcycles, but it's beautiful."

"Thanks." He grins with pride. "Pete down at the garage in town hooked me up with one of the mechanics. Do you know Aidan?" I shrug, unsure. "Well, Aidan sold this to me at a great price. There are a few things I still have to do to it, but it's drivable. Well, it's more than just drivable, but..." He shrugs like it's no big deal, but we both know this means a lot. "I just want to add some of my own touches to it when I can, and that will come. Plus, Aidan and I talked about some art I'd like him to add when I have the cash, but it's all mine."

Watching Grant talk animatedly about his new motorcycle makes my chest tight and my heart full. I could listen to him ramble about it all day and every word would sound like music to my ears, even though I'm sure I wouldn't understand most of it, but he's so happy. That's the only thing that matters to me.

"Ella." He smirks.

"Hmm?" I question, arching my eyebrows.

He chuckles softly. "I just asked if you wanted to go for a ride with me. I can't go far yet because my leg isn't ready for that, but I only drove from the other side of town, and I'm dying to go for a ride. I'd love it if you would come with me."

"Are you sure your leg can handle it?" I ask, sucking my lower lip between my teeth. I don't want to diffuse his fire, but I can't stand the thought of him getting hurt again. The possibility has my stomach instantly roiling in protest.

He holds my gaze, insisting, "I would never risk your safety if I wasn't one-hundred percent positive my body could handle it."

Exhaling in relief, I return his smile and nod in agreement. "Okay, then, I trust you. I'd absolutely love to go for a ride with you."

His grin brightens and he walks closer to the bike with me in tow. "Good, because I bought you your own helmet."

I gasp, my mouth dropping open in surprise. "You bought me my own helmet?" I repeat in awe, my heart clenching with unrestrained hope. That must mean he's not planning on leaving right away, right?

He chuckles, the low sound vibrating through my body. "Your very own. Here," he offers, reaching around the other side and coming back with a black helmet with a thick pink stripe all around the bottom edges, giving it the perfect feminine touch.

"Thank you, Grant." Without thinking, I push up on my tiptoes and press my lips to his, relief enveloping me the moment he kisses me back. Taking advantage of this gift, I stick my tongue through his parted lips and sweep the inside before tangling briefly with his. I moan into his mouth, feeling needy with my body tingling and attempt to press closer. Suddenly, I lose my balance and fall back on my heels, breaking our kiss. I laugh as his arm tightens around me, holding me up. "Thank you," I repeat breathlessly, looking into his eyes.

He grins, nodding. "You're welcome. Let me go shower quick and throw on some jeans and we'll go for a ride."

"Okay."

"You might want to throw on a pair of jeans too. Gotta protect those gorgeous legs of yours," he growls playfully. Reaching out, he gives my ass a light tap, making me jump. He winks as he turns around, heading inside.

Feeling giddy, a giggle escapes. I love this playful side of Grant. We've had our moments, but this feels like I'm seeing a side of him I've never known, and I love it. I want to see all his sides; the good and bad. I know we need to talk, and we will later, but this feels right and I don't want to mess with it. He deserves to have his moment, his time to celebrate being here and doing well after his accident, and I'm going to enjoy it with him.

I can't wipe the smile from my face as I watch him disappear into the bathroom with a pair of faded blue jeans in his hand. I've been wanting to see him in jeans for a long time. I guess that day is today and I can't wait.

There's no denying the air is electric between us. I'm sure he feels it, no matter how much he denies it, insisting it's not anything more than physical attraction and lust. Sure, we have that, but there's so much more. I'm sure it can't just be me. He must feel it!

Sighing, I wonder if that will be enough to let me in.

"Forget about it for now, Ella," I chastise myself as I step into my room to change. Looking in my closet, I stare at my clothes. Maybe I should do a little more than just jeans. I need to find something that will make him drool.

41

Grant

I STAND AS ELLA WALKS OUT OF HER ROOM STRIDING TOWARDS me. My eyebrows hit my hairline as I let my eyes drift over her, starting at her feet, adorned in black ankle boots with a one-inch heel. She's dressed in dark blue jeans that look like they were painted on, along with a pink t-shirt emblazoned with a white graphic on the front across her chest, the shirt falling just above her belly button, exposing her ivory skin, and leaving me breathless while making my mouth water.

"Um," I gulp down the lump in my throat. She tilts her head to the side, arching her eyebrow in challenge as she flutters her eyes at me. Damn. She knows exactly what she's doing. "Got a jacket to cover the middle?" I ask and lick my lips.

She giggles, the sound going straight to my cock. "Don't you like it?" she prods playfully. "I thought it was okay."

I smirk and shake my head in amusement. "You know I do," I state, the words coming out in a growl.

She blushes, her skin nearly matching her shirt. "I have a jean jacket. Will that work?"

"Sure," I grumble.

"Are you alright?"

"You keep teasing me like that and we'll never get on that motorcycle," I mumble under my breath.

"And that's a bad thing?" she taunts, the corners of her lips twitching up as she stares at me.

My head falls back as I burst out laughing, feeling lighter than I have in a long fucking time. I look at her and shake my head, clearly amused. I have to admit, I'm enjoying this playful side of her. "Let's go, Angel."

She grins, grabs a jean jacket off the hooks by the door and slips it on. Pausing, she looks me up and down. I'm dressed in a long-sleeved black ribbed thermal, but no jacket. My black leather coat got destroyed in the accident along with my motorcycle. Until I get a new one, my long sleeves will have to do.

She licks her lips, announcing, "Okay, I'm ready." She steps up next to me and gives my ass a firm pat, taking me by surprise. Leaning towards me, she whispers in my ear, "I like you in these jeans."

Her hot breath on my neck gives me chills. I take a deep breath as she turns her head and rushes out the door, but not fast enough that I miss every inch of her exposed skin turning a deep shade of red, making me laugh harder. "This is going to be fun, if she's not the death of me," I mumble under my breath.

As we walk outside, I take her by the hand as we stride towards my new ride, my fingers already tingling with anticipation. Stopping next to my motorcycle, I reach for the helmet I just bought her first and help her strap it onto her head, adjusting the straps as necessary. I grin as I look down at her, placing a chaste kiss on her lips. "You look fucking adorable."

She grimaces, obviously not liking my choice of words. "Adorable?"

I laugh. "Yes, adorable, but sexy as hell too." I give her another kiss, not able to stop myself.

She shrugs, her bright smile back on her face, making my heart skip a beat. "I can live with that," she concedes, her eyes sparkling.

Forcing myself to turn away from her, I unlatch my new black helmet and pull it over my head, clipping it in place.

Throwing one leg over the seat, I climb on, leaning back to kick it off the stand. I grab the key and turn the ignition, placing the key back into a small compartment. The familiar routine settling me as I turn the run switch on, the sound of the fuel pump priming hits my ears before I push the on switch, starting my bike. I take a deep breath, exhaling slowly as I relish the feel of the engine running between my legs. Damn, I missed this.

I look over to Ella and smile, holding out my hand. "Come here," I urge. She grabs my hand and steps towards me. "Do you see the pegs to put your feet?"

"Yes." Without further instruction, she lets go of my hand and grabs my shoulder for support as she climbs on behind me without hesitation, giving me her trust, even after seeing my accident. The thought is a little overwhelming and I pause, taking another deep breath and exhaling slowly before I speak again. "Wrap your arms around me and hold on tight."

"Okay."

"Follow my lead as we ride. Lean with me when I lean. Don't fight it." I freeze, my words giving me pause, making me wonder if I should stop fighting us, but that's way too much to process right now, and I quickly pull myself back to the present.

She wraps her arms around me, leaning towards me, her head resting on my back as she gives me a squeeze, making my insides quiver and warming me from the inside, out. "I'm ready," she announces.

Clearing my throat, I mumble, "Hang on." Then, I release the brake and put the bike in gear as I roll out onto the road.

"I will," she concurs, just before I speed up and take off. Ella squeals in excitement, laughing as she holds me tighter, widening my smile. I drive along the shoreline, taking it easy as I stay close to the beach, letting her enjoy the view, wanting her to feel comfortable and safe. Besides, I know I shouldn't go far. My cast has only been off a few hours, and with all the nonuse, it feels weak and unbalanced. I may not like it, but that's the way it is. There's no way I'll push myself too far, especially when I have her to look out for. I would never put Ella in harm's way.

As we ride, I feel more relaxed and at ease than I have in a long fucking time. It's like I'm finally taking back control of my life, and that's exactly what I need. I have the power of the bike beneath me and I'm in control. The feeling of being on a motorcycle again is freeing. Part of it is probably getting my casts off, but the accident took a lot away from me that I took for granted, so much more than I ever imagined.

Adding to that, I have my angel behind me with her arms wrapped around me. That's a feeling I'm not used to. It's over-powering, and I wouldn't want it any other way. It makes me question if maybe I'm wrong. Having her with me feels like she's exactly where she's meant to be, and that scares the shit out of me. I know I don't deserve it, but maybe I could have more. Maybe she's something or someone I could keep. Maybe I could stay.

I swiftly dismiss the thought. She's not property. She's a woman who makes her own decisions, and she would expect me to open up to her. Although I wouldn't blame her, that's not possible. I just can't do it. Even if I did, she wouldn't see me in the same way anymore. How could she? She doesn't know who I am. She believes she wants me, wants us, but she doesn't have the whole story, and I can't share all the darkness that eats away at me and consumes me from the inside out. She deserves the light. I don't have anything to offer her but darkness.

She tightens her hold on me, her head resting on my back, as if she knows it's exactly what I need in the moment. My chest tightens as I shake away my dark thoughts, reminding myself to focus on the here and now. I have a fantastic new motorcycle, and I'm on a ride with my angel pressed up against me. It doesn't get much better than this; it's time to enjoy the moment and forget about the inevitable. Everything will fall apart soon enough; I don't need to dwell on it.

I slow down and pull over to the side of the road, taking off my helmet as I look out at the ocean, the waves crashing into the shore. Twisting around, I look back at Ella, smiling broadly. My chest clenches, prompting me to turn my body further and tilt my head towards hers, kissing her lips. "What do you think?"

"Mm," she murmurs, kissing me again and making me chuckle. "I love it! I love the feel of the wind whipping against us and holding you, being pressed up against you, and moving with you around the corners, letting your body lead the way," she attempts to explain, not realizing the connotation of her statement.

Her words send heat straight to my groin. She has no idea what she does to me. I'd already been riding half hard, now I'm going to have to ride home with a steel rod between my legs. I kiss her again with a low groan. She leans towards me to deepen the kiss. My tongue dives in to meet hers, but I soon pull back, leaving both of us breathless with me suddenly desperate to have her.

Tilting my head down, I press another quick kiss to her lips. Grinning, I shake my head and swiftly tug my helmet back on and click the strap into place. I lean towards her, advising, "Hold on," letting her know we're about to go.

"Okay." She curls into my back and tightens her hold around my middle. "I'm ready."

I give her hands a squeeze before reaching for my handlebars and rolling out. With the sweet taste of Ella on my lips, I turn my bike around, veering towards home, contemplating all the ways I want her and where the hell we go from here.

42

Ella

AS I FINISH MY LAST BITE OF PIZZA, I WIPE MY HANDS AND mouth on my napkin, dropping it onto my plate. I glance at Grant from underneath my eyelashes as he sets his plate down, wondering where his head is at. It felt like he was a new man today. Getting his casts off and getting a new motorcycle seem to have turned him around, at least in some way. I wonder if that means his outlook on us has changed. I'm not sure.

It feels like his thoughts regarding a relationship are embedded much deeper than what he's shared with me. I just wish he would open up to me. I want a chance with him, but I'll start small if that's all he's able to give. Then again, even if he's never able to give me more, I know I need to try. I repeat my mantra in my head, no regrets.

"That was good pizza," Grant mumbles, leaning back against the cushions as he lays his hand on his stomach. "A good end to a fantastic day."

As I nod my head in agreement, I sit back. I bend my knee, bringing my leg up on the couch and twist, facing him. "Your cast came off, some insurance came through, a new motorcycle, a ride along the ocean and pizza. What more could you ask for?"

He chuckles, quirking his eyebrow in challenge as he licks his lips. "Oh, I can think of a few things."

My face heats, a smile tugging at my lips as he reaches out, tucking a loose lock of my hair behind my ear. "Thank you again for taking me for a ride," I reiterate, remembering the feeling of being wrapped around his body, his muscles relaxed and sharing his body heat. "I had so much fun, and I would really love to do it again."

He nods and turns his head towards me, grinning. "I'm happy you enjoyed it. And we will do it again. I promise."

My eyes widen and I quickly try to school my features as I nod in acknowledgment. My heart skips a beat, filling with hope with his one simple vow. I don't believe he's promised me anything until now. Does that mean he's considering more with me? Will he break his stupid rules for me? Will he stay?

Maybe I'm reading too much into it. He could just be talking about tomorrow or the next day. That doesn't mean he's staying.

"Is your leg sore?" I ask, changing direction without even realizing I'm doing it. I'm nervous about pushing him any further, but I also know I should try. I need to know what I'm getting myself into because the more time we spend together, the more my heart gets involved. Then again, knowing the truth won't do me any good, unless it's what I want to hear. But what if it's not?

He heaves a sigh, reluctantly admitting, "My leg is a little sore, but it was worth it. Hopefully, I'll be able to build my strength back up quickly."

I nod in understanding, preparing myself to abruptly change the subject again, this time intentionally. I hope it won't ruin his mood, but it must be done, for me. As I take a deep breath, I attempt to gulp down the butterflies suddenly consuming my insides, trying to gather the courage to tell him about Nate. Maybe I don't have to tell him, but for my own sanity, I need to get it off my chest. I don't want to hide anything from him.

Lifting my head, I square my shoulders and look him in the eyes. I watch him closely as I declare, "So...I have something I want to tell you."

His whole body instantly tenses, going rigid as his eyes go dark, losing the light that's been in them all night, squeezing my heart. I watch his Adam's apple bob up and down, his gaze never wavering before he rasps, "What do you have to tell me?"

A swarm of bees erupts in my stomach with his defensive reaction. I hate his lack of trust in me, but I remind myself, I have no reason to feel nervous. I did nothing wrong; but I did promise myself I would always be honest with him, and this is something I would want to know if our roles were reversed. It doesn't matter that he's not my boyfriend. He's important to me.

"Well, while y'all were gone at physical therapy today, I kind of had a surprise visitor," I mumble, suddenly picking imaginary lint off my jeans.

He scoots closer and reaches out, his fingertips running along my jaw until he reaches my chin, leaving goose bumps in its wake. Gently, he tilts my head up until I meet his narrowed gaze. "Who was your surprise visitor?" he questions, dragging out each word, quietly demanding an answer.

With a heavy sigh, I release the breath I didn't realize I was holding and force out my answer, "Nathan."

He sucks in a quick breath, his hand at his side tightening into a fist as he clenches his jaw. "What did he want?" he seethes.

"Well, he wanted to apologize."

He startles, dropping his hand in his lap and giving me a look filled with doubt. "Apologize? For what?" he challenges, arching his eyebrows.

"For being an asshole to me since you've been around, and especially for how he treated me last night."

He sits back, a look of puzzlement on his face. "Huh," he mumbles. I stare at him, waiting to see if he's going to comment further, desperate to know what he's thinking. I thought he would have more of a reaction, but maybe I'm wrong about his feelings for me. "That's it?"

I wince, not looking forward to this part. His low chuckle echoes through the room, sounding both dark and ominous. "No," I concede, barely shaking my head.

"Of course not," he grumbles, grinding his teeth. "What else did he say?" he questions, oddly making me feel better for asking.

"Well, he um, he also told me he's still in love with me and he wants me back," I reveal, closely watching his reaction. I suck my lower lip between my teeth, waiting and hoping to see something.

He stiffens briefly before his body sags into the couch, his gaze veering away from me, distancing himself. "No surprise there, but what did you tell him?" he prompts, staring blankly at a spot in front of him, his whole body already claiming defeat.

My heart clenches and I inch closer to him, placing my hands on each side of his face and tilting my head up, begging him to hold my gaze through my simple touch. "I told him the truth, Grant. I don't love him. I don't want him. He's not who I want," I emphasize each statement, hoping he sees the truth in my words.

I stare into his eyes, now a darker shade of gold as I watch the pain, torment and indecision run through them. "Ella," he murmurs, sounding lost and desperate. He closes his eyes, his hand falling to his temple as if he's in complete agony and trying to shut everything down and lock it away. He drops his hand into his lap and slowly opens his eyes, giving me a glimpse into his tortured soul before he swiftly closes it down, shutting me out.

"Grant?"

Gently, he removes my hands from his face and carefully places them in my lap, making my heart sink. He breaks our stare and turns his head away from me, whispering something unintelligible under his breath.

"Grant," I probe, his name a plea on my lips. My heart pounds, overwhelmed with the feeling I'm starting to lose him with my confession. I hate it. I'm not ready to lose him; I don't think I ever will be.

He shakes his head without even glancing in my direction. I watch helplessly as he stands, grabbing the pizza box and the rest of our garbage from dinner. Turning, he strides towards the kitchen without bothering to say another word and completely shattering my heart in the process.

Tears prick my eyes and spill over as my heart lodges itself in my throat. I'm so confused. One minute he acts like he wants this, wants me, and the next, he pulls away and shuts me out. Why can't I get through to him? Why won't he talk to me? Does he really not want any part of what I'm offering him? If there's even a chance to have anything at all between us, I need to try, but I feel like I'm fighting a losing battle.

I know why I'm putting myself through this; I've already lost my heart. I think I see the same in him, but why can't he see it? Why can't he trust me and let go? Why won't he talk to me, let me be there for him, support him? I just want him to make an effort, no matter how small to know he's trying. Is that really too much to ask?

43

Grant

I FINISH THROWING AWAY THE GARBAGE, FEELING LIKE THE biggest asshole in the world, but that's nothing new. But I can't help it; I don't know how to deal with all these fucking feelings.

She tells me she wants me and I'm too much of a pussy to even respond. Everything about the moment overwhelmed me, and I didn't know what to say. Heaving a sigh, I shake my head, frustrated with myself.

I need to go back in there and say something, but what? I don't know what I can give her. She deserves more than me. This feels like it's all too much. My chest hurts as if I'm being stabbed, making it hard to fucking breathe. I close my eyes, focusing on breathing in and out.

My eyes flutter open and land on a picture of her with her sister, held to the refrigerator with a small yellow turtle magnet. I step closer, looking at the photo. The two of them have their arms around each other and they're both laughing, their eyes bright with pure happiness.

I've never seen anything more beautiful than Ella when she's happy; her joy lights up the fucking world. How can I walk away from that? How can I bring so much darkness to her light? She's like my sun. I don't want to be the one to ruin that, ruin her; it would fucking kill me. I may deserve it, but she doesn't.

Either way, I can't just leave her in there after she was brave enough to tell me what she wants. I need to go back in there. Taking a deep breath, I turn and force myself to walk back into the living room, finding her sitting on the couch with her head in her hands. I wince, my chest tightening, hating myself even more for her tears. I'm not worth it.

Cautiously, I approach, making my way around to the other side of the couch. As I sit down next to her, I softly murmur her name, "Ella?"

She sniffles and wipes her eyes as she lifts her head, looking into my eyes with defiance. "What?" she questions, splintering my already battered heart.

I lean towards her, mumbling my apology, hating to see her hurting, and despising myself even more knowing I'm the one that made her cry. "I'm so sorry, Angel. I'm such an asshole. This just feels like so much, I don't know how to react," I ramble, attempting to explain what I'm thinking without really giving her anything. "Please don't cry, Ella," I plead, struggling to breathe. Not able to stop myself, I reach out, tenderly wiping away her tears with the pads of my thumbs.

Shaking her head in denial, she mumbles, "I just don't understand, Grant! One minute you're sweet, funny, kind, attentive and you look at me like you want to devour me whole and the next you're pushing me away and telling me you can't do this, whatever this is, but you won't give me any reasons."

I flinch, briefly looking away, but I can't deny even a little bit of her claim. "You're right, and no matter what I say or do, it's never because of you. It may sound like a copout, but it's because of me, every single time."

"That doesn't help," she mutters, shaking her head. Taking a shaky breath, she tilts her head, looking at me with a question in her eyes and defiantly blurts out, "Does it have anything to do with your scars?"

I gasp and flinch as if she just punched me. I clench my jaw in frustration and hurt. "Ella," I grunt, "I can't..." I trail off, shaking my head, pain clawing its way up my throat.

Seeing my reaction, her glassy eyes widen and she apologizes instantly, "I'm sorry. I didn't mean to..."

I shake my head, interrupting her, "Don't apologize. You have no reason to. It's not your fault. It's just not something I can...I just can't go there. I can't...fuck!" I stammer, frustrated, not able to think straight.

"Grant, it's fine," she mumbles, shaking her head as she wipes away her tears. "You've been honest with me about what this is and can be right from the start. Just because I don't understand, doesn't mean you have to explain anything to me. It's on me that I want you and you don't want the same thing."

My eyes widen, shocked by her statement. "Ella," I mumble, shaking my head and attempting to pull her into my arms, but she doesn't move. I settle for her allowing me to rest my hand on her thigh, needing to touch her. "That is so far from the truth! I want you, more than I can even begin to express!"

"I'm not talking about sex."

I huff a humorless laugh, muttering the words before I even realize I said them aloud. "I'm not either, Angel."

She looks up at me in confusion, her eyelashes clumped together from her tears. "What? I don't understand."

Heaving a sigh, I move in front of her so I'm facing her. I slide my hands up her sides, over her shoulders, up her sleek neck and weave my fingers into her hair. I can't hide from her anymore. Restraining myself is not doing anyone any good, especially not my sweet girl. I brush away more tears, tears demanding I give her something. She deserves it.

I hold her gaze, take a deep breath and mumble my truth. "Ella, I want you more than I want to take my next breath. The air vibrates around me anytime you're near me, and it takes everything in me to hold myself back from taking what I want. You are the light to my dark. You help me thrive and be a better man, but I'm terrified I'm going to be the one who brings you down. I don't deserve someone as incredible as you. You're everything I'm not. You're gorgeous on the outside, beautiful on the inside, and all of it together makes you the sexiest woman I've ever met. Every day I spend with you, I feel like the luckiest asshole in the world, but I know you deserve better. I can't be the one to darken your life and slay your spirit; it would kill me. You're my angel," I proclaim as if she's the most important person in the world, and to me she is.

"Grant," she whimpers my name as more tears begin escaping out of the corners of her eyes, leaving a trail down her cheeks, and squeezing my heart.

"Please, don't cry, Angel," I plead desperately.

Shaking her head, she insists, "These are happy tears."

I huff a laugh. "Happy tears?"

She nods and wipes her tears away, clasping onto my hands still holding her face. "Yeah, that was beautiful, Grant."

My heart clenches seeing the glimmer of hope in her eyes. "Ella," I mumble, my voice full of regret.

She looks up at me in question. "Hmm?"

"I can't stay. I don't know how long I'll be here, but I can't stay. I guarantee the day will come that I'll have to leave. I'll finish my physical therapy, and then I'm not sure what's after that, but I need you to remember I can't stay."

She sighs and nods her head in understanding. "I know you're leaving. You've always made that perfectly clear, but what you don't understand is I care about right now, and you're still here. You're acting like you're already gone."

"I'm trying to protect you."

"I don't want you to protect me! I can make my own decisions, and I want to be with you while you're still here," she insists vehemently.

"Ella," I attempt to interrupt. She doesn't know what she's asking. She deserves so much more than anything temporary, especially from someone like me. "I don't ever want to be the one who hurts you."

She huffs a humorless laugh. "Don't you get it? You're hurting me now!" she argues, making me flinch.

"I'm sorry." My chest aches, feeling completely lost. I have no idea what I'm supposed to do.

"Grant, I don't want you to apologize, I want you to try!"

"I have been trying."

Shaking her head, she refutes my claim. "No, you haven't. You've been holding yourself back. You push me away the moment we start getting close. You've been making my decisions for me from the beginning, telling me how it's going to be between us without giving me a choice, just like everyone else." She pauses, shaking her head. "Maybe you don't understand, but after everything I've been through when I was sick, I can't live like that anymore."

"Ella..."

Ignoring me, she continues, "I've told you before I refuse to let everyone else make my decisions for me, saying they know what's best for me. Every time someone else chooses for me, I'm the one who is forced to live with the consequences, and I refuse to do that anymore! Life is too short! I will regret it if I don't take advantage of as much time as I can with you. I choose you, Grant!"

I gasp, slightly stunned as she pauses, taking a deep breath as she stares into my eyes. She chooses me, no matter the price.

She wipes away her tears, begging me to understand. "Don't rip away my chance to choose what I want like everyone else! Taking away my choice would hurt me more than anything else you could ever do to me."

Her words leave me breathless. I stare into her eyes, feeling like I've been thrown into the abyss and she's there trying to save me again. "Angel," I mumble, my forehead dropping to hers, knowing I'm relenting. I can't say no; I'll do anything for her.

She's right. I can't take her choice away from her; that's one thing I refuse to do. She may hate me if she knew my history, my story, but I won't be the man who takes away her choice. I feel both worthless and like the luckiest asshole in the world with my decision, giving her the power to choose, no matter its impact.

"I choose you, Grant," she repeats, staring into my eyes. "No matter how long you'll be here with me, I choose you. And if anything you've ever said to me is true like you claim, at least let me choose!"

My heart thrashes against my ribcage, and I gulp down the lump in my throat, terrified for what could happen after this, but it needs to happen, for her. Taking a deep breath, I force myself to mumble words that are so much harder than she can imagine, giving her the control of our temporary future, "I choose you. What do you want, Ella?"

44

Ella

HOPE RINGS IN MY EARS AS I REPEAT HIS WORDS IN MY head, making sure I heard him right, *"I choose you. What do you want, Ella?"*

My heart pounds like a jackhammer against my ribcage, making it feel like it's about to burst. I pull him closer, attempting to catch my breath before I answer his question. "I want you, Grant," I rasp, barely able to get the words out.

Pushing forward, I press my mouth to his, my lips tingling the moment we touch. I poke my tongue out, licking the seam of his lips, begging for entrance. His mouth parts, giving me access as a soft whimper escapes my mouth. Tilting my head further, I attempt to deepen the kiss, but he pulls back, not allowing it. "Grant," I mumble, my breaths coming out in quick pants, "I thought there was no more holding back?" I question desperately.

He shakes his head, the corners of his lips curving up in amusement. "I promise I'm not holding back anymore. I couldn't even if I wanted to, but I don't. But I think there's something to be said for a little patience. Don't you?" he teases.

I feel myself blush from head to toe, and he grins with a twinkle in his eyes, letting me know he got what he was after. "I bet I could make you speed things up," I taunt, licking my lips. Reaching down, I lift the hem of my shirt.

"I know you could without even trying," he emphasizes with a growl.

"Well, then, let me try."

He laughs as he stands, scooping me up into his arms and cradling me against his chest before I have a chance to react. My hands wrap around his neck, and I hold on, my shirt falling back around my waist. "Not yet." I frown, making him laugh harder. "You're adorable when you don't get your way."

"There's that word again."

"I like it," he growls, nipping at my lower lip.

"Should you be lifting me? I don't want you to hurt yourself; your casts just came off," I remind him. Although, I like being here in his arms. He's never held me like this, but the last thing I want is for him to push himself too far, especially because of me.

"I don't plan on getting hurt. Think of it as my kind of physical therapy," he suggests, smirking. "I'm taking you to your bed. I want to see you spread out underneath me as I lick every inch of your skin."

Breathless, I rasp, "Well, you're not going to hear any more arguments from me." I press my face into his neck and inhale his salty, masculine scent. My tongue shoots out, wanting a taste. I lick him in short strokes from his collarbone to his ear and nibbling his lobe.

Suddenly, I'm on my back and he's hovering over me, his tongue delving into my mouth, searching for its mate. My tongue meets his, licking and twisting, fighting for dominance, at the same time, not caring who has it. I moan into his mouth, needing more and at the same time feeling like it's too much. My hands weave into his hair, holding on and tugging him towards me, desperate for a way to get closer. Tilting his head, he dives deeper as my body vibrates with need.

My hands slide down his back, giving his ass a light squeeze before I move them up, grasping the hem of his shirt and tugging it upwards. "Off," I grunt over his lips, the only word I'm able to force out between kisses, between breaths.

Tearing his mouth away, he leans up, pulling his shirt over his head with one hand and throwing it on the floor, instantly returning to my lips. I've never seen him move that fast. He reaches for the bottom of my shirt, attempting to do the same. "Sit up," he urges, swiftly tugging my shirt over my head, immediately followed by my bra, tossing both onto the floor. His eyes sweep over my body, bringing color to my exposed skin. "I love when you blush," he murmurs under his breath. "So beautiful." Pausing, he looks me in the eyes, holding my gaze. "Angel, you are so damn sexy, you honestly take my breath away."

His words prompt a quick intake of air, while my heart skips a beat. Slowing our pace, he leans towards me, kissing me deeper, our tongues moving with their own sensual rhythm in a slow dance. His hand glides up my side and around my breast, swirling inwards and grazing my nipple, eliciting a soft whimper from my lips.

My hands skate over his shoulders, down his back and up, exploring his body as he breaks our kiss. He looks into my eyes, his liquid gold irises filled with lust. He tips his head down, brushing his lips along my jaw and down my neck, licking my skin at the hollow. Taking his time, he continues kissing and licking a trail down to my chest, his hand moving to the other side as his mouth takes over. His tongue follows his lips as he kisses and licks my breast, slowly working his way to my taut peak. He sucks my nipple into his mouth, his tongue twirling around as he sucks again, repeatedly flicking it with his tongue. "You taste so sweet."

Reflexively, I arch my back, pushing my chest towards him, the tingling sensation of my breasts feeling like it's too much and at the same time, not enough. "Grant," I gasp.

He rolls my nipple between his teeth and sucks, releasing it with a pop. Glancing at me, he licks his lips, hungry for more. He moves to the other side without hesitation, giving it the same attention. My hands return to his hair, moving back and forth, grasping and tugging, more desperate for him by the moment.

Slowly, he runs his hand down between my legs, his fingers skimming over my core through my jeans. His hand cups my pussy, applying pressure with his palm. "Too many clothes," I mutter, barely comprehending my own words, but knowing what I want.

He releases my other breast with a pop and glances at me, grinning. "I agree." I watch as he leans up, unbuttoning my jeans before tugging down the zipper. He stands and I reach down, arching my body off the bed as I help him shimmy them down my legs before he tugs them off and drops them without thought. Pausing to take me in, he licks his lips and groans, mumbling incoherently under his breath. Reaching towards me, he slips his fingers into the sides of my black lace underwear and eases them down my body, tossing them to the floor as he stares, his eyes roaming every inch of my body.

Ready to climb back on, he moves his knee to the bed, but I lean back on my elbow and put a hand up, halting him as I shake my head. "No," I insist instantly bringing him to a halt. "I wasn't just talking about me. Your jeans need to come off, now," I demand.

His body relaxes as he gives me a crooked smile. He chuckles. "Yes, Ma'am." I watch him closely, my mouth watering as he unbuttons and unzips his jeans before shoving them down and kicking them off onto the floor. It's almost surreal to see him like this with no casts as a barrier between us, but then again, it is a first for us.

"Boxers too," I add, grinning salaciously.

"Very demanding, aren't we?" He gives me his crooked smile that leaves me breathless as he steps out of his simple black boxers, adding them to the pile and returns to the bed, climbing over me. As he brushes my hair away from my face, he caresses my cheek. Pressing his lips to mine, he kisses me, moaning into my mouth, the vibrations giving me goose bumps and heating me to my core. His hand skims down my body, leaving a trail of fire, before brushing over my core.

My hips buck up, reflexively searching for his touch. "Grant," I beg, unable to put my thoughts into words.

"Tell me what you want," he demands, but all I can do is whimper in response and kiss him again. He caresses the inside of my thigh and slides his fingers over my folds to my clit, circling it briefly. He slips one finger inside, then two. "Fuck, you're wet," he groans, breaking our kiss. I lick my lips, savoring his taste. "I love how fucking wet you are for me, Angel," he mumbles as he moves his fingers in and out of me at a torturously slow pace.

My head falls back as his mouth returns to my breasts, lavishing them with attention as he continues his slow assault on my pussy. I arch my body off the bed, pushing my breasts towards his mouth and my core towards his hand. "More, I need more," I plead. As my breathing picks up, so does his pace, his fingers slip in, curling towards my g-spot inside while his thumb rubs my juices over my clit, rubbing in slow, deliberate circles.

He lifts his head, his free hand going to my nipple, rolling the rigid tip between his thumb and forefinger as he watches me. "That's it, Angel," he encourages. "Cum for me." He pinches my nipple and my clit, while curling two fingers inside me.

"Ahh," I moan, barely breathing. An inferno burns in my belly as my vision blurs and darkens, just before I fall over the edge, the inside walls of my core, squeezing and clenching his fingers over and over again in a hard spasm, vibrating through all of me. I huff a breath as I slowly come down from my climax, my body loosening and relaxing into the mattress.

After a few controlled breaths, I become aware of his fingers gently caressing my cheek, bringing me back to the present. My eyes slowly flutter open, focusing on the gorgeous man looking down at me with awe and need. "Grant," I whisper his name, overflowing with emotion. My chest remains tight as I look into his golden eyes.

He grins, satisfied with my response. "You are the sexiest thing I've ever seen when you cum," he declares licking his lips.

My eyes drift to his chin as I feel my body heat in embarrassment, although I honestly don't know how after we just shared something like that. He chuckles softly, mumbling under his breath, "Damn, Ella. You have no idea what you do to me." Sealing his declaration, he tips his head down, pressing his lips to mine, kissing me tenderly, and prompting me to be ready for more.

45

I'M SO OVERWHELMED WITH THIS WOMAN. MY ENTIRE BODY tingles in anticipation and need with every look, every sound, every damn touch. I caress her cheek, watching her as she comes back to reality, her eyes sparkling as she looks into mine. A grin tugs at my lips. "You are the sexiest thing I've ever seen when you cum."

Her eyes lower as her skin turns a beautiful shade of pink. Damn, I love it when she blushes. Chuckling softly, I mumble under my breath, "Damn, Ella. You have no idea what you do to me." I press my lips to hers, kissing her tenderly to let her know how I feel without words I don't know if I will ever be able to express.

As I break our kiss, I look down at her and bring my other hand to my mouth, licking my fingers clean one by one as she watches me, her eyes widening. I press my lips to her now plump ones. Groaning, she kisses me back with fervor, urging me on. Her hand falls to my chest as she nudges me back. Afraid to push her too far, I lift my head and look down at her gorgeous form, her blonde hair splayed out beneath her like a halo, making her look like the angel she is.

"Grant," she whispers, my name a desperate plea on her lips. The soft sound sends a shock right through me.

"What do you want, Angel?" I repeat the same question as

before, not wanting to assume a damn thing.

"I want you, Grant," she reiterates with confidence as she gives me a gentle tug towards her. Her words alone overwhelm me.

"I love hearing you say that."

She grins and drags her lower lip through her teeth. I lean down, sucking it into my mouth. She giggles as I release it and gives a light shake of her head. "Do you have a condom?" she asks, breathily.

Nodding, I mumble, "Yeah, in the other room."

"Go," she urges, making me chuckle.

"Okay." Leaning in, I give her a chaste kiss before pushing off the bed. "I'll be right back." I stride towards the door without grabbing any clothes. Why bother? Hobbling across the hall, I feel her eyes on me. Pausing, I glance back at her and offer her a cheeky grin, hoping to see her blush. "Are you staring at my ass, Ella?"

Her eyes widen and she grins. "Yes," she squeaks, her cheeks and other parts of her turning that beautiful shade of red I love so much.

Chuckling softly, I continue into the guest room, grabbing a box of condoms from the nightstand and rushing right back to her. I set the box down on her nightstand, opening it and pulling one out, setting it down on the bed next to her. "Here," I murmur, wanting her to know she has control of what happens between us.

She reaches up towards me, her hands gliding up and down my arms, leaving a burning trail in her wake. Searching for another reaction, I playfully taunt, "You can look and touch all you want, Angel." She blushes a deeper shade of red, heat pouring off her, giving me what I want. "I know I'm going to as long as you'll let me."

"Please."

My hands skim up her thighs, and then my fingers graze over her folds. Bending over, I lean towards her, my tongue following the same path, causing me to moan in satisfaction at the salty and sweet taste of her velvety skin. "Mm."

"Grant, please, no more foreplay. I just want you," she insists, nudging my shoulders back. "I need you."

Pausing, I look at her to make sure I'm reading her right, but I see nothing but confidence and desire in her eyes. As I lick my lips in anticipation, I reach for the condom, all my blood instantly going to my cock. She watches me with wide eyes as I rip open the plastic. I toss the wrapper on the nightstand and swiftly roll the condom onto my hard cock, leaving room in the tip for my inevitable load.

I crawl back over her body like a predator about to devour my prey and adjust myself at her entrance. Stopping, I look into her sparkling blue eyes, now a darker shade. I reach up, brushing her hair out of her face and kiss her lips tenderly, barely able to hold myself back, but knowing I need to. Maintaining her gaze I ask the question, hoping for the words I need to hear, "Ella, are you sure this is what you want?"

She takes a moment to calm her breaths before she speaks, staring intently back at me. "I know this with you is exactly what I want. I've never wanted anyone more than I want you right now. You are what I want, Grant." Her words cause my heart to skip a beat before it soars. Hearing those words from her sweet lips sets my body ablaze. I'm practically vibrating with need and desperate to claim her as mine.

Readjusting, I line up at her entrance again. As I lick my lips, I take a deep breath to calm myself down, hoping to make this last when I already feel like I'm about to explode. The things this woman does to me has my body overreacting to every little thing, and I need to figure out how to handle it. Slowly, I start to push in and she gasps, instantly tightening her hold on my biceps, causing me to freeze, my entire body taut. "Are you okay?"

She takes a deep breath and smiles, opening her eyes, she looks up at me with a look I don't understand. As she exhales, she bends her knees, one at a time, skimming them against my sides as she lifts them and wraps her legs around my back. I grit my teeth, holding my breath and trying not to move as I wait for her verbal response. "I'm absolutely fabulous," she murmurs breathlessly.

Her words send chills down my spine, forcing me to exhale harshly and prompting me to thrust all the way inside with one quick movement. I groan, loving the way her head falls back in ecstasy, while she takes me in, squeezing me. "Ella, you're so tight. You feel so fucking good. I don't know how long I can last," I mumble, forcing out the words.

"That's okay."

"It's not, but I want you to cum again first," I insist, brushing my lips against hers. Leaning up, I pull out, and swiftly thrust in again, going deeper. I let out an involuntary growl as she moans, her fingers digging into my back as she arches her hips off the bed, meeting my next thrust. Needing a better angle, I readjust, wanting to hit her g-spot. I watch her face for her reactions as I continue moving and smile salaciously the moment I succeed, my hips thrusting harder and faster. My head tilts down, sucking her nipple into my mouth and letting it go, watching it bounce back. "So good," I rumble, my insides burning deep in my core and I struggle to hold myself back.

"More," she groans.

"You want more?" I repeat breathlessly. I tilt back a little more and continue thrusting. My hand, beginning to shake, slips between us, finding her clit. I brush my thumb back and forth over it, as I continue pushing myself inside. Her pussy feels like liquid fire, burning through as it squeezes my cock with each thrust. *Ella first, Ella first*, I repeat in my head, struggling to hold myself back from my release.

"Grant," she mumbles, desperately panting my name. "Grant, I'm...I'm going to...I'm going to cum," she gasps in warning.

I thrust harder, putting more pressure on her clit. Both of us groan, the sounds of skin slapping against skin echoing in the room. "Fuck, Ella," I groan as I feel the first tight squeeze of her orgasm around my cock.

"Grant," she screams my name as she arches her hips towards me, attempting to hold them there as her insides repeatedly clench me tight.

She squeezes me one more time and I feel her body begin to relax as she slowly comes down from her high. My hand moves from her clit to her hip as I thrust in again and again. My vision flashes white, as my body bursts, exploding and releasing right behind her.

Heaving a satisfied sigh, I collapse on top of her, careful not to crush her. "Wow," she murmurs.

"You got that right, but I'll make it better next time." That was faster than I'd hoped, but also like nothing I've ever experienced. How is that even possible?

She laughs in response. "That's never...I mean, I've never... while having sex before," she stammers awkwardly, her skin heating, turning beautifully pink.

I lift my head, my eyes wide with surprise. "You've never had an orgasm during sex?" I say the words, watching her turn a deeper shade of red. "Really?" I smirk.

She huffs a laugh. "Don't get too cocky."

"You always cum first," I say with a mischievous grin. "No matter how hard it is."

She rolls her eyes at my innuendo and giggles, the light sound making my heart clench. I tilt my head down and give her a chaste kiss. "I'll be right back. I need to get rid of the condom." I want her to know I'm not leaving, but I'm glad for the excuse, needing a moment to myself.

She nods and I pull out of her, immediately feeling the loss. I stand up, rolling off the condom and tying it off as I walk into the bathroom. I toss it in the garbage can and wash my hands, trying to process what happens now. I've never felt that much during sex before, but I can't tell her that. More than anything, I don't want to hurt her. I'll just do what I can to take care of her while I'm here. I don't know what else to do. It feels like I'm constantly fucking up, but there's no way I can say no to her.

Grabbing a washcloth, I run it under warm water, twisting out the excess. Taking one more deep breath, I attempt to relax and make my way back to Ella. I find her with the sheet pulled up and tucked underneath her arms, her soft ivory skin on display. Holding up the washcloth, I mumble, "Let me clean you up."

Her eyes widen, but she gives me a small nod in acknowledgment. I tug the sheet down, my heart speeding up at the sight of her naked body. Gulping hard, I attempt to focus on the task at hand. She watches me as I reach up, gently wiping between her legs before I toss the washcloth on the pile of clothes on the floor. "Thank you," she murmurs, blushing.

I grin, loving that look on her as I cover her back up with the sheet, as much for my own sanity as hers. Slowly, I lay down next to her, reaching out for her. Grabbing onto her hips, I roll her onto me, draping her body across my chest. I close my eyes and inhale deeply, savoring her soft scent mixed with sex as I press a kiss to the top of her head.

As I open my eyes, I run my fingers through her silky hair, watching as her eyes flutter closed. She appears exhausted, content and truly happy. I like that. I wouldn't mind being the one to put that look on her face every day of her life, but I don't deserve that kind of happiness. Besides, I don't think she would be here if she knew. With my chest tight, I stare at her flushed cheeks, the whisker burn along her collarbone and her kiss-swollen lips, wondering how I got so lucky and knowing it can never last because of me; because of my past.

From the moment she saved my life, I should've known I was fucked. I've never met anyone like her, my angel. My fall, when it comes to her, seems to be inevitable. But I deserve it.

Now, I just need to find a way to protect her from me.

46

I BEGIN WAKING UP, MY MIND STILL FOGGY WITH MY DREAMS, Grant at the forefront of my mind. I'm warm and too comfortable to move, but I see the sun shining even through my closed eyelids, urging me to wake. With a soft sigh, I let my eyes slowly flutter open and take in my familiar surroundings with an unfamiliar but wonderful twist. A soft gasp escapes my lips, and I quickly snap my mouth shut, not wanting to wake up Grant. I smile to myself, my heart full and happy my dreams from last night are a reality.

I'm draped over Grant's chest with his arm wrapped protectively around me. I lift my head and rest my chin on my hand, in the middle of his chest, looking up at his sleeping form. He appears so calm and peaceful as if he has no worries and all the time in the world to be here with me. I'd be happy waking up like this with him every day. I exhale slowly and turn my head, resting my cheek on his hard chest. A smile pulls at my lips as I listen to the steady beat of his heart, the continuous soft thumping soothing me.

My thoughts drift back to last night and I feel myself blush as my smile grows. I've never felt that good or that desperate when I'm with someone, but Grant seems to have a way of overwhelming my senses and putting me over the edge. My insides quiver, thinking about what he does to my body and what I want to try with him. With just a look from him I feel sexy, desired, and confident, vibrating with need for him. Everything about it is surreal to me.

The way he looked at me as if I might disappear at any moment, combined with the way he kisses me as if he may never have another chance, and the way he touches me like I'm a dream come true has me filling up with hope, happiness and admittedly even love. What we have together feels explosive, but it also leaves me feeling giddy with the kind of happiness I fought for even before I knew the man that could help me get to that place—this man. He makes me strive to be more for me and want to do everything he'll let me do for him, as I'm finding, he needs his independence as much as I need mine. I think that's part of the reason we understand each other so well. My insides tingle in anticipation of what could be if he continues giving us a chance.

I recognize I may be setting myself up for heartbreak, especially when he continues to insist he will be leaving, but he doesn't seem to be in a hurry to go, at least not yet, and his casts are now gone. Realistically, he could leave any day, but I can't let him slip through my fingers without trying. I'll deal with the repercussions when or if he goes, but I need to take the chance.

Things could be different if he would only allow it to happen. Until then, I'll savor all my time with him and hope he changes his mind because more than anything I want him to choose to stay. I want him to choose us, to choose me.

My fingers lightly trace the thorns on his chest, attempting to push away my thoughts and focus on today, a day off. I want to spend the day with Grant; hopefully he'll want the same. I know he has therapy, but besides, I wonder what we could do. Maybe I can get him to go out on the water with me. I'm sure he would like it. I grimace, thinking it might not be very easy until he's able to get his leg stronger, giving him more balance. Balance is kind of key to paddleboarding; I guess I'll wait on that suggestion. I'm sure he'll want to go for another ride on his motorcycle.

Grant begins shifting under me, and I quickly push away my thoughts. He mumbles something I can't comprehend under his breath. The feel and sound of his heartbeat picks up its pace, pounding harder as the beats become erratic under my cheek. Then, he flinches and groans as if in pain, his body going taut. "No."

I gasp and lift my head, gently caressing his chest where my head had just been lying, trying to calm his growing anxiety. "It's okay, Grant. I'm right here. It's just a dream," I whisper repeatedly, attempting to help.

"No, no, no," he grumbles, groggily.

Suddenly, he jerks away from me, shoving me out of his arms, startling me as I fall back on the bed. "Ah!" I yelp in surprise.

"No!" he repeats a little louder. His eyes fly open and he sits up, scrambling back and looking around, his orbs wide and frantic as he gasps for breath. His eyes settle on me and he locks onto my gaze. I watch a flurry of emotions quickly pass through his eyes from fear and agony to relief, embarrassment, and regret; an emotion I know all too well.

I can't help but wince, hoping it's not me giving him most of those emotions. His eyes truly are a window to his soul.

"It's okay," I repeat.

"Angel," he whispers.

My heart aches seeing him look so lost and vulnerable. I want to reach out to him, but I'm afraid he'll reject me in his state and pull away again. That's the last thing I want.

"Grant," I mumble, hesitantly. "I think you were having a bad dream," I tell him what he already knows, hoping he'll talk to me about it. "Are you okay?"

He grimaces and blurts out, "I'm fine."

"It's okay to have bad dreams," I murmur, maintaining a soothing tone.

"I said I'm fine, Ella!" he snaps, making me flinch. He winces at his own reaction and sighs heavily, running his hand through his hair in frustration. Taking a deep breath, he exhales slowly and apologizes. "I'm sorry, Ella. I warned you, I'm fucked up," he mutters under his breath as he shakes his head in disgust.

I reach out for him, my hand cautiously sliding down his arm until I reach his hand, covering it and giving it a light squeeze in encouragement. "We all have our baggage, Grant. Let me help you carry your load."

He shakes his head dismissively, not even glancing in my direction. "I told you, I'm not good for you."

"That's not true." Biting my lip, I scoot closer, flipping my hand around and underneath his, I link my fingers with his. He looks down at our joined hands, staring at them as if puzzled. "What was your dream about?" I ask, gently urging him to open up.

He shakes his head as if pulling himself out of the fog and glances at me before returning his gaze to our hands. "You don't want to know."

"I do," I argue.

As he runs his hand down his face, he scoots further back against the headboard. I move with him, both of us remaining quiet for a few minutes, lost in thought. I sit close to him, holding his hand and waiting patiently, letting him know I'm here for him in any way he needs. He finally opens his mouth and huffs a humorless laugh. "You really don't."

"I do. I want to be here for you. It doesn't matter to me what it is. I just want you to know I'm here for you."

Sighing again, he rubs his hand over his face and shakes his head in disbelief. "This is part of my dark, Ella. My past is pretty fucking dark." I give his hand another squeeze in both encouragement and support, remaining silent. "I'll admit I made a catastrophic mistake a long time ago, and then I made a lot more trying to deal with it or fix it. I've been paying for it repeatedly ever since," he grumbles, his voice sounding hollow.

After a while of watching him stare mutely into space, I realize he's not going to continue. Taking a deep breath, I decide to speak, hoping he doesn't shut me out, and at the same time, grateful he's still here. "Everyone makes mistakes, Grant. Even if whatever is haunting you is something that can't be fixed, maybe if you talk about it, maybe that will help you figure out a way to find some peace."

He shakes his head in denial, his expression tortured. "Not with this," he proclaims confidently. "I won't ever have peace, but I accepted it a long time ago." I watch his Adam's apple bob up and down as he attempts to gulp down the lump in his throat.

"Everyone deserves to be happy, Grant."

Ignoring my comment, he shakes his head. "I'll keep my promise to you, Ella, because I would do absolutely anything for you, but you need to know, I will never be good enough for you."

"Grant," I murmur, shaking my head, immediately dismissing his comments. I hate seeing him like this. Even if he won't talk to me, I wish he would at least let me be here for him.

"It's true, Angel," he emphasizes, interrupting me. "You're too damn good for me, and that's just the way it is," he states with conviction. "You deserve to be happy, and I'll always end up bringing you down or holding you back. That would only make me hate myself more."

"That's not true. I love spending time with you, and you make me feel like I could do anything." He gives me a sad smile as if my words are only to appease him, but that's so far from the truth.

My chest aches, my heart breaking for him, desperately wishing he would let me in so I could help. Whatever it is, I know we could tackle it together if he'd allow it. He gave me such a small piece of his past, without really giving me anything at all. I may not know what happened to him or the kinds of nightmares that are eating at his insides, but I can guarantee it's all killing him from the inside out. I need to figure out a way to find out what happened to him and help put it to rest, but I have no idea where to begin.

47

Grant

WE RETURN TO THE SMALL PATIENT EXAM ROOM, MY LEG and arm both sore from my workout. I scoot up on the wooden exam table covered with an ugly teal cushion, the thick strip of white sanitary paper down the middle for protection crackling loudly with every move I make. I glance up at Ella and smile as Laine sets me up with the TENS unit to stimulate my muscles on my leg. It basically sends electrical impulses through electrodes placed on my skin. It's incredibly surreal to both feel and watch your own muscles repeatedly contracting and relaxing when you're not doing anything to instigate the reaction.

"Thank you for letting me come with you today," Ella murmurs, watching my leg muscles start to jump. "That's so strange." She giggles.

"It feels weird too," I concur, chuckling. "And of course, I don't mind you coming with me. Although, I still haven't quite figured out why you wanted to." I smirk, arching my eyebrow in question. After the way we woke up this morning, I can't believe she's still here and putting up with my shit. "I'm sure it's not much fun for you just watching me go through all this crap," I complain, gesturing to the pads on my body.

"I don't mind." She shrugs like it's no big deal. "I think it's interesting. Plus, I like knowing what you're doing every day, and now I can picture it," she claims, surprising me with her simple answer. She leans towards me and whispers conspiratorially, "And I didn't mind watching you work out, either. It got me hot for later."

Laine's eyes widen and he arches his eyebrows, letting me know I'm not the only one who heard her comment. I chuckle and glance at Ella, her cheeks suddenly dark pink with embarrassment as she glances towards Laine, comprehending it too. "Um...I mean..." she stammers, trailing off as she realizes there's no fixing that one.

"Anyway," Laine mumbles, respectfully ignoring her comment, "your arm is healing fast, but we still have some work to do on it to strengthen it and balance you out. As you probably know, your leg still has quite a ways to go, but we'll reassess everything in a couple weeks after you get some more work in."

"Got it."

"I'll be back in a few minutes. Try to sit and relax the best you can with the machine working you." The corners of his lips, twitch up, clearly amused. "I just want to check on one of my patients I left with one of the other therapists really quick."

"No problem," I mumble, knowing I'm not going anywhere anyway. "Thanks," I add before he walks out the door.

The moment the door clicks shut, Ella glances at me and prods, "How are you feeling?"

I smirk and arch my eyebrows in challenge, knowing that's a question she hates hearing. She scrunches her nose up adorably and ducks her head in realization, the color returning to her cheeks. "Sorry."

Chuckling, I murmur, "It's okay. I love seeing you blush." Her cheeks heat further, making me grin. Finally responding, I admit, "I'm doing okay. I'm a little sore, but I'll be fine, and it's better every day. It feels damn good to be moving again like normal. I still feel a little off-balance, or uneven, but all this shit seems to help."

She nods. "Good." She tilts her head to the side and licks her lips, assessing me, making me wonder where her mind is headed, while mine instantly dives towards the gutter. Her lips quirk up in amusement as she confesses, "It's actually a little weird for me to see you walking. That's new for me."

I laugh in response and attempt to shake away my naked thoughts. That's not at all where I believed she was going with that sexy look on her face. "I get it. It's kinda surreal knowing you've never seen me walk before." She laughs, shrugging. I shake my head, conceding, "It's still crazy for me to think about all the simple things I took for granted before my accident. I honestly don't know what I would've done without you."

Ella blushes. "I'm glad I can be there for you."

"Me too."

A loud bang echoes down the hallway, causing Ella to gasp and stiffen, bringing both our gazes to the door in curiosity. Several heavy footsteps stomp quickly down the hall, followed by what sounds like doors rapidly opening and closing. "What are you doing? Ma'am, you can't be back here! Ma'am, excuse me, I said you can't be back here and you can't go in there! You need to stay out of the patient rooms! I need help! Will someone please call security?" we hear a woman yell from somewhere down the hall.

Ella pales instantly and slowly inches towards me, quickly linking her fingers with mine, her anxiety written all over her face. My stomach twists with concern, needing to protect her. I reach around her back with my free hand and wrap it around her, pulling her close to me attempting to comfort her. "It's okay, Angel. I'm right here, and I promise I wouldn't let anything happen to you." I'd die first to protect her. I press my lips to her temple as I caress her arm up and down in support.

A soft gasp comes from the doorway, prompting both of us to turn towards the sound. A woman dressed in black capri pants and a white, ribbed, V-neck shirt with light brown hair and tear-filled, soft, familiar golden-brown eyes encircled with wrinkles and bags underneath stands in the doorway holding her trembling hand to her mouth. She has a thin, petite build, adding to her frail, tired appearance. "It is you," she cries.

I gasp at the sound of her voice, my heart dropping into my stomach like dead weight as I stare at the woman. I'm suddenly frozen in place, feeling like I'm going to be sick. I struggle to take a breath as I feel all my blood drain from my face, leaving me cold. She looks like she's been through hell and back again, but it's her. "Mom?" I rasp, barely able to utter the word.

"Grant!" she sobs, her shoulders shaking. She stumbles into the room and throws her arms around me, squeezing me tight. "It is you. It's really you. My baby," she sobs hysterically, collapsing against my chest.

All the chaos going on around me quickly becomes muf-fled. I'm unable to move, my arms frozen as I sit completely stunned, feeling as if I'm in a fog and this moment is anything but real. As I take a deep breath, I bring my gaze to Ella's. My mouth hangs slightly open while I continue clinging desper-ately to her hand as if it's my only lifeline. I feel a few tears escape out of the corners of my eyes, leaving a trail down my cheeks, overwhelmed and completely at a loss. What...the... fuck.

Ella's free hand flies to her mouth, covering it in shock as she stares at the scene in front of her—a scene even I'm not able to process. I finally force myself to lift my arm from around Ella's back and slide it around my mom to return her hug, without letting go of Ella's hand. I can't let go; I need her strength to get me through this moment.

A blur of movement out of the corner of my eye distracts me, dragging my attention away from the woman who raised me. I turn my head in what feels like slow-motion and I'm met with another overpowering sight. A man stands in the doorway in khaki pants, a light gray button-up shirt with the sleeves rolled up and the top button open. He appears older than the last time I saw him with his dark hair now peppered with shades of gray, and his familiar green eyes, now surrounded by a few wrinkles stare back at me with astonishment, relief, exhaustion, and deep-seated pain.

Unfortunately, every bit of that falls directly on me.

An intimidating, broad, bald man, standing at about six-feet, three-inches and wearing a black security uniform stalks into the room, pulling me out of my daze and back to reality. I hold my hand up from around my mom and shake my head at him, gulping hard before I attempt to speak. "It's okay, they're my parents," I declare, my voice hoarse.

My mom continues to sob against my chest, nearly inconsolable, as my dad finally steps into the room. Cautiously, he approaches us, wrapping his arms around us both and murmuring something into my head that I'm too stunned to even hear.

I feel Ella try to move away to give us our moment, but I can't do this without her. So, I tug her hand closer, gripping it tighter and holding it against my heart, not able to let her go. My automatic reflex telling me more about how far I've fallen for this woman, no matter how hard I've tried to maintain my emotional distance. I grimace at the irony; my realization comes just in time for all my shit to be brought to the table and laid out in front of her. It won't be long before my past sends her running far away from me.

Ella

SITTING ON THE BACK OF GRANT'S MOTORCYCLE WITH MY arms wrapped tightly around his stiff frame, I lean my head against his back, completely stunned as I continue going over the scene I just witnessed in my head, attempting to process.

Grant hasn't spoken. He hasn't said a single word since he claimed they were his parents. He just continued clinging to my hand as if begging me not to leave him. Little does he know that's the last thing I want to do. I'm thankful I could be there for him. It's ironic they showed up today; the first time I accompanied him to one of his appointments since he left the hospital, but I just had this feeling I needed to be there for him after the way we woke up, and I'm grateful I went.

I have no idea what happened to all of them. So many what-ifs keep running through my mind. I'm completely at a loss. He said his family was no longer around, but I didn't think this is what he meant.

How deep of a hole is he in? Is he in trouble? What is he running from? I can't even fathom all the endless possibilities, but an array of nightmares continue going through my head. I'm almost desperate for him to talk to me. Whatever it is, I want to help him, but without any answers, I'm so confused and feel utterly helpless while he seems so lost. I hate it.

The smell of the salt air indicates we're getting close to

home. Carefully, I peer around him, realizing my house is only a few blocks away. I glance behind us, his dad driving a white Ford Edge, his hands tightly gripping the steering wheel as his mom sits in the passenger seat, appearing as if she's still crying, but I wouldn't blame her.

Thankfully, the other patients seemed understanding and security didn't have to do anything; plus, I'm grateful Laine let us stay in the room until everyone calmed down enough to drive home. Watching Grant's mom clinging to him, afraid to let go, terrified he would disappear, was overwhelming. It broke my heart to watch his dad nearly pry her off Grant, while Grant looked on, appearing helpless, defeated, and weighed down with guilt. I've never felt so powerless in my life, and with my history, that's saying a lot. The only way they could get her to agree to let him go and follow behind was if I gave her my address and phone number in case we got separated. Even then, she tested my number immediately, verifying the connection. But with the way Grant's driving, keeping up with him hasn't been an issue.

We pull into the driveway and he parks his motorcycle right next to my Jeep. I reluctantly release him with a sigh and climb off, fumbling with my helmet. "Come here," he urges, breaking his silence. Unclipping it for me, he sets it down and reaches for me. I close the distance between us as he cradles my face in his hands, tilting my head down to rest on his forehead. "Thank you," he rasps, his voice overflowing with emotion.

My heart clenches. "You don't have to thank me. I just want you to know that I'm here. Please let me be here for you." I hope this isn't the beginning of our end. I'm not ready for him to let me go. I don't want him to leave.

He nods, almost imperceptibly, although I'm not sure if it's in acknowledgment or acceptance. He tips his head forward and presses his lips to mine. I push towards him, needing to be closer as our lips move in a slow, sensual rhythm, shooting shivers down my spine. Everything about this kiss feels different somehow; it feels like more.

Slowly, he pulls back, breaking our kiss. He looks into my eyes, his own showing so much vulnerability, making it difficult to breathe. "This isn't going to be an easy conversation," he warns, grimacing.

As I nod in understanding, I hold his gaze, proclaiming, "I will stay right by your side. I promise I'm not going anywhere." As long as he doesn't want me to go. I hope he doesn't.

Relief washes over his face, instantly followed by mine as he leans in, kissing me again, hard and chaste before he releases me, exhaling harshly. He climbs off his motorcycle and we turn towards the house, making our way up the walkway as his parents get out of their car.

We walk inside, waiting for them to follow and shut the door behind them. He reaches for my hand, entwining our fingers together. I give his hand a gentle squeeze in encouragement as he tugs me to the couch and sits down, pulling me down next to him. It's exactly where I believe I need to be. I wouldn't want to be anywhere else.

"Are you two married?" his mom blurts out, desperate for some insight into her son. She frantically glances back and forth between the two of us, her eyes full of curiosity and at the same time devastation.

My eyes widen and I gasp in surprise, taken aback by her question. For the first time, I recognize the big picture, just how little they know their own son and a touch of the impact it's had on all of them. The reality crushes me. I've only gotten a glimpse of what it's done to him and I can already tell that's only the tip of the iceberg. "What?" I whisper, still processing the question.

"Well, you're living together, right? This is your house?" she probes meekly, suddenly unsure of her own assumption. Then she grimaces and shakes her head in frustration, tears again welling in her eyes.

"Well, sort of," I answer, scrunching up my nose as I think about all the times he told me this was only temporary.

Her eyebrows draw down in confusion. "Sort of?" she echoes shaking her head. "How can you be sort of married?"

Grant huffs a humorless laugh and shakes his head. "No, Mom, we're not married. I should be so lucky," he mutters. My stupid heart flutters with glee at his comment, although it's such a difficult time for him, I don't want to read into anything he says one way or another. "This is Ella," he states, looking at me with pride, making my stomach flip-flop. "She's my girl, and she's my angel. She saved me, and I've been staying here with her in her house ever since."

"What? What do you mean she saved you? What happened?" his dad inquires, fraught for more information.

Grant sighs heavily and runs his free hand through his hair before dropping it on top of our clasped ones. "A couple months ago, a small hurricane hit the coast here," he begins, adding, "I think it was only a level one or something." He pauses shaking his head.

"Only," I huff under my breath. Only he can downplay a hurricane.

"Anyway, I had just left my last job, and I was trying to make my way up the coast. I started looking for a safe place to pull over to wait for the storm to pass through and a strong wind gust got ahold of me, making me feel weightless before my bike dragged me a few feet and I skidded across the ground," he elaborates, matter of fact.

His mom gasps, her hand flying to her mouth in terror at the image probably running through her head. "Grant!"

Ignoring her, he continues, "Ella saw it happen, and she came to my rescue. It was already pouring rain, and the roads were nearly deserted. If it weren't for her, I wouldn't be alive." He glances at me, a flicker of admiration in his eyes. "She's my angel."

My chest clenches at the thought of something happening to him, and my hand falls protectively to my chest, covering my heart. I take a deep breath, attempting to hold myself together as the images from that night flash through my mind. What if... Quickly, I shake my head, trying to rid myself of that nightmare. "I'm thankful I was there," I murmur, barely breathing.

"Me too," he concurs with a stiff smile.

"So, you've only been here for a couple months," his dad surmises, arching his eyebrows in question. "Where were you the ten years before that? Better yet, why did you leave at all?" he challenges, his voice cracking on the last word.

"You really want to know, *Dad*? You really want to know what happened? Where I've been? What I've been doing? And how fucked up my life is?" he taunts, glaring at his father as he shakes his head in disgust, as if his dad is the one to blame. Is he? Grant begins shaking, suddenly looking like he's about to erupt.

I'm not sure I can help, but I'll sure as hell try. I gently squeeze Grant's hand and move myself into his line of sight. "Grant, look at me," I urge, cradling his face in my hands, one hand still gripping his. "Take a deep breath. Slow down and breathe," I prod tenderly, steadily holding his gaze. "Breathe in and out..."

Thankfully, he attempts to do what I ask, breathing in through his nose and out through his mouth a few times before speaking. "I'm good." His pale cheeks, deep breathing and eyes frantically searching mine beg to differ.

"Why don't we take a few minutes and maybe get some water," I suggest, desperate to help him. I don't care how long they've waited; they can wait longer. I don't care about anyone right now, except the man sitting in front of me, and I've never seen him looking so scared and vulnerable. I just wish I knew why.

He nods and rasps, "Yeah." Then he kisses me on the lips and stands, still grasping my hand. Without looking in their direction he tugs me along, and I willingly follow him into the kitchen, hoping he'll let me in.

49

Grant

I GULP A FULL GLASS OF WATER AND SET IT ON THE COUNTER as I take a breath, glancing at Ella. She's everything I fucking need. She feels like my strength right now. Honestly, I don't know if I could do this without her, and that scares the shit out of me. I'm afraid I'll damage her with all my crap. She's so beautiful, inside and out. So perfect.

Time has run out. It's time for my parents to know the truth, and what Ella is going to hear will open her eyes to my ugly, beaten, and battered soul, and I'm terrified I'll either hurt her or she'll run away screaming. I'm honestly not sure what would be better, but I believe our end is inevitable and so close I can taste it, making me sick to my stomach.

"Thank you," I rasp, my chest tight.

She smiles softly as she steps towards me, pressing a tender kiss to my lips. I close my eyes, savoring the feel and taste of her, not sure how long she'll continue to share herself with me. I'll take whatever she's willing to give. She pulls back, resting her hands on my chest as she looks into my eyes. "Grant, if this gets to be too much, they can leave and come back tomorrow," she suggests, uncertain, biting her lower lip.

I gulp down the lump in my throat and nod in agreement. "You're right. Telling them about my recent motorcycle accident was probably the easiest part of the night," I concede, grimacing at the reality of my statement. "There's no way in hell I'll be able to get through everything tonight. It's too damn much." That reality overwhelming me.

"I'll be right by your side," she reiterates, calming my nerves.

I nod in acknowledgment, too scared to ask if she means it. I'm grateful for everything Ella does for me, but I also can't help but wonder how long her words will remain true, despite her intentions. That fear almost seems to be taunting me more than my confession.

Closing my eyes, I take a deep breath, exhaling slowly, attempting to regain my footing. My chest aches as if I just went ten rounds in boxing and lost. I have no idea where to even begin. This is not something they'll want to hear, but I can't run anymore.

Glancing through the doorway, into the living room, I watch as my dad comforts my mom, holding her and rubbing her back. I did that to them. They don't deserve this; I don't deserve them. This whole situation is my fault. Fuck. I heave a sigh, relenting. "We should go back," I whisper, knowing it's the last thing I want to do. "I guess it's time to tell them everything."

"Are you ready?" she prods, her eyes full of empathy.

"I'll never be ready," I mumble, revealing my heartbreaking truth. "Let's go," I urge as she gives me a sad but encouraging smile.

Holding her hand for strength, I force myself to move. We make our way back into the living room and I sit down, immediately pulling Ella close to my side. I look up, watching my parents as my dad eases down onto the arm of the chair my mom's seated in, keeping his arm around her back in support.

"I can't believe we finally found you. We've missed you so much, Grant," my mom whimpers, making me cringe.

"I'm sorry, Mom. I'm so sorry. I never wanted to hurt you. I didn't want to hurt any of you!" I can't believe they've been chasing me since I left, I don't want them to waste any more time on me. I'm not worth it. If confessing everything can't do anything else, at least it can help them realize that ugly truth.

"Then why did you leave without even a goodbye? To us? To Matt? He was absolutely devastated," Mom cries.

"Or even letting us know where you were going?" my dad interrupts.

Grunting, I run my free hand through my hair before dropping it into my lap. "You want to know why I left?" My stomach churns, a storm brewing inside me. "When I finally left, I left to protect everyone I love, especially Matt." I pause, shaking my head, my thoughts whirling. "But there was a shitload of other reasons that piled on before I hit that point. I didn't want to go; I didn't have a choice," I claim, my voice cracking.

"I don't understand," my mom utters, shaking her head, her voice unsteady. She brushes away more tears as she stares at me.

"I know you don't." I take another deep breath, hoping I'll be able to get this out. I glance at Ella out of the corner of my eye, wondering most of all if she will still be by my side supporting me after all this is over, but I'm out of time. This is the end of the road.

"Please," my mom begs for answers.

Again, I run my hand through my hair, flustered, tightly gripping the ends, I groan as I let go. Looking between my mom and dad, I finally ask, my voice surprisingly steady to my own ears, "Do you remember when I told you I'd gotten involved with a woman I shouldn't have, and I didn't know how to get out?"

"Yeah," my dad prods, dragging out the word, his eyebrows drawing down in confusion. "I remember."

"Do you remember me telling you she hit me?" I push, watching him closely.

My dad pales, nodding his head. He gulps hard and whispers hoarsely, "Yes, but when we talked about it and I asked questions, you acted like it could've been an accident. Those were some serious accusations, Grant."

I laugh humorlessly and grumble, "I'm fucking well aware." Grinding my jaw, I steel myself and continue, "Well, I downplayed what she did to me because I felt like an idiot. Anyone I got the courage to try to talk to laughed at me and dismissed my claim as bullshit. So, I stopped trying." I shrug as if it were inevitable.

"Oh, Grant!" my mom whimpers as Ella's hand tightens around mine.

Ignoring them both, I blurt out, "That's when I started drinking and getting high." I huff a humorless laugh and shake my head. "You know the game I fucked up when the scouts were there for me?" I prompt, not waiting for a response. "After the game, I wanted to kill myself. I even thought about how to do it."

"No!" My mom's choked sob echoes as she covers her mouth, and Ella's soft gasp hits me hard in the chest, but I push forward needing to get it out now that I've started.

"I thought getting a football scholarship was my last chance of getting away and escaping my reality."

"You should've come to us!" my mom argues, tears streaming down her face.

"I fucking tried!" I retort, wincing as she flinches away from me. Shaking my head, I attempt to explain what it was like for me. "I was sixteen the first time it happened. She got pissed I didn't show up when I said I would. I went there four hours after I had planned because I went to the bonfire with my friends and had a few beers. She broke a wine bottle over my back that night. I refused to go to the hospital because I'd been drinking and I didn't want to risk getting kicked off the football team or ending up with a record."

"But why would you go back to this woman after that?" my mom questions, her disbelief clear as she desperately tries to understand.

I give her the simple answer. "Blackmail, threats, power." I shake my head in disgust. "Take your pick," I spew bitterly.

"We could've helped you," my dad declares, his own regret and guilt evident in his voice. "I could've helped you," he emphasizes, thinking as a lawyer he can solve most anything.

Shaking my head, I argue, "She had too much on me. Besides, I'm the reason it started in the first place."

"If someone hits you, it's not your fault," my dad insists. "Ever!"

"He's right," Ella whispers from my side, her voice barely audible.

Turning my head, I glance at her, seeing tears in her eyes and the evidence streaking down her cheeks, causing my chest to spasm. I reach up and wipe her tears away with my thumb. "Don't cry for me, Angel. I'm not worth it."

"You're always worth it!" she insists, her tears falling faster.

I shake my head, but I see no point in arguing. Sighing, I turn back to my parents, agreeing with them. "I don't think it was my fault when she hit me. I just didn't see a way out. It was my fault I got involved with her in the first place." With another shake of my head, I run my hand through my hair, overwhelmed with defeat.

"Who was she, Grant?" my dad pushes. "You need to stop protecting her and tell us who the hell she is!"

I huff a sullen laugh and look at him with wide eyes. "You think I'm protecting her? After everything I've been through, you think that's what this is about?"

"What else should we think?" he challenges, narrowing his eyes at me. "You refused to tell us then, and we still don't know who she is now, years later!"

"It's not about protecting her, and it never has been. That bitch can go to hell!" I yell, clenching my free hand into a fist.

"Then what was it about? And who the hell is she?" he repeats.

"At first it was about protecting me and my future, then it was about protecting you, but most of all it was about protecting Matt!"

"What does Matt have to do with this?" he probes, my mom mirroring his expression of bafflement.

"Besides public embarrassment, she also threatened him," I reveal, seething all over again as I say the words aloud.

My mom gasps and my dad rises, beginning to pace back and forth, silently fuming. Suddenly, he halts in front of me and stares into my eyes with his jaw clenched tightly and slowly repeats, "Who is she, Grant?"

Taking a deep breath, I exhale slowly, averting my eyes as I feel my embarrassment and guilt consuming me all over again. "Mrs. Stone," I hoarsely declare, enlightening them as I force the words from my mouth.

My mom wails, releasing another choked sob in pure anguish as my dad's hands clench into fists, his eyes dark with fury. He seethes, clarifying in a deep, gravelly voice, "Mrs. Stone as in Amy's mom? Matt's Amy?"

Instantly dropping my gaze, I gulp down the lump in my throat and nod my head with shame overwhelming me. I attempt to tug my hand away from Ella, but she only holds on tighter, swamping me with hope I know is too damn early to grasp onto.

Tears flood my eyes, and I fight to keep them back as everyone takes in my confession. If I let go, I may never recover.

50

Ella

I'M SO INCREDIBLY HEARTBROKEN AND DEVASTATED FOR THIS man, my entire body aches. How could someone take advantage of him like that? Manipulate and abuse him? Threaten him and his family? Rip away his future? I can't believe people like that even exist, but this beautiful man is living proof, surviving nothing but pure evil. How in the hell could he possibly think any of it is even remotely his fault?

I wipe away my tears, knowing it's a useless effort. I want to help him. I need to help him, but how? My chest aches, feeling like tiny pinpricks poking at me from the inside out. I can't believe there's more to this story, but knowing everything I do about him, and what he has already shared, I know there's so much more that's bound to shatter me; I can only imagine what it's done to him. It's obvious his guilt alone is eating him alive, and for something he shouldn't even feel responsible for; it's not his fault!

After a few minutes of everyone processing Grant's confession, his dad finally breaks the silence, asking, "How?"

He sighs, running his hand through his hair, not meeting anyone's gaze, but thankfully still holding onto my hand. "After Gia and I broke up, I was upset. I was working at the Stones' house, like I did most Sundays. Mrs. Stone was the only one home. I think I was mowing the lawn when she came outside and brought me a bottle of water. She noticed something was wrong and asked if she could help. I told her I was fine, but then, I admitted Gia and I broke up. She insisted I take a break and have a beer with her to talk. Of course, I thought that was a great idea. The next thing I know, we're doing things in her kitchen I didn't plan on," he discloses, looking at our joined hands as if he expects me to pull away. "For a while, she would call me whenever Mr. Stone wasn't home, and like a fucking idiot, I kept going back." He scrunches up his face in disgust, hating himself.

"Weren't you a sophomore when you and Gia broke up?" his mom inquires, speaking up as she wipes her nose with a Kleenex.

He nods, refusing to lift his head. "Yeah."

"You were barely sixteen!" she reiterates, grief stricken. My eyes widen, stunned by the truth. He was a minor and being abused by an older woman in more ways than one, whether he admits it or not. My blood boils, furious at this woman for what she did to him.

He cringes and mumbles his acknowledgment, "I know."

"You're not responsible for any of that! She is! It doesn't matter if you agreed or not, you were too young to give your consent!" she claims.

"I knew what I was doing," he argues, trying to shoulder the blame. My hand tightens around his, wanting to tell him it's not his fault, but knowing he won't listen, especially right now. He's been running for so long, and this whole time, he only needed someone to listen to him, fight for him and protect him. He didn't deserve any of this. My stomach twists into knots, knowing how much he lost.

"You were only sixteen!" she repeats. "She knew what she was doing, and she had no right! She seduced you and stole my baby."

"Your mom is right, Grant. Even the law is on your side," his dad reiterates.

"What side?" he retorts in disbelief. "The only side I was on was getting laid." I feel myself tense in response, but quickly attempt to force myself to relax. He doesn't need my jealousy adding any pressure to this complicated situation.

"Grant!" his dad admonishes in warning.

"What?" he prompts defiantly. "It's true! I had an affair with a married woman. It doesn't matter how old I was when it happened, especially since at first it was what I wanted!" he argues. "I'm the one who made the stupid decision to pursue it. That's on me!"

"Grant," his dad mumbles his name, shaking his head in disagreement, disappointment, and remorse. "It doesn't matter what you wanted. Since you were a minor, that's a punishable offense. That's the law!"

"I'm the one who started it, and I'm the one who continued it." Ignoring his dad, he resumes, shaking his head, "It doesn't even matter. The problem with her started when I was interested in someone else, and I wanted to end it with her. That's when all the other bullshit came into play, like the blackmail and threats."

I take a deep breath and exhale slowly, preparing for what else he could possibly say after revealing all of that. His confession is breaking me, but not how he thinks it will. I'm livid this happened to him. I hate how much blame he's putting on himself. This isn't his fault. I just have no idea how to convince him he's not culpable.

"Explain it to us," his dad pleads.

Sighing, Grant's gaze becomes unfocused as he continues, suddenly appearing as if he stepped out of his own body and begins talking about someone else's life as he speaks. "I didn't know she had cameras hidden some of the times we were together. She threatened to share the videos with my friends. I'd not only lose the chance of dating anyone, but my reputation would've also been demolished along with yours."

"Grant," his mom mumbles as she stands and takes a step

towards him. He holds his hand up, insisting, "I'm sorry, but I need space if you want my confession. Please, just wait until I'm done."

She nods stiffly and sits back down as his dad insists, "We don't care about our reputation! We care about you!" He pauses, taking a deep breath before adding, "And Grant, those videos are proof that could put her away for a long time. She would never use something that could condemn her. Did you see any of these supposed videos?" his dad probes, while his mom grips the arms of the chair so tightly, her knuckles turn white.

"It doesn't matter right now, Dad! Stop going into lawyer mode if you want to hear this. Just listen as my dad!"

His dad presses his lips tightly together and nods rigidly. "Fine," he grumbles, "but I will come back to it."

Ignoring his comment, Grant continues, "I'd show up like I was supposed to, but she started getting pissed at me for other things, and she'd be sure to let me know it. I ended up with more cuts and bruises, but everyone assumed they were from football. And I would never get rough with a woman, even her," he spits with disgust.

"That bitch will pay for this," his mom mutters venomously, taking me by surprise. Then again, I can't imagine how I'd feel if it were my child. Knowing this happened to the man I'm falling in love with is already unimaginable. I sniffle, no longer bothering to wipe away my tears.

He keeps talking as if no one else has said a word, "I started partying more, drinking, and smoking pot to deal with it, and what do you know, she used that for blackmail too. I just kept making stupid fucking decisions," he berates himself. He pauses, gulping down the lump in his throat.

Shaking his head, he mutters, "She was really close with Coach. Did you know that?" he questions, not waiting for an answer. "She could get me suspended, kicked off the team, kicked out of school and whatever else, ripping away all of my dreams like they were nothing, so I kept going back to her and taking whatever she threw at me, both literally and metaphorically."

His body begins shaking, and I reach out with my free hand, hoping to calm him. Resting my head on his shoulder, I rub his back in soothing circles while tears stream down my face and he keeps talking, revealing more of his pain and suffering.

"I got to a point where I felt like football was the only good thing I had left in my life. It was my outlet to release some of my anger and resentment as well as my escape. It used to be my favorite thing to do, but either way, it was still there for me when it felt like nothing else was. I was going to work my ass off and get that scholarship to any school that fucking wanted me and get far away from her."

He shakes his head, laughing manically. "She knew what I planned and started threatening Matt," he spits out with pure hatred. "Matt followed Amy everywhere back then. He was always there. Taking Amy away from him was her obvious solution and the easy part. But she planned on hurting him and ruining him too. She had ways to do it. I couldn't let her." His voice cracks, overwhelmed with emotion. "He was only twelve at the time. He had his whole fucking life ahead of him. She'd already ruined so much. I couldn't let her destroy him too."

"Oh, Grant," his mom stammers with unbearable pain.

"The night before the big game, she was pissed at me as usual, and she took her anger out on me. She didn't go easy on me. Then again, she never did, but sometimes it was worse than others. I was sore as hell, but I was determined to not only get through the game but thrive in it. I took something to help with the pain. I didn't think I could get through the game without it, and it fucked me up. Another stupid decision, and I lose my one shot," he mutters with pure self-loathing.

"Please stop being so hard on yourself," I whimper into his

back. I hate hearing him beat himself up. Nothing about what he went through was easy.

"After that, I gave up," he proclaims, making me wonder if he heard me at all. "I didn't want to live. I'd barely been surviving as it was, but I thought about what it would do to Matt and both of you if I ended my life, and I knew I couldn't put any of you through that. So, I figured out another way to deal with it, and I made an agreement with Mrs. Stone," he confesses, resigned.

I gasp in surprise. "An agreement?" his dad prompts, shocked, echoing my thoughts.

"Yeah. I got the courage to stand up to her. I told her I wasn't going to be her boy-toy or her punching bag anymore, and she wasn't going to do anything about it. I knew the only way she'd listen to me would be if I found a way to blackmail her or threaten her right back, so I did. I would disappear and she would let me go if she wanted her secrets as well as mine to remain hidden. I told her I had pictures I would share with her husband and the police."

"Pic..." his dad begins.

Pointing to his dad, he immediately interrupts, elaborating, "Before you say anything, I was eighteen in the pictures, so the only issue it would cause her would be a possible divorce. I just didn't tell her that and hoped she believed me. I didn't want her anywhere near Matt." He sighs heavily, his shoulders sagging with defeat. "Anyway, she agreed to let me go without repercussions as long as I didn't come back. I didn't have anything left anyway, and the least I could do was protect all of you after everything I did to ruin our family."

His last statement crushes my heart, eliciting a whimper from my lips. I wrap my arms around him and hold on tight, attempting to soothe both of our souls.

"She did this to you, Grant. She did this to us," his mom whimpers emphatically. "None of this is on you."

He sighs, his shoulders sagging as I try to hold us both together, feeling completely helpless. After finally hearing his story, I wonder if he'll ever really let me in.

Grant

AN EERIE SILENCE SETTLES OVER US AS I SIT ON THE COUCH
with Ella leaning against me on one side and my mom sitting
next to me on the other, hugging me tightly, her tears finally
beginning to slow, most likely drying out. Everything about
this moment is surreal—my confession draining me physically
and emotionally, leaving me exhausted. I feel like I just ran a
seven-day marathon and then jumped in the ring, begging for
a fight.

"You shouldn't have wasted the past ten years of your life
chasing after me. I'm not worth it," I mumble again, guilt consuming me for all the time they squandered.

"We haven't wasted anything! Especially knowing we've
finally been led right back to you," my mom emphatically insists.
She obviously believes it, but I wonder if I ever will. Why would
I? "But even if we weren't here with you right now, I'd still
be looking, Grant! I had to know you were okay," she cries,
desperate for me to believe it.

I flinch, not accepting her statement, but not arguing with
her either, knowing it would be futile. "I'm sorry," I mutter,
overwhelmed with shame and remorse, at the same time believing I didn't have much of a choice.

After a few minutes of silence, she softly questions, "Grant,
what did you do after you left home? Where did you go?"

Sighing, I admit, "I'll be honest, Mom, I was fucked up for a long time. I know it's not what you want to hear, but I drank and smoked pot, and I even popped some pills trying to numb the pain. I just kept moving, going from one party to the next. Eventually, I found myself in Arizona with a job at a garage, and they were willing to train me and help me get the education I needed to become a mechanic. I got myself into rehab and took advantage of it, even specializing in motorcycles."

"You were always in the driveway working on yours," my dad murmurs, lost in a memory. The corners of his lips curve up in a smile as he adds, "Matt was always following you around with the wrench you gave him and his toy toolbox."

My heart clenches, recalling those same memories. "Is Matt doing okay?" I inquire anxiously.

"He seems to be. He's still close with Amy," he reveals, watching me closely. "He hasn't been answering my calls lately. Hopefully we'll talk to him soon."

I nod my head in acknowledgment, wondering if he'll ever forgive me, or if I'll ever even see my little brother again. I'm sure he's not so little anymore.

Sighing, I run my hand over my face in complete exhaustion. I glance at my mom and then my dad, knowing I need some time to myself and hope they understand. "I'm sorry to do this after all this time, but I need to ask you to go."

My mom stiffens and has a quick intake of air. Her face goes white as a sheet as she mumbles my name in fear, "Grant."

I wince, knowing that's my fault too. Shaking my head, I insist, "I promise I just need to rest, and I need some time to myself to process all of this bullshit. I've tried not to think about any of it for years." It never worked, but I always fucking tried.

My dad nods in understanding as my mom pleads, "Please, don't run this time, Grant. I don't think I could handle it again."

I gulp hard, my throat feeling like sandpaper. "I'm not running, I promise. I just need some time. Please," I request, my voice cracking.

As my dad steps towards me, I stand, reluctantly releasing Ella's hand and my mom. He clasps me around the back, patting it firmly, and I return the gesture. "Please, let us help. We need this too, more than you realize." He steps back with tears in his eyes and straightens, clearing his throat. "It's damn good to see you, Son."

His simple sentiment sends a shiver down my spine. My heart lodges itself in my throat and I give him a firm nod. He reaches out, helping my mom to her feet. She wobbles slightly and then wraps her arms around my waist as my hands reflexively fall behind her back, holding her close. "I'm so sorry, Mom." I say the words I'll say until the day I die.

She shakes her head, unable to speak. My dad eventually gently pulls her away, promising, "We will see him tomorrow. He needs to rest."

Reluctantly, she leans on him for support. Looking at me, she rasps, "I love you, Grant. We love you."

I nod as my chest tightens not able to respond, but mostly because I don't deserve it. Dragging my feet, I walk them to the door, closing it behind them.

With a heavy sigh, I turn and look back at Ella, her red, puffy eyes, and tear-streaked cheeks, looking more beautiful than ever. My heart remains stuck and I gulp hard, needing to speak. "Thank you," I rasp, my voice cracking.

She opens her mouth to respond, her voice barely above a whisper. "You don't ever have to thank me for something like this. I told you I'd be here, and I meant it."

Her words help tip me over the edge, and I feel the dam break and a flood of emotions swallow me whole. My shoulders begin to shake as my tears fall and a sob escapes my lips without my consent. I lean my back against the door, sliding to the floor, not able to take another step. I'm completely overwhelmed, my emotions crushing me. Everything I've fought so hard to avoid comes flooding back, and I'm no longer able to keep it buried. My head falls into my hands as I cry, grieving for everything I lost, everything I endured and everything I put my family through. Shame, guilt, and grief completely overwhelm me, pulling me into the darkness.

Barely a moment later, I feel her arms wrap protectively around me. She murmurs words of comfort I'm not able to comprehend, too lost in my own head, my own devastation—destruction created by me. Leaning on her, I let go. I cry harder than I ever have, feeling like it will never end, but for now I have an angel watching over me, and I couldn't ask for anything more in this dreaded moment. I just try not to question if she'll be there when I open my eyes.

52

Ella

DEEP IN THOUGHT, I SIGH SOFTLY, CURLED UP AGAINST GRANT in my bed. Mindlessly, I run my fingers over his chest in a continuous figure eight pattern as he sleeps, passed out from pure exhaustion. I can't believe what he's been through. It's overwhelming just thinking about it. Not really being able to comprehend it makes it difficult to put myself in his shoes and figure out how to help him. I do think I finally understand why he tries to push me away, although I still don't agree with it. It just makes me more determined than ever to hold onto him, be there for him, and help him to the other side of all this chaos and devastation.

Thinking about that woman enrages me like nothing I've ever felt before, igniting a fire inside me. She's like a tornado destroying everything in its path, leaving nothing but destruction. I'm shocked to find out she's not only married, but she's also someone's mother. Hopefully she's a better mother than she is a person, but that thought contradicts itself. There's no way that's even a possibility, and that terrifies me for this girl, Amy. From the sound of it, his brother Matt sure seems fond of her, and Grant obviously adores his brother, knowing how protective he is.

Listening to Grant tell us about everything that happened to him, at least a glimpse of it, brought on indescribable pain.

Every part of me inside and out reacted, the torturous ache spreading like wildfire throughout my body. I know he left a lot out, not wanting to give us too many details of his abuse, but his physical and emotional scars say more than even words can do. My tears kept flowing, making me think I really did have an endless supply as he spoke, but they did eventually dry, leaving me with a headache and an overwhelming helplessness I didn't think possible. After hearing his confession, I know things will only get harder.

When his parents reluctantly left and he broke down, I shattered right along with him. I've never seen a man so vulnerable and broken, and knowing he let his guard down with me obliterated my heart as it began piecing it back together again. That's what I want to do for him, help piece him and his heart back together again; if he'll only let me.

Grant begins to stir under me, groaning and squirming. "No, please, no!" he begs, sounding desperate.

"Grant, it's okay," I murmur softly, gently nudging him in an attempt to wake him from his nightmare. "It's only a dream."

He begins thrashing and I jump back, not wanting him to accidentally hurt me. I can only imagine he would blame himself for that too. "Ella, no!" he screams, startling me.

He gasps and his eyes fly open as he frantically looks around the room, taking in his surroundings. He sees me, sitting on the other side of the bed and relaxes only slightly. "Ella," he whispers my name on an exhale.

"Are you okay?" I prod, attempting to keep my emotions in check. I know better than to assume anything.

He sighs heavily and runs his hand through his hair and then back down his face. "Yeah, I'm alright."

"You were having a bad dream and you yelled my name," I inform him. His eyes widen in surprise and he stares at me, trying to read me. "You told me, no," I elaborate, watching him for his reaction.

He winces and sighs heavily. He holds his hand out and

reaches for me. "Come here, please."

"Okay." I take his hand and scoot closer, giving him my trust as I wait for his explanation.

"I've told you almost everything, I might as well keep spilling my guts," he mutters his poor attempt at making light of the situation.

"What was your dream about?"

"It's just a dream," he mumbles grinding his jaw, telling me it's so much more. I arch my eyebrows in question, waiting for him to continue. He groans. "Do you want all the ugly details or the short version?"

"I want the details. They may be ugly, but not because of you, not to me. I want to know what haunts you, so I can help you heal."

He winces and clears his throat, averting his eyes as he begins to speak. "When it got bad with her, she started getting creative to get what she wanted from me. I was over working on their yard and Matt and Amy were there playing. They were twelve at the time and I had just turned eighteen. I stopped to help them fix a remote-control car they were driving around the front yard. Then, I told Matt to go get the one from my room so they could race each other. They were excited and wanted to walk there together; it was only about a mile and I'd rather they be at our house than hers," he adds, shrugging like his reason is obvious.

"I imagine."

"Anyway, when they left, she was livid, not that they were gone, but that I was flirting with her twelve-year old daughter."

I gasp in disbelief, "What?"

He huffs a humorless laugh and grimaces, trudging on. "She put something in my water. I'm still not even sure what it was, but I know she did. I wasn't even drinking or taking anything at the time." He winces at his own statement. "I don't mean like a date-rape drug, but something she probably had in her house and it made me feel...off; I guess I'd say it made me feel foggy and weak." He pauses, gulping as he glances at me uneasily.

"It's okay," I insist, attempting to encourage him to speak. "You can tell me. I'm not going anywhere."

He clears his throat and continues, looking away, "She handcuffed me to her bed, slapped me across the face and then fucked me, telling me I was hers. Then, she got a large metal serving spoon and beat my chest and back with it as hard as she could as punishment for lusting after her daughter, leaving welts that lasted weeks. To finish me off, she took the metal serving fork and dug it into my shoulder until I screamed for mercy."

He pauses again, refusing to look at me as I recall the teardrop shaped holes near his shoulder, my hand immediately drifting to the spot on his arm. "Grant..."

"In my dream, it was my memory, except you stomped in at the end, stabbing me," he whispers so quietly I have to strain to hear him.

I whimper, my tears easily replenishing and cascading down my cheeks. "Grant, I would never hurt you."

His head snaps to mine and he pulls me into his chest, quickly reassuring me, "I know you wouldn't. My head is just fucked up after reliving all that shit in the past twenty-four hours. It's too fucking much to handle, and yet you're still here."

"And I'm not going anywhere! I want to be here with you."

"But I don't understand why, Ella," he argues, shaking his head. "You're too good for me. I'm so broken; I'm not worth the trouble!"

Vehemently shaking my head, I deny his claim, "That's not true, Grant. You're an incredible man with so much heart. When you love, you love hard. Look at your brother as an example. You have so much to give."

"Even if I have a lot to give, that doesn't mean I deserve to have it. Not everyone deserves a happily ever after, Ella. I ruin everyone who dares to love me. Why would I want that for anyone I love or care about?"

I pull back, looking into his eyes as I place my palm adoringly on his cheek. "You've been punishing yourself for over ten years for something that wasn't your fault." He opens his mouth, I'm sure to argue, but I keep talking, stopping him. "It's true, Grant! But even if you don't believe it, don't you think you've endured enough? Don't you think it's time to move on and let yourself live? Don't you want to let yourself love again?" I challenge, waiting to see what he does and hoping he wants to do it with me.

"Ella..." he murmurs my name.

53

Grant

I THINK I'M ALREADY IN LOVE AND I WANT ALL OF THOSE things, but I know I'm not good enough for her. I reach up, weaving my fingers into her hair and hold her gaze. "You're too fucking good for me, Ella." Then I crash my lips down on hers, suddenly desperate to touch her, feel her, and taste her. I stick my tongue out, licking her lips, pushing in the moment she gives me entry. She moans into my mouth, the sensation going straight to my cock. I tilt my head, moving closer and deepening our kiss.

She pulls back gasping for breath as she whimpers my name, "Grant."

My lips instantly seek hers, not giving her a reprieve. I wrap my arm around her back and lift, scooting her down the bed, while my other hand continues to hold her head captive as I devour her, licking, twisting, exploring, and savoring her sweet taste. I groan, her soft, needy whimpers, telling me she wants this, wants me as much as I want her. Carefully, I pull back, talking onto her lips, "I want you, Ella. I need you."

"Please, Grant," she replies, just as fraught with desire, giving me permission to completely let go of my inhibitions.

Quickly sitting back, I pull my shirt over my head and toss it on the floor. I lean down and kiss her, sucking her bottom lip into my mouth and releasing it as I reach for the hem of her shirt, giving it a gentle tug to ask permission.

Sitting up, she raises her arms in response. I swiftly pull it over her head, tossing it on the floor next to mine, obeying her silent request. Her hands fall to my chest and begin skating over my body as she kisses along my jaw. She sticks her tongue out, tasting my skin behind my ear before she nibbles my lobe. Placing soft kisses under my ear, she works her way down my neck, making me moan in pure pleasure, "Ahh."

"Grant, I want you in my mouth."

Shaking my head, I deny her request. Her eyes widen in surprise and I quickly explain, "I need to be inside you, Ella. Please."

She licks her lips, her eyes full of heat and nods in agreement. "Grab a condom."

"Let me get you ready first." I flick her bra open in front and shove the soft, silky black material away, exposing her breasts. I cover her breast with my mouth, my tongue swirling around before I suck the taut nipple into my mouth, eliciting a moan from her lips as her body arches towards me. Releasing it with a pop, I move to the other side, giving it the same treatment until I hear her guttural moan.

I unbutton her jeans and tug the zipper down, moving my hand to the waistband of her panties. "I'm already wet, Grant. Just take them off."

A grin tugs at my lips, enjoying her statement and subsequent request. Delving my tongue into her mouth, I find its mate before I stand, obliging her. I tug off her jeans, followed by my own, leaving them in a heap. My hands hook in my boxers, ready to tug when she abruptly sits up, her boobs bouncing, making me gasp. "Ella," I warn.

She grins mischievously. "I'm done being patient." Without delay, she pulls her panties off and flings them on the floor before laying back down. She smirks and stares at me as her hand falls between her legs. My breathing instantly becomes ragged as my body burns with desire, watching as her fingers skim over her folds.

Groaning, I kick off my boxers and swipe a condom off the nightstand, quickly climbing back over her with a possessive growl, eliciting a playful giggle. "I would love to watch you touch yourself, but now is not the time."

She arches her eyebrows in challenge. "Oh, really?"

Instead of responding, I kiss her, slipping my tongue inside, our tongues instantly fighting for dominance. I reach down and slip my hand between us, finding her folds completely soaked. I groan and break our kiss, talking over her lips, "Fuck, Ella, you're right. You're so ready for me."

"Condom," she reiterates.

I lean back and pick it up off the mattress, ripping the black square open with my teeth. I slip the condom out of the package, tossing the garbage towards the nightstand before I roll it over my thick, hard, shaft, Ella watching my every move as she licks her lips. I hover over her, this time kissing her slow and sweet as I readjust over her entrance. Her hips buck up towards me, eliciting another groan. "Ella," I rasp.

"Please," she begs. I shift, no longer able to hold back. With one quick, hard movement, I thrust deep inside her, reveling in her wet heat. Her head falls back with a moan, my own answering grunt inevitable.

Slowly, I begin moving, finding the perfect rhythm between us as I look down at my angel, her blonde hair spread out behind her like a halo, knowing this is my heaven.

Searching for an angle to hit her g-spot, I slide one hand down to grasp her hip while the other reaches down her leg, bending it and folding it towards her, resting it at my hip. I grin as she moans, her eyes rolling back in her head. "Grant, yes, right there, yes, please," she pants, poking my fire higher.

Her walls swell, burning, squeezing, prompting me to pump into her harder and faster. My breathing becomes erratic and my body boils, sweat dotting my brow. A tingling begins deep in my gut, spreading to my tightening balls, letting me know

I'm struggling to hold myself back from falling over the edge. "I need you to cum, Ella," I plead desperately, knowing I'm losing my fight, but she needs to be first. Always her.

She arches up into me, thrust for thrust, groaning as her walls begin to clench. She screams my name, "Grant," as her insides spasm, shoving me off the cliff and I fall over the edge, thrusting hard and fast, pausing deep inside her as she milks my cock dry.

"Fuck," I mutter as I collapse on top of her, holding most of my weight off her, not wanting to crush her. Taking a moment, I rest my head on her forehead as we both pant to catch our breaths. I press my lips against hers, moving in a beautiful rhythm, savoring her before I reluctantly pull back with a groan.

"Let me get rid of this and I'll be right back." I brush my lips over hers and push up off the bed. As I stride to the bathroom, I remove the condom, tying it off before tossing it in the garbage and washing my hands. Grabbing a washcloth, I run it under warm water, squeezing away the excess.

Rushing back to Ella, I find her lying in the same spot I left her, looking completely sated, causing me to chuckle in satisfaction. She opens her eyes and smiles at me as I lay down next to her mumbling, "I brought this to clean you up."

"Thank you." She sighs happily as I carefully wipe between her legs and toss the washcloth on the floor with our clothes.

"I'm happy to help clean you up anytime." I lay down and pull her into my arms, her hand falling to my chest.

"That was wonderful," she murmurs, her lips brushing my skin, leaving goose bumps in their wake.

"Just wonderful?"

She giggles, ignoring my question. "How are you feeling?" she prods, kissing another spot on my chest, hoping to ease my worries.

"After that, I'm fantastic," I tease. She gives me a playful tap and I chuckle softly. Then, I quietly admit, "Better with you."

She doesn't respond, but I feel her fingers running over the rough skin of my scars under my tattoos, making my stomach twist. There's no point in hiding them anymore, she knows what they are, but the blatant reminder tells me why I'm no good for her, especially after everything she's been through. She deserves to stay in the light, not having me drag her into my darkness. Is this just my chance to say goodbye? To have one woman who's compassionate about my past, even if it's only for a moment in time? I'm honestly not sure, but like I promised, I will never regret any time I spend with her. I hope she feels the same.

34

Ella

I KISS GRANT GOODBYE, WAVING AS HE LEAVES FOR HIS physical therapy appointment. I have a few errands I need to do today, and I want to clean up the house. I asked Hannah to take my shift today, telling her I wasn't feeling the best. I just couldn't do it.

After the emotional rollercoaster the other day, Grant and I spent the whole day in bed, but I think we both desperately needed it, especially him. Now I'm struggling to wipe the smile off my face, making me feel a small pang of guilt as if I'm happy for his pain, but we both know that's not true. I try to push my feelings aside, knowing he would want me to be happy.

At the same time, it's hard not to let his past get to me. I hate what he's been through. I hope Grant feels better today. Sometimes it's hard to tell when he tries to hide it from me. I know he's dealing with a lot, having so many painful memories resurface can bring back a lot of insecurities too. I'm just trying to be there for him while he works through it and trying to be strong for him, although that's not always easy.

He did tell his parents he would see them today, too, and I wanted to give them some time together to catch up without me in the way. Of course, they all claim I'm not in the way, but ten years is a long time to go without seeing your son. They've been calling or texting constantly since they left that night. I don't really blame them for being afraid he's going to slip away again. I feel the same, but he's never left me, at least not yet. I grimace, once again hoping he decides to stay.

Spinning on my heel, I stride towards my bedroom, ready to get to work, hoping it will distract me from worrying about Grant. Grabbing a white, plastic laundry basket out of my closet, I grip the sides, collecting all the dirty clothes off the floor, both mine and Grant's, and tossing them in, my cheeks flushing as I remember how they got there. I giggle, amused I'm blushing at the memory even standing in the room all alone.

Crouching down, I swipe a shirt off the floor before straightening and lifting the basket. My vision suddenly becomes blurry, a wave of dizziness washing over me. Slowly, I set the basket down, focusing on a spot on the wall as I concentrate on my breathing, attempting to hold myself together until everything slowly comes back into a clear view.

I grab a bottle of water off my nightstand and gulp half of it down, thinking I might be dehydrated. Glancing at the time, I realize it's already after two and I haven't eaten any lunch yet. I'm sure it's just because I'm hungry. I make my way to the kitchen and make myself a peanut butter and strawberry jelly sandwich, my stomach feeling like it can't take much else.

Taking my time, I bring my sandwich into the living room with a fresh bottle of water, setting the water down, and keeping my sandwich on a paper plate in my lap. I begin nibbling as my cell phone rings, interrupting my lunch. I glance at the screen and smile at my older brother's face. Swallowing my food first, I answer. "Hi, Dec."

"She finally answers!" he announces, sounding relieved. "Where the hell have you been, Ella?" he questions, making me wince. I know I don't have to tell them my every move, but I also know they worry about me.

"I've been here, but Grant's parents showed up unexpectedly. We've been spending some time with them."

"Wow, you met his parents. I didn't even think you were

dating, and now it sounds serious," he mutters sarcastically.

"Dec," I say his name in warning.

"Ella," he murmurs, mirroring my caution and making me laugh. "You sound really good," he observes, a smile in his voice.

"I am, mostly. I just feel a little off today," I admit, hoping he doesn't blow it out of proportion. "But I'm happy."

"You're not feeling well?" he probes, ignoring the rest.

I should've known. I don't know why I didn't keep my mouth shut. "I'm fine, Dec. It's just been exhausting the last few days."

"Hm," he mumbles, pausing. "Exhausting how? What exactly have you been up to? Have you talked to the doctor?"

A soft sigh escapes my lips. "No, but I will call the doctor if I need to, and I haven't been doing anything crazy, I promise."

"Okay. Well, maybe you should get some rest."

"I will."

"Is Grant around?"

"No, he had physical therapy, and then I believe he was planning on spending some more time with his parents while they're here. Why?"

"Just asking, don't get so defensive. I haven't seen you in a few days, and I was calling to see if I could bring dinner over or something."

"I guess I could do that." I wonder if that was really his plan all along, or if me saying I was feeling off made him come up with a reason to visit.

He chuckles softly and sarcastically mumbles, "Don't sound too excited."

I giggle, knowing he's not offended, but I placate him anyway. "Dinner sounds good, Dec."

"Alright, I'll be there in a couple hours."

"Okay."

"Ella?"

"Yeah?"

"You really do like this guy, don't you?" He sounds as if he already knows my answer and he's okay with it.

"I really do, Declan."

"Alright, well, I'll see you in a couple hours. Please rest until then," he pleads.

"Got it, Doctor Dec," I tease, smirking.

He laughs and disconnects the call without responding.

I set my phone down with a smile on my face, feeling a sudden sharp pain in my back, making me wince and accidentally dump my sandwich onto the floor. I close my eyes and focus on breathing in and out until the pain subsides before I peel my sandwich off the floor. "Great," I grumble irritably, not in the mood to make another one.

My stomach churns, feeling a little nauseous. Reaching for my glass, I take another sip of water before curling up on the couch. Declan's right, I need to rest.

I pick up my phone, dialing Grant, assuming he's probably in the middle of therapy, but he'll get the message when he's done. "Hey, Grant. It's me. I know you're probably in the middle of your physical therapy, but I was wondering if you could swing by here quick before you go by your parents' hotel?" I inquire nervously. I hate having to ask, but I think I need to this time. "I just need you for something, but hopefully it will only take a minute. I'll show you when you get here."

I don't want to worry him, so I don't elaborate on my request, but after everything I've been through, I feel better when someone checks on me when I'm not feeling right. I know Dec will be here in a couple hours, but I don't want him to rush over here when everything is probably perfectly fine and Grant could be by in about thirty minutes. Besides, just seeing his face and his sexy smile always makes me feel better.

I close my eyes, a headache coming on making me groan. "Damn," I mumble to myself and try to go to sleep.

I'm not sure how much time passes when I feel a gentle hand on my arm, attempting to nudge me awake. Prying my eyes open, I find Declan hunched over me, his eyebrows drawn down in concern. "Gabriella, are you alright?"

Barely able to move I lick my dry lips, my tongue peeling away from the roof of my mouth, telling me I need water. I start to shake my head but stop, the small movement feeling like my head is being run over by a truck. "I don't feel so good, Dec," I mumble, my voice shaking. My whole body feels weak as I open my mouth again, attempting to ask for a glass of water, just a moment before my head spins and everything goes black.

55

Grant

I GLANCE AT MY PHONE AS I WALK INTO MY PARENTS' HOTEL in the next town over. Genesis Beach is too small a town for a hotel. A missed call notification from Ella lights up my screen, along with a voicemail. My thumb hovers over her name, hesitant to call her back or listen to the message, my mind already overwhelmed. Heaving a sigh, I decide against it for now, slipping my phone back in my pocket as I make my way up to their room on the third floor. Forcing myself to trudge down the hall to the door, I knock and wait.

Barely a moment passes before the door swings open and my mom crashes into me, throwing her arms around me and hugging me tight. "You're here! I started to think you were just a dream."

My heart clenches, feeling like shit. I fuck everything up. "I'm sorry," I murmur, knowing I will never be able to say those words enough.

"Come in," she urges, tugging my hand as she pulls me into the room before reluctantly releasing my hand.

"Glad you could make it, Grant." My dad smiles, relief evident in his eyes.

Shifting uncomfortably, I take in the junior suite, with a king-sized bed, a desk, a kitchenette, as well as a small, round table near the window with three chairs; a simple white and mahogany theme. Pausing, I take a deep breath and make my way to one of the chairs and sit down. Exhaling slowly, I attempt to ease my anxiety, running my hand over my face, my nerves causing my stomach to turn. "I um, wanted to come talk to you and let you know what I've been thinking," I begin, needing to just get it over with.

My mom sits down in the chair next to mine, her hands suddenly shaking. "What is it?" she asks as my dad lowers himself into the seat across from me.

I gulp down the lump in my throat, but it doesn't help. Taking another deep breath, I plunge ahead. "I need to take a few days to myself. I was thinking I'd just take a ride along the coast, but I want you to know where I am. I'm not just going to take off on you again. I promise." With a glance at both my parents, I see their anxiety clearly skyrocketing.

"Grant..." my dad begins.

Swiftly interrupting, I emphasize, "Listen, I know you have no reason to trust me right now, but after everything I told you the other day, you must at least understand why I left, even if it's just a little bit. But this time, I'm promising you I won't disappear. If you call, I will answer when I can. Hell, I'll even schedule a time to talk to you every day if you want, and you will see me again. I'm just completely overwhelmed being thrown back into my past. Besides seeing my family again, it's not a place I ever wanted to be again. I need some time to think everything through and figure out a way to move on," I explain, having no idea what that might look like.

My dad sighs heavily and nods his head in understanding, looking away, attempting to hide his emotion. "I get it, but I don't like it," he mumbles quietly.

My mom's tears return, making my heart feel like it's about to break all over again. "Why don't you stay and find someone who can help you, like a psychologist?" she suggests, pleading. "Is Ella able to take the time to go with you?"

I wince, still unsure about how to handle things with Ella,

but hoping a couple days to myself will help straighten out my thoughts and feelings. "She's part of the reason I need to get away," I finally concede.

She gasps, her eyes widening in surprise. "Did something happen between you two? You seem so good together."

Sighing, I shake my head and admit, "No. Honestly, I'm crazy about her, and I feel like I've won the lottery every time I'm near her."

"Then, why would you walk away from her?" she pushes.

"She gives me so much, and all I do is take from her. I have nothing to offer her." I grind my jaw. "The only thing I do is bring darkness to her doorstep. She's better off without me." My chest clenches tightly, making it difficult to breathe.

"That's not true! But since I know you won't believe me, don't you think that should be her decision?" my mom challenges.

I flinch at her choice of words, knowing Ella will hate me for taking her choice away, but maybe that's for the best. If I give her the chance to make the decision, I know she'll tell me to stay, but at what cost to her? She's always thinking of everyone else but herself, and she needs to be first, always. "I'll end up ruining her like I have everyone else I love," I rasp hoarsely. "I can't do that to her."

"Oh, Grant," she whimpers, shaking her head. She stands and steps over to me, wrapping her arms protectively around me. "What happened to you is not your fault," she repeats, her voice hoarse. "We don't blame you; not even for running. We just want you back."

I close my eyes, feeling like a tornado is brewing inside me as I soak in her love. I never realized how much I missed this, how much I missed them. I guess I tried to push it out of my mind. "I'm so sorry," I reiterate, crushed for everything I did to them.

After a few minutes, I release her, gently nudging her back. "We love you, Grant. We always have, and we always will."

"I love you, too," I state, the words foreign on my tongue. And saying the words aloud makes my chest feel like it's being squeezed, trying to make me burst. My hand falls to my chest, rubbing the ache, attempting to ease the pain. "I need to go."

My mom gulps hard and nods in acknowledgment. "I need to hear from you every day for a while, even if it's just to tell me that you're okay," she declares, leaving no room for argument.

"Okay."

"We'll be here waiting for you," my dad states.

My eyebrows draw down in confusion. "You're not going home?"

Shaking his head, he stresses, "We need more time with you. We'll be here waiting."

My chest tightens as I step towards my dad, embracing him, grateful for his declaration. He pats my back firmly before pulling back. Still holding my hand, he suggests, "I'd listen to your mom's advice when it comes to Ella. She knows what she's talking about, and if she means that much to you, that's when you hold on with all you've got and throw everything in the ring to fight for it. Fight to be the man we know you are and the same one you think should be by her side. Fight for her, Son. That's what she deserves."

I nod and gulp down the lump in my throat, releasing him. But I can't stop my train of thoughts, wondering if that would be enough; if I'm enough.

My mom leans in, giving me another hug, begging as she clings to me, "Please, call me in the morning."

"I will, Mom, I promise." I know I can't put them through that again after seeing them, and now that they know the truth, maybe we can rebuild our relationship and have one another in our lives.

My emotions bounce all over the place with so much going through my head as I stride out of the hotel. I climb on my motorcycle and ride out, heading north, my thoughts consumed with Ella and what her reaction will be when I don't come home. My chest tightens, making it difficult to breathe, but I don't know what else to do. I'm a mess, and I need to get my head straight.

This is how it's always been for me when I'm dealing with something; I ride, finding somewhere new, but even I'm not sure that's what's best this time. I already feel like I've lost a part of me the further I go. I push myself forward, believing I'm trying not to be selfish and do what's best for Ella. She's my priority. I ride until I'm low on gas, then I stop, filling up and grabbing a bite to eat before rolling out again. Finally, I stop for the night when I can no longer keep my eyes open. I check into a motel and crash from pure exhaustion.

In the morning, I gather my things and leave, wanting to get a couple hours of driving in before stopping for breakfast at a truck stop diner. I walk in, the black, white, and red fifties-style diner a familiar setting. As I grab an empty stool at the counter, I reach for a menu, quickly skimming it.

An older waitress, petite with short gray hair in a pixie cut wearing black pants and a white button-down shirt with a white half-apron tied around her waist leans over the counter, asking, "What can I get you?"

"Can I have two eggs over-easy, bacon and hash browns with a coffee, please?"

"You got it." She nods and spins around towards the kitchen.

Reaching down, I pull out my phone and lean on my forearms against the counter. I see several notifications of missed calls and texts, but I'm not surprised with the way I left. With a heavy sigh, I unlock my phone and tap my mom's number.

"Grant?" she answers on the first ring.

"Hi, Mom. I just wanted you to know I'm okay."

I hear her sigh of relief over the line before she whispers, "Thank you."

My stomach twists, but I ignore it, clearing my throat. "Listen, Mom, I don't mean to cut you short, but I just sat down to eat some breakfast and I have some other messages I should check."

"That's okay. Thank you for calling, and although I want you to call me tomorrow, you can also call again later if you'd like. I'd love to hear from you."

"Got it. Thanks, Mom. I love you," I mumble, my voice cracking. The words still cause a stabbing pain in my chest.

"I love you, too, Grant. We love you," she emphasizes tearfully.

I disconnect the call and take a deep breath, trying to pull myself together. As an attempt to distract myself, I open my text messages, shocked to see I don't have a single one from Ella, but I have several from her brother, Declan. I grimace and open the texts, figuring I deserve any mud he slings my way.

Hey, man. Let me know if you beat me back to the house.

Where are you?

Grant, where are you? I need you to call me right away.

It's urgent! Call me!

Man, where the fuck are you?

Check your fucking messages and call me!

You asshole, just when she needed you most.

My heart drops into my stomach, knowing something's not right. This doesn't sound like the normal, "Fuck you," message I expected. Holding my breath, I open my voice mail, my call from Ella still unanswered along with three messages from Declan.

With my hands shaking, I tap on Ella's message first. Listening to the sound of her voice makes my heart race, but all she really does is ask me to stop at the house before I go see my parents, not giving me anything out of the ordinary.

Steeling myself, I hover over Declan's messages, a feeling of dread washing over me. I tap the first one as the waitress sets my breakfast in front of me. Glancing up, I force a smile and nod in appreciation, my phone glued to my ear. "Hey, Grant, it's Declan. Listen, I just hung up with my sister and something isn't right. I don't want to worry you or anything, but she's not feeling well, and with her history, we don't take any chances. I'm going over there right from work, but could you please stop sooner to check on her and let me know how she is? Thanks, man," he adds, disconnecting the call.

Panic begins clawing at my throat as I tap on the next one, no longer hungry as I struggle to swallow my anxiety. "Hey, Grant, it's Declan again. I really hope you check your messages. I got to the beach house a few minutes ago and Ella doesn't look good. I have her in my car and I'm driving her to the hospital. Meet me there," he insists, leaving no room for argument.

I exhale harshly as I reach for my wallet, pulling out a bunch of bills and throwing them onto the counter as I struggle to stand, barely breathing. I tap on the last message, my throat dry, my empty stomach churning. "What the fuck, Grant? Where the hell are you? They're admitting her and I'll tell you the details if you answer your fucking messages! She needs you!"

My heart thrashes against my chest as I begin running towards my motorcycle as I tap his name, returning his call. "Where the fuck are you?" he rasps accusingly.

"How is she?" I spit out, ignoring his question, desperate for answers.

"She's going into surgery now. They found another tumor on her spine, and we won't know anything until they come back with the biopsy results," he reveals, his voice cracking.

"Fuck," I mutter. I clench my chest, feeling like I'm having a heart attack. "I'm on my way, but Declan, I'm not that close. Please, keep me updated. I'll be watching my phone."

"I gotta go," he declares dismissively, not bothering to respond to my request, but I don't blame him.

Quickly, I start my ride and roll out, hating myself more as each second passes. I should be by her side. I'm such an asshole! "Please, don't let anything happen to Ella, not my Angel," I beg. I continue praying, something I haven't done in years, as I speed south down the highway, struggling to keep my vision clear and desperate to get to her. I should've never left her side.

56

Ella

I BLINK MY EYES OPEN, FEELING GROGGY AND SORE. I ATTEMPT to lick my lips, my mouth feeling dry and pasty. "Grant," I mumble, wanting to see his face.

"He's not here, Gabriella," I hear Nate's low voice at my side.

As I take a deep breath, I pry my eyes open further and look around the room, the stark white and pale blue indicating I'm in the hospital again. I grimace and groan, trying to remember what happened to get me here, but I'm not sure. I open my mouth and rasp, "What happened?" my voice coming out scratchy.

"Take it easy, Ella," Nate advises, gently patting my arm. "You're okay, but you're in the hospital. How are you feeling?"

"Not great. What happened?"

"You need to relax. You just had surgery."

"Surgery?" I echo, confused.

"Yeah," he sighs, sounding exhausted. "Declan found you half-conscious at home and brought you here. We found a tumor on your spine, and they had to do surgery to do the biopsy because of the location. With your history and your current state, of course they wanted to do it right away."

"Where's Declan?" I ask, ignoring the part about surgery. I'm familiar with the process since I've had these before, and it doesn't matter what he says until he comes back with the results. Only then we'll decide what to do. I've found it's not worth it for me to stress about it until I can get some real answers.

"He should be right back. He stepped out to answer a call." I nod in acknowledgment. "In the meantime, I need to know more about how you're feeling, and I'm going to do a quick assessment.

"I'm fine," I mumble, ignoring him as he goes through the regular checks. "Why are you assessing me?" I question, curious where the nurses are. Besides the fact he shouldn't be my doctor.

He clenches his jaw, attempting to hide his frustration with me without success. "Because I'm here, and I don't want to leave your side."

My eyebrows draw down in confusion, finding the way he said that odd. I open my mouth to ask what he's talking about when Declan walks in, his eyes full of relief as he meets my gaze. "You're awake."

"I am," I confirm hoarsely.

"How do you feel?"

I grimace at his question and mumble, barely able to speak, "I'm okay. Nate said you found me. Thank you."

He nods his head, giving me a sad smile. "You scared the shit out of me when I found you," he admits, briefly avoiding my gaze.

I wince. "I'm sorry." I hate how much they've had to drop everything to take care of me.

"I'm just glad you're okay, Ella."

"Where's Grant?"

Ignoring my question, he informs me, "I just sent Mom and Dad home to shower and change, but they'll be back soon. Finn and Char were both here too, but they both went home to do some homework. They'll be back later tonight."

"Okay, how long have I been here?" All of that sounds like

a lot to happen in just one day.

"Ah, I guess this is your third day here. You've been here for two nights," he clarifies, rubbing the back of his neck.

"Where's Grant?" I repeat my earlier question, finally processing Nate's response. "Nate said he's not here. Where is he?"

"He's on his way. He should hopefully be here soon," Declan claims, avoiding my stare.

Nate huffs a humorless laugh and shakes his head in displeasure. "Why don't you tell her the rest of it, Declan?" he probes, arching his eyebrows in challenge. Declan gives Nate a look of warning.

"What's going on?" I prod, confused and annoyed, my voice coming out like I just swallowed a porcupine.

"Your boyfriend hasn't been here yet," Nate announces, more than happy to share the disparaging news.

"Why?" I push, looking at Declan, feeling my chest tighten and my stomach churn. Did he leave me? Is he already done? After everything we just went through?

"He left for a couple days, but he's been riding back since he found out you were in the hospital, and he should be here today; very soon," he emphasizes, glaring at Nate.

"He left?" I echo, attempting to hold back my tears. My heart squeezes. I knew this day would come.

"I knew that asshole would break your heart," Nate mutters in contempt. "He's not worth it, Ella. You should be with me. I can watch out for you and care for you as well as love you. You need me, and I want you. He's not worth your effort."

Taking a deep breath, I exhale slowly, attempting to gather my thoughts. "Nate, I appreciate what you do for me, and you're a wonderful doctor. You know I loved you once, but I'm sorry, I just don't feel that way about you anymore. I'm grateful to have Grant in my life. He is worth it, no matter how long he remains in my life. Nothing in life is guaranteed."

Nate sighs heavily, relenting. I look away and close my

eyes, not wanting to show them how much it hurts. My heart clenches as if I'm being stabbed in the chest, betraying me as a tear escapes from underneath my eyelids. How could he just leave me?

Grant

I RUN DOWN THE HALL, SLOWING AS I GET CLOSER, TRYING to read each room number, not wanting to miss hers. I haven't eaten since I left yesterday morning to come back. I've been too sick to think about food, too worried I made the biggest mistake of my life when I walked away from her without even saying goodbye. I still can't believe I was stupid enough to leave. I should've come home. I should've been the one who found her and brought her to the hospital. They say sometimes time can make all the difference. If something happens to her, I'll never forgive myself.

I run my hand over my face, my two-day old scruff scratching my hand. I spot her room number and take a step towards the doorway when I hear her ex-boyfriend's voice grating over my skin. "I knew that asshole would break your heart. He's not worth it, Ella. You should be with me. I can watch out for you and care for you as well as love you. You need me, and I want you. He's not worth your effort." I freeze, holding my breath, terrified for her response.

"Nate, I appreciate what you do for me, and you're a wonderful doctor. You know I loved you once, but I'm sorry, I just don't feel that way about you anymore. I'm grateful to have Grant in my life. He is worth it, no matter how long he remains in my life. Nothing in life is guaranteed."

I release my breath with her sweet words and step into the room, needing my eyes on her. My heart leaps at the sight of her, and I take a moment to calm my anxiety. "Ella, Angel," I rasp, overwhelmed at the sight of her in a hospital bed with an IV in her arm and oxygen tubes in her nose. I can't believe I wasn't here for her.

She turns her head towards me with tears in her eyes and whimpers, "You're here."

My heart clenches at her reaction and I quickly rush to her side. Carefully, I embrace her, afraid I'm going to hurt her. "I'm so sorry I wasn't here," I profess, my voice catching.

"You're here now," she murmurs, barely audible.

I press my lips to her forehead, taking a deep breath and inhaling her scent, feeling comforted just being near her. I let my forehead fall to hers and press a soft kiss to her lips. "And I'm not going anywhere, I promise."

"We won't get the biopsy results back until tomorrow," Declan states. I straighten and glance at him. He looks me up and down and smirks. "You look like absolute shit, man."

I chuckle softly and mumble, "Thanks. I had somewhere I had to be." I glance at Ella in adoration. "Nothing else mattered." A few tears escape out of the corners of her eyes, and I swiftly wipe them away with my thumbs.

"Fuck me," Nate mutters under his breath. Declan and I both huff a laugh, but he quickly covers his up. "I'll go see to a few other patients, and I'll be back to check on you in a little while. Okay, Gabriella?" She nods, keeping her eyes pinned on me. "Great," he mutters. "Call me if you need me before I return."

I press another kiss to her lips and brush her hair off her face. "I'm sorry."

"I'm going to step outside for a little while and make a few phone calls," Declan declares. "And give you guys some privacy."

"Thank you," we both respond, not looking in his direction, but we know he's gone when the door clicks shut.

"You left me," she states, the hurt evident in her voice.

My chest tightens painfully. "I'm sorry, Ella," I swear, knowing it's not enough. "I don't even know what I was doing. I talked to my mom and dad. I promised them I wouldn't disappear, but I needed some time to process everything, and I guess I'm used to doing it alone on the road."

"Did you get the time you needed?"

"No, but I got the clarification I needed," I answer honestly.

"What?" she asks, her eyebrows drawing down in confusion.

"You never left my head, the further away I would drive, the more crushed I felt. Then, when I finally picked up my phone, I saw all these missed texts and messages and it felt like I was having a heart attack." I rub my chest at the phantom pain. "As I started reading the texts and then listening to Declan's messages, I've never hated myself more than I did in that moment. I've never been so terrified in my life. I couldn't breathe. I called Declan, hopped on my bike, and headed straight for you. I kept running these terrible scenarios through my head; I just needed you to be okay." I struggle to breathe as I wipe my tears away.

Ella reaches for my hand and holds it tight. "I don't know what's going to happen."

I nod in understanding. "I know, but whatever happens, I want to be by your side if you'll let me. I know I have a lot of shit to work through, but I plan on doing whatever is needed. I want to be the man you deserve, Ella. If you're still willing to put up with my bullshit, I will do everything I can to be better."

"You want to try?" she whimpers, a choked sob escaping. "Really try?"

"I have to try because I have fallen so deeply in love with you, Ella. I don't think I can do this without you. I'm going to fight to be the man you deserve."

Another soft sob escapes her lips as I wipe away her tears. I look into her eyes filled with hope as she questions my claim. "You think you love me?"

I huff a laugh and press my lips to hers. Pulling back, I hold her gaze, emphasizing, "I don't think, Angel, I know. With everything that happened in the last few days, I have absolutely no doubt in my mind about how I feel, it just took me a little while to put it all together and get here. You've saved me in more ways than one, and I will be forever grateful. But you have brought me back to life with your endless positivity. I don't know where I'd be if it weren't for you. And as I've said before, I will do anything for you as long as you'll let me. I love you, Ella."

She cries as I kiss her again. Then, she pushes up off her bed, attempting to deepen the kiss. I pull back, laughing. "I'm pretty sure I'm not supposed to get you all riled up, and that's doctor's orders, not Doctor Nate's orders." I smirk.

She giggles and falls back to the bed, closing her eyes with a small smile on her face. "Grant?" she whispers.

"Yes?"

"I love you, too," she states, her voice soft, while the words echo in my ears. I gasp, my chest tightening as she squeezes my heart in the palm of her hand, controlling me in a way I never knew I wanted without even trying. "And Grant?"

"Yes, Ella?" I grin.

"My brother is right. You really do look like shit."

Laughter erupts from my chest as I reach for her hand, entwining our fingers together. She smiles and closes her eyes. I stand, watching her fall asleep, for the first time in my adult life a sense of peace, contentment and love washes over me, the thought overwhelming. Reaching out with my free hand, I scoot a chair up to the side of her bed, refusing to let go of her hand.

It's not long before Declan returns, standing in the doorway. "Are you two good?" He narrows his eyes on me.

I smile and nod. "Yeah, we're good, really good. Thank you, Declan."

He crosses his arms over his chest and meets my gaze. "I

didn't want to stress her out, but if you fuck up like this again, you will not have things so easy," he threatens.

"I wouldn't have it any other way."

58

I LOOK DOWN AT ELLA, LAYING IN THE HOSPITAL BED WITH her blonde hair spread out around her like a halo. She's so beautiful. How does she remain so positive after everything she's been through? I don't understand, but that's part of why I'm falling so hard for her. She gives me hope every time I look at her or even feel her in the room. I can't help but wonder how she's allowing me to sit by her side holding her hand, praying to a God I haven't prayed to since I was a child, begging for her to be okay. If anyone deserves to be okay, it's Ella, my angel.

My chest tightens, and I press my lips to the back of her hand, careful not to scratch her with my thickening whiskers. Declan told me he would stay with her while I go home and shower, but I'm not leaving her side. I washed up in the bathroom, grateful for the toothbrush he brought in for me when he returned.

Her parents stand on the other side of the bed, while Finn stands next to me. "She'll be okay," he claims confidently. "She always is." I want to believe it's true, but I just nod, continuing to pray as I watch her sleep.

"She's being released today," her dad mumbles.

My head snaps up to meet his gaze. "They don't wait for her results before discharging her?" I question, surprised.

He shakes his head. "No. The results should come back

today, but sometimes it does take longer, and they won't even look at what to do next until those come back. We'll bring her home with us so we can take care of her. You're welcome to come by anytime you wish."

"No," I refuse, shaking my head.

Both her parents look at me confused. "You don't want to come by to see her?" her mom questions.

"No," I grimace and shake my head, starting over. "No, I mean I want to bring her home. I want to be the one to take care of her in her own home."

They both look at each other and then at me, uncertain. "It's not easy. You have to treat her wounds and…"

I shake my head, interrupting them. "I don't care if it's hard. It could be the hardest thing I've ever done, and I would still want to do it. I want to take care of her, please." They don't respond, and I open my mouth to plead my case when Declan steps into the room.

"I think she would want to go home with him," he declares, surprising me. "Why don't we wait until she wakes up and we can ask her. She's old enough to make her own decisions now," he reminds them. I smile to myself, knowing she would appreciate those words of support, no matter what she decides.

Her mom forces a pained smile and concedes, "You're right. We'll ask her when she wakes up what she wants to do."

I breathe a sigh of relief and smile somberly at Declan, thanking him with a nod of my head. Her mom looks down and then holds up her phone. "Charlotte wants an update. I'll be back," she announces as she turns and walks out of the room.

I brush my lips across the back of her hand again and a small smile tugs at her lips as she begins to stir. I do it again, wanting to see her sparkling blue eyes looking back at me. She giggles softly, her eyes fluttering open and landing on me. She smiles and whispers my name, "Grant."

"Hi, Angel," I murmur.

Her smile grows. "Is that really you under there?" she teases.

I chuckle softly in response, my free hand rubbing my chin. "It tickles."

"You get to go home today," I tell her. She grins in response.

Her dad leans down, kissing her on the top of her head, interrupting our moment. "How are you feeling, Ella?"

She sighs. "I'm okay, Dad. I'm just a little sore and tired. I'll be fine."

"I have to leave in a few minutes to get Finn to school so he can play in his game, but Mom can stay, and I'll be back right after."

"It's okay, Dad. I'll be leaving today, and Grant's here," she murmurs, smiling at me. My heart skips a beat and restarts, galloping out of control.

"What am I?" Declan jokes.

She grins playfully. "Sorry, Dec. I didn't see you there."

"Gee, thanks," he mutters, smiling wide.

"Well, what about when you're discharged?" her dad asks, anxiously waiting for her response. I imagine letting go can't be easy for them when they've always been the ones to care for her when she's sick, especially when they've all been through so much, but like him, I hold my breath in anticipation.

"Grant can bring me home," she informs him. Then she pauses, glancing hesitantly at me and inquires, "Can you bring me home? Do you mind helping me, or should I go to my parents' house until I'm better?"

I release the breath I'd been holding and smile down at her. "I'd be happy to bring you home and take care of you."

Her body settles back into the bed as she relaxes, grinning. Glancing at her dad, she proclaims simply, "Grant has me." Her words fill me with pride and hope, tightening my chest.

He nods his head and kisses her on her forehead again. "Okay, Sweetheart." He lifts his head and focuses on me. "Let us know when you have her settled, and we'll be over to see her," he informs me, entrusting me with his daughter. I can imagine it's not easy.

"I'll take good care of her," I promise.

He forces a smile and nods his head firmly, his eyes watery. He clears his throat and looks back at Ella just as her mom steps back into the room. "I love you, Ella. We'll be over to see you in a little while."

"I love you, too, Dad," she mumbles. Glancing at her brother, she prompts, "Good luck at your game, Finn!"

He grins as he steps closer to his sister. I move back to make room for him but maintain my hold on her hand. Leaning down, he gives her an awkward hug and mumbles, "Thanks, Ella. My first touchdown will be for you," he claims, making her laugh. I love that sound.

"Thanks, Finn."

"Feel better so you can come to the next one."

"I'm working on it."

"I guess we have to go, but we'll see you later," her mom mumbles as she walks to the other side of the bed and bends over, hugging Ella. "I love you, Gabriella."

"I love you too, Mom." She waves as they all walk out of the room.

Declan clears his throat and moves to the other side of the bed. "It looks like he's got you covered," he states, nodding in my direction. He crouches down, giving Ella a hug. Then he straightens, staring at me and quirking his eyebrow in challenge, "Right, Grant?"

Nodding, I swear, "I've got her."

He reaches out to shake my hand, but I offer him my left, refusing to let go of her hand. He chuckles, shaking it awkwardly, and then pats me firmly on the back. "I'll see you kids later," he jokes as he strides out of the room.

Ella reaches out and runs her hand through my hair as I kiss the hand I'm still holding, my chest feeling tight and my stomach turning, my fear and concern for her overwhelming. "It's going to be okay, Grant."

I attempt to gulp down the lump in my throat as I look at

her in wonderment. "How do you do that?"

Her lips twitch and she arches her eyebrows in question. "Do what?"

"You know I'm having a hard time with this. I just want you to be okay. I want to be everything you need, but you're the one who remains so positive and strong all the time. How do you do that after everything that gets thrown at you?"

"Honestly, it's not easy, but I have a chance; I have hope, and that's what matters to me." She purses her lips in thought. "I've found I can't dwell on the negative when there's so much of it in this world." She gives my hand a comforting squeeze. "I guess I choose to live in the moment and take advantage of every single one I'm given. It's what got me through all those years I was in and out of the hospital, all the small moments. It makes every good moment seem brighter." She shrugs her shoulders like it's no big deal.

"You have no idea how incredible you are, do you?" I question, not expecting an answer. "Your bright light is one of the reasons I fell in love with you," I confess as I brush her hair back from her face. "You make it seem like it's possible to pull out of the darkness," I rasp, feeling vulnerable, but she makes it so easy to be. "I'm following your light."

59

Ella

GRANT FINISHES CHANGING MY BANDAGES, TENDERLY PRESS-ing his lips at the edges of the gauze covering the small incision before he pulls my shirt back down with a satisfied smile on his face. "There, you're all done."

"Thank you." He nods and scoops me up in his arms, holding me close to his chest. My arms reflexively reach up, hooking around his neck as I laugh. "I can walk, you know," I proclaim, leaning into him as he strides down the hall.

"I know, but I want to carry you sometimes," he claims, his eyes sparkling. He tips his head, lightly kissing my lips. I push my head up, attempting to deepen the kiss, but he pulls back, grinning. Heaving a sigh, I relent and curl into him, inhaling his scent. "Besides, I still have a lot of making up to do," he asserts as he pulls the sliding glass door open and steps out onto my back deck, closing the door behind him.

He sets me down in one of the Adirondack chairs facing the ocean, but I don't let go of my hold around his neck. He crouches down in front of me, his hands falling to my knees. Sliding my hands around, I rest my palms on his cheeks, looking into his eyes. "Grant, I already forgave you, and after everything you shared with me, I understand why you left. The important part to me is that you came back and you're here now."

"I don't deserve you," he mumbles in awe.

"You do, and I'm going to convince you it's true because just like you believe I'm your light, I believe you're mine." I notice his quick intake of air and lean towards him, pressing my lips to his to emphasize my point. Jutting my tongue out, I lick his lips. He groans, opening for me, his tongue flicking out to meet mine licking, twisting, and dancing together in a slow, sensual kiss, eliciting a moan from me as my body tingles to life.

He slows our kiss and pulls back, resting his forehead against mine as we both catch our breath. "I fucking missed you, Ella."

"Then, next time you leave, take me with you."

"You can count on it."

"Good. I've always wanted to travel."

He grins and kisses me again. I meet him eagerly, kiss for kiss, and lick for lick before he begins his retreat again, making me groan in protest. He chuckles softly and reminds me, "You've only been home from the hospital for a few hours."

"How could I forget," I mumble sarcastically. "But what does that have to do with you and me and what I want to do to you?" I challenge defiantly.

He groans. "Damn it, Ella. You drive me crazy."

A smile tugs at my lips. "I like that."

"I promised I would take care of you."

"And you will definitely be taking care of me," I taunt playfully.

"Ella..." He laughs, shaking his head in amusement as the muffled ring of my cell phone comes from inside. "Saved by the bell," he jokes. Standing swiftly, he chuckles as my hands slip from his neck. He jogs into the house. Returning quickly, he hands me my phone before it goes to voicemail. "It could be the hospital."

I heave a sigh and glance at the screen, an unfamiliar number lighting it up. Squaring my shoulders to gather my courage, I slide my finger over the screen, answering the call while

Grant stares at me in anticipation, clenching his jaw. "Hello?"

"Hi, Gabriella," a deep familiar voice sounds over the line.

"Nathan," I mumble, surprised to hear from him. I notice Grant stiffen and reach for his hand, giving it a squeeze. "I didn't recognize the number."

"I'm calling from one of the staff quarters."

"Ah, makes sense. What's up?"

"I'm actually calling because I have your lab results. They just came in, and I didn't want you to have to wait until they come across your doctor's desk. Plus, I wanted to be the one to tell you that you're going to be okay. Everything came back negative. The tumor is benign," he announces, his own joy evident.

I release the breath I didn't know I was holding, my hand falling to my chest with pure relief as tears fill my eyes. Grant swiftly crouches in front of me with fear shining in his eyes as he takes in my teary gaze. Quickly, I shake my head, not wanting him to get the wrong idea. I gulp down the lump in my throat and mumble my appreciation, trying to smile at Grant to give him some comfort. "Thank you, Nate," I rasp, my voice shaky.

"As you know, your regular doctor will follow up with you on what's next, but Ella, I'm really happy for you."

"Thank you," I repeat, gulping down my emotion. "I gotta go tell my family."

"Okay. I'll talk to you soon, and I'm here if you need anything."

I nod even though he can't see me and disconnect the call, focusing on Grant. "It's not cancer," I choke out, happy tears overflowing and streaming down my cheeks.

He breathes a sigh of relief, his whole body relaxing almost instantly. Then he picks me up, spins around and sets me in his lap, holding me tight. He presses his face into the crook of my neck, inhaling deeply, mumbling, "Thank fuck."

We sit like that for a few minutes, relishing the news and

being in each other's arms when I finally register his phone has been ringing repeatedly. "Um, Grant?"

"Yeah," he mumbles without moving.

I giggle softly. "I think someone is desperately trying to get ahold of you. You should probably answer that." He heaves a sigh and leans back, looking at me. "I should call and let my family know about the results anyway."

Sighing, he nods in agreement and reluctantly loosens his hold on me. "I'll give you some privacy to talk to your family."

"You don't have to, but thanks."

He nods, giving me a chaste kiss. Then he stands with me in his arms, setting me carefully back down in the chair as he answers the call. "Hello?"

He steps away, walking towards the house and disappearing inside. I take a deep breath, inhaling the salt air as I relax back into the chair. Momentarily, I sit, watching the waves crash over the sand, grateful for this moment.

Not wanting them to wait any longer, I reach for my phone and unlock it, tapping on my mom's name. She picks up on the first ring. "Hello?"

"Hi, Mom."

"Ella, how are you feeling?"

I sigh, feeling all the stress of the last few days drain out of me. "I'm good, Mom. Nate just called, and the tumor is benign," I announce without preamble. I've learned to just spit it out when it comes to things like this.

A strangled cry of relief echoes through the line, followed by, "Thank God."

I hear her call to my dad just as Grant steps back out onto the deck with his eyes wide and his face pale. My mom says something, but I don't register what she says, with all my focus on Grant. "Mom, can you let everyone else know?" I request. I assume she agrees and I mumble, "Thanks. I gotta go." I disconnect and set my phone down, my heartbeat turning erratic.

Cautiously, I stand and approach him, stepping directly in

his line of sight. Reaching up, I cradle his face in my hands, tilting his head down, desperate for him to meet my gaze. I look into his eyes, searching for answers, and I'm chilled by the haunted look in his hazel orbs. "Grant, what's wrong?" I urge, panic churning in my gut.

"That was my dad," he states, his voice hollow. He takes a few deep breaths before he continues. "He's leaving for the airport and flying home right away to help Matt. He got arrested last night for beating the shit out of Amy's boyfriend."

60

Ella

RINSING THE SOAP OFF THE BOWL, I CAREFULLY SET IT IN the drying rack as memories of the last few days wash over me. Grant has been so worried about his brother but focusing his attention on taking care of me to keep his mind occupied. I'm grateful his dad is returning from Massachusetts today, saying everything is okay with Matt. Although he's anxious to find out what happened, knowing Matt will be okay brought a smile to Grant's face again. He took off early this morning to take care of something before his dad got back, wanting to make sure everything gets done.

Yesterday he told me has an idea he wants to share with Pete and Aidan, but he wouldn't tell me much else until he spoke to them, not wanting to get his hopes up, and I can't stop thinking about it. He scheduled an early meeting with them at the garage. I dry my hands, glancing at the time on my phone for maybe the hundredth time in the past hour, anxiously waiting for him to return home.

The front door swings open and Grant walks in, grinning the moment he sees me standing in the kitchen doorway in my bare feet with his black t-shirt draped over me like a gown, hanging off my shoulder. I wanted his scent around me while he was gone today. I've relished every minute at home with him the last few days while I healed, and he continued his physical therapy, but I knew it would quickly be coming to an end.

"How'd it go?" I prompt, excited to find out about his proposal.

Without a word, he stalks towards me, his eyes liquid gold. Reaching for me, he cradles my face in his hands as he tips his head down, molding his mouth over mine. My lips part and he slips his tongue inside, sweeping and tasting me. I whimper into his mouth, his kiss igniting me instantly. I push my body towards his, looping my leg around his, trying to get closer, feeling his hard length press against my belly. "Damn, you look sexy in my shirt," he mumbles over my lips, his voice a hoarse whisper, sending shivers down my spine.

"If you like me in this shirt, you should see what's under it," I declare as I lick my lips, my cheeks tinging pink. I know I'm playing with fire, but we haven't been together since I've been home from the hospital. It hasn't been that long, but every kiss, every touch, every look taunts me, daring to push me over the edge, and I just can't take it anymore. I want him!

His eyes flash and he groans as his lips fall to my neck and his hands slide down my sides to the hem of my shirt. He slips his hands underneath, slowly gliding them up my thighs, cupping my bare ass. "Fuck, your naked under here?" he questions breathily as he leans back, looking into my eyes like he's already done for.

I smirk and playfully taunt, "Maybe." He growls in response, crashing his lips to mine as he plunges his tongue into my mouth, kissing me desperately. He picks me up, grasping the hem of the shirt and pulling it over my head as he sets me down on the cool, smooth counter, completely exposing me to him as he breaks our kiss.

"How did I get so lucky," he mutters with a shake of his head. "You are the sexiest woman I have ever seen, Ella." He groans as he kisses me again, his hands sliding to my breasts, gently kneading. I weave my fingers into his hair as his lips move down, kissing and licking a trail down to my breasts, his mouth replacing one of his hands over my nipple as he sucks it into his mouth. I arch my back towards him, needy for more.

He skates his free hand down between my legs as he continues his assault on my breasts. His fingers brush over my core and back again, making me moan his name in desperation and desire, "Grant."

"Put your hands on the counter behind you and lean back a little bit," he instructs. I do as he says making him moan in appreciation, his hand running over the hard length of his jean covered cock. I lick my lips, watching him in anticipation, with my nipples in taut peaks, still tingling from his touch and his wicked kiss.

He lifts both hands to my thighs, gliding them up towards my core. My breath hitches, becoming ragged as he inches closer, nudging my legs apart. He slides one hand through my folds and then the other. "So wet," he murmurs, my juices dripping, begging for his touch. He leans closer, his tongue licking me from my core to my clit as he pushes two fingers inside my pussy making me cry out in pleasure and surprise.

"Grant," I rasp, reaching for him.

"No. Sit back so I can look at you like that while I devour your pussy like it's my last meal," he insists. I gasp, my eyes widening. My body shakes in anticipation while I lean back as directed, not able to give him a verbal response. "Don't move," he demands, biting his lower lip and releasing it. "You're fucking gorgeous."

His hands spread my legs as his mouth covers my pussy, his tongue pushing inside my core and curling before retreating and licking up to my clit. "Ah," I moan as he sticks two fingers inside me, curling towards my g-spot, while his mouth and tongue methodically go to work, licking and sucking my folds and my clit. His fingers pump in and out of me, his tongue, swirling around my clit, licking, nibbling, and sucking. I pant, barely able to breathe, my body on fire as my hands itch to touch him, struggling to follow direction. "Grant, I c...can't..." I beg, not quite sure what I'm even begging for, but knowing I need it. "Please."

His tongue licks and his mouth sucks harder, adding more pressure, while adding a finger inside me and pumping faster. "Yes, more," I rasp but I can't take any more. I feel a burning flood me deep in my core, his name a scream on my lips, "Grant," as relief slams into me, his moan vibrating over me, adding to the fire. My walls squeeze his fingers repeatedly as my vision blurs. He continues licking and sucking me until I come down from my climax, with a satisfied sigh.

Sliding his fingers out of me, he licks them clean while holding my gaze. Then, he steps between my legs and tugs me to him, pressing his lips to mine and pushing his tongue in, giving me a taste of myself. He pulls back, resting his head on my forehead and catches his breath. "I want to cum all over your tits, but not today."

"Why not?" I ask as I lean forward and reach for him, just now realizing he's still fully clothed. I unbutton his pants and tug the zipper down. "I need these off."

He kicks his shoes off and yanks his jeans and boxers down, kicking them onto the floor before admitting, "Because right now I need to be inside you. It's been too long." He's right it has been too long. With the surgery on my back, although the incision is small, my restrictions were big, including no sex, which changes today, and we're not waiting another moment. I reach for the hem of his shirt and lift, pulling it over his head and tossing it on the floor. Freezing with wide eyes and my body tingling, I stare at him standing naked in my kitchen, his firm muscles now appearing more balanced than I've ever seen as well as incredibly defined, making my mouth water.

I reach for his cock and wrap my hand around his hard length, stroking him up and down, eliciting a groan of pleasure from him. He picks me up and I wrap my legs around his waist as he strides out of the kitchen while he kisses me, unwilling to wait. "Where are we going," I mumble breathlessly over his lips.

"Condom," he mumbles, making his way to my room, my core rubbing against him. He walks us into my room and lays me down on the bed, immediately reaching for a square packet out of the nightstand. He rips it open with his teeth and swiftly rolls it on. Then, he lays down, hovering over me, kissing me soft and slow as he positions himself at my entrance.

My hips arch up towards him, wanting him, needing him, desperate to have him. "I want you, Grant," I whisper over his lips.

Granting my request, he slowly eases in, filling me, pushing all the way in, and stopping at the hilt with a satisfied moan, sending shivers down my spine. He looks into my eyes and tenderly kisses my lips as he pushes my hair out of my eyes. Then he kisses me again, his tongue pushing towards mine, soft and slow like a waltz, causing butterflies to erupt in my stomach along with the burning desire. He pulls out and then pushes in again and again before breaking our kiss. "I love you, Ella," he murmurs. He thrusts again and breathlessly repeats, "I love you so fucking much."

Overwhelmed with emotion, I lift my legs and wrap them around him, moaning desperately, not able to speak. He begins picking up his pace, my hips bucking up to meet his. My head falls back onto the bed, no longer able to maintain our kiss. I rake my hands over his back, clinging to him as he pushes into me faster, kissing my neck, my collarbone, my chest, repeating the words like a mantra, "I love you, Ella."

My heart feels like it's going to burst, my insides about to combust, my core burning with my orgasm already approaching again. I gasp and groan, not able to mutter his name, every part of me feeling like it's all too much. He thrusts faster and harder. "I need you to cum, Angel," he begs, "Cum for me."

I do as he says with a scream, my insides squeezing his cock, his movements almost immediately becoming erratic. I continue pulsing as he pushes into me as deep as he can maneuver, hitting my spot again as I continue to contract around him, lights flashing before my eyes. My body finally begins coming down and I exhale harshly, just as Grant collapses partially on top of me with a groan.

As we slowly catch our breath, I cling to him. Eventually, I lower my legs from around his back, my whole body moving like jelly while I'm completely sated. I look at him, needing him to see the truth in my eyes as I finally murmur, "I love you, too, Grant."

He grins, his eyes bright with happiness as he kisses me. Our mouths move slowly in sync before he reluctantly pulls back. "I should get rid of this condom." I nod and he kisses me again. As I moan into his mouth, I feel him twitch inside me. With a groan, he pulls back. "I need to get rid of it now."

Slowly, he pulls out and I instantly feel the loss. I smile, watching his glorious backside as he strides to the bathroom and quickly returns, holding up a washcloth. With a nod of my head, he steps towards me, climbing back on the bed and gently wiping me clean before he tosses the washcloth on the floor and pulls me into his arms.

I curl into his side as my fingers begin running over the lines of his tattoos on his chest, pressing my lips there. "So, how did it go with Pete and Aidan?" I ask, repeating my question from earlier.

"Good." He grins. "Looks like I have a job."

"That's great!" I glance up at him and wait for him to elaborate.

"I'll help out at the garage some, but Aidan and I are going to work together to fix and accessorize motorcycles and even build custom ones. He's extremely talented at the artwork and small details, and I'm good with the other side. Pete will recommend us to customers, and we'll do the same, but Aidan and I will be more of a specialty."

"That's fantastic! I'm so happy for you! This sounds like it couldn't be more perfect." I lean up and press my lips to his, feeling his excitement practically radiating off him. "And I like that this new job will keep you here," I add selfishly, kissing him again.

He grins, giving me his crooked smile I love so much. "I never thought I'd say this again about anywhere, but I'm happy I'm going to be staying too. In fact, I wouldn't want it any other way," he murmurs his agreement over my lips, deepening the kiss.

The doorbell rings, startling us both, and my eyes widen in surprise. "Get dressed and answer the door," I urge, gently pushing at his chest, knowing he can be ready to walk out of the room much faster than me.

He chuckles, quickly standing and tugging his jeans on, going commando before grabbing a white t-shirt off the dresser. "Coming," he calls as he leaves the room while pulling the t-shirt over his head.

I jump up and push the door shut, searching for my clothes, before making my way to the bathroom to clean up, wondering if his dad is already here or if it's someone else checking on me. I laugh and shake my head. Well, I guess I better get moving.

61

Grant

MY DAD SHOULD BE HERE ANY MINUTE. MY STOMACH HAS been twisting like a tilt-a-whirl waiting to find out more about what happened with Matt. It seems like everything has worked out, but the way my dad said he had to talk to me about it, it felt as though he were insinuating it had something to do with me, and that makes no fucking sense.

A knock at the door pulls me out of my thoughts, and I quickly stride towards it, yanking it open. I find my dad on the other side dressed in khakis and a light blue button-up shirt with the sleeves rolled up to his elbows. He runs his hand through his hair, looking exhausted. "Hi, Grant," he murmurs, offering me a sad smile.

"Hey, come on in. Mom didn't come with you?"

He shakes his head. "No, she doesn't need to hear this all over again. She already knows what's going on, and she hasn't been sleeping. I told her to get some rest and she could see you later."

I nod, gulping down the sudden lump in my throat and taking a step back as he enters, closing the door behind him. "We can talk in here," I suggest, gesturing towards the living room.

"Okay," he concurs, trudging further into the room as if approaching a death sentence, only increasing my nerves.

"Would you like anything to drink?" I offer as more of a distraction than just remembering my manners.

He shakes his head. "No thanks."

I nod and sit down on one end of the couch as my dad lowers himself into the recliner. He sighs as he leans forward, resting his elbows on his knees. Then he glances up at me, his green eyes appearing flat and anxious, leaving me uneasy. "You said Matt was okay," I blurt out, my nerves suddenly a whirlwind.

His eyes widen, realizing what I must think. "He is, he's okay," he insists, nodding. "He's in love with Amy."

"Huh. I'm not really surprised." I shrug my shoulders. "He's been chasing her around since we were kids." A thought suddenly slams into me. "Is that why he got into a fight with her boyfriend?"

He winces and shakes his head. "No." He pauses and takes a deep breath, gulping down the lump in his throat. "Matt found out her boyfriend was abusing her both emotionally and physically, and he lost it."

I gasp, my mouth dropping open in shock. "What?" I ask, even though I heard every word. I clench my fist, my blood boiling with anger for a man I don't know and my heart breaking for the bubbly, petite blonde I remember growing up, knowing Matt would follow her anywhere. "What happened? Is she alright?"

He nods. "She's stronger than we all realize," he states, his voice cracking. I tilt my head, assessing him, feeling like his comment is cryptic.

"Please tell me she pressed charges against him."

"Unfortunately, no."

"What?"

My dad puts his hand up to stop the rant he knows is coming. "She ended up making a deal with him. She wouldn't press charges as long as he wouldn't. She did it to get Matt off the hook," he confesses, grinding his jaw.

"Shit," I mumble under my breath, running my hand through my hair and back down my face before dropping it in my lap.

"Exactly."

"Matt should be thanked for hitting this asshole, not have to go to jail. I would've done the same damn thing!"

"I'm sure you would have," my dad mumbles, nodding. "No man worth anything ever hits a woman."

Out of the corner of my eye, I see Ella step into the room, drawing my attention. She looks gorgeous wearing basic black jeans and a white ruffled t-shirt, with her hair pulled up in a high ponytail, still damp from her shower. She sits down next to me as she greets my dad, "Hi, Mr. Young. Do you mind if I join you?"

Smiling, I immediately link my fingers with hers, lifting her hand to my lips and kissing the back of it. Before he even has a chance to respond, I advise, "Ella stays. She's my home. I know there's more coming, I can see it in your eyes and I can feel it in my bones. But whatever it is, she can hear it. I tell her everything."

My dad nods in acknowledgment and takes a deep breath, exhaling slowly. "Okay. So, when I was home, Matt told me he thought there was a possibility Amy's mom had been abusing her for years, but she had never confessed anything. He just saw so many signs."

I hear Ella's breath hitch and I clasp her hand tighter, already knowing this conversation isn't going anywhere good, my heart sinking further by the second. I brush my lips over her hand again, the simple gesture bringing me comfort, although I shouldn't be surprised hearing this with everything I've been through.

"I got a call from Matt when I was on my way back and he confirmed it." I wince, wondering if I could've done something long ago to prevent it. "He confronted Mr. Stone, and he's not letting Amy out of his sight. He asked if there was anything we could do to help her. I didn't give Matt any details, but I did tell him she was part of the reason you took off, but you would need to share that story with him. That's one of the things that further tipped him off about her. He's always had his doubts, but..." He pauses, his emotions overwhelming.

"Dad..."

He shakes his head and starts again, "Mrs. Stone always tried to keep the two of them apart. She hated your brother, but he never understood why." He shakes his head, pausing to get his emotions under control again. "She started abusing Amy when she was only twelve years old," he chokes. "But Grant, just because that's about the same time you left, it's not your fault. Don't you dare think about taking the blame for her twisted actions."

I gasp for breath, my chest tight like I've gotten the wind knocked out of me by a bowling ball. If she's been harassing my brother and her own daughter since I left, why did I stay away from my family for all those years? My ears start ringing as I feel Ella's hand cupping my cheek, attempting to calm me and pull me out of the abyss before I fall into the darkness with guilt consuming me.

I force myself to focus on her until I can hear her words. "It's okay, Grant. It's not your fault. I'm right here," she murmurs softly. I breathe in and out slowly, closing my eyes as I brush my lips against hers, reminding myself she's still here, standing by my side. With her, I know we can get through this together. "It's okay," she repeats, comforting me.

I kiss her again and mumble, "Thank you." She smiles at me in encouragement. I momentarily rest my forehead on hers. "For the first time, I don't feel like I have to do this alone and it's all because of you. I know I can tackle this as long as you're here with me. I love you so much, Ella."

"I love you, too, Grant." She presses her lips to mine. "I believe you're strong enough to tackle anything, but I'm not going anywhere, and together we're stronger. I'll be right by your side," she reiterates, my heart beating for her.

Taking a deep breath, I exhale slowly, turning towards my dad with determination. "I'm not letting her get away with this. I want to make her pay for everything she ever did to me," I declare vehemently, "and for everything she did to Amy and Matt. I left to protect everyone I love, and leaving only took away more from all of us and gave her the power to control the board." I pause, shaking my head in disgust. "I want her to pay for what she took away from all of us! Where do we start, Dad?" I know he will know exactly how to handle this and what we need to do. I wouldn't be surprised if he already has a plan.

Epilogue

2 years later

Ella

GRANT WALKS IN FROM THE GARAGE, HIS BLACK G & A'S Cycles Specialty Shop shirt smeared with grease. He grins, striding straight for me. "Hi, Angel. You look beautiful." Reaching for me, he cradles my face in his hands and kisses me slow and tender as if he has all the time in the world, leaving my knees feeling weak. He pulls back, looking into my eyes adoringly. "How was your day at the center?"

I smile, loving my new job. The hospital worked with the health department to open a new center called Breaking Cycles, giving kids in difficult situations, physically or emotionally, an opportunity to thrive. It's similar to a Boys and Girls Club, but they offer specialty healthcare on site, always having a Physician's Assistant (PA) or a nurse practitioner (NP) along with other available specialties as needed including social workers, psychologists, speech therapists, occupational therapists, and much more. I went back to school for social work, and I'm working there with the after-school program until I'm completely certified and trained. Laine's program helped spur the new center.

"It was good! We have a new boy that started coming

today. He's only ten years old, and he's such a sweet kid, but he's quiet. I guess it's just him and his mom now. His dad recently went into the system, and his mom works two jobs. It's heartbreaking, but I know I can help pull him out of his shell."

"I don't doubt it." He grins. His confidence in me astounds me.

"I love having my own thing."

"What do you mean?" he asks, his eyebrows drawn down in confusion.

"With my brothers and Char," I mumble, shrugging my shoulders. "For the longest time, Dec was always the smart one, Charlotte was always the talented one, Finn was always the athletic one and I was the sick one, but now I'm the one who helps people."

Grant gives me a look I can't quite decipher and presses his lips to mine, our mouths moving in an easy rhythm. Then, he pulls back, resting his forehead on mine. "Ella," he rasps. "You've always been the one who helps people, but you're so much more than that! You have the biggest heart I've ever known. You bring happiness wherever you go with your positivity and light. You kickstarted my heart, breathed life back into me and brought my soul back from the dead, breaking the cycle."

My chest tightens, my heart full as he continues. "Therapy helped, but that's nothing compared to what you've done for me. You are the reason why I can picture a future for myself again and why I started dreaming again when I believed there was nothing left for me but nightmares. It's why you're my Angel, you did more than save my life the day you scraped me off the road. You are the heart, the light and the soul of your family and ours."

Tears spring to my eyes, his words overwhelming me. "Grant," I whimper, barely able to breathe. I wrap my arms around his waist and rest my head on his chest, holding on tight.

"Don't cry, Angel," he murmurs, attempting to wipe away

my tears with his thumbs.

"I love you, Grant."

"I love you too, Ella." A cocky grin tugs at his lips as he looks down at me.

I freeze, my heart skipping a beat as I finally process the last word of his speech, ours, as in our family. I push back and look up at him, suddenly shaking. "Grant?" I question, not wanting to assume anything.

He chuckles softly and brushes his lips over mine. "I had a whole thing planned, but I've already given you most of my speech," he jokes. My breathing picks up and my heart begins to race as I wait for him to finish his statement. "Wait here," he instructs.

Ignoring his request, I follow him out to the garage. He laughs as he walks over to his workbench, opening his toolbox, and pulling out a small, square, black velvet box, making me gasp. He turns to me and takes both of my hands in his, his forehead falling back to mine. "What I said before is true. You are the heart, the light, and the soul of everything I know in life. I don't ever want to even imagine life without you by my side." He steps back enough to take a knee in front of me. Holding up the box, he flips it open with a click. "Please make me the happiest man in the world and become my wife," he pleads. "Will you marry me, Ella?"

I nod, and murmur, "Yes," as my tears flow freely. I hold out my shaky hand and he takes it in his, steadying me. I don't even bother looking at the ring as he slips it on my finger, the man in front of me all I care about. He stands and picks me up, pulling me into his arms. "I love you," I whisper into his ear. I lean back, wrap my legs around his waist and press my lips to his. He tilts his head, deepening the kiss, and I moan into his mouth as our tongues twist, lick, and stroke.

He pulls back and rests his forehead on mine, grinning as we catch our breaths. "I had a whole grand proposal planned after the game," he enlightens me, taking me by surprise.

I shake my head, insisting, "This was perfect. Now we just need to celebrate. Do we have time before the game?"

He groans in frustration, admitting, "That's why I wanted to wait until afterwards."

I giggle rubbing my core against him. "Well, you could fuck me right here, and we could both cum fast and then take our time later," I suggest, blushing. "I'm already soaked for you, Grant." I reach between us and rub my hand firmly over his hard shaft.

He groans, "Fuck, Ella, you know you drive me crazy when you talk dirty and your skin turns that perfect shade of pink." He sets me down on his workbench, tugging my jeans and panties down. Then he slips his fingers down to my pussy, sliding them through my folds. "Yes, you are," he agrees on a moan. "Are you sure?" he asks, hating to rush.

"I want you now!"

Giving me what I want, he unbuttons and unzips his jeans, pulling out his dick, and stroking as he rubs my clit. He wraps one arm around me, bracing his other arm on the workbench as he lines up at my entrance. "Fuck, I don't have a condom out here," he suddenly remembers.

"I don't care. It's only been us for over two years, and I'm taking the pill again," I remind him, wanting to feel him inside me.

"Are you sure?" he repeats, barely restraining himself.

"Please," I beg.

In one quick move he thrusts inside me so deep, my head starts to spin. He begins moving in and out, the hot, smooth, feel of his dick against the walls of my pussy already has me panting for breath. "Grant."

"I'm not gonna last, Ella. You feel so fucking good, squeezing me. Ugh," he groans.

I lift off the workbench, his pace already frantic. He reaches between us, flicking my clit as he pounds into me. "Yes, please, yes!" I rasp, already feeling a blazing inferno in my core. "Harder, yes!" I pant. "Grant, yes, yes!" I scream, my insides already squeezing his cock, my vision blurring as I milk him, barely breathing, and I feel him falling over the edge right along with me.

He pumps into me again, and again, holding himself inside me as he releases a guttural groan and I feel him cum inside me, lengthening my climax as I spasm around him. His forehead finally drops to mine as we both gasp for breath.

"Damn, woman," he mumbles accusingly. He sighs as he picks me up, instructing, "Wrap your legs around me and don't rub against me until we get in the shower. I don't want us to leave a trail." He smirks.

I bury my face in his shoulder, my face turning tomato road as he chuckles softly, walking us back into the house. "We need to do that again," I murmur.

He bursts out laughing before mumbling his agreement, "Yes, we do."

Grant

I saunter out of the bedroom with a huge smile on my face, feeling completely sated after round two in the shower with Ella. My heart squeezes, emphasizing the fact she's mine forever. I can't believe she said yes. So much for an elaborate proposal, with our families there to witness it. This was so much better; it was perfect for us. We've been through so much in the past two and a half years, but I don't believe for one second that I would've been here without her. Now it's my personal mission to do everything I can to treat her like the angel she is for the rest of our lives.

Ella steps out of the bedroom, dressed in a red and white football jersey with Finn's number on the back, dark blue jeans and white sneakers with her hair pulled back in a French braid down the middle of her head. I grin. "You look sexy, Ella, but you have to change your shirt."

"What?" Her face drops, making me chuckle.

"I have a present for you, and I want you to wear it tonight."

"I'm already wearing your present," she teases, wiggling her fingers. "And I have to wear more than just your ring to the game?"

A low growl passes through my lips as I nibble her lower one, eliciting a giggle from her as she wiggles away. "I have another present I want you to wear."

Her eyebrows draw down in confusion. "But I want to support my brother."

I smirk and shrug my shoulders like I don't care, but I do. "You will be there cheering for Finn louder than anyone else in those stands." She smiles as I reach for her, taking her hand.

"Do you think he's ready for tonight?" she prods, sounding nervous for him.

"You don't need to worry about Finn. Your brother is going to slaughter the other team tonight. His arm is better than mine ever was."

"I hope you're right." She smiles.

"I am." I grab the white paper bag from my black duffle bag next to the couch and hand it to her, not able to wipe the smile from my face. "Here, open it."

She looks up at me with wide eyes, then she slowly tosses the tissue paper to the side and pulls out a red and white football jersey, just like the one she's wearing, except this one has, "Young," written on the back in bold letters with additional small writing on the front by her right shoulder stating, "Mrs. Coach."

She laughs. "Oh, my gosh! This is fantastic! I love it!"

"You can wear what you want, but it would be a fun way to tell our families you agreed to marry me. I wasn't going to give it to you until tonight or tomorrow, but since I couldn't wait to pop the question..." I tease, trailing off.

She glances at the one carat princess cut diamond with

a smaller stone on each side and a yellow gold band. It looks perfect on her finger. I can't wait for everyone to know she's mine. "Thank you," she murmurs and sniffles.

I lift her chin, looking into her watery eyes. "What's wrong?" I question, my stomach turning.

She shakes her head and grins. "Nothing. These are happy tears." She closes the distance between us and kisses me softly. "I love you."

Now that I hear those words coming from her lips, I don't think I could ever hear them enough. "I love you, too, Ella."

She pulls back and reminds me, "We have to go, the coach shouldn't be late for his own game." I grin, still grateful I found a way back to football. It went from tossing a football with Finn in the back yard and giving him some tips, to him asking me to work with him on his technique. I've never seen a kid so talented. He's a natural, and the difference in his game has been tremendous. Finn's friends soon began asking me for private training sessions and I obliged, enjoying having football back in my life in some capacity. I didn't realize how much I missed it until it fell back into my life.

After working with the boys, the coaching staff noticed a huge difference in their players, who all shared who had been working with them. Then, when the high school coach retired last year, they called me up and offered me a job just through various recommendations. At first, I wasn't sure since Aidan and I were just starting out with our new business and I didn't want to miss any time with Ella when she wasn't busy with work or school. But they practically begged me to take over the team, and I finally agreed. I absolutely love it, and Ella constantly tells me how happy I appear doing it. She's right.

"You should get going. If your brother and Amy get here before you leave, you'll never get out of here. And they should be here any minute."

"You're right. I'm really looking forward to seeing them and my parents."

"I understand. It's your first family reunion since the trial wrapped up." She reaches out and squeezes my hand, acknowledging the impact of today.

I'm thankful Mrs. Stone is doing some time, although the statute of limitations passed for assault against me, but it hadn't for sexual assault. Add in the repeated assaults to a minor, her own child at that, and she was charged and sentenced for several back-to-back crimes, getting twenty-plus years. I'm not sure how long she'll actually stay there, but she's damned either way, and the weight I feel lifted from my chest is indescribable.

I see the same kind of relief in Amy's eyes, and it shatters me for her, but she has my brother. They're good for each other. Matt has always looked at Amy the way I look at Ella, and I'm thankful their rough road led back to each other and even more grateful they're back in my life. The four of us have been through so much shit, and now that we're finally on the other side of this nightmare, we're stronger than ever. "It's a good day," I murmur.

I shake myself out of my thoughts, needing to get out of here and focus on the game for the next couple hours. "Wish me luck."

"Good luck, Coach," she proclaims and kisses me on the lips. I never knew life could be this good, and I'll be forever grateful for this angel in front of me.

Acknowledgements

Writing this is the part that's overwhelming. There's so many I want to thank and I don't want to forget anyone!

As always, thank you to my family, Michael, Tyler, Allison, and our dogs, and my mom, my dad in heaven and my sister, as well as my extended family. I appreciate your constant love and support more than anything! I wouldn't be able to do what I love without you.

Thank you Trista and Ryon for giving me this chance with Atmosphere Press! I'm truly grateful for the opportunity. Alex, thank you for keeping me on track and answering all my questions. Although it's the same process, everyone works a little differently and I appreciate your advice.

I don't even know where to begin when it comes to you, Asata. I'm truly thankful for your time, effort, advice and so much more. You are really good at what you do and that's putting it mildly. I'm lucky I've had the opportunity to work with you and I really looked forward to talking with you. I hope I have the chance to work with you again. I can't wait for the day I get to read your book. Thank you Asata, as well as Chris and Sara for your expertise and all you did for my novel.

As for Ronaldo and your team, I love how you were always on top of everything, no matter how many messages I sent. Your creative process was impressive and it made putting the cover together so much fun! Plus, I'm thrilled with the results. Thank you! I also need to thank the photographer, Steve for your incredible pictures. Of course, having a model like Vinny helps!

Vinny, I've really enjoyed getting to know you and working with you. I hope you love the cover as much as I do. Thank you for your updates, staying on top of everything across the pond, including communication with the photographer, as well as doing more than I could ask. I hope to work with you again soon! Thanks to my good friend and incredible author, Jill for introducing us! One day all three of us have to sit down for a drink!

This book had a unique start, and I didn't know if this one would ever be published. It has taken me longer than any other, but I'm thrilled with the results! Thank you to Natasha of Sinful Desires and all the incredible authors in that group – I appreciate and adore all of you! You inspired me to write this one. Thank you to all my friends on Wattpad for your support.

Dina, I'm so grateful to you for helping me with the final preparations of my manuscript before submitting to the publisher and giving me advice whenever needed. It means so much to be able to run over ideas with someone who knows where I'm coming from and the direction I'm trying to go.

Nick and Ayana, thank you for your help, patience, and support. I'm immensely grateful to you both for all you do to help with getting my books out there!

To all my 'SteamQueen' Ladies, you are incredible women, writers, supporters, and friends! I'm so thankful for you! Thanks to all my Beta readers, my ARC readers, my street team, and my fans who have read, shared, or reviewed my books. I greatly appreciate every single one of you! I love writing and being able to share it with all of you! I hope you continue to read, share, and enjoy! Thank you!

About Atmosphere Press

Founded in 2015, Atmosphere Press was built on the principles of Honesty, Transparency, Professionalism, Kindness, and Making Your Book Awesome. As an ethical and author-friendly hybrid press, we stay true to that founding mission today.

If you're a reader, enter our giveaway for a free book here:

SCAN TO ENTER
BOOK GIVEAWAY

If you're a writer, submit your manuscript for consideration here:

SCAN TO SUBMIT
MANUSCRIPT

And always feel free to visit Atmosphere Press and our authors online at atmospherepress.com. See you there soon!

Connect with the Author

Official Author Website

www.nikkialamersauthor.com

Linktree for All Author Links

https://linktr.ee/NikkiALamersauthor

About the Author

Award winning author **NIKKI A LAMERS** has always had a passion for reading and writing, especially romance. She grew up in Wisconsin with her sister, mom, and dad. She always loved reading romance books and watching romance movies with her dad, something they both enjoyed. After college she lived in Florida for a few years working for the "Happiest Place on Earth," where she met her husband. She now lives on Long Island in New York with her husband and two kids. She spends her free time reading or hanging out with friends and family. She would love to spend more time traveling, visiting new places and meeting new people as well as continue creating stories, each of her characters becoming part of her family.

www.ingramcontent.com/pod-product-compliance
Lightning Source LLC
Chambersburg PA
CBHW021335150726
47989CB00005B/1991